The RELUCTANT MIDWIFE

Also by Patricia Harman

The Midwife of Hope River
Arms Wide Open: A Midwife's Journey
The Blue Cotton Gown: A Midwife's Memoir

The RELUCTANT MIDWIFE

A HOPE RIVER NOVEL

patricia harman

wm

WILLIAM MORROW

An Imprint of HarperCollins*Publishers*

P.S.™ is a trademark of HarperCollins Publishers.

Designed by Diahann Sturge

ISBN 978-1-62953-401-5

This book is dedicated to the healer in all of us.

Life can be hard,
but if we hold hands
we can make it across the river.

Acknowledgments

I'd like to thank first my husband, Tom Harman, for his support of my writing. He will do an extra load of laundry just to give me time at my computer; also, my staff at Partners in Women's Health Care who have to put up with the changes in my schedule for book-related events.

In addition, I thank my editor, Lucia Macro, and her wonderful staff, as well as my agent, Barbara Braun. They have helped me give birth to another Hope River Novel. Also, I can't fail to mention the midwives, muses, and patients who have inspired me.

And last, dear readers, I thank you for your letters and e-mails of encouragement. Writing a book is in some ways a lonely endeavor. You have doubts: Is it good enough? Will people like it as much as the last book? I keep thinking of you. I tell the story for you, knowing the women and men of Hope River give us courage, give us hope, help us heal.

Somewhere in Appalachia, there's a small white house with a blue door. In the back, behind the barn, is a graveyard. Two women kneel in the tall yellow grass.

Under a rock are three babies, two of bone, one of spirit. There are fresh graves too, where black and white sleep together, eight in all.

The women have flowers in their hands, bouquets of daisies, yellow mustard, and pink phlox. One of them makes the sign of the cross. One of them can't stop crying.

From the private journal of Becky Myers, RN,
reluctant midwife
Wild Rose Road, West Virginia, USA
1934–35

The RELUCTANT MIDWIFE

Spring

1

Highwayman

"Holy hell, what's this?" I say to Dr. Blum, who doesn't seem to notice the beat-up black DeSoto with a table tied to the top that's pulled over on the side of the road. A young man, wearing a wool plaid jacket, stands on the berm, waving his hat. "Help. Stop!"

The newspapers warn us about highwaymen out to do no good, robbers who pose as distressed travelers in these hard times, lure do-gooders to help them, and then at gunpoint take all their money and valuables. Slowing, I see a woman in the front seat, her feet on the dashboard and her face wild with pain. It's only that face that compels me to stop.

"Oh, for god's sake, that doesn't look fake, does it?" I ask the doctor, backing up to see what's happening. My passenger doesn't answer, but then he never does. "Here goes nothing." I put my leather pocketbook in the doctor's limp hands and cover it with his coat. "If the man is a thief, unless he puts a gun to your head, don't give this up. It's all we have," I command, jumping out of the Pontiac. Blum doesn't blink.

"What's the problem?" I yell to the stranger. "Your lady okay? I'm a registered nurse."

"Oh, thank god, ma'am. I'm Alvin Norton. . . . It's my wife,

Bernice. She's having a baby. What should I do? It's another forty miles to Torrington."

"She's having the baby *right now*?"

I remember the first baby I ever saw born, a premature infant too little to breathe, with a double cleft lip that ran up to his nose. It was a precipitous delivery in the emergency ward and the mother was hysterical. Still in training, I'd been left to labor-sit while the other nurses went on break, and ever since then, I've approached childbirth with dread.

I push those images away and run for the passenger side of the auto, where I find a blonde of about twenty, vomiting out the window.

"It's coming!" she says, her green eyes wide.

"What should I do? What should I do?" Alvin asks again.

"Well, the first thing is . . . get her bloomers off."

The man blushes, sets his hat on the hood, and pulls off the woman's wringing-wet pants while I throw off my worn wool coat. It's old but it's the only one I have.

"Can you roll on your side, Bernice? Put your head up by the steering wheel and open your legs? My name is Nurse Becky." The woman squirms around and props one leg up on my shoulder.

"Sir, if the baby is truly coming, I'll need a blanket or something to wrap it in. If it's not time yet, maybe you can make it back to Butler Mills. There might be a doctor there." I sound so calm and confident, but my whole insides are shaking.

"Yes. Yes!" The father is running around like a chicken with its head cut off.

"In the suitcase!" the woman yells. "Blanket in the suitcase! Ughhhhhh!" A hairy orb about the size of an apple is already showing. The infant peeks out and then retreats, not ready to enter this hard world, I imagine. I try to act as if I do this all the time, but cold fear grips my stomach.

As a registered nurse, I've assisted physicians at scores of deliveries, but the rawness of emotion and the blood and the goo have never appealed to me, and then there is still the vision, deep in my psyche, of that first deformed child. . . . I'd rather set a broken arm, assist with a hysterectomy, or clean a ragged wound.

I have even been present when a midwife delivered the baby of a homeless woman in a tent, pitched under a stone bridge, and the outcome was healthy, but I still didn't like it. What was it the midwife said to her frightened patient?

"Push a little," I say, trying to imitate her soothing voice, as cold sweat drips down the side of my face. "Push a little . . . Blow a little . . . Push a little . . . Blow a little. Your baby is almost here, Bernice." The father comes back, holding a crocheted white baby blanket. I hate to get it bloody, but it's apparently all he could find.

"We're on our way to her mother's in Torrington," he explains between contractions. "Where we were going to stay until her confinement, but the baby's not due for two weeks. Will it be okay?"

"Ughhhhh!" growls the woman again and I ignore the nervous father, all my attention on his wife. I have no idea what I'm doing, so I just put my hands around the baby's head and hold on, trying to keep the mother from tearing.

What a strange way to come into this world, I reflect, *one human being squeezed out of another.*

"Push a little. Blow . . ." The head is out.

"Oh my God!" the father exclaims, holding himself up on the open car door.

"No pushing now, Bernice! Blow. Let me check for a cord around the neck."

"Urghhhh!" the mother growls again and the whole baby swivels and comes out on the seat.

"It's a boy," Alvin announces before I have time to look. "Oh, Nurse! Oh, my sweet Bernice." He runs around to the driver's side and strokes his wife's sweaty yellow hair. She is smiling; her leg still perched on my shoulder.

"Is it okay?" Bernice asks.

I give the lustily crying baby a once-over, looking, as I always do, for any anomalies, and quickly wrap it in the beautiful blanket, cord still attached.

"Just fine. A healthy male infant." *Now where to put the child while I attend to the afterbirth?*

"Do you have something soft? Another blanket?" The new father comes up with a worn chenille bathrobe to make a temporary bed for the infant on the floor.

"I have to push again!" the mother groans.

"Mother of God! Is there another one?" That's the dad.

"No, it's the placenta, the organ that gives nutrition and oxygen to the infant. You wouldn't have a bowl would you?" The father holds out his nice felt fedora and I plunk the whole slimy afterbirth into it.

Then Bernice squirms around and sits up. I hand her the crying, beet-red boy, still attached to the mess in the hat, and she begins to sing to him. *"Sleep, baby, sleep. Your father tends the sheep. . . ."*

Alvin sits down on the running board, his face very white. "I don't know how to thank you, ma'am. Will they be okay, until we get to her mother's?"

"Yes, but take them to a doctor or nurse right away, someone who can cut the cord properly. I don't have a pair of sterile scissors. This is important. Don't do it yourself. It has to be sterile, and then a special dressing goes over the stump."

"Thank you," Alvin says again. "I have a few dollars. I'm sorry it can't be more. I just got laid off at the Cumberland Lumberyard. That's why we're moving to Torrington, to live with her folks. Had to leave everything but what we could stuff in the car. You're an angel sent from heaven, Nurse."

"No, you keep the money. We don't need it. We're almost home."

"Thank you, Angel," the mother says, and I realize she thinks that's my name. *Angel!* Bernice's eyes are closed and she has the blissful expression of a person who's just experienced an earthquake or a wildfire and come out alive.

Alvin finds a towel, which we put between the mother's legs. I show her how to rub her uterus to be sure it stays firm and assist her in getting the infant to the breast. Then I take my coat off the hood of the DeSoto, say good-bye, and go back to the Pontiac to wash my shaking hands with water from a bottle I'd refilled at the last gas station.

"So," I say to Dr. Blum, dropping back behind the steering wheel, my heart still pounding. "I delivered a baby. Did you see that?" Blum is snoring and drool is running down his chin. I look at him sadly, my once brilliant colleague, now a baby himself.

The Doctor

"You did this on purpose, didn't you?" I hiss at my charge. "To punish me, and for what? I didn't have anything to do with your losing your mind."

The waitress, a bleached blonde, watches through the back window of the Four Leaf Clover Cafe just outside Oneida, West Virginia, and I catch a glimpse of myself in the glass, a small woman with a short light brown bob, an aquiline nose, a pinched mouth, and a puckered brow. Nurse Becky Myers, fallen on hard times.

The doctor just stares at a spot about a foot in front of him, seeing whatever nightmare he imagines or seeing nothing at all. The mountains leer over us, sandstone covered with red maple just budding. I blow out and begin the cleanup.

For more than seven years I worked with Dr. Isaac Blum, as his part-time surgical nurse while I ran the Women and Infants' Clinic

in Liberty, West Virginia. Then, in 1930 when the bottom fell out
of the economy and the clinic lost its state funding, I followed him
to Perrysville to be his office nurse in the private practice he shared
with his brother for another four years.

I'd always admired Blum, the kind of physician who delivered
babies, did surgery, made house calls, stayed up all night at the
bedside of a sick child, and still saw patients in the office the next
morning. He was a brilliant diagnostician and a careful surgeon,
with gentle, competent hands.

I'll admit he wasn't perfect. He often talked like a professor,
used big medical terms that the patients couldn't understand, and
he lacked social skills, but I always smoothed things over. We were
a team, and when you face life-or-death together, year in and year
out, you form a strong bond.

Now, here I am, a forty-two-year-old registered nurse with an advanced degree in public health, taking care of a grown man who
poops his pants, can't talk, and requires complete care just to survive. Maybe, I sometimes think . . . he doesn't want to survive.

Blum's collapse a year ago was a sudden one. After his wife
plunged down the bank of the James River and died in that auto
crash, it was like someone pulled the plug, and his life force just
swirled out of him. It took two days to find her body, trapped
under the ice.

I wasn't a relative or even his lover, but like a good nurse, I took
over his full-time care. What else could I do? Watch him starve, or
rot away in his own feces? Thinking it was temporary, I moved him
into the spare room of my rented apartment and devoted all my time
to his recovery. . . . Only he didn't recover, and we lived on his savings until it ran out. A year of grief later, his brother, Dr. Leonard
Blum, senior partner and owner of their two-person practice, finally
washed his hands of him.

"For god's sake, Isaac," Leonard yelled, the last time we saw him, just two days ago. "I have a living to make and a family to support. You can sit there like a living corpse and starve if you want to, but I can't carry the practice alone. I'm bringing in another physician." He slammed the door and roared away in his Packard.

I'd just brought Isaac home from Johns Hopkins (my last hope), where, after studying him for four weeks, the neuro men recommended experimental electrotherapy. They'd shoot a strong current through his brain and hope the pain would jolt him out of his lethargy, but I drew the line at that. (If Blum ever came back and had lost even one brain cell, I'd get the blame.)

Then, just yesterday, our landlady, Mrs. Jenkins, knocked on my door and stood there, her chin up and hands on her hips.

"Nurse Becky," she said. "You owe three months' back rent and my patience is as thin as snow in Atlanta. Twenty thousand people in the U.S. are being laid off every day and my husband is one of them. These are hard times, and I'm going to put you out if you can't pay by Friday. We need the cash."

I had only forty dollars, not enough for one month's rent, let alone three. The rest of the doc's money had gone to Johns Hopkins, but that night, Blum shocked the pants off me. As I was putting him to bed, he spoke for the first time in more than a year.

"Go home." His voice creaked like a door hinge that needs oiling.

"*We are home, here in Perrysville, Virginia.*"

"No." He shook his head. "Other Virginia!"

By this I realized he meant *West* Virginia, where he still owned a house and his old clinic. *So . . .* having no other options, I loaded up what I could and we escaped in the night.

Now, we follow the wooded ridge on the county road past small farms with grass so green it makes your eyes sing, past waterfalls that cascade down sandstone cliffs, past mountain streams that laugh for the joy of it, and as we begin our descent my spirits rise. The old worried Becky is replaced by the *other* Becky, the optimistic one.

"We should be in Liberty in another ten minutes," I say to my mute companion. "The electricity at your house may be turned off and it will be dusty and dirty, but we can manage." The doctor doesn't comment, but then I don't expect him to.

Finally, after twenty hours in the Pontiac, we enter a high mountain valley, and I feel my tight stomach soften. There in the distance, I catch sight of a familiar landmark, a winding ribbon of silver they call the Hope.

2

A Poor Welcome

"Explain to me exactly how this happened," I demand from Mr. Linkous, the attorney who has, for the past ten years, handled Dr. Blum's affairs in Liberty. It's only my training as a nurse that keeps me from screaming.

Isaac is seated at my side, immobile, hands balled up on his knees, eyes fixed on the attorney's framed diplomas mounted on the wall behind his desk. (It's so sad, really. When I first knew him, you could see his mind working in his very blue eyes, like minnows darting through a clear mountain stream.)

"Well." The pale young lawyer clears his throat and flips his fountain pen back and forth between his fingers. "I was left in charge of paying Dr. Blum's mortgage and taxes when he and Mrs. Blum joined his brother's practice in Charlottesville, but last year he stopped sending funds. I wrote him three times."

Here he frowns and taps a file on his desk that I assume holds copies of the correspondence. "I wrote to his brother too, November first, 1933, then I put a notice in the papers here and in Charlottesville on January first, 1934, but there was no response. Short of traveling to Virginia or paying the mortgage and taxes myself, there was no choice."

"We were in *Perrysville*," I snap, as if that makes a big difference. "It's about thirty miles outside of Charlottesville."

"The house, all its contents, his clinic, and two acres were put
up for auction by Mountain Federal on . . ." Here he consults the
documents again. "February twenty-fifth, 1934. Mr. Churchouse,
an investor from Charleston, bought the property for a song. I'm
sorry." The prematurely balding attorney closes the folder, as if
that puts an end to it.

"So we have *no* place to live? He has no *home*?" I'm getting a
little hysterical now.

Linkous glances at the doctor, then back at me. "What happened?" he asks in a whisper. "I'm so sorry. Was it a stroke?"

I'm too upset to sugarcoat it. "The nerve doctors aren't sure.
Maybe a stroke, though they can't determine the source of the
damage. Maybe shock at his wife's death."

The lawyer's dark eyebrows shoot up. "I heard about Mrs. Blum.
A tragedy. She seemed a fine woman." I know what he means. She
was a looker.

Back in the Pontiac, I stare out the window at the boarded-up
stores on Main Street. *What now?* Blum sits like a manikin from
Levy's Dry Goods. We have only ten dollars, not enough for gas to
get back to Perrysville and no family that either of us can turn to.
I have never felt so alone.

When I left Liberty four years ago, Wall Street had crashed and
a few stores had closed, but farmers, miners, tradesmen, and their
families still came to town for necessities. Now, all along Main, I
see only two autos and one very swaybacked horse attached to a
cart. For Sale signs are everywhere. At first glance there are only
a few shops left open, the grocery, the barbershop, Stenger's Pharmacy, and the Eagle Theater, but that's apparently only on Satur-
days. Farther down, there's a bar with a neon sign and Ida May's
House of Beauty, but that's all.

"Welcome home," I reflect out loud, flopping my head back on the leather driver's seat. I could be working at Walter Reed Hospital right now in a clean white uniform and a starched hat. Instead, I sit hunched in a cold car, nearly destitute, a caretaker of a mentally incapacitated ex-physician with no place to live and no place to go. It's not like I'm Dr. Blum's wife or sister, for god's sake, I'm just his last friend, well, almost a friend—actually more of a colleague. I look over at the poor fellow and straighten his collar.

For a moment I consider renting two rooms at the Barnett Boardinghouse and trying to find work in Delmont, twenty miles up the road, but I know, just by looking at the number of men on the courthouse steps, that there will be no jobs there either.

The same out-of-work miners, loggers, mechanics, and laborers who were sitting on the benches four years ago, when I lost *my* job, are still here, only then there were only five or six of them. Today there must be twenty lounging about, smoking Luckies and corncob pipes, hoping for some kind of day work. I watch as one spits a wad of tobacco on the sidewalk, and it's here the tears come. I really have no idea what to do next.

"Mr. Linkous should have at least taken us home to his house for the night," I complain to my mute companion. I get no response, but I continue my one-sided conversation.

"After filling the gas tank three times, we have only ten dollars." I scramble through my change purse, and add, "And forty-five cents. . . . Not enough to get us back to Perrysville, and anyway, where would we go when we got there? We still owe three months' rent to the landlady and can't ask for shelter from your brother."

"We have the Pontiac, only six years old." I take a deep breath and go over our assets. "We have two strong bodies. We have twelve years of higher education, but only one mind, between us." Here my voice breaks and Blum looks over.

Then he speaks again, the second time in a year. "Patience."

"Patience! Are you out of your mind?" At this, I actually

smile because *he truly is out of his mind.* "If you think we can just sit here *patiently* on the corner of Sycamore and Main and someone will come to our rescue, you are sicker than I thought!"

Then I get it: *Patience Murphy, the midwife.*

Shelter

"Patience Murphy!"

Once again Blum amazes me. It's like his once brilliant mind is hibernating, and for a moment it sticks its nose out of the cave and makes an observation.

The midwife of Hope River, Patience Murphy, was one of my only friends when I lived in Liberty four years ago. You'd think there'd be others, but for a single professional woman in a small mountain town, there weren't many options.

A few people reached out to me when I first left the Coal Miner's Mission at Scotts Run and took my job as the Union County public health nurse. The pharmacist Mr. Stenger and his wife invited me to dinner, but their five wild children drove me nuts, and I never followed up with a reciprocal invitation.

The schoolteacher, Marion Archer, took me shopping in Torrington, but she talked so much I couldn't stand it. Then there was Priscilla Blum, Dr. Blum's wife. She and Patience . . . they were my *almost friends* . . . and the doctor . . . but that was purely professional.

Patience Murphy and her young colored assistant, Bitsy Proudfoot, live only ten miles out of Liberty on Wild Rose Road. We can be there in thirty minutes. Maybe Patience will allow us to stay with her for a few days. I'd be grateful even to sleep in her barn.

I start up the Pontiac and roll down Main Street, past the closed shops, past the courthouse, the train station, the fire station, the water tower, and the Saved by Faith Baptist Church.

As we cross the stone bridge over the Hope, I feel Dr. Blum straighten and look down at the water. On the far side two men are fishing. They raise their hands in salute and I wonder if they recognize the doc or are just being friendly.

It hadn't occurred to me, until now, that when people hear that Dr. Blum is back, they might expect him to restart his practice. I tighten my mouth. It isn't often that I let myself feel the whole weight of his tragedy. Mostly I just do my duty as a nurse, puzzled and angry, wondering how I got into this.

I know the answer, of course. I just never thought it would go on and on. *Now what can I do?* Leave him on the steps of a poorhouse or abandon him to the state asylum for the insane? I've been in those hellholes, and you don't do that to someone you care about.

As I turn onto Salt Lick, a wind comes up and I'm almost run into a ditch by a green truck, the kind that they used in the Great War, now filled with young men in khaki uniforms. When the guys see me, they yell out their catcalls. "Hey, baby!" "Hi ya, doll!"

CCC, CIVILIAN CONSERVATION CORPS, it says on the cab. As part of Roosevelt's New Deal, the feds are hiring young men from all over the country, giving them work to do in rural areas instead of going on the dole, and I suppose I shouldn't be surprised to see them here, even in Union County.

Their whistles give me a lift, but only for a minute. From a distance they can't tell I haven't put on makeup in two days nor washed my short dark hair since we left Perrysville. They can't see the lines of worry and sadness around my brown eyes.

The shadows are long and it's nearing six by the time we labor up Wild Rose Road, past the Maddock farm, where Sarah Maddock, the crippled woman, and her husband, an engineer, from Huntington, live. The Maddocks moved to her family's place after she was brought down by polio some ten years ago.

At the end of the gravel lane, sits Patience Murphy's home, a small two-story white cottage with a periwinkle blue door. The house was in no great shape when I last saw it, but it looks way worse now, and the picket fence that I used to love is gone. What's more, Patience and Bitsy have let the yard go. The grass has grown up and a branch on the big oak in front swings in the wind like a broken arm.

"Hello!" I call, jumping out of the car, but Dr. Blum doesn't follow. Unless I guide him, he won't move at all, even if he's hungry or thirsty or has to pee. He's a wind-up toy, without volition, and I'm the winder.

When I step up on the porch and look through the cracked window, I see Patience's old sofa, but no piano and no paintings on the wall. That's one of the things that impressed me about the midwife the first time I came here, her display of original artwork, something you don't see much in the mountains except in the homes of the coal barons, bankers, and railway executives. I also was interested in her small bookcase with two shelves of novels, children's books, and medical texts.

It's dawning on me now that no one lives here, but just to be sure, watching carefully for copperheads, I head out through the tall grass to the barn behind the house. The double doors creak as I peek in. What am I afraid I'll find? Dead animals? The skeleton of a midwife I once admired hanging from the rafters? My imagination is too fertile. Always has been.

What I discover is . . . nothing. There are no signs of recent life, not a cow or a horse or even a chicken. Shafts of pale light shine down from the loft and the air smells of dust and old manure.

On the way back to the house a flash of lightning catches my eye and then the dark clouds growl, like dogs giving warning. *Thunder is scaring the frost out of the ground.* That's what the old-timers say in Vermont.

With a sinking heart I must face the facts. Patience Murphy is gone. Then the rain comes, cold tears.

3

Roughing It

Last night, as soon as there was a break in the weather, I ran for the car and got some supplies. Then, after a cold supper that I'd packed before we left Perrysville, I put Dr. Blum to bed on the dusty sofa and I lay down with an old army blanket on a bare mattress upstairs.

Looking around, it's clear that Patience and her friend Bitsy have been gone for months, probably years. There's nothing in the kitchen cupboards, no pots or pans, only a few tiny mice droppings, and the house smells faintly of mold.

The wood cookstove is still here, as is the heater stove and an old metal lantern, but we have no dry wood to make a fire or kerosene for light. The midwife never did have a phone or electricity. As in most of rural America, the power and telephone lines haven't reached into the hollows or up the mountains, and now with the Great Depression, the farmers won't get them for years.

Luckily, I'd stowed a few candles in our emergency kit, and sometime after midnight, before I fell into a troubled sleep, I got out my nurse's notebook and tried to think about our situation. It wasn't good.

Problem: Two Adults. Impoverished and Homeless.
(I can't believe I'm writing this about myself! How could this happen to a woman like me?)

One male physician, age 45, 6' 2" and 164 pounds at last weigh, fit enough but quite useless.

One female nurse, 42, 5' 4" and 128 pounds, with two college degrees but no survival skills. She's not even a good cook.

Ten dollars and forty-five cents. (I actually got out of bed, opened my pocketbook, and counted the change again, wishing, like anything, that I'd taken Alvin up on his offer of a few dollars for assisting at his wife's emergency delivery.)

Food: a half loaf of bread, a chunk of cheese, three apples, and a Hershey's Bar left from our stop at the Four Leaf Clover Cafe.

Two heavy wool blankets from the trunk of the car.

Our clothes.

Some medical books and equipment that I suppose we could sell, but who would want them?

I lay here, now listening to rain slash the side of the house and thunder roll away over Spruce Mountain and wonder what could have happened to Patience and Bitsy. There were rumors that the KKK was out to get them, and that thought makes me sick.

Somewhere in the house, water leaks through the roof, a steady *drip, drip.* Twice I hear the doctor moan in his sleep, and once I think he's crying, but it stops.

Another Life

This life of poverty is new for me; counting pennies, sleeping on a bare mattress without proper linens, not knowing what we will eat tomorrow or where we may go.

I was born into a life of ease in Brattleboro, Vermont, the

youngest child of Dr. Donald and Martha Farenthold, but my life wasn't trouble free. Father was a drunk and not a jolly one, though no one in town knew the shadow we lived under.

A respectable member of the community, Dr. Farenthold was sober at his medical office and the hospital, but as soon as he got home, he'd fall into his big chair, open a medical journal, and uncork the bottle. By nine he was plastered and we lived in fear that someone would need him in the night and we would be exposed.

In the early days, Mother tried to divert him with outings and family games, but he would get belligerent. Sometimes he'd even bash her around. To stay away from him, she volunteered for various charitable organizations, the Children's Home Society, the Red Cross, and the Lutheran Women's Club.

Then, when I was fourteen, Mama got uterine cancer. . . . Ironic, a doctor's wife dying of a treatable disease. She could have had a hysterectomy if they'd found it in time, but by then my parents were hardly speaking.

Our home, a big Victorian with a white picket fence around the lush lawn, not ten minutes from the Connecticut River, had been anything but peaceful, but after Mother died, it was a tomb.

For a few years, we had a maid and a cook, but eventually Father ran them off, and my brothers and I had to fend for ourselves. Darwin and William, nine and ten years my senior, who attended Amherst College just down the road, left for Harvard Medical School as soon as they could. That left Father and the house to me.

I was a pale child, bookish and withdrawn. In school, even if I knew the answer, I was hesitant to raise my hand. Though pretty enough in an old-fashioned way, I didn't date, didn't participate in sports or girls' clubs, just got all As and went home to try to keep Father from burning the house down or doing something else self-destructive.

As soon as I was seventeen, just like my brothers, I applied for college. Girls didn't go to university much in those days, but I argued that it would secure my future in case I never married.

"An attractive girl like you! You'll get hooked before you get your degree. It's a waste of my money," Father whined, looking over his glass of amber liquid.

But I proved him wrong. I graduated from the University of Vermont with a teaching diploma in May of '14 and didn't marry for another six months. Luckily, Father was pleased with my choice, a young physician, Dr. David Myers, whom I'd met at a Chautauqua in Burlington.

Following our honeymoon in New York, father sobered up for a while. We moved into a new Sears Roebuck Craftsman house that he had built for us, and by September, David had set up a practice.

Everyone expected us to conceive right away, but we were having too much fun. We canoed the backwaters of the Connecticut River and danced in the ballroom of the Copley in Boston, but by late 1915 the party was over.

War in Europe was on everyone's mind, and David began talking about joining the medics. You'd think I'd object, but I actually encouraged him. I was young. What did I know of the horrors of combat? My brothers were already in Spain, and I would have joined too, only I was a girl.

Within the month, David contacted a second cousin in Winnipeg and signed with the Canadian Army. Many of the young men from Vermont and Maine were doing the same.

Our last night together, we walked the banks of the Connecticut, as the full moon rode the ripples, breaking into little shards of light. The June air smelled of honeysuckle and growing things. I was twenty-three. He was twenty-eight, and we had our whole life before us.

"You are so lovely," David told me, pushing a shock of his thick black hair back from his forehead. "Always stay this way, so beautiful with moonlight on your face."

I laughed. "I'll be old someday. Will you still love me?"

"Always, but you'll never be old. Not to me. I'll always see you like this."

"Even when I have strands of gray in my hair and wrinkles around my eyes?"

"You'll never be like that."

"If you say so." I mocked him and did a little jig, my hands on my hips in the silver moonlight.

"Trust me on this. Look at you; you're too full of life." He grabbed my hand and we ran along the grassy bank.

The next morning he left on the train for Montreal, so handsome in his new Canadian uniform, leaning out the window, waving. I never saw him smile like that again.

Gunshot

At dawn, a deafening blast rips open my dreams. Before I'm truly awake, I'm at the upstairs window of the little house with the blue door, staring down at a lean, leathered man wearing a black hat pulled down to his eyes, his firearm aimed at Dr. Blum, who is walking through the wet grass in his long underwear, straight at the gunman.

"No!" I yell, flying down the stairs, missing every other step and twisting my ankle at the bottom.

"No!" I yell again, slamming through the screen door, running toward the armed man to shield the doctor. "Don't shoot."

The man lowers his double-barreled shotgun, and I see that it's

Mr. Maddock the neighbor from down the hill. I had met him once or twice when I made home visits to his paralyzed wife.

"Miss?"

"Don't shoot," I call again. "It's me, Becky Myers, the home health nurse and . . ."

"Well, what are *you* doing here? I called out to that fellow twice that he was trespassing, but he didn't answer, just glared with those crazy blue eyes . . . then he started to come for me and I fired a warning shot into the air. There are hoboes all over these hills taking up residence anywhere they like, tearing up property, stealing and selling whatever's not nailed down."

When I drag the doctor back to the porch and sit him down, I notice the front button of his union suit is undone. Maybe he was on the steps trying to relieve himself when Maddock showed up. (If it's true, this is a first and would show some progress.)

"This is the doctor. Doctor Blum. He's not himself," I explain to Mr. Maddock. "It's a stroke . . . or some kind of brain attack." (I'm making this up to keep it simple, and a stroke is something people in Union County might understand.)

"I brought Dr. Blum home, thinking the mountain air might do him some good, but when I got to Liberty, Mr. Linkous, his attorney, told me the bank sold his house."

Here, Maddock enters the yard. When he cracks open his shotgun and removes the shells, I take a long, shaky breath. The sun is just rising over the mountains, golden through the still bare branches of the oak.

"I used most of the gas we have left to get to Patience's house, but no one's here. . . ."

Maddock steps closer, his eyes like black marbles inspecting Dr. Blum. "He's gone queer, all right. Used to be a sharp fellow. Stroke, you say . . ." He pushes his black hat back a little and squints. "I didn't hear you come up the road last night or I would have stopped you."

"It was almost dark. Can we stay a few days? We won't harm anything. Just until I figure out what to do next?"

"I'll tell the missus to make you some biscuits." I take this as a yes and am grateful.

"Have Patience and Bitsy been gone long? There's not much in the house. Nothing in the barn, and the lawn isn't mowed."

"Moved out around the time you left. Whole damn country is moving like a bunch of ants hunting for food. I try to keep the weeds down when I have time." He kicks at the grass and some pieces of the picket fence that used to surround the cottage.

"So who owns her house? Patience didn't just leave it, did she?"

"I imagine she and her husband still own it . . . or the Mountain Federal Bank." He never looks at me when he talks, but he can't take his eyes off the doctor.

"Her husband?"

"The animal man. The vet."

"You mean Dr. Hester? I didn't even know they were courting. Did they all leave together?"

"No."

I have to squeeze for each tiny bit of information and it's slower than picking burrs off your socks.

"So where are they now?"

"Bitsy, the colored girl, and that colored fellow Bowlin went east to Philly, to be with her brother, Thomas Proudfoot, the one they thought killed a white man."

"And Patience?"

"Why's he staring like that?" Maddock indicates the doctor.

I glance back at Blum, who sits gazing without expression at the same spot one foot from his face, a man sleeping with his blue eyes open.

"I don't know, Mr. Maddock. We don't know. It's like he's not home anymore."

"Don't let him come down to my place. I don't want him around my Sarah. I'll shoot if I see him. He was right sharp the last time I saw him." He says this last part again.

"I know. It's a tragedy. But Patience, where did *she* go?"

Maddock raises his chin toward the ridge covered in spruce that rises behind the barn.

I turn to look back.

"On the other side of Spruce Mountain."

"On the other side of the mountain?"

"Yonder," he says again. "The midwife and her baby."

Good Samaritan

Driving back down Wild Rose Road and around Salt Lick, I am almost gay. "Well," I say, turning to my companion, "things are looking up. Did you hear what Mr. Maddock said? Patience isn't gone; she just moved to the other side of the mountain. Oh, I hope they say we can live in her house for a while! It's not bad, really. I could fix it up. Then maybe I can get a job. Probably not nursing . . . But what will I do with you? I can't leave you alone."

This had never occurred to me. "Oh, well, don't get the horse before the cart. First things first . . . We need shelter . . . then warmth and firewood . . . then food." (I can't believe my life has been reduced to such basics.)

As we bounce down the dirt roads, still slick from last night's rain, I glance at the gas gauge. One-quarter full. We have just enough to get to Patience's house to ask for permission to live in her cottage and then get to town at some point for supplies.

As a physician's daughter and a physician's wife, then later as a single professional woman, I have never been particularly frugal, never needed to be, but with no job and no income, I will have to start now.

I glance over to check on Blum, but he is staring out the passenger window, his face impassive, a little spit on his chin, and I reach over to wipe it off with my hanky. That's when I hit the rough place in the road and blow a tire!

"Dammit! Dammit! Dammit!" I curse, pounding on the steering wheel. With the economy busted, most states' coffers are as empty as a robin's nest in December and the roads have all gone to hell. I get out to look. I have never changed a tire in my life!

A jack is used, I think, to lift up the auto, and there's a spare in the back, but how do I get the flat tire off the wheel? "Oh, Blum! Why don't you pull yourself together and help me?"

The able-bodied Dr. Blum sits vacantly, gazing at the pussy willows just beginning to open along the road. He doesn't even know the Pontiac's stopped.

Irritated, I remove the gear and luggage from the trunk to get at the jack, his medical bag, two boxes of books, my art supplies, and his surgical instruments, though I don't know why I brought them.

I'm sitting in the wet grass in the ditch with tears in my eyes, trying to figure out how the jack works, when a low hack driven by a black man wearing a yellow slicker pulls up to the side of the car.

"Ma'am." He steps out of his vehicle and tips his broad-brimmed straw hat. "Preacher Miller of the Hazel Patch Baptist Fellowship. Can I be of some assistance?"

I catch his eyes on Blum, probably wondering why the man still sits in the car while the woman struggles with the jack.

"It's me, Reverend, Becky Myers. I met you one time at the hospital in Liberty. The home health nurse . . . It was after the cave-in at the Wild Cat Mine. You were one of the men who brought in the bodies. And that's Dr. Blum. You probably met him sometime too. He's . . . He's not well." I leave it at that.

"Miss Myers!" The preacher tips his hat once more and gives me a big smile that lights up his dark face. His eyes are brown and soulful. "So nice to see you again. I heard you and Dr. Blum moved away to Virginia. Are you back to set up your clinic or just visiting?"

"No, we're back. It's a long story. Right now I'm trying to find Patience Murphy, the midwife. Mr. Maddock, on Wild Rose Road, told me she's married to the vet. Am I headed in the right direction?"

"Not far at all." Reverend Miller is already rolling up his sleeves and soon has us back on the road.

"Just two miles ahead on the left. You'll see a sign that says Daniel Hester, DMV, Small and Large Animals, with a little sign below, Patience Hester, Midwife, Small and Large Women." He chuckles at the joke. "Say hello for me."

4

Reunited

As we pull across a small wooden bridge that spans a bubbling creek and into the tree-lined drive of Daniel Hester's farmyard, my heart leaps. Here I hope I will find friends.

The two-story stone home, with a porch on two sides, is surrounded by mowed grass. I can tell Patience lives here, because there are bunches of herbs hanging under the porch eaves: tansy, feverfew, mint, and echinacea are the ones that I recognize, but there are a dozen more. The midwife is also an herbalist and uses them to help heal her patients.

There are chickens in the yard scratching for insects and four horses and three cows in the field. The cowbells tinkle, but other than that it's so quiet, I decide Patience and Dr. Hester must both be out delivering babies, a little boy or girl for her, a calf or lamb for him.

Unsure what to do, I take Blum's arm, head for a wooden bench under one of the giant weeping willows, and take a seat. The long drooping branches are just budding out, covered in yellow, like palpable sunshine, and with the tip of my finger, I reach out to touch them.

We don't have to wait long. Within twenty minutes, a dusty black Olds rolls across the bridge and stops behind our Pontiac. My friend has come up in the world. She once rode a horse to births, before that a bicycle.

I take my time rising, watching as Patience gets out of the vehicle. She's a small woman, thin, but sturdy, and pretty, with high color. Her brown hair, which she used to wear long, is shoulder length now, and she peers through her wire-rim glasses at our Virginia license plate.

"Hello!" she calls out, looking around, and when she turns, I'm startled to see she has a toddler on her hip.

"Over here." I step from under the long willow fronds. "Patience! It's me, Becky Myers." If I had been apprehensive at all, my questions about our friendship evaporate in the time it takes a wide smile to rush across her face.

She plops the child on the grass, and with open arms runs toward me, her red-and-black-plaid farm jacket flapping like wings. "Becky!" Laughing as we embrace, we almost fall over. Though the midwife is small, she's as strong as a pony.

"Chiggers," I say indicating the baby. Patience doesn't get it. "Chiggers," I repeat, thinking she must not know about the troublesome insect that burrows under the skin and itches like crazy. "On the grass. They're everywhere in Virginia. Very much a problem for the young and tender."

"Oh, chiggers. Yes, we have them. Danny gets them once or twice in the summer and me too, but since it's cooler here in the mountains, they're not so much of a problem. You *are* the same old *worrywart*, Becky Myers! Come inside."

It's then that she sees Dr. Blum, still sitting immobile on the bench under the weeping willow. "Oh, you have someone with you! A new beau?" She's probably kidding, but I don't find it funny.

"No, it's Dr. Blum. He's not well. The physicians at Johns Hopkins think it's a stroke or maybe catatonia." I wave my open hand in front of his face. "Anyway. He's all gone. . . . We've come to ask for your help."

Kindness

At the kitchen table in the stone farmhouse, Patience and I catch up over coffee. Silent as a sphinx, Dr. Blum sits staring into space on a stool in the corner.

I take in the room. . . . There's a green enamel wood cookstove against one wall with a wooden box filled with split oak, shelves filled with glass canisters of beans, cornmeal, and flour, and a sink with a small red metal water pump. In the corner is a large Frigidaire, which means that the Hesters have electricity and probably a phone. This must be heaven for Patience, who used to live without any such conveniences.

"What happened?" Patience asks in a low voice, indicating the doctor with her eyes.

I tell her the story, how Priscilla Blum died when her auto crashed through the guardrail into the ice-covered James River and how, after that, the doctor just collapsed, lost his mind.

"Up until then he'd been his normal self. He'd actually done four surgeries earlier that day. One was an emergency appendectomy that went horribly wrong and the patient died on the operating table. . . ."

"Maybe the two deaths on one day were his breaking point, or maybe he had a stroke from the stress." That's Patience.

"Maybe so."

"He's lost so much weight." She studies the doc and I look at him from her eyes. She's right. He's lost around twenty pounds and his once strong jaw has gone slack. Not only that, his brown hair is thin and dry. Not a healthy-looking specimen.

"I feed him, feed him with a spoon three meals a day," I respond defensively. "But he doesn't care about food or anything. I was sympathetic in the beginning. Really, I was, but I expected his disability to be temporary. Now, I don't know. . . . I'm just frustrated. In all this time there's so little improvement."

"This happened a year ago?" We watch as Danny, Patience's toddler, approaches the doctor and runs a little metal truck up his leg. For just a moment, I think Blum sees him, but then he goes back to the blank stare again.

"Yes, a year ago, during a snowstorm. Like I said, as a last resort, I took him to Johns Hopkins, but it cost a fortune, and they were no help. After about a year, his brother, the older Dr. Blum, had no sympathy at all. He bellowed at Isaac to snap out of it, thought he was faking. Just a few days ago, he abandoned us altogether and we were left on our own. . . ."

Here I trail off. I don't tell Patience how I prayed on my knees for my colleague, to a God I couldn't locate. I don't tell her how at first I would stroke Isaac's head and his shoulders after I bathed him, hoping I could bring him back. I don't tell her how once or twice I slapped him, I was so mad.

We both turn to the sound of an auto rattling up the drive. "It's Daniel," Patience says, standing.

From the kitchen window, I watch as the veterinarian opens the trunk of his Ford Model T, removes a satchel, and sets it on the top of the car. Then he pulls out some rope and pulleys and other bizarre-looking veterinarian equipment and carries it into the barn. He's a tall man, with an outdoor look, wearing a long brown canvas coat.

A few minutes later, the kitchen door slams open and the vet comes in and picks up his little boy. "Who have we here? I wondered about the Virginia license plate!" he says with a lopsided grin. His light brown hair is receding in front, and his large hands are chafed and rough.

"It's Becky Myers and Dr. Blum!"

"Well, hello! What brings you back to Union County?" He leans over to shake the doctor's hand, and when there's no response, frowns and looks at me with concern.

"Dr. Blum is . . . I don't know how to put this . . . disabled." The vet looks him over as if assessing a lame horse.

"What can he do?"

"Nothing."

"No one knows what's wrong with him," Patience puts in. "It might be the shock of his wife's death, a stroke, or possibly catatonia. Remember? We heard about her accident."

I take up the narrative a second time, giving the history and what the doctors proposed. "The neuro men at Johns Hopkins said there was nothing they could do, except electroshock treatment and there was no guarantee with that."

"So why'd you come back?" That's Daniel, looking deep into Dr. Blum's pale eyes. "A damn shame! So why'd you come back?" he asks me again.

"Well, he told me to."

"That doesn't sound catatonic."

"It wasn't a conversation, just one word . . . no, three words in all. . . . After his brother disowned him. We were out of money and owed three months' back rent. Since he couldn't take care of himself, I'd moved him in with me, and I was tearing my hair out about a probable eviction when he opened his mouth and offered an alternative. 'Home. West Virginia.' "

"That's all he's said in a year?" Patience moves to the sink to pump water.

"Yes. That's about it . . . until yesterday when he spoke again. After the lawyer told us that his house had been sold . . . we were sitting on Main Street in his Pontiac, broke with nowhere to go. I'll be honest, I was crying when Dr. Blum spoke for the second time. 'Patience' he said. At first I thought he meant to be patient and have faith, then I realized he meant Patience, the midwife.

"We drove up to your old house on Wild Rose Road, hoping to find shelter and found you were gone, but camped there anyway, feeling lost. Mr. Maddock was the one who told us you'd moved to the other side of the mountain." Here I clear my throat and take a moment to get up my courage.

"I was hoping we could stay there for a while, take care of the empty house for you. . . ." I trail off, suddenly embarrassed. Asking for help isn't something I'm used to.

"Of course . . . of course," Patience reassures. "You'd be doing us a favor. We thought of selling the place, but no one can afford to buy it now . . . except the very rich, who are already hovering like vultures, taking advantage of the foreclosures and bottomed-out land prices."

Here her face gets pink and her voice crackles. Hester reaches over to pat her arm. The midwife, I recall, has always been something of a leftist, sympathetic to the poor and suspicious of the rich.

"There've been hundreds of drifters and homeless passing through, but we've been reluctant to just let a stranger move in," Daniel adds, standing to let his dogs in, two beagles and a three-legged mutt. "We might even have some furniture in the barn and some of Patience's kitchen things and linens. You could stay here with us for the night, and in the morning we'll look around." He stands and gives his wife a kiss on her neck.

"Come on, Blum. Time to milk." He takes a bucket and then pulls Blum through the door.

I shake my head. He still doesn't get it, or else he's trying to prove some point, and I watch through the kitchen window as the men cross the farmyard.

Hester has his arm linked through Blum's as if they were old chums and they probably *were* associates, both college-educated doctors. Tears come to my eyes for what's been lost, tears for the vet's kindness, tears for the long, lonely way ahead. I wipe them with the back of my hand, before Patience can see, then I tell her about my emergency delivery on the roadside yesterday.

"I must say I was proud of myself," I end the story. "Bernice didn't even have a perineal tear."

"Sounds like maybe you have a knack for this. Maybe you should be a midwife," Patience kids me. She knows that being near a woman in labor terrifies me. "Anyway, you should keep track of your births. Start a journal with the dates, names, and details of what you think is important. You never know when you might need it."

"It's not like I'm going to attend many more deliveries, but you're probably right. If something bad happened, the board of medicine might someday investigate. I'm a registered nurse."

Patience shakes her head, laughing. "Becky. Becky. Becky."

"Well, they might!"

April 2, 1934

Emergency delivery near the intersection of the National Turnpike and Route 26. I assisted a male infant to be born in an auto to a Mrs. Bernice Norton and her husband, Alvin. (I was more nervous than usual because I hadn't seen a baby born in five years. The Blum brothers stopped doing home deliveries when all the women started going to the hospital in Charlottesville.)

It's interesting that, though I was terrified, some of what I'd seen Patience do in the tent with the hobo girl came back to me and I was proud that Bernice didn't tear. It was her first baby, a healthy male infant, weight unknown. Only a small amount of bleeding. They went on to Torrington to her mother's home with the cord still attached and the placenta nestled in Mr. Norton's hat.

5

Wild Greens

Today I cannot be sure, but I think the doctor reacted when our new dog, Three Legs, licked his hand. It may have been reflex, but he appeared to reach up and ruffle his fur.

I shouldn't really call the golden mutt *our* dog. He's really *mine*. I feed him and I take him in and out of the cottage to do his job, but it's Isaac he's taken a shine to. The vet says it's sometimes that way.

At first I was horrified to be given a pet. We scarcely have enough food to feed ourselves, but what could I do? The veterinarian and midwife are our benefactors and I wasn't in a position to argue. Daniel led Three Legs right up to Blum, who sat in the gray, weathered rocking chair staring into space. Then the vet took Isaac's flaccid hand and made him stroke the dog's big yellow head.

"See," he addressed the canine. "This is Dr. Blum, your master. Do whatever he says." Here he winked at me, acknowledging the irony . . . since Blum never says anything.

It's been more than a week since we moved into the little house at the end of Wild Rose Road and we are slowly getting adjusted. I've replaced the glass in the broken window and repaired the roof. Patience and Dr. Hester generously brought over a box of linens, dishes, a rocking chair they found in the barn, and two braided rugs. They also gave us a basket of meat, eggs, milk, and bread, which we needed badly.

Now, Dr. Blum and I sit on a wooden bench on the porch while I sort through the dandelion greens I've picked for our midday meal.

"It seems wrong that I have to eat the weeds that other people pull out of their front yards . . . like I've failed somehow," I say to my mute companion.

Blum's expression is as blank as the blue sky, but I shrug and keep talking. "I know there are people poorer than us, but just look at you. You're wearing some of Daniel's old work clothes, a flannel shirt with a hole at the elbow and frayed denim pants. I'm wearing a pair of stained slacks and an old sweater, torn at the waistband."

I stop myself and stare out across the fields. . . . "No, that's wrong. I have to stop feeling so sorry for myself and try to look for the positive.

"For example, look at the base of the old oak where daffodils are blooming in clusters, and in the distance see how the river glimmers in the morning light. There is always the Hope." I think this is funny, and when I look over at Blum, for a moment he appears to share my amusement, but I'm probably wrong.

Job Hunt

"Okay, Dr. Blum," I start out at breakfast. "I can't put it off any longer. This morning we are going into town to find some kind of work."

To get ready for my job-hunting expedition, I settle on a brown skirt, a yellow middy, and brown flats. My town clothes are a little out of date, but of good quality, and I worry that I won't look as desperate as I truly am. I also worry about the doctor, unsure what I will do with him if I *do* get a job, but decide I'll cross that bridge when I come to it. At the last minute I spiff him up too, with a shirt and a tie.

Our trip into Liberty is uneventful until we cross the Hope River. Just before the bridge, a large newly constructed billboard confronts us.

"JOBLESS MEN KEEP MOVING. WE CAN'T TAKE CARE OF OUR OWN. —LIBERTY CHAMBER OF COMMERCE." I read the sign out loud and cringe, wondering how people will respond to a *jobless woman*. As in most small towns, people get employment through family and friends, but we have no family and not many friends.

The first stop I plan to make is the grocery store, which thankfully is still open. (So many of the stores are not.) As I cross the bridge, a sleek red Packard with a silver winged goddess on the hood comes up behind us and honks. *Why such a hurry?*

On Main Street, I pull up to the curb and watch as a driver in black exits the Packard and opens the back door. A woman of about fifty, wearing a white coat and hat, gets out and waltzes into Ida May's House of Beauty. She trails a fur stole, and it occurs to me she could be a movie star, but then why would she be in Liberty?

"Okay, Dr. Blum. I have to go into the general store. You must stay here. Do not move from this seat! Do you understand?" I slow my speech, pounding out each word, take his chin in one hand, and turn his face to mine. "Do you understand? Don't move!" Of course he makes no response, and why do I think he would?

The little bell on the glass door of Bittman's Grocery rings when I open it, but there's no one behind the counter and many of the long wooden shelves are bare. "Hello!" A man wearing a clean, worn brown apron steps out of the back carrying a case of canned pork and beans.

"Good afternoon, Mr. Bittman," I say, and put on a bright face. "Do you remember me, Becky Myers? I was the home health nurse in Union County a few years ago."

"Yes, of course. My wife, Lilly, went to your baby classes with our first child, and you were friends with Mrs. Blum. I was sorry to hear of her death and . . ." Here he hesitates. "And the doctor's infirmity. Mr. Linkous was in and told me what happened."

The grocer is a tall, lean thirty-year-old with arms so long his wrists show at his cuffs. He has brown hair and brown eyes, and at a distance could be a ringer for the actor Gary Cooper.

"*Infirmity* is putting it nicely, because he can't speak or do anything for himself. I hoped by bringing him home, he might heal, but so far, there's little change."

Bittman clears his throat and squints. "I heard about the mix-up with the bank and the doctor's house, and we are right sorry for that. Mr. Linkous feels bad too." He looks around the empty grocery. "You probably noticed, we're one of the last places open . . . but we're still holding on." Here he picks up a rag and starts wiping the counter, studying the pitted wood as if there were some spot that needed polishing.

"The doctor and I are living in Patience Murphy's old place. . . . I'll need a few pounds of white beans, a small ham bone, and a tin of lard . . . two pounds of flour and an onion. How much will that be?"

"One dollar and five cents. The ham bone is only nineteen cents a pound, a good deal."

I make my purchases, still trying to get up my nerve to ask about work. Silence swallows the air between us. Finally, I spit out the words. "Do you know of any jobs, Mr. Bittman? I don't mean just nursing, anything at all. I'm our sole support now. . . ." I trail off and then add, almost under my breath, "I would even work in trade, take barter instead of cash. . . ."

"I'm sorry, Miss Becky. There's no work anywhere. You see how it is. Even *able-bodied men* can't find anything. Half the county has moved on. . . . Hey, Junior," he calls. A little kid with red hair sticks his head though the open door of the back room. "Bring out that box of apples for Miss Becky."

"No, please. I can't afford them."

"Oh, there's no charge. They're headed for the trash or Mr. Mintz's pigs. Bottom of the barrel went bad and spoiled, but if you cut off the rotten places you can make some nice applesauce. I'll carry them out to your car."

"Well, thank you. Thank you so much. I'm sure we'll love them," I murmur as we load the crate into the trunk. Bittman stares at the doctor through the passenger window, then taps the glass.

"Howdy, Doc." When there's no response, he taps again and then shrugs. "You take care now, Miss Becky, and don't be a stranger."

Three blocks down Main we pull up to the curb, this time at Stenger's Pharmacy. I repeat my instructions to my mute companion, this time shortening the command: "Stay!" Like he's Three Legs the dog. "Stay!"

Another Try

As if the six-inch gap will entice passing customers in, the front door of the pharmacy is propped open. "Mr. Stenger?" I call, pushing it wider and looking around. Except for a scrawny orange cat on the counter, the shop appears vacant. "Mr. Stenger?" I call again louder, and a short, round man with a balding head and one lazy eye comes out of the back carrying a bucket and mop. He wears a long white cloth coat with a crooked red bow tie, and the store smells like carbolic acid and something sweet, probably Lilly of the Valley Toilet Water. (I used to buy it here in better days.)

"Oh, hello. I didn't hear you come in. . . . Is that Becky Myers? Nurse Becky! I heard you were back." He leans his mop against the wall, moves toward me, right arm outstretched and I shake his soft hand. My hands were soft once too, but as I look down I notice a little grime under the nails. Without hot running water, *I've become a country girl.*

"What can I do for you?" Stenger asks. "Is the doc all right? I heard he'd suffered some sort of fall."

"No, not a fall. We don't know of any injury. Some of the specialists at Johns Hopkins thought he might have had a stroke. Others say it's catatonia, a neurological condition brought on by hysteria or maybe shock."

"I know about catatonia. Part of my training was at the State Asylum for the Insane in Weston. You'd see those people, the cata tonics, walking around carrying a doll or dancing with a broom. It's like they're ghosts."

"Yes, that's what he's like, a ghost of himself. It's pitiful really."

The pharmacist shakes his head and leans on the counter. "So what can I do for you, Miss Becky?"

"I need to find work." I don't lead up to it this time, just dive right in.

"Whew! You and everyone else in the good old USA. Papers say twenty-five percent of the nation is unemployed, but in West Virginia it's worse." He indicates the headlines in the *Charleston Gazette* on a newspaper rack in the corner: UNEMPLOYMENT REACHES 80 PERCENT IN UNION COUNTY.

"That's like no jobs at all. Eighty percent! Most of the mines have shut down. . . . Hear about the strike in Toledo?" He pushes last week's paper across the counter. AUTO-LIGHT STRIKE IN TOLEDO. 2 DEAD. 200 INJURED, reads the headline. "Six thousand union strikers fought fifteen hundred National Guardmen."

"Listen, Mr. Stenger, I know it's bad all over, but I'm desperate. Can you think of any work at all?" The pharmacist turns back to his mop and bucket. "I wouldn't ask you, but we're almost out of money. We have no supplies put ahead and. . . ."

In better times I would never have gone on like this. Mr. Stenger sets the mop aside and reaches under his white pharmacist coat for his wallet.

"No, I didn't mean *that*! I have never asked for handouts. I just need a job." He pulls out a two-bit piece and forces it into my hand. I have no choice but to accept it or the coin will fall in his bucket.

"Don't tell the missus," he says, going back to his work. "You see what even a trained pharmacist has come to—I now mop my own floors."

"I could do it. I would be glad to."

"The store is closed now, Miss Myers." He rings the water out of his mop and swishes it across the wooden floor, almost chasing me out, and we're both so embarrassed I don't say good-bye.

Despite the fact that this twenty-five cents will help keep us going for another week, it burns in my hand, and my cheeks burn too. *How embarrassing!* And Mr. Stenger's calculation of my ability to get work is more dismal than I imagined. I blink back the tears, ashamed by my weakness, and step off the sidewalk.

That's when it hits me. The passenger-side door of the Pontiac is half open and Dr. Blum is gone.

Lost

"Mr. Stenger!" I run back to the pharmacy and pound on the glass door. The pharmacist opens it, but holds the orange cat back with one foot. "The doctor! He's disappeared. I hate to ask you, but can you help me find him? He could get run over or hurt by someone who doesn't understand his problem." I wring my hands like a heroine in a silent movie.

"Now, now, Miss Myers. Don't cry. Liberty isn't very big. We'll find him." He slips off his lab coat, locks up the pharmacy, and joins me on the cracked walk. "He can't have gone far. You head down to the courthouse and ask the fellows on the steps. I'll head up toward the church."

Frantically, I hurry along past the closed sweetshop, the closed dry goods shop, and the volunteer firehouse, but Isaac has vanished! How many times have I wished to be free of him, now he's gone! I should have been watching him closer.

Embarrassed, I ask the men lounging on the benches if they've seen a strange fellow in a white shirt and tie, with a vacant look, walk by. They all shake their heads and look at me funny so I turn and run back to the car.

Where could the doctor have gone? Like Mr. Stenger says, Liberty's not a very big town. You can pretty much see the length of Main by standing out in the street. Could he have wandered down an alley?

Just then I spy Mr. Stenger leading the doc by the arm in my direction.

"Where did you find him?"

"He was in the soup line down at the Saved by Faith Baptist Church, three blocks away. The fellows weren't sure if he smelled the hot food or just wandered there by accident, but one of the drifters gave him a cup and pushed him in line. They could see there was something wrong with him, thought maybe he was deaf and dumb." The doctor still carries an empty tin cup and there's food on his face.

Stenger eyes the cup. "No one knew he was a physician, thought he was a bum just panhandling through town, until he got up to the front of the line and two of the church ladies serving food recognized him. They'd heard you were back so they sat him in a chair with a cup full of beans and that's where I found him." "He fed himself?" I ask, amazed. "He hasn't done that since he took his spell." Stenger doesn't get the significance. "You fed yourself!" I say to Blum, almost laughing, but he doesn't seem to hear.

"Well, all's well that ends well," Stenger intones as he opens the glass door to his store and then says brightly out of habit, "Come again, Miss Myers."

On the way out of town I make a point of going past the church to see the soup line. There are dozens of fellows, mostly white with a few colored mixed in, and I'm happy to see that the African Methodist Episcopal and the Saved by Faith Baptists have joined forces and serve all races.

I study the men as we drive by: thin, hollows under their eyes, cheeks sunken in, clothes greasy and torn, and I wonder where their women are. Staying with the children and kin, I imagine. But the men must leave home and keep on looking for work. They can't stop. Whatever it takes, just like me, they must find work.

The Joes in the line turn to stare at our vehicle, and one tall fellow in overalls waves with the stump of an arm. That's Holly Wetsel, I realize. One-Arm Wetsel! The doc saved his life a few years ago when men from the sawmill carried Holly to the clinic in the back of a pickup. He'd run his hand through the roller and crushed it so badly it couldn't be saved. Isaac amputated the torn stump and stopped the bleeding, while I provided the anesthesia. He didn't charge a cent for the surgery. That's how he was . . . generous when you didn't expect it, but otherwise a skinflint.

As we pass the church, Isaac turns. His face doesn't change, still the blank stare, but there's a shift of the head in what looks like a nod. Maybe he's thanking the men in the soup line. . . . I take a deep breath. Not likely.

6

Horse Shoe Mine

"Thanks for coming with me, Becky," Patience says as we bump in her Olds down Salt Lick Road. "It's a lot more fun to have a pal at a delivery and also safer if something goes wrong." I'm bracing my feet against the floorboards wondering how I got into this.

Thinking it over, there wasn't much choice. Blum and I were at the Hesters' returning their push mower when Patience got a call and the person on the phone mentioned blood. Then when Patience asked me to come with her to the delivery, what was I going to say? *"No thanks, I'm busy?"* She clearly thought I'd be happy to attend, as if assisting a woman in labor was a big honor.

Daniel gently led the doctor off to the barn. "Come on, old buddy. I got something to show you. We'll leave the birthing to the ladies."

"I get so tired sometimes," Patience goes on as she expertly bounces around another hole in the gravel road. "But since Mrs. Potts died, I'm the only midwife in Union County. . . ."

"When we get there, can you sort through the birth satchel and resterilize the scissors and whatever else we'll need? I just had a delivery yesterday and didn't get around to it. This is Thelma Booth's fourth child. She's been calling me every few days with one thing and another."

Patience takes a sharp left and passes a wooden sign that reads HAZEL PATCH.

"You know about Hazel Patch? That's where Reverend Miller and his Negro followers live. It's a village of about a hundred folks who migrated up from the southern part of the state to work the Baylor Mine, until the cave-in in '24, when seventeen of their men were killed, seventeen men and two boys.

"They say you could hear the trapped men calling for help, but no one could get to them through the boulders. They screamed for a week and then the cries got weaker, and then they stopped. Those who weren't killed won't go underground again, no matter what, and now make a living as subsistence farmers.

"I spent a lot of time in mining camps," Patience goes on. "Did I ever tell you? I was married to a union organizer for the UMWA, the United Mine Workers of America. The camp we're going to today isn't unionized. It's abysmal. The houses are little more than the shacks that the hoboes build under the bridge in town."

She takes another sharp turn and follows a narrow gravel road along a bubbling creek where the water is a shocking golden color and the rocks are covered with orange slime that comes from acid runoff out of the mines.

"I worked at Scotts Run as a public health nurse when I first came to West Virginia," I tell her. "Up there, even some of the non-unionized camps had nice schools and churches and a clinic with a doctor, but that was over ten years ago."

"That's the way it should be. Unions, just by their presence, stand for improved living and working conditions, but now that the economy has fallen apart, the coal barons can do anything they want. They know the men won't strike. It's not like there are a lot of jobs to choose from and they're lucky they have one."

As we continue into the hollow, I see shacks perched on the hillside and a company store, but nowhere a clinic or school. Miners, wearing metal hats with lights on them, their faces so black you can only see their eyes, are just coming out of a massive dark hole. Some of them lift their heads as we pass, but only one fellow waves.

Thelma

"You remember Thelma?"

"I saw her at my Women and Infants' Clinic, years ago. Had to explain everything to her twice; she's a little slow."

Patience takes another sharp turn and we pull up in front of a plain wooden miner's house, all one story. I'm surprised, in such dismal circumstances, to see that the trim around the windows is painted a sea green, with a matching sea-green door. Purple pansies bloom in green window boxes in an attempt to bring cheer to an otherwise gray world.

"Miss Patience!" cry three freckle-faced kids sitting on the porch. "Miss Patience! The midwife! Ma, the midwife is here." You'd think she was Santa Claus.

"Okay, baby dolls, you calm down!" A very pregnant redhead, with an angelic freckled face comes to the door.

"Come in. Come in. Why, Nurse Becky, I didn't know you were in town. I'll make us some tea."

"Thelma! What are you doing out of bed?" Patience squeals. She rushes forward, pushing the children aside. Fresh blood is visible on the insides of the woman's calves and stains her worn pink house slippers.

"For god's sake, you're bleeding, Thelma! Becky, can you bring in the birth satchel? I'll get her back to the bedroom. You children stay here. Where's your father?"

"He's working in the mine, down under," the oldest boy, around eight, answers. "Might do a double if he can. We need the money." Patience sighs and propels Thelma down a narrow hall.

"Will Ma be okay?" the boy says, turning to me. "That's a lot of blood."

"The midwife and I will take good care of her," I hedge.

"Will she be okay?" he asks again.

A cloud, like a hand, has moved over the sun.

Blood

When I step into the small bedroom with Patience's birth satchel, Thelma is lying on her side, crossways on the sagging iron bed, folding clean laundry, and singing to herself. *"Happy days are here again. The skies above are clear again. So let's sing a song of cheer. Happy days are here again."*

"Thelma, I want to check the baby's heartbeat. Can you roll on your back?" Patience asks sweetly, though by her expression anyone—but Thelma—could tell she's angry. "Do you know when you last felt the baby kick?"

"Probably last night. No, maybe yesterday. It's been quiet today."

The midwife holds out her hand and I know what she wants: the metal stethoscope. Her lips are drawn thin and tight. For all we know this baby could already be dead. Mrs. Booth is so clueless, it's possible.

"It's okay, Thelma. It's okay," I whisper in her ear as Patience moves the stethoscope up and down and then across the bulging mountain of abdomen. The air in the room gets thicker as the minutes go by, and I remember that the last time I went to a delivery with Patience she only had a Pinard stethoscope, a wooden hornlike tube. She must have inherited this new metal one from the late Mrs. Potts, the colored midwife who in years past delivered half of Union County.

Finally, Patience pushes her drooping wire-rim glasses up and begins to tap her finger in the air while staring at the gold timepiece she wears on a ribbon around her neck, and I know by watching her that the fetal heart rate is normal. We both take a deep breath and Patience breaks into a smile.

"Your baby is fine, Thelma. Nice and strong. But why are you bleeding?" She turns to me. "It might just be bloody show."

"That's a lot of blood," I note. The mother rolls on her side and goes back to folding the laundry, as if our conversation doesn't concern her.

I study our patient. *"Happy days are here again . . ."* She has a pensive, faraway look in her eyes, and Patience and I each place our hands on Thelma's abdomen at the same time. Her uterus is rock hard. We wait for her singing to stop and the uterus relaxes.

"She's singing through the contractions," Patience whispers, then she nods her head toward the door.

"What do you think?" she asks me as we stand in the narrow dark hallway.

I hesitate, not sure if Patience knows the medical terms, but then remember she's studied the whole of Delee's *Principles and Practice of Obstetrics*, a medical text that her mentor, the midwife Mrs. Kelly left her. Bitsy, her young assistant, had also studied it when they used to attend births together.

"It could be an abruption," I offer. "Have you ever seen one?"

"Yes." Patience's face grows gray. "But she's not in severe pain. Usually, in abruptions there's terrible pain, so most likely it's a placenta previa with the placenta at the edge of the cervix or, God forbid, completely over it."

"Do you think we could get her in the car and make it to the hospital in Torrington?" I ask.

"Maybe. If she's only a few centimeters, we might try, but it's three hours to the hospital so I guess I have to check her. It's her fourth and we might not make it."

We both know that doing a vaginal exam in a situation like this is dangerous and not just because the West Virginia Midwifery Statute of 1925 forbids it. Patience could accidently poke a hole in the placenta and that would cause a life-threatening hemorrhage.

"Thelma." Patience tries to get the mother's attention. "I need to check you. I will be very careful, but you mustn't move or squirm around." She pulls on her sterilized red rubber gloves and holds out two fingers. "Oil," she says and I pour a little from the brown bottle she carries in her bag. *Happy days are here again.*

Tamponade

I hold my breath and watch Patience's face as she slowly moves her fingers into the vagina.

"Seven centimeters," she finally says. "Completely thinned out and the head well engaged." Then her eyes widen. She mumbles a curse and removes her fingers, as a handful of blood leaks out on the bed. "A partial previa. I can feel the placenta where it's come loose on the left side, about an inch of it. I think we need to get her out of bed."

"Out of bed?" (This seems unusual and if I didn't have so much respect for Patience, I'd think she was crazy.)

"There's no way we can get a mother of three, who's already seven centimeters to the hospital in time. So it's better to get the baby out quickly. Also the pressure of the head on the edge of the placenta might slow down the blood loss."

"You mean like a tamponade? Dr. Blum told me about this."

"I don't know the word *tamponade*," she whispers back, "but it's like when you put pressure on a wound."

Once on her feet, Thelma begins to sway and to sing again, but she's almost yelling the words with each contraction. *"Happy days are here again! Happy days are here again!"*

I run down the hall to the kitchen, throw the midwife's scissors for cutting the cord in a pot of water on the cookstove, then run back again and straighten the bed. "Happy days are here again!" I didn't know such a pretty woman could yell so loud, but at least she's not screaming like so many women do. The contractions are only two minutes apart and the bleeding has slowed.

I get rid of the unfolded laundry, run down the hall a second time, grab the pot of hot water, and set it on a towel on the bedroom dresser where it can cool. *"Happy days are here . . .* Ugggggggh!" It's more of a growl than a groan and I nervously point to the bed, asking Patience with my eyes if it's time for the patient to lie down.

The midwife shakes her head no. "Here, Thelma, do like me." Both women squat on the wooden floor. In between contractions, there's the *drip, drip, drip* of red and I wipe it up.

"Be ready for anything," Patience whispers. "The baby may come out floppy if there's been too much blood loss. . . ." I begin to shake inside, and to quiet my nerves try to take deep breaths.

"What?" the mother cries. "What about my baby? Is it okay?" Patience reaches for her stethoscope and listens for a brief moment.

"The baby's fine," she reassures and that may be so, or possibly not. She didn't spend a lot of time listening. "Now bear down like you mean it!"

"Oil," she orders again and I pour a little of the oily golden liquid on her fingers. She wipes it around the woman's vagina and two pushes later the head is out. "Wait! Blow!" There's a rubbery cord around the baby's neck. She eases it off and the baby drops into Patience's clever hands. She holds the blood-covered, dark-haired, wailing infant out to me and when she reaches out her chubby little arms, I almost choke up. It's as if light has burst my tired heart open. I don't know how else to say it. Light.

May 5, 1934

Today I accompanied the midwife, Patience Hester, to the bedside of Thelma Booth, mother of four who was in advanced labor. Thelma was bleeding heavily and we were concerned about an abruption or previa. Since there was no time to get her to Torrington, Patience, had her stand for the last bit of labor to create a tamponade. The bleeding slowed and a healthy 5-pound, 6-ounce baby girl was born a few minutes later. The father, Wally Booth, a coal miner, at the Horse Shoe Mine, could not come home for the next twelve hours because he was working two shifts in the hole, so Patience and I had to stay the night.

The midwife slept with the three children in their bed and gave the broken-down sofa to me. All night we could see the lights from the coal trucks going up and down the road and we had only bread and milk for supper.

7

Prayer

Outside, another day fades. Inside, flames crackle in the heater stove and there's the cozy smell of woodsmoke. Yesterday, I discovered a small pile of split oak under the porch, enough to build an evening fire, but it won't last long, and hopefully it will soon be warm enough that, except for cooking, we won't want a fire. Lamp oil will always be needed, but for now we have the three candles I brought from Perrysville. I am loathe to spend our last dollar on kerosene, because we might need it for food.

I let out a breath and stand up. "Bedtime," I tell the doctor and begin our ritual.

First, we march to the outhouse. I wait outside while Blum relieves himself. Then he waits for me. This is progress, I have to admit; I used to have to stand right beside him and hold his male organ. Next, we return to the kitchen to wash in the white enamel washbowl and then brush our teeth with baking soda.

This is one of the things Dr. Blum and I have in common . . . or *had in common*, I should say. . . . We once shared a keen desire for scrupulous oral hygiene, and I still spend at least two minutes on each of us brushing with our Reputation toothbrushes. Isaac sits on a wooden kitchen chair in a trance with his mouth as wide as a baby bird's. I actually think he likes it.

Finally, I remove his clothes and pull on his long white cotton nightshirt. Then I lead him to the sofa and cover him with Patience's green quilt. (He still refuses to go up the stairs to the other bedroom.)

My day is almost over. I blow out the candle and for a minute sit in the rocking chair next to him. "Now I lay me down to sleep. I pray the Lord my soul to keep . . ." I whisper. "If I should die before I wake, I pray the Lord my soul to take. . . ." Before I'm through with the children's prayer, Isaac is already snoring.

That's when my real prayer begins, a prayer with few words. "Thank you for all that we have and help us get through tomorrow. Help us. Help us get through tomorrow."

Tomorrow, I think. *Tomorrow or the next day, though I dread it, I will look for work again.*

Intruders

At dawn as yellow light slides over the mountains, I wake to the sound of someone clunking around downstairs.

Yanked out of a net of strange dreams, I sit up in bed, the hair on the back of my neck standing on end. Definitely movement . . . and I fear the worst . . . that one of the traveling men has come into our house, one or several!

A woman alone with a companion who's no help; we are sitting ducks. And where's our guard dog, Three Legs, when I need him? I yank on my pants, pull a sweater over my head, and rush down the stairs, yelling more aggressively than I feel, "Who's there! Who the hell is down there?"

I discover Dr. Blum standing in the middle of the front room looking lost and holding his penis. Three Legs stands at his feet looking up with a big, wet grin. "For god's sake, Isaac!" I admonish. "What the hell are you doing?" It's clear what he's doing, he's trying to go to the bathroom, but we have no indoor toilet and no porcelain potty either. Still upset, I roughly push him out to the porch and point to the rail, waiting to see if he will get the idea. He doesn't.

"Oh, Isaac! *Come on!*" I howl as he pees on the porch floorboards. Then I let out the breath I was holding. "Sorry . . . You just are so much work to take care of!"

"The truth is, I was scared, you know?" I continue my monologue. "I was scared! I pictured a couple of vagrants stumbling around downstairs, rough men who could hurt us." I am still shaking, almost crying, and I have to wipe my eyes before I can see. Finally, I calm myself.

It's then that I realize the importance of Dr. Blum's action. He was actually trying to take care of himself. Somewhere between unbuttoning his long underwear and opening the door and walking to the outhouse, he apparently forgot what he was doing, but he was actually trying. *He was trying.*

Summons

"Come on, Blum," I command. "Just get in the car." The doctor and I are dressed for another day of job hunting, and though I put on a little makeup, my mood is not great. After talking to Mr. Stenger and Mr. Bittman last time, I feel sure that looking for work will be futile, but I have to keep trying.

I stop with one foot on the running board. A pickup, throwing dust, is moving our way. It pulls up in front of the gate, and a muscular man with thick, dark hair and a small beard jumps out. He's wearing the regulation farmer's coveralls in striped denim and the cloth stretches across his biceps. "You the nurse?" There's the bulge of chewing tobacco in his right cheek.

I fold my arms across my chest. "I am."

"My name's Simon Markey from over Snake Hollow. My wife's paining bad and Patience Murphy, the midwife, said I should get you. She said to tell you *come fast*."

"What's the trouble? Is Patience already there?"

"No, ma'am. She's in Delmont delivering another baby. I called her at home and the vet told me where she was and then when I tracked her down, she told me to fetch you, that you'd sit with my woman until she could get there."

Oh, Patience! How could you do this? Even looking for work sounds more fun than sitting with a woman in labor.

"She'll likely be back in Union County within an hour or two. We need you bad, ma'am."

"Is this your wife's first baby?"

"Yes and she's not doing well. Please come. She's crying something awful."

"Did you leave her alone?"

"Neighbor girl's sitting with her now, but she don't know nothin'. Just a kid. Never saw nothin' born before but a calf and a set of kittens."

I let out air in a long sigh. *My favorite things!* Blood, goo, fear of something being wrong with the baby, and a screaming woman . . .

"Well, I'll have to bring my charge. He's disabled and I have no one to watch him."

"You mean Dr. Blum? I guess I can mind him if you tend to my honey. He's not dangerous, is he?"

"You've heard about him?"

"Most of Union County has by now. They say he's not himself. Brain injury in an auto accident or something." I don't stop to contradict another variation of Isaac's story. It's as good an explanation as any, and though Blum wasn't actually *in* the accident he became a victim.

"Okay, Isaac, change of plans." I run back inside for my black leather nurse's bag. "We're going to a delivery. Hopefully, Patience will be there soon."

Maybe we'll earn a dollar, I think. Maybe Mr. Markey is one of the few farmers in the area who are still doing well. Who knows? I consider with optimism, maybe we'll earn a whole fiver.

The anxious father-to-be takes off in his truck, spitting gravel, and I follow in the Pontiac, trying to keep up.

Dahlila

The Markey home is a surprise. It rests on a flat overlooking the Hope Valley and though his road, "Snake Hollow," sounds forbidding, the setting is beautiful. The two-story brick dwelling, once painted white, looks out across the hills to the spruce, pine, and hemlock mountains on the other side of the river, and his fields are green and cut short by the black-and-white cattle that graze there. I'm just getting out of the car, taking in the idyllic setting, when a scream cuts the fresh air.

"Eeeeeee! I can't do this anymore! Simon Markey, you better get in here! I can't take it, I tell you!"

Simon looks at me apologetically. "You go on in, Nurse. I'll watch your mister."

He's not my *mister*, I want to tell him, but decide to let it go.

God knows what the rest of Union County thinks. Simon hands
me my satchel and nods toward the house. A thin, dark-haired girl
with a prominent overbite runs out the door.

"Gotta go now, Mr. Markey. Ma will be needing me at home."
She doesn't stop to say good-bye. Just runs off down the dirt road
on her bare feet, her black braids flying. I can't say I blame her.
With the next scream, I feel like running myself.

"What's your wife's name again?"

"Dahlila."

"Dahlila," I whisper under my breath. *Dahlila, you better stop
screaming, because I can't take it.*

"Hello?" The screen door creaks behind me as I enter a well-
appointed parlor with a new blue-embossed davenport, matching
wing chair and rocker, oak end tables, and a whatnot shelf with
a collection of glass and ceramic dogs and cats. The floor is covered with a flowered carpet too nice to walk on, and in the corner
there's a shiny coal stove with a silver ornament on top. A radio
on an end table is turned up high and a blues song, "Hard Times
Now," blares throughout the house, probably Simon Markey's attempt to drown out the screams.

*"You heard about a job, now you is on your way. Twenty men
after the same job, all in the same ol' day. Hard times, hard times . . ."*
(It could be my theme song.)

"Dahlila? It's Nurse Becky Myers, come to sit with you. Patience, the midwife, sent me." My reference to Patience is supposed
to give me legitimacy, though in the arena of childbirth, I'm a fish
out of water.

"Dahlila?" I call softly again, pushing the door open at the top
of the landing.

"Are you okay?"

"No, I'm *not* okay! Do you think I sound okay? I thought this
was supposed to be easy."

A woman in her midtwenties, with one long blond braid coming undone, sits in the middle of a rumpled four-poster bed. The sheets and blankets have fallen to the floor and her bottom half is naked. On top, she still wears a striped pink satin chemise.

"You thought having a baby would be easy?"

"My sister says it is. I can just hear her. 'If the doc hadn't checked me, I wouldn't have known I was in labor! Forty-five minutes later my baby was born.' "

"Well, that isn't usually the case. Mostly it takes a long time, at least half a day, sometimes two."

"Two!" She begins the high-pitched wail again and I realize I've made a tactical error. "No. No. No! I can't do it. I won't. Get that man in here. Simon, I will kill you! I swear I will. This is all his fault for wanting a son."

She starts to huff with contractions and I wonder when Patience is going to get here. She better hurry or I'll have to do this delivery myself. My stomach grips at the thought of it, and my eyes get tight around the edges.

"Dahlila," I say when her contraction is over, being careful not to upset her again. "Watching you, I have a feeling your baby will be here sooner rather than later. I'd like to get the bed made and things ready for Patience. Do you think you could help me? Just be a little quieter so I can think."

The woman drops her shoulders and takes a big breath, then another. She's has a Northern European look, lean and tall, the kind of woman you'd picture in a movie, lounging against a bar in a low-cut dress, only her flawless skin is makeup-less and her blond hair is tangled and matted. "You think so? You really think the baby might come soon?"

"Oh, yes. I'm almost sure of it. When did the pains start?"

"This morning about six when I got up to use the bathroom."

"Has your water bag broken?"

"No, nothing."

"Have you voided recently?"

The girl looks embarrassed. "You mean tinkled?"

"Yes, urinated or defecated. Where do you usually go? Do you have an indoor water closet?"

"Oh, yes. Simon had it built when we first married. He is so good to me."

"Why don't you go down the hall and see if you can *tinkle* while I change the linens. It's not good to labor with a full bladder, makes it hurt more too." Here she stops for a minute to do her huffing and I glance at my watch. The contractions are every four minutes.

Grateful I thought to bring Dr. Blum's delivery pack in my nurse's bag, I quickly lay out what I think Patience will need while Dahlila goes down the hall to the bathroom. "Mr. Markey," I yell down the stairs. "Do you have hot water and sterilized linens? I want to get every thing ready." No answer. "Mr. Markey?"

Tarnation! Where is he?

Two doors away, I can still hear the laboring mother breathing through her contractions. "Stay right there on the commode, Dahlila. I have to be sure we have warm water and a few other things."

"Mmmmmm," the girl says.

Solo

It takes two trips up and down the stairs, but at last I'm back in the bedroom with a pot of hot water and the bundle of sterilized sheets and rags that Dahlila must have fixed up.

"You okay?" I yell in her direction, though I figure she is, since she's no longer screaming.

"Mmmmmmmmmmmm," she says again.

There's nothing like the efficiency of a nurse, and within minutes the bed is prepared, padded, and ready. I check the cradle in the corner and open the curtains, hoping to catch sight of Patience speeding this way, but there are just the green peaceful fields. Simon and Dr. Blum are nowhere in sight. Maybe it's better that way.

Just then, it comes to me that I haven't yet checked the fetal heartbeat, which is actually the first thing I *should* have done, so I dig out my stethoscope and hurry down the hall to escort Dahlila back to the bedroom. I'm alarmed when I get there to see her leaning over the sink, her fingers gripping the porcelain.

"Come on, Dahlila, let's get you back in bed." I half pull her down the hall to the bedroom, but before she can climb back into the four-poster, she has another contraction and gets down on her hands and knees on the floor. "Oh no, that's not the way! Look, I've made the clean sheets all nice for you, and I need to check the baby's heart. . . . Honey!" Dahlila rotates her hips in a strange, erotic way.

"Mmmmmmmmmm!" she groans.

"Honey . . . ?" Then her water bursts and all hell breaks loose.

"It's coming!" she gasps.

My stomach gives a lurch. *Patience really isn't going to get here in time!*

"Dahlila, try panting. I need you in bed so I can see what's happening, okay? Dahlila!" I insist. "I *really* need you in the bed."

"Can't!" She's down to one-word replies. "Mmmmmmmmm!" I picture the baby's head descending.

There's nothing else for it, I must get down on the floor to look.

"Pant, Dahlila. Pant!" I make my voice strong like Patience's and pull on my sterilized rubber gloves. "The midwife should be here any minute. You can do it. Let me see where the head is." *It better be a head. If not, we're in very big trouble.*

"Mmmmmmmmmm," the mother groans again and I'm relieved when I see a nice hairy orb.

Again, I try to think what Patience would do. I want to wait for her to get here, but I still haven't checked the fetal heartbeat, and the stethoscope is back in the bathroom where I dropped it next to the sink.

Maybe it's better to get the baby out and not fool with listening to the heartbeat. (Better a live baby than a heart rate to write in my nurse's notes.)

"Dahlila, look at me. I need you to listen and do exactly what I say." I try to sound firm and hold her green eyes with my brown ones, but I'm pretty sure my voice is shaking. "When you feel an urge to push go with it. If it stings, stop for a minute and pant. Pant and let your opening stretch. It's going to burn like fire for five or ten minutes and then it will be over and you will have your baby."

"Oh, I can't. I can't!"

"Yes, you can! We can do this together." This is said with *much* more confidence than I feel.

I have no oil like Patience uses, so instead I dip one of my sterilized rags in the pot of warm water and hold it against the young woman's vagina. I'm just going on instinct here, hoping it might help her stretch.

"MMMMMMMMMMMMM!"

"Slow it down, honey . . . the head's almost out." "*Hard times. Hard times,*" the radio booms.

"Oh! Ow! Ow!" Dahlila cries.

"One more little push." There's no time for keeping the head flexed the way Patience does, or maneuvering the shoulders like Dr. Blum does, and maybe it's just as well, because with the woman on her hands and knees, I probably wouldn't do it right anyway. With the next push, the whole baby rotates and falls into my lap.

"I did it!" Dahlila cries, and the baby boy, startled to be here, cries with her. Downstairs, the front door flies open.

"Everyone okay up there?" It's Patience and Simon.

"You okay, babe?" That's the father.

"You okay, Becky?" That's Patience, and on the radio we have a new song. *"New day's comin', As sure as you're born! There's a new day comin', Start tootin' your horn . . ."* Now Dahlila and I are both laughing. Laughter just bubbles up. I sit back against the bedstead, still on the floor, covered with blood and amniotic fluid. Dahlila's eyes meet mine in joyful hysteria and I bite my lip to get control. This makes us laugh all the harder. Finally, I clear my throat.

"Everything's fine. Patience, you can come up, but please wait a few moments, Mr. Markey."

Ten minutes later the placenta is out and Patience has stitched a few tiny tears. Some women, she tells me, are built better for childbirth than others, but if you're careful and let the head deliver slowly most won't have more than a few skid marks. Finally, we get the new mother between the clean sheets. We wash her face and hands and give her the baby, now wrapped snug in the sterilized blanket. Mr. Markey doesn't wait for permission. He bounds up the stairs.

"I did it," the young mother cries proudly. "I made you a baby."

The father doesn't say a word. His eyes are on the wonder of this new life and the beautiful woman before him. He just sits on the chair and sobs.

There's movement in the hall and when I turn, Dr. Blum is leaning against the doorframe. It's then that I see something I've not seen before, not even when he was in his right mind. His eyes are wet too.

May 16, 1934

7-pound, 3-ounce infant boy born to Dahlila and Simon Markey of Snake Hollow. (Baby was weighed on an extra old-fashioned hanging scale that the midwife had given me.) I was supposed to just be there just for support until the midwife could get there, but the baby arrived before she did. Patience made it for the placenta and she repaired two tiny tears.

The six chickens I received were not payment enough for the dozens of gray hairs I got, but I did learn a few things. The warm water compresses were something even the midwife had not tried and seemed to offer the mother some comfort. Also, getting the woman out of bed apparently lessens the pain (I did not know this), and the baby often comes quicker. Dahlila delivered her baby boy on the floor and we both laughed our heads off.

8

Healing for Money

"Hello," a man calls from out in the yard just as I'm cleaning Dr. Blum's face, readying him for the trip into Liberty we'd abandoned when Mr. Markey sped up the road and begged for my assistance.

We both go out on the porch to find another stranger standing in the road, a handsome guy, clean-shaven, with shoulders as broad as a truck and a low voice that comes out like gravel running along a stream bed. "Hello," he says again.

Surely he has the wrong house. He's standing next to the shiny red Packard I'd seen in town last week, the one with the silver winged goddess on the front of the hood, and he wears a black uniform with a little chauffeur's cap.

"Are you the nurse, Rebecca Myers?"

"Stay!" I hiss as I push Dr. Blum back inside and take the steps down into the yard. "Yes, I am."

"There's a medical emergency at the Barnett Boardinghouse. Mrs. Bazzano asked me to bring you. It's her son . . . her eight-year-old son."

"A child? What sort of an emergency?" (At least it's not a woman in labor!)

"It's his breathing. He's having an air attack. Old lady Barnett recommended you."

"I'm not a physician, you understand? Can't you take him to the hospital in Torrington? There are specialists there."

"No, we can't go into Torrington." From the corner of my eye I catch sight of Isaac as he takes this moment to come back outside and stand at the rail to piss.

"Dr. Blum!" I shout, but it's too late. He's already taken his pecker out and is spraying a long one right toward the driver. The man steps back a few feet and stares in amazement.

"He's a doctor? If he's a doctor, you can both come."

"Sir, your name?"

"Nick Rioli. I'm the driver for Mrs. John Bazzano and her children. *Mrs. John Bazzano of Pittsburgh.*" He says this last part as if it's significant and I take it that they come from money or fame.

"Well, listen, Mr. Rioli. I think you can see that the doctor is not right, clearly not able to help anyone, and you've caught us at an inopportune time. We're on our way to town for an employment interview."

This is a fabrication, but I need something more impressive than *I have to go out and look for a job.* "You really should get the boy in the auto and head for Torrington *right now.*" The fellow just stands there, his arms folded in front of his body, making it clear he's not leaving.

"Mrs. Bazzano is prepared to pay." Here he pulls out a black leather wallet and holds a crisp ten-dollar bill between his fingers, an attractive bribe. I haven't seen that kind of cash for months and my eyes are glued on the green. It doesn't take long to make a decision.

"Okay, Mr. Rioli. You've convinced me." I hold out my hand for the tenner. "We were going into Liberty anyway. I'll follow in our own vehicle and go to the job interview later, but I have to make myself clear: If the boy is seriously ill, I may not be able to help him.

"On the other hand, if I *am* able to help him, it will be another ten dollars." I'm shocked by my boldness. *Healing for money. What would Florence Nightingale say?*

Wings

Twenty minutes later, the doctor and I are sitting in the back of the opulent Packard with springs so flexible I can hardly feel the bumps in the road. The silver winged replica of the goddess of speed propels us toward Liberty and I regret that the driver wouldn't let me bring my own vehicle, but then I wouldn't get the smooth ride.

"So." I speak loudly, to be heard over the roar of the motor. "Can you tell me more about the child, Mr. Rioli?" Dr. Blum sits next to me, our medical bag in his lap, riding along in his usual silence. "Has the boy had breathing attacks before? Does he have any medical history? Any recent exposure to TB or anything like that? And why can't you go into Torrington?"

The driver clears his throat and watches me through his rearview mirror. "The boy goes to an asthma specialist in Pittsburgh, but he's never been this bad before. He's having one attack after another."

"Any recent colds or croup?"

"Yes. It started with a cough. We were on our way to White Sulfur Springs to take the cure, but had to stop for a few days when he became ill, and now he's started getting short of breath."

"You mentioned the family name, John Bazzano, but I don't know anything about them."

"In this case," says the driver, "that's just as well."

A few minutes later, as we cruise past the soup kitchen at the Saved by Faith Baptist Church, I shrink down, embarrassed to be seen riding in the limo while the hungry men stand in line for free food. They cannot know by looking at us that until an hour ago, the doctor and I were close to destitute ourselves.

"Why is it better that I don't know the family?" I turn back to the driver.

"Don't you read the papers?"

"Not lately, no."

We pull up into the drive of Mrs. Barnett's Boardinghouse, a two-story white clapboard building with porches on both the upper and lower levels and around two sides. A neat white picket fence encloses the yard, and there are twelve-foot-tall white snow-ball bushes out front.

Two men in dark suits sit on the porch, in rattan chairs, playing cards. The shorter one has a small mustache and smokes a cigar. The other has big chompers with a gap in front and they both rise as we approach. Mr. Rioli parks in the back, and I notice there's only one other vehicle, another smaller late-model Packard.

Despite his urgency to get me to the sick child, Joseph stops for a minute and turns around in his seat. "Nurse Myers," he says in that deep rattling voice. "You seem like a smart lady. I don't know about the doc . . ."

"He's disabled now." I defend my old colleague. "A few years ago, you couldn't have wanted a better physician. He's a surgeon too . . . or was."

"No doubt," the chauffeur allows, but I can tell he doesn't buy it. "What I want to say is . . . For everyone's sake, don't ask too many questions about what you see and hear inside this house."

I frown. "As a nurse, I never talk about my patients, except to other medical professionals."

"Well, I'm warning you, keep that to a minimum too. I mean it."

The men from the porch are approaching the Packard and Nick gets out and opens the door for me.

"Any trouble?" the taller of the two asks, and I see now he has one blue eye and one brown. Still, he's a handsome fellow, well groomed with a recent haircut. Both men tip their hats.

"Nah, smooth sailing," says Nick. "Don't be alarmed by the gentleman in the back. I'll take the lady inside. Can you guys keep an eye on him; he's the nurse's charge, harmless she says, but a mute."

"Yeah."

"Just don't let him wander," I interject. "He doesn't know what he's doing and might scare someone or get hurt." I pull the black medical bag out of the car, just as a woman cries out.

Blue

"Oh, not again! Not again! Joey. Joey. Stay with me, Joey," a woman screams. Mr. Rioli grabs my arm as we race up the stairs to find in the front bedroom, the fancy lady I'd seen in town kneeling next to a bed. To the side, on the floor, I can see a child's pale feet and I can hear his labored breathing. The room is filled with exotic-smelling smoke so thick I almost choke.

"Ma'am," I introduce myself. "I'm Rebecca Myers, registered nurse. Can I help you?" When she turns I see that her face is red from crying.

"Oh, thank the Lord!"

"Mommy?" a voice from behind us interrupts.

"Hush, Allegra. Go back to the other bedroom and keep your sisters quiet. The nurse is here."

"But we're hungry."

"*It doesn't matter!* Go ask Mrs. Barnett. Go!"

The older child leaves and I don't get a look at her because I'm now on my hands and knees with the mother, helping the boy to sit up. He's a handsome kid, but his sandy-blond hair is sweaty and matted and his lips are blue. He breathes out with a high-pitched whine, and then coughs. Over and over he coughs and tries to push his air out.

"Nick," I order. "Open the windows. We have to get some of this smoke out."

"But Mrs. Barnett said it would make him better."

"I know people say breathing incense helps, but I'm a nurse, if you want me to help, you have to do what I say. Open the windows."

I pull out my stethoscope and listen to the child's lungs and heart. His respirations are rapid, forty a minute, and there's a marked expiratory wheeze.

"It's okay, Joey. Breathe with me. In . . . Out . . . In . . . Out." The child's eyes, in his blue-white face, focus on mine and he makes a low moan, like wind being forced through a narrow pipe.

"Oh, Joey," the mother sobs. "My little Joey. I'm so sorry. If only your father were here. I'm so sorry." Her tears fall on the boy's head as she caresses it and I see that her emotions are louder than the boy's breathing.

"How long has Joey been having these spells?" I try to settle her down.

"It's his sixth fit today—before that he would have one or two a month, but he fell ill from the night air, or maybe it's a reaction to the greenery—we had an inhaler but he's used it up and I wrote down the medication we need and had Anthony take it to the pharmacy, but the pharmacist said he didn't have it—he told Anthony we might be able to get some in Torrington, but we don't want to go back there . . ." Her sentences run on like the Hope River flooding with chunks of ice in March.

I take my glass thermometer out of its metal case and put it under the boy's arm. The mother looks surprised.

"I can't put it in his mouth. When he breathes like that it won't be accurate." Then I wait the two long minutes during which the boy and the mother begin to calm down.

"It's ninety-nine degrees. Close to normal. What else have you tried?"

"Anthony got him some Schiffmann's Asthmador Cigarettes at the pharmacy, the last pack they had, and blew smoke in his face, but it didn't help."

"Okay, I'm going to run to the pharmacy myself to see if Mr. Stenger has some epinephrine somewhere in back. I'll get your driver to take me. Maybe, since the pharmacist knows me, I can persuade him to help. Epinephrine is what's in the inhaler, right? It's the medication the doctor from Pittsburgh gave you?"

"I think so."

"Yes, that's what they use. . . . Mr. Rioli!" The driver is listening to everything, just outside in the hall.

Getting away from the house gives me some time to think. If the boy keeps going on like this, he could go into cardiac arrest and the next asthma attack could be his last . . . or the one after that. I'm just praying that Mr. Stenger will be able to find some epi stashed away in the back. Even a few drops could be used in the child's nose.

"Step on it, Nick," I order as we peel out of the drive. It isn't until we get to Main that I remember Dr. Blum. Hopefully, he's still on the porch with his babysitters.

"Little Joey going to be okay?" the chauffeur asks me.

"I don't know. I'll do what I can. It depends on if we can get some kind of medication with a bronchodilator in it. Status asthmaticus can be fatal."

"Status what?"

"Status asthmaticus . . . asthma attacks that go on and on with-out a break."

Long Shot

The chauffeur, knuckles white and jaw clenched, grips the wheel as we head into town, but our trip to the pharmacy is fruitless. When Mr. Stenger insists he has no epinephrine, we leave in a hurry after wasting precious time.

"What now?" Nick asks.

"Let's go back to the Barnett Boardinghouse and I'll call the local vet and see if he has any medication that might help. He lives out in the country. Maybe he'll bring us something."

"I could go get it, if you tell me where. I could persuade him."

"What's with you anyway? I thought you were going to get rough with Mr. Stenger back there?"

"I just . . ." (The blush moving up his baby face surprises me.) Before the driver can answer . . .

"Hey! That's the vet!" A black Model T with a dent in the rear is moving away from us down Main. "Can you catch him?"

The Packard shoots forward, horn blaring, and the Ford screeches to a halt. I jump out while we're still rolling. "Ill child with asthma," I yell to Daniel Hester. "We need epi."

"Where?" Daniel yells back, standing on the running board.

"Barnett Boardinghouse."

"I'll have to go home. I have a little there."

"The boy is critical," I offer, as he speeds away, then bite my lower lip. The sun is too bright for early May. It should be softer. The shadows are too harsh and I don't know why I care so much about one little boy of one apparently very rich family, but I do.

On our return to the rooming house, we find the child has fallen asleep and is breathing quietly, but it doesn't last. An hour later, his eyes snap open and lock on to mine. He sits up in bed, puts his hands around his neck, and looks around wildly.

"Breathe in . . . Breathe out . . . Look at me, Joey! Do it like this. I know you feel like you can't get your air, but breathe slower. In . . . Out . . . In . . . Out." The boy starts to cough again and it's all we can do to keep him in bed. Once, he sits up so hard his head hits my nose and it begins to bleed, dripping red on Mrs. Barnett's white sheets.

"Nick," the mother shouts. "Help, Nick. We need you. This time it's worse."

There's the sound of heavy feet coming up the steps and when I look up both Daniel Hester and Nick Rioli are trying to make it through the door at the same time. The vet is wearing dirty blue coveralls and smells like manure, but he's here and I feel less alone.

"This is the animal doctor I told you about, Mrs. Bazzano, Dr. Hester. He has the epinephrine." The vet kneels on the floor, touches the shaking boy on the arm, and then opens a leather bag like I carry.

"How much does he weigh?" Hester asks Mrs. Bazzano.

"Sixty pounds at his last doctor's visit. Maybe less. He's not been eating the past few days." Daniel fills a syringe from a glass vial. I had expected some kind of inhaler, but now that I think of it, his patients probably don't use inhalers and an injectable will work faster . . . *if* it works.

"Uhhhhh. Uhhhhh. Uhhhhh." Joey makes a strange noise as he forces air in and out. Then he stops breathing altogether and falls back.

"Arm." Daniel orders, and I pull up the boy's nightshirt sleeve. The vet doesn't bother with cleansing the skin, he just jabs the needle in and pushes the plunger. "I'm not sure I have the dose correct," he whispers. "I gave him what I would give a good-sized dog. I have a little more if it doesn't work."

Then we wait. Thirty seconds. I'm holding my breath along with Joey, wondering how long you can go without air before your heart stops. I count the seconds in my head. Thirty-four, thirty-five, thirty-six, thirty-seven. At last Joey gasps! Relief is almost instantaneous.

Mrs. Bazzano and I look at each other and I wipe her tears. She pulls a white hanky out of her pocket and wipes my bloody nose.

9

Ice Pick

It isn't until dusk three days later that Dr. Blum and I leave the Barnett Boardinghouse. Nick and one of Mrs. Bazzano's men had retrieved our Pontiac and, thank God, I'd asked Daniel to check on our six poor chickens still locked in the barn. I'm not much of a chicken farmer, but I know the birds have to eat and he took them some feed.

The chauffer slaps Blum on the back as we stand in the driveway getting ready to leave. "Well, old buddy," he wisecracks, "I expect you'll beat me in poker the next time I see you." The men have taken a shine to the doctor, always setting him up with a hand of cards when they play. Not that he ever actually joined them. He just sat where he was, holding the fan of cards in front of him like the other Joes. "He has a real poker face," they kidded.

Mrs. Bazzano and the children, including Joey, wave from the porch.

The vet had offered to take Isaac home with him days ago, but Mrs. Bazzano was paying me two dollars a day, renting our rooms, and feeding us, so we happily stayed. Also I didn't want to leave until the order for three asthma inhalers came in on the train.

Before I turn up Wild Rose Road, I stop at the Hesters' place. Inside I can hear Patience playing the piano, something familiar, "*Oh! Susanna, Oh don't you cry for me, For I come from Alabama with my banjo on my knee.*"

A few minutes later at the kitchen table over coffee and gingerbread cookies, I tell Daniel how much I appreciated him helping me out with Joey. "I wanted you to know what it meant to me, your help at the bedside. You saved the boy's life. Here's something from the child's mother." I hold out a ten-dollar bill. "Mrs. Bazzano also asked me to tell you how grateful she was."

"Bazzano?" Patience asks. "Bazzano?" She turns to Daniel. "You didn't say who they were. That's the Bazzano family from Pittsburgh?"

"Yes," I answer quickly. "Somewhere near Pittsburgh."

"Don't you know who they are?"

"I know quite a bit," I answer smugly. "The lady said her husband owned a restaurant, but he was killed in an accident last year and they had to leave town. I figured they were deep in debt or something. Nice woman, but she has her hands full with five children, and the little boy, so sickly."

"Don't you know who they *are?*" Patience asks again. Both Daniel and I shrug. "That's *John Bazzano's family*. The Pittsburgh mobster! The *late* mob boss. He was assassinated in New York City last year. *The ice pick murder?*

"We read about it in the newspaper, Daniel, *right here at this table*. Bazzano was stabbed some twenty times in the chest with an ice pick and discovered a few days later in a trash bin. It was big news."

"*That* John Bazzano?" Daniel now recalls the story, but I draw a dead blank. Most likely it happened around the time I was dealing with Dr. Blum's illness and had stopped reading the paper.

"The ritual murder was in retaliation for Bazzano wiping out three brothers in a rival Pennsylvania gang. *All three*. Can you imagine?"

I swallow hard. "Those people were mobsters?"

In the end Patience holds out her hand and takes the ten-dollar bill. When times are hard, it doesn't matter if the money is dirty or the money is clean.

Windfall

"*Old MacDonald had a farm. E-I-E-I-O,*" I sing to Dr. Blum as I scrub our linens on the washboard in the big galvanized metal washtub. It lightens my load to have a little money in the money jar. "*And on his farm he had a chicken. E-I-E-I-O.*" The sound of a motor interrupts my song as a battered green pickup truck loaded with wood pulls into the yard.

What now? It's Reverend Miller from Hazel Patch, the Negro pastor who changed our flat when we first returned to Union County. A tall, young black fellow sits in the front beside him.

I hurry outside, pulling Blum along. "Why, Reverend, how nice of you to stop by. Won't you come in?" I inwardly cringe, knowing I have nothing to serve them, no biscuits, no apple butter, not even coffee.

"No need for that, ma'am, though I thank you kindly." He tips his straw hat and wipes sheen from his wide handsome brown face. "We brought you some wood. A tornado touched down in Hazel Patch in April and wreaked havoc. We're trying to get the hillside cleaned off. I just dropped off a load to the Hesters, and Patience said you could use some too."

"I thought tornados didn't happen in the mountains."

"Oh, they happen, but only every ten years or so. Where do you want us to stack it?"

I survey the bed of the truck. That's a lot of wood! Some of the trunks are six inches, some only four, but still good for the cook-stove. "To the side of the house I guess."

"This is Nate Bowlin." He indicates the young man with him, a tall fellow of about eighteen who's eyeing Dr. Blum as if he were a ghost. The physician still stands next to me and I note that his pants are ripped and hitched up too high, like an unkempt scarecrow or one of the homeless men down by the river, and I'm suddenly embarrassed. I hadn't given any recent thought to how we're dressed when we're out on the farm because we don't usually get company.

"Be right back," I say to cover my discomfort, then I lead Blum into the house and sit him on the davenport. "Stay."

Returning, I find the wood almost all stacked in a pile taller than I am. The Reverend and Nate finish up. "Could I offer you a few dollars? I just got paid for a nursing job. That's a lot of firewood."

"No. No." The Reverend puts up his hand. "You need what you have."

He opens the truck door and I think he is going to leave, but he stops, takes off his hat, and looks toward the blue door. "We've been praying for the doctor. Any change?"

I shrug, surprised. "Not much. Maybe a little. One day he got up and dressed himself."

Reverend Miller shoots me a big smile and his very white teeth illuminate his dark face. "Well now. That's something!" he says as if dressing yourself was a real accomplishment. "The Lord works in mysterious ways."

Woodpile

"Okay, Blum. Time to get to work." I'm dressed for the outdoors in old slacks and a plaid cotton shirt that Patience gave me.

Her old six-foot-long crosscut saw hangs on spikes under the porch and I carefully carry it out to where I've lined up two saw-horses I found in the barn. Sometimes I think the doctor is making progress and other times he seems like a little boat bobbing along without rudder or sail. I plunk a straw hat on his head and once again my loneliness hits me like a locomotive loaded with coal.

Get a grip, Becky, and quit feeling sorry for yourself. If you expect to have cooked food this summer and heat in the fall, you have to cut up this wood. I lay the first log, about eight feet long and the width of my forearm, up on the sawhorses then give Isaac one of the handles.

Just then, I hear another car whining up Wild Rose Road. Two cars in one day! We're getting to be Grand Central Station!

"How ya doing?" the vet asks, jumping out of his Model T and going straight toward Dr. Blum. He reaches out to shake hands, and when Isaac ignores him, he picks up the doc's right mitt and pumps it. "Glad to see you. Here let me give you some help." Blum is still standing with his left hand on the saw handle and Daniel Hester takes my place and begins to pull and push.

"Bitsy and I used to store our firewood under the porch," Patience tells me, gathering little Danny up and climbing out of the passenger-side door. She plops her little fair-haired boy on the steps and gives me a hug. "It stays nice and dry there. . . . I'm so sorry we don't get over more. . . . Our life is crazier than the Pittsburgh Zoo. Are you doing okay?" She studies my face.

I shrug and smile to show that I'm game, just the good old out-doorsy girl living the good old farm life with the good old catatonic boy. My act doesn't fool her and she nods toward Isaac. "Pretty hard, huh?"

I turn away. If she only knew the tears that I'm hiding. "We're making it. Pastor Miller brought the wood and I found the two-person saw under the porch. Thanks for thinking of us. Do you want to come in? I don't have any coffee or anything."

"That's okay. Put on the water. I brought you a jar of peppermint leaves I dried last fall. We can have tea."

Patience follows me through the blue door with her little boy and gives him his red metal fire truck to play with.

"Oh, the house looks so pretty. Do you have everything you need? Is there anything more I could lend you?"

"No, Patience." I smile, looking around the room at the white walls, the shining windows, at the sofa covered with a blue-and-green quilt, at the white curtains I made of muslin that Patience donated, at the bookcase that now holds our books, mostly medical. I have even set out my paints and brushes in a clear quart jar, and on the back wall hung one of my paintings, *Purple Iris on a Hillside*.

"You've given us all this! All I need now is a job with cash money. I can't live on your charity forever. There has to be something."

"Times are tough. . . . There aren't many jobs, Becky." Patience stares out the window. "Try not to worry. We'll share what we have and you'll share with us. That's how people get by nowadays. The thing is, you can't have too much pride." For the first time, I notice how worn she looks.

Outside, there's the *swish, swish, swish* of the two-man crosscut, and when I look through the window, I see the vet and the doctor, pulling back and forth equally. There's the sheen of sweat on Isaac's face, and when Daniel stops for a break, he takes a swig from a silver flask and then holds the same flask to my charge's lips.

I am horrified at the offer of liquor to a catatonic, but Patience laughs, looking over my shoulder. "Boys will be boys!"

I could run out and stop them, but I hold myself back. Dr. Blum is actually working, and the pile of cut firewood grows.

"Did you hear there's a CCC camp going up south of town?" Patience asks, dropping back into the rocking chair. "Camp White Rock. They're going to build a state park, plant trees, clean up the forest, and build a lookout tower for wildfires."

"A state park! That's just what we need in times like these, a place to picnic."

Patience seems embarrassed to have to tell me. "It's not the park that's important. It's the money that it'll bring into Union County. Also the CCC means jobs for young men all over the country. The wages are small, but they get plenty of food and a place to live. It's part of Roosevelt's New Deal. The fellows also get a check for twenty-five dollars a month sent home to their families, so in the end families and women benefit too."

"What if a woman doesn't have a husband or a son? What if all she's got is a man too addled to pull his end of the two-person saw," I snap, acid leaking out of a rusty car battery. Patience puts her hand to her mouth, shocked by my bitterness.

"I'm sorry," I apologize. "I'm just worried is all. Even if I find work, I don't know what I'll do with Dr. Blum."

"You could leave him with me."

"I don't think that would work—what if you had to go to a birth?"

The midwife adjusts her silver wire-rim glasses. "I take Danny with me sometimes."

"Danny's different. He's little and cute. Anyone would want to help take care of him. Dr. Blum isn't cute; in fact, to some people he's downright scary."

"Danny is cute," she admits, then counters my negativity: "But you have to have faith. If you can't find a job, you have us and if you do find a job, we'll figure something out."

Then she changes the subject. "On Saturday I have to go into Liberty to see Lilly Bittman. You remember her? She's pregnant again and cramping. The blind girl who married the shopkeeper at Bittman's Grocery? A sweet woman with bright red curly hair?"

"Cramping? I didn't even know she was pregnant. I was in the store a few weeks ago, but Mr. Bittman didn't say anything. How far along is she?"

"About five months. She's worried she's going to have the baby too early. I gave her husband strict orders to keep her in bed."

"When I go in to look for work again, I can see her," I offer, happy to have something I can do to help my patron. "Save you a trip. My money from Mrs. Bazzano isn't going to last forever."

"Would you? I'd be grateful. Daniel has to travel so much; the cost of gas is killing us."

I look at Patience in her thin yellow dress. Her cheekbones are hollow and I know mine are too.

Summer

10

Blue Skies

It's time to go job hunting again. The thing is, the humiliation at Stenger's, when the pharmacist gave me a quarter, still stings.

To prepare, I dress my mute companion in a clean white shirt and at the last minute decide to give him a tie. Dr. Blum was always a nice dresser. Snappy, you might even say, because Pricilla, his wife, bought all his clothes and *liked her men to look attractive*. I smile. The pretty blond flapper had a way with the fellows, but Dr. Blum was so busy he never noticed.

I use a little lipstick and dress myself up too, in a pale green blouse, plaid pleated skirt, and hose, my last pair. I want to look professional, but I must be prepared to take anything—charwoman or laborer on a road crew.

Before we leave, I adjust the back seams in my stockings, hoping I have them straight, then I get out the money jar and stuff the last ten-dollar bill Mrs. Bazzano gave me in my pocketbook. It isn't until I've loaded Blum into the auto that I remember my nurse's bag. I'd promised Patience I'd look in on Lilly. That's where I'll make my last stop, I decide. I'll see the pregnant woman and pick up the few groceries we need.

We are most of the way into Liberty, just crossing the bridge over the Hope River, when the gray clouds break open and a patch of blue illuminates my heart. I promised myself that I would try to see things more positively. *Look at the daisies covering that field! Look at those two bluebirds sitting on the fence!*

Things aren't so bad, really. There are many who are poorer than the two of us. I think of the people in the Midwest where nothing can grow because of the drought. I should count my blessings. The important thing is to have hope, not to give up even in the face of despair.

Why, look at Dr. Blum and me, all dressed up like any middle-class couple, driving along in our late-model auto! *"Blue skies smiling at me!"* I croon at the top of my lungs, but no one can hear me except the doctor, and you'd swear he was deaf. He doesn't react, doesn't tap his toe or cringe, either one. *"Bluebirds singing a song . . . Nothing but bluebirds all day long!"*

Captain Wolfe

We park in front of the pharmacy, between a horse cart with two mules and a green army truck with wood sides. CIVILIAN CONSERVATION CORPS it reads on the door.

When I enter the building, I'm surprised to see Mr. Stenger's wife at the counter talking to a tall man in a CCC uniform. I'm glad it's her. Mr. Stenger may still be miffed about the scene with Nick Rioli when we tried to buy the epinephrine. It makes me tense just thinking about it. Also, I don't want him to give me another quarter.

"Will the young man be okay?" Mrs. Stenger asks as she wraps up a collection of medical supplies—a compression gauze, cotton balls, and Merthiolate. She's a pretty lady, with her dark wavy hair tied back, and she wears her husband's long white lab coat that droops almost to the floor.

Mrs. Stenger, I remember from my previous years in Liberty, is an inquisitive, college-educated woman of about fifty, with five children whom she raises like wildflowers.

"I'm sorry we don't have a physician in town anymore," she goes on in her low voice. "Are you sure you don't want to buy a sling or some plaster? What if you need to make a cast?"

"No, this should be fine. The boy's arm doesn't seem to be broken, just scraped and bruised. He was clowning around and fell off the truck. Fifth District is sending Dr. Crane from Camp Laurel tomorrow." The CCC man strokes the head of the purring orange cat on the counter.

I'm feeling shy, but have to speak up. "I'm a registered nurse. Is there anything I can do to help?"

"Oh, Nurse Becky. I didn't recognize you." That's Mrs. Stenger. "My husband told me that you and Dr. Blum were back in town."

"We've just returned from Virginia, Dr. Blum and I, but Dr. Blum is not well."

As I move toward the counter, I can see the man is nice looking with a straight jaw and small, flat ears, but a scar down his cheek mars his handsomeness. A military injury from the Great War, I imagine. Most of the CCC officers, Patience told me, are from the army reserves, and General Douglas MacArthur is in charge of the program.

"I know first aid and can even set a broken arm."

"Thank you. I appreciate the offer, but we'll be okay." The gentleman salutes and limps toward the door. From the looks of him, his face was not the only part of him wounded. Still, he carries himself well and doesn't seem outwardly disabled. He turns at the door. "Miss? Miss . . ."

"Rebecca Myers," Mrs. Stenger offers.

"Miss Myers, if you're ever interested in helping out at the camp, we accept volunteers. . . . It's Camp White Rock. Do you know where it is?"

"I've heard of it. I can get directions."

"Then I hope you'll come by." He gives me a smile and I see that his teeth are strong and white.

"I'll think about it. I'm caring for Dr Blum in his convalescence, so that makes it complicated, but I'll think about it."

"Just ask for Captain Wolfe." He salutes us both again and then turns with a snap and marches down Main.

Gray Skies

"Becky, Becky. Becky," Mrs. Stenger gushes coming around the counter as if we were once best friends. "It's so good to see you and oh, my holiness . . . the captain . . . what a man. He was nearly killed in the Invasion of Lorraine. . . . So how is the doctor? How is he? Terrible! Terrible! What's his condition, anyway?" The woman floats around the counter flapping the long white medical coat and looking like the older sister of the actress, Joan Hopkins, same dark hair and big eyes.

I take a deep breath. "He's stable, but he's suffered some kind of brain damage." I keep the story short, wanting to stay on task.

"Such a tragedy. And you, dear, you must come to dinner." I ignore the invitation and get on with my mission.

"Well, Mrs. Stenger . . ."

"*Lucille*," she commands. "Call me Lucille."

"Lucille, I know many people are worse off than the doctor and me. I've seen the soup lines, but I *have* to find work. Do you know of *anything*? Any work at all? It doesn't have to be nursing. House-work or cleaning, or clerking in a store? Anything?"

Mrs. Stenger doesn't answer at first. She walks back behind the counter and starts putting a new shipment of Lydia Pinkham's Vegetable Compound on the mostly bare shelves.

"I'm sorry, dear. I'll keep a lookout, but times are tough and men must have work first . . . for their families. I'm not sure this was the best place to come back to. Surely, it would have been better to stay in Virginia. Doesn't the doctor or you have family?"

I don't know how to answer this, so I just say, "No."

It's too shameful to admit here in West Virginia, where kin always takes care of kin, that Blum's own brother kicked him out. And it's too sad to admit that I too am alone.

Rich Girl, Poor Girl

For the next hour, with Blum in the car, I swallow my pride and walk up and down Main, visiting every establishment.

How did this come to be? Rebecca Myers, a college graduate, wandering the streets of a small mountain town, unemployed, almost destitute. I quickly review my downward spiral. *State funding for my Women and Infants' Clinic cut . . . Moved to Charlottesville when offered a job as Dr. Blum's office nurse . . . Priscilla Blum's life cut short by her tragic crash into the James River . . . Dr. Blum withdraws into silence and neither of us works for over a year . . . All savings gone . . . Eviction imminent . . . Escape in the night . . . Return to Liberty. Now here I am . . . impoverished, alone, walking the streets, looking for work, any work at all.*

Not quite any *work! Get a grip, Becky.*

Pulling myself together, I continue my search and poke my head in Sheriff Hardman's office at the courthouse. He comes around from behind his desk and shakes his head.

Since I last saw him, his hair has thinned and the scar on his chin, from a knife fight long ago, is more prominent, but he's still a big man, someone you wouldn't want to mess with.

"I don't need cash money. I'd work for food." *God, this is hard! I feel like I'm begging.*

"I'm sorry, Miss Myers. I'll let you know if I hear of anything. Can I walk you out to your car?" At the side of the Pontiac, he looks in at the doctor and taps on the window. Isaac doesn't blink, doesn't even turn his head. The sheriff taps harder and studies the side of Blum's stony face. "Damn shame," he comments, then tips his hat and turns away.

Only two last places to go and my fruitless day will be over. I need to get gas and some kerosene, then a few supplies at the grocery, where I'll check on Lilly Bittman, the young pregnant woman whom Patience is worried about.

I stop first at the Texaco station where Loonie Tinkshell, the owner, comes out wearing khaki coveralls and a cap like a military man. He salutes like one too and wipes a long strand of his hair off his forehead leaving a line of grease. "Hi, Miss Becky. Dr. Blum." Loonie is not really loony; people just call him that. His Christian name is Louis.

"Car trouble?"

"No, we just need a fill-up and some kerosene, but can you check the oil?" I notice the prices on a handmade cardboard sign: 10 CENTS A GALLON FOR GAS. 5 CENTS FOR KEROSENE. CASH MONEY! NO CREDIT!

A few minutes later, I pull out my ten-dollar bill to pay for the gas and feel ridiculous. Loonie looks at the paper money, looks at me, and then without saying anything walks into the station to get me my change. It takes him five minutes. Damn, now he will think I'm a moneybags.

Just because I feel bad, I tip him two dimes, but then I feel worse. In a couple of weeks, I'll need those coins.

Looking Up

I am surprised when I enter the Bittman's Grocery to find more shoppers than last time. Two women and a man move up the three aisles in slow motion, probably trying, like me, to maximize the nutrition they can get with their meager cash. One woman carries a pale thin child with a cleft lip on one side, and I shiver remembering the first baby I delivered. The little boy reaches out when they pass the pickle barrel, but doesn't make a sound and the mother pulls his hand back.

I step up to the counter. No point looking at things we can't afford. B.K. Bittman greets me in his brown apron. His short dark hair sticks up like he forgot to comb it and his hazel eyes have a worried, haunted look.

"Miss Becky, how can I help you?" he says in a monotone.

"Good morning, Mr. Bittman." I fumble in my jacket pocket, looking for my short list. "How's Lilly?"

B.K. holds my gaze. "Poorly. Did you know she's in the family way?"

"Yes. The midwife told me." I don't need to explain which midwife; there's only one, since Mrs. Potts passed away and Bitsy moved to Philadelphia.

"Could I see Lilly? I told Patience I would stop by." I set my little leather nurse's bag on the counter as if this makes my visit official.

"Yes, sure. We'd appreciate it, but just so you know, I can't afford to pay. Can I gather the things on your list while you visit?"

The grocer opens a door to the rear and shows me up a set of steep wooden stairs that lead to the couple's apartment.

"Lilly, honey," he yells, "Miss Becky, the home nurse, is on her way up."

"Hello," I call, entering a kitchen with a sink full of dishes, leftovers still on the table, and a back door that leads down another set of stairs to the alley.

"I'm in here." Lilly's voice draws me toward a bedroom where a pale young redhead sits up in bed, a book on her lap and three books on the bedside table. The startling thing is her eyes, aqua blue. She turns in my direction, though I know she can't see me. The books are in Braille.

"Miss Becky. It's so nice to have you back." She reaches out for my hand and her soft fingers run up and down my wrist, her way of connecting since she can't meet my eyes.

"Thank you," I answer formally. "Most everyone has been very nice, but it's been a hard landing. I thought the economy was bad near Charlottesville, but it's much worse here. I can see people are really suffering. Anyway, enough about me! How are *you*? Patience said you're pregnant again. I take it this is a good thing?" Here I raise my eyebrows waiting for her response and glance at her small protruding abdomen. It's strange to use my face to convey concern when Lilly cannot see it.

"Yes, we were very happy. It took five years to get pregnant last time, four years this time and we were wondering if it would ever happen again. Now I'm not sure. I mean, we still want the baby very much, but you heard about the cramping. I'm afraid I'm going to lose it.

"B.K. and Patience insist I stay in bed and they're probably right, but there's so much to do. Did you see the kitchen? The housework has gone to the devil, and B.K. needs help in the store . . ." She shrugs. "And . . . and if I'm going to lose the baby anyway, I might as well get up."

"Have you been to the doctor's in Torrington?"

"Yes, I went there a few weeks ago to see the specialist, Dr. Seymour. He wanted to admit me, but Boone Hospital has become a rat hole. There's no money for upkeep. You even have to bring your own pillow and, anyway, we couldn't afford it." She's still stroking my wrist. Back and forth. Back and forth.

"And then there's B.K. He's wearing himself thin. I can't see him, of course, but I *feel him*, his ribs sticking out. He's trying to hide it from me, that the store's in trouble, losing money. I used to tend things when he did deliveries, but I can't anymore. They call this the Great Depression, but it's not just the economy, it's everything." I see the tears in her unseeing eyes and she wipes them away.

Getting down to the point of my visit, I change the subject. "So how bad are your pains? Any bleeding or leaking of fluid?"

"The tightening comes and goes. It's worse when I get up and sometimes my back hurts. The baby's still moving, so I know it's alive. No water leaking. My last baby was born in the caul, so I guess I make strong water bags." She lets go of my wrist and puts her hands across her belly, holding the new life in. "Do you want to feel it?"

"Oh!" I say when the fetus bumps my hand. Then I pull out my stethoscope, place it on Lilly's lower abdomen, and consult my watch.

"The heartbeat is strong, a hundred and thirty-five beats a minute. I think if you stay in bed, there's a good chance all will be well. When is your confinement? Do you know?"

"Patience says I'll have the baby in the fall, but my God, I can't lie around that long. Bittman's Grocery is a two-person operation. We've been thinking of finding a deliveryman. That would take the pressure off B.K. and I'd feel better about staying in bed. The problem is they'd have to have a good vehicle. Most of the guys without jobs don't have reliable transportation."

I go on alert, like a hunter who has just seen a four-point buck. "How much could you pay?"

"Do you know someone? They'd need chains for the winter."

"I'm thinking of *me*. I have a six-year-old Pontiac. We have chains and *I* could do the deliveries. Dr. Blum, you probably heard, is disabled now, but he could carry the heavy boxes and I'd be careful to not let him scare people. What do you think?"

B.K. enters the room, sits on the edge of the bed with his hand on Lilly's leg, and joins the conversation. "We couldn't pay much, only gas, two bits for a delivery and maybe your groceries at a discount. We were thinking of a man, but you'd do this for us?"

"I'm a good driver. I got us all the way here from Virginia . . ." I'm almost on my knees, though I still sit on the bed.

"Well, let's try it. I'll call you the first of the week and you can get started."

That puts the damper on things. "I'm sorry, we don't have a phone."

"Oh," Lilly says, dropping her head in disappointment, but then jerking it up, the red hair flaming around her pink face. "But that's okay. We'll just tell people that deliveries are only on Mondays and Thursdays now."

"It's set then?" Can you stay for our midday meal?" B.K. asks.

"No, I have to go. The doctor's in the car, but I'll see you Monday. There will be deliveries for sure, then?"

"Yes, I already know of three. Yes, for sure. I'll memorize the directions so that you can write them down." Lilly is like a new woman and I am too.

11

Goose Attack

"Damn!" I curse, as I turn around for the third time and reverse my course on County Road 92. "We've been up and down this stretch two times and I still haven't seen a swinging bridge."

Finally, I spot it, almost obscured by the tall grass. I pull up in the gravel, find the boxes of groceries Mr. Bittman has prepared, and motion Dr. Blum to help me. When he doesn't respond, I open the passenger door and haul him out.

"Here!" I yank out his arms so I can set the box in them. "Follow."

I take the smaller carton and wind my way down a narrow path that leads to the wood-and-cable contraption that spans the creek. Dr. Blum is right behind me and I don't know if it's safe for the two of us to cross at the same time, but I guess I'll find out.

With each step, I hold my breath as the swinging bridge bounces and sways. *Don't think about the water and rocks below,* I tell myself. *Just keep your eyes on the white house on the other side.*

Across the field, four blond barefoot girls sit on the porch and they can't stop giggling. I suppose my fear must be hilarious to people who travel the bridge a few times a day. Finally, a woman comes out, wearing a blue housedress with tattered lace down the front. Her golden hair is pulled back in a bun.

"Sally," she yells. "Go down to the bridge and help that lady. Those are our groceries and I don't want her dropping them in the creek."

The oldest girl saunters over with the other ones following.

"Ma'am," she says with a curtsy, when I reach dry land. "I'm Sally. Can I take the parcel for you?"

It's not heavy, but I'm shaking so bad, I give it over gladly, happy to have the solid earth under my feet. "Nice to meet you, Sally. How old are you?"

"Almost ten." She's such a pretty, well-mannered child.

"Fifth grade then. Where do you go to school? Does the school bus come all the way out here?"

"It still passes by, but I don't go. My shoes were too small and Ma says it would be shameful to go to school barefoot." This takes me aback. I hadn't really thought about the impact of the Great Depression on children, except maybe for the lack of nutritious food. Moments later, the sound of honking interrupts my thoughts as four huge geese come running from the barn, their necks outstretched and their vicious yellow bills open and ready to bite.

I jump up on a hay wagon and pull Dr. Blum with me.

"Help!"

Willa

"Girls!" the mother shrieks. "Get those birds away!" She comes off the porch flapping her apron and the troop of little blondes, laughing their heads off, drives the flock out of the yard. The biggest goose circles around behind the barn, a mean one with a black head and red eyes, and comes back, but Sally chases him all the way down to the creek. Embarrassed, I climb down from the wagon. Blum jumps down too.

"So sorry," the woman of the house apologizes. "The geese aren't used to strangers and they're as fierce as guard dogs. That big one bit the Fuller Brush salesman in the butt. . . . My name's Willa Hucknell."

"I'm Rebecca Myers from Bittman's Grocery. I guess you figured that out."

"Lilly told me there'd be a new delivery person but I pictured a man. Would you like to rest a spell after that torment? I've just made some coffee."

"Okay, but just a minute," I respond, knowing it would seem rude to refuse. "We have three other deliveries to make."

I follow Willa into the neat kitchen dominated by a long wooden table and surrounded by nine wooden chairs. There's a sink with a pump, a white cookstove, and a pie safe in the corner. The pine floor is shiny and clean.

Willa gets out two blue chipped mugs and pours coffee into them and I notice then that she's pregnant. "How far along are you?" I ask, wondering why the heck, in times like these, the Hucknells need more children. Then I remember, not every pregnancy is planned and birth control is hard to afford.

"Just four months; I'm showing earlier every time." She rolls a cigarette, lights it with a wooden match, and sits down at the table, blowing smoke out the side of her mouth. "So what's wrong with the sawbones?" she asks boldly.

"No one's sure. He's not dangerous or anything. I just have to lead him around."

"It's a shame," Willa responds. "I wasn't crazy about him when he doctored here. Kind of a cold fish, but he was a good physician. We don't have one now."

I take a sip of the black coffee and keep my eye on Blum through the kitchen window. He's still standing in the grass in the front yard and when one of the small girls picks up a stone and throws it at his shoe he doesn't flinch.

"This coffee is good," I tell my hostess, "but I can't stay long. The groceries are three dollars. It's twenty-five cents for the delivery." Mrs. Hucknell turns toward the pie safe and rattles around in a money jar while I try not to look.

"My husband, Alfred, is employed by the PWA, the public works thing, on the Pennsylvania Turnpike at Bald Knob and he needs the truck for his job. That's why I have to have groceries delivered. The girls miss their daddy, but we were getting so far behind, the bank threatened foreclosure. Him going away to work is the only way we could keep the farm, and he only gets home once a month to see the little ones."

"You and your children live here alone? Keep the farm up and everything?"

"We do the best we can. We don't grow crops since Alfred left, just our garden, the chickens, a cow, and the hay fields, but we hold on all right. I get a neighbor to bring us wood . . . or coal, if we can afford it.

"It's hard for everyone now," she goes on. "At least we have a place to live and we have the girls. We are rich in girls!"

"Just girls? No boys?"

The woman looks over at me and takes another long drag on her cigarette. "Yes, but Alfred keeps trying to get him a son, says every man needs a namesake."

There's laughter on the porch and I see that the pebble game has escalated into a teasing song with the children circling the doctor. "*All around the mulberry bush. The monkey chased the weasel. The monkey thought it was all a joke. Pop goes the weasel!*" The "pop" is shouted right into the doctor's face, but he doesn't blink and the girls think that's hilarious.

Mrs. Hucknell slams through the wooden screen door. "For shame on you, Sally, and you a big girl! You leave Dr. Blum be! He's the one that delivered you right in this house ten years ago."

The mother turns to me as I stand in the doorway. "For the twins, Sunny and Sue, who're five, I had Patience, the new midwife. The last one, Sonya, I birthed myself. She's four." She plunks down next to her children and commands their attention. "We must be kind to those who help us in this troubled world, even if they turn funny later on," she instructs, nodding at the doctor.

Sally hangs her golden head. The little ones move in close to their mother and she strokes their flaxen hair. For a minute, I'm sad I don't have children. How nice it would be to have their small, soft warm bodies against me.

But that's not all there is to mothering, I remind myself. There's feeding and bathing, mending their clothing, teaching them right from wrong, and keeping them out of danger until they have enough sense not to be a danger to themselves.

Anyway, I have Dr. Blum to care for. . . . I smile to myself (not without bitterness) and drink up my last bit of coffee.

Mrs. Stone

The next week my deliveries go without mishap and because I can park close to the homes, I don't need Dr. Blum's help; I just roll down the windows and leave him sitting in the car.

There's the Indian family, the Hummingbirds, who live in a large log house on Dark Hollow, then Charley Roote, an old veteran of the Spanish-American War who lives on the next farm, and finally, a widow, Mrs. Stone.

The tiny lady, about five feet tall, using a cane with a silver lion's head for a handle, meets me on the side porch of her two-story brick farmhouse. In the back is a barn with a wire fence around it and about two dozen goats of all colors and breeds, some little, some big, some with horns and some with droopy ears. "Oh, sweetie, thank you so much. I didn't know the Bittmans were using a delivery girl." The tiny white-haired woman ushers me into her kitchen where my eyes go wide. The room is a blaze of white; white walls, white cupboards, a white-and-yellow-checked linoleum floor. On one open cupboard, displayed on flowered shelf paper, are dozens of white ceramic cookie jars, decorated with red, yellow, and blue flowers, each one different, an amazing collection. On the other shelves are seashells of all sizes and shapes and a few carved wooden sculptures, the kind you might get in Africa or India.

Mrs. Stone pulls open the door of the shiny white fridge and takes out a jar of brown liquid. "Can I give you a cup of ice tea? Won't take a minute. I need one myself. I'm just a mess today." She has a high voice, almost like a little girl, and she indicates a round oak table covered with papers.

"What did you say your name is? I'm Mrs. Stone, but you can call me Sparky." I decide to let Isaac sit in the car another few minutes, while I take in the pleasant surroundings. Mrs. Stone interests me.

"My name is Becky Myers. Have you lived here long?"

She answers, standing with her back to me, so I can't see her face. "Just a year. I've lived overseas most of my life. I'm originally from Connecticut, but my husband was in the Foreign Service. This was his mother's homeplace. He died on Christmas, right after the crash."

"That must have been terrible, losing your husband around Christmas." I have a feeling she's leaving a lot of heartache out of the story. "Was it a long illness?"

"No. He jumped. Jumped from the Brooklyn Bridge." My head jerks up and I almost choke on my tea. "He didn't even leave a note or say good-bye. Just went off to work in the city like it was any other day. I suffered, of course, floated like a lost soul, but then I came back to myself and moved here. . . . What else can you do? Life goes on."

She sits down across from me and offers the sugar bowl, decorated with flowers like the rest of the collection. Her hands are small and dotted with brown age spots, but they look strong.

"I'm so sorry. Was it money, like you hear about? All those suicides at the beginning of the Depression, twenty thousand around the world, I read somewhere."

"I guess, but if it was debt he didn't tell me. That's the worst part, not knowing. It was months later the lawyers brought me in and told me we'd lost everything." Here she runs her veined hands over the piles of correspondence on the table.

"Paperwork! That's why I'm in such a frazzle. More tea?" I place my palm over my glass to indicate I'm good.

"My stomach is just in knots." She stares at the stacks of folded and wrinkled documents in front of her. "I hate this sort of thing; can't find what I'm looking for, but I know it must be here.

"When we inherited this farm in '25, my husband remarked *specifically* that the deed said *mineral rights included*. I didn't understand why that was important. In Connecticut we never heard of such things.

"Later, he told me the history, how the farmers in Appalachia, back in the 1800s, were tricked into giving up their mineral rights for a few measly bucks and then the oil and coal barons came in and tore up their land. He said his grandpap was wise to refuse to sell, a stubborn old coot! He just wouldn't sign.

"Now, yesterday, this young man, wearing a suit and tie, just a whippersnapper from Pennsylvania Oil and Gas, comes by saying *they* own the mineral rights and want to bring in a crew to drill for oil. I may be over the hill, but I'm not senile. How dumb does he think I am?"

"What's wrong with an oil well? I see them along the road. Once the company drills, they just put in a pump, one of those rigs that go up and down. Gas is a byproduct and you could get it free to heat your house like a lot of farmers do. Some folks even heat their outhouse. Seems like a good deal."

"Give them an inch, honey, they'll take a mile! You see what they did to the Harrod farm on North Run?" I shake my head no.

"Brought in those big trucks and drilling machines, and now their road and fields are nothing but a rutted mess and that beautiful creek that used to have nice brook trout in it is dead from the muddy runoff. This farm is all I have left and they're not going to ruin it!"

"Maybe you could go to the county assessor. They must have copies of the deeds. I hate to leave, Mrs. Stone. The tea was refreshing, but Dr. Blum is sitting out in the car."

"Dr. Blum?" We step out on the porch. "Well, why didn't you bring him in?"

"No, you don't understand. Dr. Blum has had a misfortune. Physically, he's fit, but he has no intelligence and I take care of him."

Sparky Stone walks right up to the car and whacks the door to startle the doctor, but Blum doesn't blink. "What do they say about him, his physicians?"

"Well, they don't say much, just that's he's had a stroke or maybe he's catatonic."

"I've never trusted doctors. Never needed them much either," Sparky comments, still staring at Blum. "Next time you come, Miss Becky, bring the man in."

The old lady reaches through the open window and strokes Blum's jaw with one bony finger, then turns his face to hers and looks into his eyes as if searching for something. I may have imagined it, but I swear light flies from her eyes to his, then Blum blinks and the curtain comes down.

Oranges

Back at Bittman's an hour later, I check on Lilly, who's being a good girl and staying in bed and then give B.K. his money. He writes the proceeds in his notebook and turns over my pay. "It wasn't too bad today. I enjoyed driving around the countryside and the people were nice, especially Mrs. Stone. She's a character. You'll want me Thursday, then?"

"Lilly is already writing down the deliveries."

I look at the oranges arranged on a tray on the counter. "How much?" I ask longingly.

"Twenty-five cents a dozen." B.K. rests his elbows on the wooden counter.

"No, I guess not. . . . I do need some basics, though, five pounds of cornmeal and three pounds of red beans. As I leave, Mr. Bittman wraps up six oranges.

"On the house," he says.

I go out into the sunshine feeling rich with my carton of food and my bag of golden fruit, but as we cross over the Hope River I see a barefoot young mother with stringy brown hair, begging just this side of the bridge with her two raggedy kids clinging to her long skirt. This is something new. I have never seen a woman begging before, and she holds a crude sign: WILL WORK FOR FOOD.

What else can I do? I slow the auto and roll down the window, peel open my parcel, and hold out two oranges.

"God bless you, ma'am," the young lady whispers. "We haven't eaten all day. Can I do anything to repay you?"

"No. No, we're fine."

Afterward, I thought of the groceries in the back. I could have given her more.

Blum turns his face away, staring down at the water where it rushes over the rocks.

12

Lawn Party

Sticky with fruit juice, we sit in the shade of a weeping willow tree on an old blanket on the Hesters' lawn. There's the smell of newly cut grass and the scent of the red roses growing up the side of the porch.

Each of us shares a slice or two of our oranges with Danny and juice dribbles down his little chin. Daniel lies on his side petting Emma and Sasha, the two beagles he says were his wife's dowry. The doctor and I lean against a bench across from them. Patience rests against the trunk of the tree.

"Is that the phone?" I ask. The double ring floats across the yard.

"Damnation." The vet mutters as he sprints for the house.

"Excuse his French. He's just tired," Patience apologizes. "He was up with Mr. Earle's sick cow last night, milk fever. Slept for a few hours today, but was hoping to have a quiet night."

"Patience!" Hester yells from the stone porch. "It's for you . . ."

With a long sigh, the midwife pushes herself up and plunks Danny Boy in my lap.

"Patty-cake. Patty-cake. Baker's man." I try to entertain him,

taking his sticky little hands in mine and making them clap. *"Make me a cake as fast as you can."* The vet ambles back across the lawn.

"Afraid she's going to have to leave. Lately, one of us is always going. It's hard. That's why we haven't been over to see you. It's always something."

A few minutes later, Patience returns with her birth bag in hand. "I wish I didn't have to go. We were having such a nice time. Daniel and I don't have much of a social life."

"None," cuts in Daniel.

"Want to come with me?" Patience brightens. "It's Mrs. Mitchell. You *know* her. The one I told you about, the woman expecting twins. I could sure use a baby nurse."

I go on alarm. This is exactly what I *don't* want to do. I'd rather face Willa's geese.

"I don't think so, maybe another time. The doc and I were driving around all day toting groceries. I'd better get him home."

"Blum can stay here," Daniel offers, supporting his wife. "I have some work in the barn, mucking out stalls. He can help."

"But Dr. Blum has his good clothes on," I argue, still trying to get out of it.

"I have a pair of coveralls and old rubber boots." That's Hester again.

"Please! It will be fun. I'll split my fee," Patience pleads. "Well, I'll split whatever I get. Sometimes it's cash. Sometimes it's food. Sometimes it's nothing. I could even split nothing!" She thinks this is funny.

I haul myself up. "You know how I enjoy childbirth. . . ."

Patience can tell I'm wavering. "Please! It would help to have company."

Daniel doesn't wait for my answer. He balances his toddler on his shoulders and leads Blum away.

Five minutes later we are rolling along Bucks Run in the midwife's dusty Olds. The oaks, maple, and hickory are covered in leaves now, a beautiful blur of summer green, but my stomach is tight, and I wonder why I agreed to this. Was it just to be nice to Patience? We owe her a lot. Was it out of some kind of sense of duty as a nurse? Was it the lure of sharing Patience's fee? I hate to think it was only the latter. I'm getting to be a money-grubber. Poverty will do that to you. Once you've been broke, you're always looking for a dime.

I'm about to ask Patience about Danny's birth, what the experience had been like for her, when she makes a sharp turn to the left, bumps across a creek through a foot of water, and pulls up in front of a dingy white two-story farmhouse with what looks like a chicken coop attached to the side.

A man waves wildly from the front steps, then runs back inside as a woman screams. Patience is already in motion.

Double Trouble

"Becky!" Patience calls.

"Right behind you." I enter the upstairs bedroom as a disheveled, unshaven father in coveralls backs out. He looks down, wipes tears from his eyes with a red bandanna, and runs down the hall.

"Asepto suction," commands Patience.

I know what she's asking for and find it wrapped in white cloth at the bottom of her birth satchel, a glass syringe with a red rubber bulb that's used to suck out the newborn's nose and mouth. As I hand it over, I get a look at the baby and my stomach drops. It's a tiny limp male, around five pounds, covered in meconium, baby poop.

Now I understand Patience's urgency. If the newborn aspirates the brown stuff that's been floating around in his mother's womb, he can get pneumonia and die. If she can manage to get it out of his airway before he breathes, his chances are better. Gently she places the pointed glass tube in his mouth and then his tiny nose, sucking out only clear fluid, no meconium.

"Thank you, Lord," the midwife mutters. "Here, get him going." She hands me the wet infant and pulls out her fetoscope to listen for the second twin's heartbeat.

"Okay, little one. Let's hear you cry. Open up those lungs." I give him a few pats on the butt and he wails.

"Is he okay? Is he all right?" sobs Lucy Mitchell. Her face is red and sweating, her golden eyes wet with tears. "I tried to wait for you, but he was coming and I couldn't stop."

Patience listens to the second twin's heartbeat as she consults the pocket watch hanging on a ribbon around her neck. "One hun dred and fifty-two beats per minute, just fine."

"One hundred and fifty-two," I repeat out loud, to remember the rate, then reach over and take the mother's pulse. "One hundred and ten." That's fast, but then she just delivered a baby unattended, which would be enough to accelerate anyone's heartbeat.

"Can you help get the baby nursing, Becky? It will bring on the next set of contractions. Sometimes there's a delay after the first twin, as the womb reorganizes itself. I need to do a vaginal exam to feel what's coming. I think it's a head, but I'm not sure."

Lucy doesn't need any help from me; she takes her nipple, gently strokes it against the newborn's cheek, and the baby opens his mouth, just the way nature intended.

"What will you need next, Patience? Scissors? Sterilized string to tie off the cord? Anything else?"

"That should be it. Oh, some more sterilized pads and Mrs. Potts's bleeding tonic. You know about that?"

I find a small brown bottle and hold it up to the light.

"It's a tincture of motherwort, pennyroyal, and blue cohosh to make the womb contract after the afterbirth is delivered," Patience explains. "I keep it ready at every delivery, but don't often use it. Twins are a special case though. The womb has been so stretched with two babies, it might need help contracting down afterward, but you probably know all this." She turns and takes off the rubber gloves, carefully arranging them on one of the sterile pads.

"Did you feel the presenting part?" I whisper, not wanting to alarm Mrs. Mitchell if the presentation isn't head down. Even Dr. Blum knew that frightening the mother could stop her contractions.

"No. It's too high," Patience whispers back and then in a louder voice. "We will just have to wait. . . . Clarence," she calls. "You can come back now. Everything's okay! Come see your new baby boy. You can bring the children."

My eyebrows shoot up. The children! Lucy is still half naked. Quickly I pull a blanket over the woman's bare legs. Certainly this never happened when Dr. Blum did a delivery!

Clarence Mitchell, having recovered himself, enters softly. He's a fair-haired fellow with a sunburned face, a few whiskers, and a band of white on his neck where his shirt collar usually covers his skin.

"Wife, you done good! Right healthy," he says about the baby and surprises me when he sits down next to her on the side of the bed. The couple's little boy and girl climb up too and Patience seems unfazed.

"Only the first baby is out. The labor will start up again soon," Patience explains as she plunks down on the other side and pulls the baby blanket down a bit so the children can see. "Look at that little sucker," she says. "He knows exactly what to do, just like a calf or a foal."

"Can we touch him?" asks the girl, who must be about six. She strokes the baby gently on the back with one finger. Timidly, I find a corner on the very full bed and sit down with them.

"Mmmmmmm," groans Lucy with a contraction, but there's a smile on her face. "Mmmmmm." It doesn't look like pain, almost pleasure.

"The labor is starting again. Let me listen to the next baby's heartbeat and then it will be time to walk," Patience says.

"We'll move out of your way, then," the father announces, leaping up.

Snow Globe

"Mmmm," the mother moans again and takes the midwife's arm. They walk and then stop, walk and then stop. While contracting, Lucy stands staring into space, rotating her hips. There is peace and a timeless feeling, as if nothing else matters.

Finally, I work my way across the room and in a hushed voice ask Patience, "Shouldn't we get her back in bed?"

"It's okay," Patience tells me. "It's not time yet. Lucy's voice hasn't dropped. When her voice changes the baby will come. I'll check her in ten minutes," she adds, consulting her gold timepiece.

"Mmmmmmmm."

"Can you lie down for a bit, Lucy?" Patience finally asks exactly at ten minutes. "I'd like to check your progress and listen to the baby again."

The second Lucy is on her back I observe something odd.

"Look, it's the water bag," Patience explains. "It reminds me of a floppy snow globe. See the bits of white in the amniotic fluid? That's vernix, a creamy substance that protects the newborn's skin while it's floating around in there. By the time the baby is full term it's mostly worn off."

I've never seen an intact amniotic sack before. Dr. Blum and the other physicians I've worked with always broke the membrane early in labor. With the very next contraction the sac pops and water squirts all over the bed.

"Whoops!" says Patience, not a bit fazed. A tiny pink girl follows with the next push.

"You okay, Becky? You're as white as a sheet."

"Yes," I lie. I've watched amputations, assisted in surgery, scraped dead tissue out of infected wounds, but this baby came so fast I didn't have time to prepare myself.

"You sure?"

"Yes," I lie again and sit down before I faint.

"That was wonderful!" The mother laughs.

Patience gives Lucy some of Mrs. Potts's herbal medicine, just in case, and she tells me not to bathe the second baby; the white vernix is healthy for her skin. Then Mr. Mitchell and the children creep back into the room and we all sit on the bed again and watch as Lucy feeds both babies from both breasts.

I have never given birth. Never wanted to. It horrified me to watch women scream and cry through labor until someone could put them under anesthesia, but this is different, and now that it's over, I see that all that we did in the hospital and the clinic and even at Dr. Blum's homebirths was more to comfort ourselves than to really help the mother.

"Isn't she wonderful?" Mr. Mitchell exclaims, taking his wife's hand and pressing it to his cheek. Six-year-old Clara crawls into my lap.

June 17, 1934

*Birth of twins, a male, Cecil Mitchell, (5 pounds, 8 ounces)
and a female, Callie Mitchell (5 pounds) to Lucy and Clarence
Mitchell of Bucks Run.*

The first twin was already out when we got there. Lucy and Clarence birthed him alone, but he was covered with meconium and the midwife had to suck out the baby's mouth and nose. Luckily the baby hadn't aspirated.

The second baby had a separate sack. That was a good thing, because there was no meconium in her water and everything went as smooth as silk. Just as a precaution, Patience gave Lucy a spoonful of Mrs. Potts's hemorrhage medicine and she only bled about 400 ccs. There were no perineal tears, but the babies were small.

Clarence said he was sorry he couldn't afford more and gave us five dollars. Patience laughed and said that was a good deal because we only delivered one baby.

13

An Idea

All week, Dr. Blum and I have worked planting our kitchen garden. We now have a nice little plot thirty by fifty feet. Nothing like the Hesters' or Maddocks' but for beginners it will do. Mrs. Maddock sent over some tiny tomato plants she had started in cans from seeds she'd saved last fall. Some will be red, some will be yellow, some with be almost purple.

Carefully, I transplanted them, digging the holes, patting the soil around their roots and watering each one. Dr. Blum helped, after I showed him how to carry the bucket back and forth from the spring.

The Reverend Miller, with his wife, Mildred, a bundle of energy and concern, stopped by with a sack of seed potatoes that they'd saved last fall, and Patience shared some of her bean and squash seeds.

Finished with the watering, we sit on the porch and stare out at our plot, or I stare at the plot, and my companion stares at the air in front of him.

"Dr. Blum. It's Sunday and we need a day of rest!" I break the silence. "I've been thinking we could go to church, but with your strange ways, people would stare, so let's go on a picnic to the

Hope River instead. What do you think?" Blum acts like he can't hear, but I know he can. He got the water from the spring when I asked him to, didn't he?

It doesn't take long to get ready. I pack two pieces of corn bread in a small willow basket, along with a canning jar of water, and a pint of applesauce I made with the Bittmans' half-rotten apples, then I take Isaac's hand like a child and lead him down Wild Rose Road.

At the Maddocks' place, there's no truck in front. They've probably gone into town to attend services or maybe they belong to the closer church at Hazel Patch. It's a colored church, but Reverend Miller is so kind, whites would probably be welcome.

As we walk, I reflect on the changes in Dr. Blum's health. Some of his actions have purpose now, though in the case of his stroll down Main Street, when he ended up at the soup line, it's hard to tell. Most important, when I show him how to do something he can copy me.

One thing is for sure: He has altered physically. When he was a physician he was tall, thin, and bookish. Now he actually has muscles and so do I. Carrying water, hoeing and digging, walking the land, sawing wood. We are both stronger.

Near the corner of Wild Rose and Salt Lick Road, I notice for the first time the square rock foundation of the small cottage that Maddock said vagrants burned down. The remains of the barn are nowhere to be seen.

This is our turning-off point and we cut across the road onto a well-worn grassy path toward the sound of the water. Here and there in the brush are the remnants of cold campfires, rusted tin cans, cleared areas where makeshift tents have been erected and then pulled down.

Patience tells me that the homeless like this spot because they can get water and they can fish. Also, no one seems to own this stretch along the river, so no farmer will come with a shotgun to run them off.

Closer to the water, in the wetlands, it's another wilder world, where purple iris and yellow buttercups bloom. Red maples, wild cherry trees, and tall oaks press into the sky. I let out my breath, breathe in and blow out again, remembering my youth, when hiking and climbing and canoeing with David used to bring me joy.

At the edge of the rushing water, we sit on the rocks and eat our corn bread with applesauce and drink our water. Dr. Blum stretches out on a flat slab of stone, his muscled arms under his head, looking up at the clouds.

I turn away and to distract myself from his handsome body, watch the schools of tiny trout darting through the water. For an hour I watch them, and then an idea comes to me. Here's a source of protein I hadn't thought about! If the hoboes can fish, why can't we? And why didn't I think of it before?

Excited, I yank Isaac up. "Come on, old buddy, let's go home and search the house and the barn. Maybe there's something we can use for a pole or a net, something we can use to get fish."

I'm on a mission now, pulling the doctor along as we hurry through the willows and low brush up to the road. This time as we approach the corner of Salt Lick and Wild Rose, I see two vagrants searching through the rubble of the burned-out cottage, looking for metal that they can salvage and sell.

"Hey, lady. Hey, mister," one of them yells. "Can you spare a dime? Or can you give a couple of working Joes, down on their luck, a bite of food?"

"Sorry," I say. "We are poor ourselves and have nothing to share." I turn over our empty basket to make my point. The truth is, I'm scared of them. The taller man with the full beard and the torn denim shirt stands up straighter.

"Well, bless you then, sister, you and your man. Don't give up hope. That's about all we have in these dark times." He turns and heads for the river.

As soon as they are out of sight I walk slower, ashamed of myself for being afraid. It's true we have little, but still we have more than they have. I just didn't want them to follow us home.

When we get back to the farm to search for a fishing pole, I discover a wealth of other tools I'd overlooked. Hanging on one of the walls in the barn, I find a scythe that could be sharpened and used to cut grass, a hammer, some nails in a tin can, another bucket, a rake . . . but no fishing pole.

Disappointed, I return to the house and find Dr. Blum sitting on the front steps with both a net and a pole. Not only that, there's a hook and a line!

"Isaac, you amaze me. Where did you find it?"

"Under," he says pointing toward the porch, and I think he's as surprised as I am to hear his own voice.

"You can talk, Isaac. You can talk if you want to," I tell him. "It's okay. I get lonely sometimes." But the curtain is already down and the lights are turned off.

Purple Iris, Pale Lilac

"Miss Becky! Miss Becky!" The girl named Sally calls from across the swinging bridge. We are on a first-name basis now, and this is my third trip to the Hucknell house. "Can I help you?" she asks.

"Sure." I hand her my box when I get to the end of the swinging bridge. (I've got the knack of crossing the metal-and-wood contraption now, just roll with the rhythm like a sailor on the sea.)

"What did you bring us?" The little girls swarm around like a flock of sparrows.

"Whatever your mama ordered," I respond. "I don't look in the boxes. Mr. Bittman, the grocer, packs them."

"How are you, Willa?" I greet the children's mother on the porch as I wipe my sweating face and arms with a handkerchief.

"About half."

I let that pass. In the mountains "about half" means you aren't swell, but you don't want to talk about it.

As usual, despite the heat wave, Blum takes his place on the porch with the four little girls. Sally has taken to reading to him from Louisa May Alcott's *Little Women* and he sits there like one of the family.

"Got a pot of coffee brewing?" I ask as I open the screen door.

"Cream?" Willa asks, not her usual talkative self. I pull out one of the wooden chairs. Taking a break with Willa has become a weekly routine and I admire this woman who is raising her daughters and caring for the farm with her husband away.

"So how's it going?" I start the conservation. Willa shrugs and when she flips her long blond hair back, I see bruises along the side of her face.

"Willa!" I point to the area.

"What?"

"Your face and neck."

"What?" When she covers her neck with her hand, the sleeve of her worn blue-dotted dress falls back and I see more discolorations on her white skin. Purple iris. Pale lilac.

"Willa, what happened?"

"It's nothing. The old man was home." She turns toward the sink so I can't see her face.

"Your husband? He was home? He didn't hit you in the stomach did he?"

"No, he wouldn't hit me there. He knows I'm pregnant again and he thinks it's a boy."

"But what got into him? I thought when he came home it was a happy time for you and the girls."

"The children maybe. They love their daddy."

"And you? I thought you loved him."

She turns and looks right at me now. "Sometimes I do, but not today. Would you love a man who makes you get all dolled up and does this to you? He's angry all the time and he takes his anger out on me. Each time we do it, he gets rougher in bed. He's in town now, probably getting loaded, throwing away money we need."

I listen with a poker face. It's something you learn when you are a nurse. Even if the wound is deep and infected, even if it smells bad, you don't let your revulsion show.

"You can't go on like this, Willa. He could really hurt you sometime." *Or kill you,* I'm thinking. "And the girls. Do the girls know?"

"Oh, yeah. I'm sure they know. He treats me bad during the day, especially if he's had a little hooch, and he treats me worse at night. That's where he has me. I never cry out. He knows I won't. It would scare the kids.

"We used to be goofy for each other, you know, but now he worries about money and losing the farm. Then he drinks."

"You told me that he works for the PWA on the highway."

"No, he quit there. He's home for a few days, then he'll start a different job at Bear Run, a laborer's position, hauling rock, building a new home for Mr. Kaufman, the big-shot department store owner in Pittsburgh. It's harder work, but a little better pay."

There's a ruckus on the porch. *"It's my turn."* Susie and Sunny are fighting over Dr. Blum.

"You sat in his lap last time!" Sunny clings to the doctor's shirt, almost pulling it off. Susie has tears in her eyes. Sally and Sonya are howling with laughter, but Isaac just sits there, like the monument of Abraham Lincoln.

"Oh, holy bejeezus!" Willa curses, leaping out of her chair. "Those vixens are so starved for manly attention, they'd follow the mailman into town. I don't know what I'm going to do with them. . . . Girls! Off!" she hollers and scatters the children away with a broom.

I follow her out, straighten the doctor's clothes, and smooth down his hair. "I guess we'd better get going."

"I'm so sorry," she says to me. "Say your apologies, children."

"Sorry."

"Beg pardon."

"Sorry."

"Dr. Blum." That's me, tapping the physician on the shoulder. "Time to go." The doctor stands.

"I'm so sorry," Willa says again.

"No harm done," I reassure, giving the woman a gentle hug so as not to hurt her bruised body. "You need me for anything, send word through Patience, the midwife. I mean *anything*. She has a phone. You know how to get her? There may be a time you have to get out of here." I whisper this last part.

All four of the girls walk us to the swinging bridge, the towheaded little ones holding Isaac's big hands. When I look back, their mother stands leaning against the peeling porch, her hand on her neck.

Boom

It's Independence Day in Liberty and the Hesters, Dr. Blum, and I stand in front of the pharmacy watching the parade. It begins with the Liberty High School band, wearing their worn dark blue uniforms, playing "The Stars and Stripes Forever." Then the Negro Drum and Bugle Corp from Delmont struts by dressed in spotless white shirts and black pants with black berets, raising their knees high and holding their proud heads back. Finally, near the end, come the Veterans of Foreign Wars. Charley Roote, dressed in his Spanish-American War uniform, is one of my delivery clients, and he catches my eye and winks.

"Daniel was in the Great War," Patience whispers.

"He never talks about it," I comment.

"He can't. He's not what you'd call a military man. He tells me stories sometimes, though. He was in charge of the horses for his platoon. One million men were wounded and died, but eight million horses also perished. It was awful. I think he felt worse for the animals than his fellow soldiers. At least the men knew what they were fighting for, or thought they did."

The horses in the parade come last, all decked out with red, white, and blue ribbons in their manes and tails, and the vet, perking up, points out the ones that he knows or has treated. Little Danny is amused by their droppings.

Now it's almost dark and you can hear the old-timey fiddle music from a few blocks away where Sycamore has been blocked off for a square dance.

"How about here, ladies?" It's Daniel, spreading a quilt out among the other blankets on the lawn around the courthouse where people are picnicking.

"Looks good," Patience agrees, and we lay out our small meal of cold baked beans, biscuits, and new potato salad.

A few minutes later, our meal is interrupted by cruel words. "Sit down, bitch! I can't see through you."

All heads turn, and in the growing dusk, I see Willa Hucknell, tending her blond brood, a few blankets away. That must be Mr. Hucknell! I've never met him before, and his words rip like a razor through the peaceful families eating their Fourth of July suppers. "I said *sit down!*"

The man, a handsome freckled-faced guy wearing a white fedora and white shirt open at the throat, sways above the picnic blanket like he's two sheets to the wind. "Are you listening, bitch? Are you listening?" He gives the woman a whack across her head. Daniel jumps up, as do several other men, even Blum and, yes, even Patience. Danny covers his ears and I pull him into my lap.

"Alfred . . . please!" Willa Hucknell begs. She must be so embarrassed, I think. To be treated so roughly in public would hurt more than the slap.

"You fuckin' 'shamed of me?" He slaps her again. *What's got into him?*

"Hey there, Alfred. You old son of a gun!" Daniel Hester winds his way through the crowd to get to the Hucknells, trying to defuse the situation. Blum follows like a shadow, increasing their bulk, if not their power. "Ain't seen much of you lately, Al. Had any more trouble with that three-teated cow?" Hester's playing the good ol' boy. He never says "ain't" at home.

Mr. Hucknell mumbles something surly and plunks himself down, and Daniel turns back to our quilt, thinking the disturbance is over, but he's wrong. Loud enough for the whole crowd to hear, Hucknell curses, "Fucking *Doctor* Hester, the *veterinarian*, but that cow never was right after he treated her. Charged me ten dollars, the *quack*."

Daniel whips back. "Excuse me. What did you say?"

A few more people rise to see what's happening, and some of the mothers lead their children away. There's a nasal laugh up front and a short, stocky man yells, "Fight!"

Here Patience gently pulls on Daniel's shirtsleeve. She's wearing her second-best dress, a navy blue shirtwaist with tiny white flowers, and in the dusk the white flowers look like stars.

"He killed out best stallion, Devil, too." The nasal voice is louder.

"Those are the Bishop brothers," Patience whispers and points into the crowd. "They'd love to start trouble." A beer bottle flies and shatters on the courthouse steps and at the same time Hucknell jumps up and pushes Daniel and Daniel pushes him back.

Then all hell breaks loose. *Boom!* Hucknell hits the vet in the face with his fist as the first of the fireworks goes off at the fairground. *Boom!* A white trail of light shoots into the night as two men rush forward and knock Daniel down. *Boom!* The trail of light bursts into red, white, and blue flowers, illuminating the crowd. *Boom!* Another skyrocket goes up. Blum gets into the scuffle and shows his new strength when he grabs one of the Bishop brothers and throws him through the air. *Boom!*

"Oh, shit!" Patience yells, heading into the melee, and I pull her back before she gets hurt.

"Somebody get the sheriff," a woman screams. *Boom! Boom! Boom! Boom!*

Then two more men rush forward, heading into the throng. The bigger of the two puts his size twelve boot in our potato salad while the small guy busts his head right into Blum's left kidney, a dangerous place, but the doctor swings around and traps the fellow in a headlock.

Boys on the courthouse steps are chanting, "Fight! Fight!" and by the rocket's red glare, bombs bursting in air, the melee gets wilder. It's as bad as a dogfight, and although originally it started with Mr. Hucknell and Daniel, all the men on the lawn are enjoying it.

Boom! Gold and silver blossoms light up the sky.

Boom! Red, white, and blue bits of burning confetti float down through the air.

Danny is crying.

Boom! White turns into red.

Boom! Boom! Boom! BOOM!

Then in the distance a siren goes off. The sheriff, alerted to the disturbance, is coming this way.

"Hester!" Patience yells.

"Isaac!" I try, but the men pay no attention.

The siren gets closer, the rotating red and blue lights of the squad car adding to the fireworks as the crowd rapidly scatters.

"Later!" growls one of the men moving off. The vet kicks him in the butt and I swear Isaac laughs.

"I can't believe you did that!" Patience berates her husband in the backseat of the Pontiac as we drive toward home. I'm at the wheel with Blum at my side. "You could've been arrested and locked in jail or, worse yet, had to pay a big fine for disorderly conduct."

Daniel grins his lopsided grin, and Patience, I notice in the rearview mirror, is smiling too.

"You think paying a fine would be worse than me behind bars?"

"Daddy was bad."

"You're right, my little man. Dr. Blum and Daddy should have controlled themselves. We're lucky no one got hurt. But goddamn that Alfred Hucknell! I can't stand to see a man hit a woman, then he called me a quack! The final straw was when the Bishop brothers got into it!"

"I'll admit when that slob stepped in my potato salad, I saw red," Patience adds.

"Boom!" says Dr. Blum, and shocks the pants off all of us.

14

Shame

Dark night and the wind slams into our little house from the west. I've been awake in bed for hours, my mind skittering from one worry to another. It's not like we're starving. We get tomatoes, carrots, new potatoes, and greens from the garden. Daniel brings us eggs and milk twice a week in exchange for Isaac's help with the vet work, and the fish have been a great addition to our diet, but we have so little cash money for kerosene, gasoline, sugar, cornmeal, and beans. I am really worried about what we will do this winter.

The delivery job is keeping us going, but just barely. There's got to be something else. I come full circle to the one place I haven't tried yet, the CCC camp.

I try to remember the name of the officer I met in Stenger's Pharmacy? Mr. Wolfe? No, *Captain* Wolfe. I was reluctant at first to go out to the camp, because of the distance and because it sounded like he wanted volunteers, but now it seems only sensible to at least see if I can get another paying job. Really, it isn't that far, just three or four miles past Mrs. Stone's place.

Across the hall, Blum snores lightly, the sound of a two-man saw cutting pine.

I picture his body, changed with the physical work. Poverty and the mountain air must agree with him. . . . Some might even find him attractive.

The wind slams the house again. Then thunder and lightning shake the window glass. The storm must be close. I pull the sheet up under my chin, remembering Mr. Hucknell and the fight, picturing the bruises I observed on Willa's neck. I'm a public health nurse, for god's sake, or used to be! Shouldn't I go to Sheriff Hardman? Would he do anything?

I run my hands over my own neck, feeling bruises long gone. It stays with me still, like a lump of black coal. The shame of it. I never told anyone.

The year was 1918 and soldiers were beginning to straggle back from the war. First came my brother Darwin, who returned from Europe without a scratch, but was struck down by the Spanish flu and died at a naval base in Boston a few months later. Twenty-five million died from the epidemic worldwide; *twenty-five million in just a few years!*

Then, before the grass even sprouted on Darwin's grave, my other brother, William, was killed in the Second Battle of the Marne. It broke Father's heart, the loss of his sons. He closed his practice, drank himself into oblivion, and passed of a stroke three months later.

I wore black, and it almost undid me, my whole family gone, but then David came home and I wore bright yellow. He was my family now and, like a daffodil, I wanted to make him happy.

We sold Father's house and moved back into our little place on High Street. We were young and in love, so I thought it would be fun, but David had changed. He wasn't the man who had left me. The first thing I noted was that he delegated all the decisions about our home to me.

"Sure, babe, whatever color you want. A red door, a green door. It doesn't matter."

"Fine, buy a new coal heater. We can afford it. Whatever you think."

He didn't shave, grew a thick, dark beard, refused to go out, and unless I purposely made a lot of noise in the kitchen, he didn't get up until noon. When I talked about restarting his medical practice his answer was always the same: "Couple of weeks. Couple of months, but not just yet. I need to rest." He shook his head and I wondered if he still heard the sound of gunshots and grenades, tanks and wounded men screaming.

Gone was the laughter I remembered, the dancing, and the joy in all things beautiful in the Vermont countryside. Secretly I was hoping for a child, something to heal us, but my husband was withdrawn and didn't care to be intimate, a big change for him.

"Do you want to talk about it?" I'd ask as we lay on our backs in our bed in the dark, not touching.

"What?"

"The war. What you did. What you saw."

"It's over now." He would kiss me gently on the cheek, almost like a sister, but he never wanted to be touched himself, and he never tried to enter me. In the night, I would wake and see him at the window, staring out into the street, smoking a Lucky Strike, a sentry on guard.

After three months, I decided I should move ahead with the practice. If David could just get started seeing patients, I was sure it would take his mind off the war. In a bold move, I leased a three-room office a block off Main.

The summer before, wanting to contribute to the cause, I'd gone to Vassar for the wartime intensive-nursing course, but the conflict ended before I could enlist. Now, I reasoned, I could be David's nurse.

I signed the lease for the office in December, but by February nothing had happened. First, David needed to renew his medical license. Then he had to reapply for privileges at the hospital. These were his excuses for inaction.

Finally, one evening in front of the fire, I decided to have it out. "What's going on?" I asked, confronting him.

David shifts in his chair and hides behind the *Brattleboro Reformer.* "I just need some time."

"But I want to understand. I want to help. It's been five months, but you resist me at every turn."

David rises and stands over me, his fists balled. "You can't understand. You weren't there. You fucking weren't there! In one day twenty thousand soldiers were killed in battles around the world. It was a fucking horror movie." He wads up the newspaper and slams out the door.

Nightmares

I never knew what would trigger the nightmares—a smell, a noise. David would throw off the covers screaming, horrified by some vision he saw. The first time I tried to wake him, he lashed out at me as if fighting a German soldier and belted me out of the bed. When I hit the floor, I thought I'd broken my arm, but it was just bruised. I was stunned, couldn't comprehend what had happened.

"Do you want a divorce?" I finally got up my nerve to ask one Sunday as we were walking to church. It seemed a safe time to broach the subject. Surely, he wouldn't explode in public. I was wrong.

"No, I don't want a *divorce!*" He stops on the sidewalk in front of the rectory. "I just want some peace and quiet and an end to your fucking nagging. Don't you get it? Men were killed right in front of me. I dragged their bloody bodies out of the trenches, tried to save them as they suffered. Sometimes I wish I'd died with them!" He shoves me away and I stumble off the high sidewalk and fall into the street.

The worst part was that Mrs. Stopper, the pastor's wife, and her three daughters, dressed to the nines, were just coming down the rectory's front walk. They stopped with shocked faces, turned around, and hurried back inside.

Once home, David apologized, wept on his knees like a character from a novel, holding me around the waist, begging me to forgive him, and I would have, but the assaults got worse. A slap here, a punch there. He was always angry. If not at me, at the mailman for leaving someone else's mail in our box, or the stock boy at the grocer for omitting an item he wanted, or his old-maid aunt, his last living relative, who called to check on him once every few days.

Three weeks after the scene in the street, David had another dream and began to scream in the middle of the night.

"No! Stop! Stop!" By this time, I'd moved to the adjoining room, but afraid the neighbors would hear, I hurried to his bed to wake him. This was a mistake.

"No! You fucking Kraut!" Believing me to be an enemy soldier, my husband grabs me around the neck. I can't breathe, can't fight him off. I yank his thick beard, tear at his hands. We roll off the bed, crash to the floor, and the impact brings him around just before I pass out. Tears streaming down our faces, we lay there panting.

"This can't go on," David groans. "One of these nights I'll kill you." He crawls to the chest of drawers and pulls out a pistol wrapped in a pair of army underwear. "Here, you must sleep with this revolver under your pillow. If I come for you in the night, shoot me. . . . Don't threaten! Shoot me. Do you understand? If you plead with me, I won't stop."

"David! I couldn't!"

"You have to. I'm out of control." He sits back on the bed and starts pulling on his clothes, first his pants, then his shirt. Forgets the boxers.

"I'll take you to a veteran's hospital! They must have a unit for ex-officers with bad dreams and outbursts. I've read about it in the paper. Thousands, maybe millions of men who saw combat have readjustment problems. They call it shell shock."

"Never! I worked in such loony bins during training. I'd be shipped to an overcrowded asylum with the rest of the whacked-out soldiers, labeled crazy, maybe even given hydrotherapy or insulin-shock treatments. You know what those places are like, men strapped in straitjackets, in padded rooms." He's tying his boots, and as I reach for him, he pushes me away. "I'd rather die!"

A month later, he stole his gun back from under my pillow and put a bullet through his brain down by the Connecticut River, right where we had once danced in the moonlight. His prediction was right. He would never see me get wrinkled and old.

15

Messenger

The sun, like a giant orange, is just coming over the mountains when I wake with a bladder so full I really have to get to the outhouse. I rise and go out into a cool morning with the promise of a beautiful day, but the rumble of a truck barreling up Wild Rose Road lifts me out my reverie.

Now who could this be? I look down at my worn housedress and bare feet, then back at the vehicle pulling up at the fence, a beat-up open hack driven by a wisp of a boy, not more than fourteen.

"I'm Chester Mink. Mrs. Wade says come quick. It's a disaster," he hollers, then adds as an afterthought, "ma'am."

I figure there must be some mistake. He's probably looking for the midwife. "You have the wrong house. Patience Murphy doesn't live here anymore. She's Mrs. Hester now, the vet's wife, and they live on the other side of Spruce Mountain."

"I know that," he responds, looking frustrated. "I been there once already and no one's home. Mrs. Wade said to fetch *you*. She says come quick!"

My first reaction is to make an excuse. I'm not used to these urgent demands. It may be okay for Patience and Daniel to rush, rush, rush, but I have enough to cope with just getting through the day. I haven't even had a cup of tea, and what will I do with Dr. Blum?

"Please, ma'am! It's an *emergency*." He jumps out of the vehicle and comes up to the porch, a thin awkward lad wearing denims that are too short, and his eyes are big in his very white face. I glance at my wristwatch. It's seven fifteen.

Trapped

Thirty minutes later, we cross the bridge over the Hope and speed down Main. Chester hasn't said a word and is concentrating so hard on just keeping the old truck on the road that I dare not ask any questions. Dr. Blum just bounces up and down, loosely rocking between the driver and me, holding my leather nurse's bag.

We turn at Sycamore, and pull up in front of an immaculate two-story brick home right behind the Saved by Faith Baptist Church. As I hop out of the truck carrying my medical bag and run toward the house, I hear crying—"Eiiiiiiiiiii! Eiiiiiiiiiii!"—long screams and raised voices. *There must have been a terrible accident.*

I don't have long to find out. Mrs. Wade, Lilly Bittman's mother, hurries out the front door.

"Miss Becky, thank God. Come in! Come in! Dr. Blum with you? That's fine. Chester, sit with him out here on the porch. No, walk him around town. Just make yourself scarce. . . . Come in. Come in," she repeats, dragging me up the steps and down a long hall to the door of a bedroom. Before I enter, I take hold of her fleshy arm. "What's happened? The screams are horrible! Chester didn't tell me anything, didn't say a word."

"You've seen babies born, right?"

My heart does a flip-flop and I immediately feel rather faint. "You tried to find Patience?"

"Yes. Yes. Chester already called at her house, but Mr. Hester said she's down in Oneida attending a woman in labor and she's been there two days. He said to get you. You're like a midwife, aren't you? Almost a midwife?"

"My experience is limited."

"Well, that fine, dear. We just need *someone*. It's Peaches Goody," the woman continues. "She's only twelve. Says she didn't know she was pregnant, then her water broke in church and there was blood all over the place. I almost believe her, that she didn't know she was pregnant, though it sounds incredible."

A hundred questions flood my mind: *Who's the father? How big is the baby? How big is the girl? What's the presenting part? Is the baby likely to be full term? How long has she been in labor?* I'd like to run right home, but that isn't possible, so I take a big breath and open the bedroom door.

What I expect to see is a young woman thrashing around on the bed, but instead find two older women hovering in front of a huge oak wardrobe, one tall and thin, one short and round, neither pregnant. They turn toward me with big eyes.

"Oh, thank the Lord, you've come, Miss Becky!" says the tall one, whom I now recognize as the teacher, Marion Archer. Her hair is pinned back from her face and it's a lot grayer than when I saw her five years ago.

"Thank the Lord!" echoes the other, Mrs. Goody, the round one, the Saved by Faith preacher's wife.

"Eiiiiiiiiiii! Eiiiiiiiiiii!" The wails come again, the sound of a wild animal caught in a trap, and I locate the source, the freestanding closet.

Before I even put down my bag, the round lady addresses the

young woman hiding inside. "Honey babe. Peaches? Honey, please
come out now. Do it for Mama. *Please.* The midwife is here. She'll
help you."

I'd like to clarify the situation, tell them again that I'm a registered nurse, not a midwife or a physician, but it doesn't seem the
right time, so instead I pull Mrs. Goody across the room. She's
dressed in a tasteful plum calf-length Sunday dress.

"What's going on?" I inquire. "Why is she hiding?"

The lady gives a long sigh. "It's Peaches, my twelve-year-old,
just a sixth grader and apparently in the family way. . . . I swear
we had no idea. She's a little chubby like me, and as far as I knew,
hadn't even started her monthlies yet. If she did, she didn't tell me."

Mrs. Goody wipes her tearstained red face. "I don't know how
this happened. She was outside running and playing kick the can
with the other girls until a few weeks ago. Then this morning, right
at the beginning of my husband's Sunday sermon, her baby bag
burst and water and blood spilled all over the place."

"We rushed her out of the church and over here," Mrs. Wade
interjects importantly, "because I've attended several home deliveries, and the pastor was having after-church tea at their house."
(I'm hardly listening, still trying to picture an overweight pregnant
child playing kick the can.)

"So why is she hiding?"

"She's in pain. I don't think she even knows where babies come
from . . . and she's afraid."

"Can't you force her to come out?"

"No. She's got a wire hanger hooked to something inside that's
holding the doors closed. I thought of getting her father to come
tear the closet apart, but before we do that, can you try? Maybe
she'll listen to you."

A preacher's daughter, wouldn't you know it! *And the poor child
now pregnant.* Apparently she'd at least ovulated one time or she

wouldn't be in this state. The Reverend Goody, tall and balding, with eyes so dark they seem almost black, is familiar to me. He's of the fire-and-brimstone variety, and Peaches must be terrified of what he'll have to say about her pregnancy.

Blum was called to his church once, when a rattlesnake bit a visiting faith healer named Sampson Lick. He would have died for sure if Dr. Blum hadn't pulled the poison out with his mouth; then the two of us took turns nursing the man all night. Even after he almost met his maker, we heard Mr. Lick went back to serpent handling. Dr. Blum was pissed as hell.

"Eiiiiiiii. Eiiiiiiii." The trapped animal cries again. When she stops, the house is so still you could probably hear a spider weaving its web.

Red Velvet

I take a long breath to fortify myself. This is not what I thought I was here for. I pictured a medical emergency, a sick baby, a man with a broken arm, or maybe a case of pneumonia. "Okay," I say. "I'll give it a try. Can you ladies step out of the room? You could call the midwife again."

"Maybe we should remain," says Mrs. Wade.

"No, I'd really rather try by myself." The women look miffed, but they do what I say, and now it's just me and the screamer.

"Peaches," I whisper, sitting on the floor, next to the wardrobe. "Peaches. This is Becky Myers. I'm a nurse, a doctor's nurse." I don't know why I say *doctor's nurse*. Maybe I think it sounds more official.

"They called me to see if I could help. Are you in terrible pain?"

A muffled "yes" comes from inside the cabinet.

"If you open the door, I can try to figure out what's wrong. Are you bleeding?"

Very quietly, she says, "There's water or pee still coming out of me, but it's dark in here, I can't see. Also, my back hurts so bad. I don't mean to scream, but it's killing me. I think I might die. I don't want to die."

"Honey. Honey. You are *not* going to die. You are going to have a baby."

There's no answer for a minute, then, "I can't have a baby. I'm a girl, not a mommy."

I change tactics. If I can only get her to come out, maybe I can help her. For all I know the infant's head may be crowning and she's sitting on it.

"Are you hungry, Peaches?"

"A little . . . when I'm not paining. Oh, no! Here comes another one. My back! My back! Eiiiiiiii!" Her howl this time is even louder than before. Then she sobs, a blubbering little kid, really.

Finally, she lets up. "What would you like to eat?" I continue. "A glass of milk? A sandwich?"

"Could I have cake?" *Typical kid!*

"I'll see. You start unlocking yourself and I'll be right back. You can call me Nurse Becky."

When I open the door into the hall, I find Mrs. Wade, Mrs. Goody, and the Archer woman hovering there, wringing their hands.

"Can Peaches have something to eat? Cake? She'd like cake. You don't have any cake around, do you, Mrs. Wade?"

"Yes, yes. I have a red velvet cake I made for Sunday supper. Can she eat in labor?"

"Well, Dr. Blum would say no. She may throw up later. But knowing Patience, the midwife, she'd probably say yes. I'm just trying to get Peaches to come out of the closet. She really doesn't understand what's going on. She thinks she's going to die."

Peaches's mother starts to cry again and mumbles over and over, "My poor baby. My poor baby."

"I'm going back. . . . Tap twice on the door when the cake is ready, but please don't come in. I'll tell you when it's time."

I enter as Peaches starts her howl again, only this time it's not quite as frantic.

"Cake on the way," I announce cheerfully. She cuts the cry short. "What kind?"

"Red velvet chocolate cake, Mrs. Wade's specialty. How are you coming with the lock?" I'm surprised when the door cracks open.

Just a Girl

"You really think I'm having a baby?"

"Well, yes. I think so. It does hurt some, especially when it's your first one, but it doesn't hurt so bad if you understand what's happening."

"But I'm just a sixth grader. How could a baby get in me? Can you make the pains stop?"

"Well, maybe . . . if I could examine you. I'll see."

I truly have no idea what I can offer in terms of pain relief. Luckily, just then there's a tap at the door. "That's the cake. There's a towel on the bed. Sit on it and we can eat while we talk." I'm surprised when, without any more coaxing, I see one pale freckled leg appear at the closet opening, then another.

Mrs. Wade opens the door and pushes in a fancy silver tray with the cake and two glasses of cold milk. She looks at me with big eyes, silently asking how things are going, but I say nothing and close the door again.

When I turn, a short, plump girl with large breasts, a body that looks sixteen, and a baby face is sitting on a green towel on the edge of the bed. She's wearing her Sunday dress, a sailor-type middy with a long skirt, but the skirt is all rumpled, blood streaked, and wet. Poor kid, I think.

"Yummy!" she says, reaching out for her plate. I sit down next to her and pick up my glass of milk. There must be something I can do for her pain. Dr. Blum always gave the mothers morphine, but that's not going to happen.

I again try to imagine what Patience would do, but realize I know little of her methods except the breathing when the head is crowning . . . and the use of oil.

"Oh, no! Here comes the pain again!" Peaches cries. "Are you sure I'm not going to die?" She begins to shake her hands in front of her as if they've both gone to sleep. "Oh. Oh. Oh. Eiiiii!" I reach over and touch her belly, which is round and hard under about two inches of fat.

"Peaches, feel your belly. See how hard it is? That's your baby trying to come out."

"Don't say that, Nurse Becky! There can't be a baby!"

Birds and the Bees

For the next ten minutes, interrupted by contractions, I try to explain the female reproductive system.

"But how did a baby get in there?" the girl asks. *Good question.*

"A man or an older boy has to get his penis inside or near a girl's privates. Then he puts in some seeds and the baby grows."

Peaches looks horrified. "It was only a dare. Don't tell my mama!"

"Did you do that with a boy, honey? It's okay. I won't tell her if you don't want me to."

"One time last fall, a long time ago, we were playing hide-and-seek in the dark, and my friend Molly's cousin from Beckley dared me to let his privates touch my privates. He didn't put his snake inside, but he rubbed it on me and afterward I was wet. I hit him in the face because I thought he'd peed on me." *Now we are getting to the heart of it.*

Another contraction but at least she's not screaming.

"Mama will hate me. She will be so mad. There have been other girls in the church that had babies, but they were in high school. I'm just a kid. You think it was the boy and his seed? Not Jesus?"

"I think it was the boy, yes."

"Miss Becky. I don't feel so good. I'm going to puke."

I grab a pillow to catch the vomit and protect the flowered carpet.

"Oh, no! Now I have to pooh!"

I go very still. We have nothing ready for the birth! And again I haven't even listened to the fetal heartbeat.

"I'll be right back, honey," I say, hoping to sound calm. "I think your baby might come soon and I need to get some things ready for the birth."

"Mrs. Wade! Mrs. Goody!" I call, running out in the hall. "Bring warm water. Bring clean linen and something to wrap the baby in!"

Behind me in the bedroom there's a low groan.

When I step back in the room with my bag, Peaches is squatting over the potty. "Ughhhh!" she groans. No crying now. Just nature taking over.

July 27, 1934

6-pound, 9-ounce female infant born to Peaches Goody, the daughter of Reverend Goody and Mrs. Goody, after two hours of pushing. Patience wasn't there, and I had to do the whole delivery by myself from start to finish. Present were Mrs. Goody, Mrs. Wade, and Mrs. Archer.

The hardest part was dealing with the patient, a 12-year-old child who didn't know she was pregnant or even how she got pregnant. She screamed through the first half of labor, but was amazing once she began to push. Peaches had one small tear, which I repaired as best I could. Blood loss was minimal.

Afterward I looked around and everyone was crying, even the new mother, whether for joy or for sorrow, I couldn't tell, but I cried too. Some will say it's a tragedy, a child giving birth to another child, but who knows what happiness this new life may bring.

I was surprised when Mrs. Goody dug in her pocketbook and gave me ten dollars, a welcome gift!

16

Threat

It has been ten weeks since I started transporting groceries for the Bittmans and during that time, the number of my customers has steadily declined. It worries me that my only source of income will dry up, and I'm sure it's a sign of the worsening economy. If it weren't for Peaches Goody's delivery, we'd really be strapped.

Even Willa has stopped needing my services, probably because her husband has been laid off and is home with his truck. Daniel said he saw him coming out of Bittman's with a big carton of groceries and another time going into the saloon in the back alley, but the vet looked away and didn't make eye contact, trying to pretend that nothing had happened on that infamous Fourth of July.

Mrs. Stone is one of my few remaining regular customers and today as I pulled into the long green drive of her lovely farmstead I found her on her porch feeding a baby goat.

"I don't know how this happened. One of the nannies, Bella, had her kids at the wrong time. They usually come in the spring. There were triplets and this one is the runt . . . just not getting enough food. The others push her out of the way."

I sit down on the steps to watch. The little black-and-white goat with droopy ears nudges the bottle like it was an udder and gives a repeated cry that sounds quite human. Mrs. Stone absently runs her hands through its fur.

"The man from Oil and Gas Company came back yesterday and this time he brought reinforcements, two other fellows in dark hats. Now they're telling me the state has a hundred-dollar tax lien on the property that never was paid.

"I'm old, but I'm not dumb. They're just trying to intimidate me. Telling me that they're going to get the sheriff to auction the place off for back taxes! I own this place free and clear. It's all paid up. They think because half the farmers in Union County are in hock, I am too."

"Did you try Mr. Linkous, the lawyer in town? Maybe he could help."

"I guess that's my only hope. Thanks for listening, honey."

To cheer her, I change the subject. "I noticed your trumpet flowers have bloomed. I love the way the vines grow over the arch in the gateway. I'm partial to picket fences. They're so homey, and the orange flowers complement your white farmhouse.

"Patience Murphy, the midwife, lets us live in her old house rent free," I go on, "a little cottage on the side the mountain, not as nice as your place, but beautiful in its own way. There used to be a picket fence there, but a few years ago someone burned it down."

Mrs. Stone blows air through her nose and tightens her mouth, a determined gesture. She places one hand over my hand and one over Blum's. I know what she's thinking. These are bad times. She loves this house and the land her husband willed her. She loves the picket fence too and what it represents, a safe haven from a rough world . . . but the Oil and Gas Company man will be back.

House of Beauty

Today, since it rained and Blum is off with the vet, I put on my second-best dress and go into Liberty to do something nice for myself. As I cross the Hope the sun breaks through, but it doesn't matter, the garden is still too wet to work.

There's not much doing on Main Street today. Only Bittman's Grocery and Stenger's Pharmacy are open. The Eagle Theater has movies on Saturday, and the Mountain Top Café and a few bars on the back street are still hanging on. Only Sam's Barbershop and Ida May's House of Beauty seem to be thriving. That's where I'm headed, Ida May's.

"Well, how you doin', honey? I was wondering when you'd visit us. Looks like you need some help!" Ida May turns from her present client and indicates my hair with a flip of her scissors and then goes back to work.

I find a seat in the corner and prepare to wait. It's the busiest day of the week, but that can't be helped. Tuesday is half-price day. Fifty cents is still too much, but Mrs. Goody's gift was an unexpected blessing and I've decided I'm just going to do it!

Ida May, who is around thirty, bottle-blond, plump, and pleasant, keeps up a running patter with whoever sits in her swivel chair. Across the room two women discuss the White Rock CCC camp that I'd heard about.

"I hate to see it," the older of the two complains in a high twang. "It's a ruination, bringing in riffraff from Pittsburgh and Baltimore, even New Jersey. My sister in Ohio said they were going to truck in African boys from Cleveland and Detroit to the camp near her, but the locals wouldn't stand for it. I hope they don't try that here. There will be hell to pay. The coloreds in Hazel Patch and across the tracks are one thing; they're decent, respectable people, but outsiders? Who knows what would happen?"

"My husband says they better keep those boys out of town, even the whites," her friend responds. "Some of them have been to prison, probably rapists and thieves."

Finally, Ida May crooks her finger at me. "You want a bob and a finger wave?" the beautician asks.

"Sure, but keep my bangs long." *Snip. Snip.* She's already started.

"So what you been doing with yourself, Nurse Becky?"

I dread this chitchat, but it's part of getting your hair done, and part of Ida May's job, to spread gossip. She's better than the *Union County Gazette.*

"Nothing much," I answer, knowing that won't be enough for the beautician. "Well, you heard, I brought the doctor back to Liberty. He's disabled now."

"Tch. Tch." Ida May looks at me in the mirror, shakes her head, and makes the sound with her tongue that means *how sad.* "You don't really *have* to take care of him, do you? You must want to. You aren't even kin." She hands me the mirror so I can see the back of my hair. "Short enough for you?"

"A little shorter? I guess I don't *have* to, but what would you do? He has no one. His brother disowned him and the doctors at Johns Hopkins can't figure out what's wrong. They say maybe he's catatonic."

"Oh!" gasps a dishwater blonde under the next dryer. "What's that?" (I knew she was listening.)

"It's a mental illness. It's like when a soldier comes back from the war and just quits talking and withdraws into himself."

"Terrible." "How awful." "Poor Dr. Blum," the hens cluck.

Finally, I'm done. Ida May shoves me under the dryer and a half hour later, pulls me out and presses in the waves with her expert fingers. The shop is nearly empty now, with only one gray-haired woman waiting for a trim.

"You look just lovely," Ida May tells me, sweeping the floor. "A darn sight better than when you came in."

I give her a smile and the half dollar I owe. I wish I could tip, but that just won't do. Outside, I glance at my reflection in the window of the House of Beauty. The salon owner is right. I look a lot better than when I came in.

Flirt

"Ma'am." The uniformed gentleman crossing Main, gives me a salute. "Do you remember me?"

"I do, of course. You're with the White Rock CCC camp."

"You're the local health nurse. Nurse . . ."

"It's Myers. Nurse Myers."

"Captain Wolfe," he introduces himself. "May I walk with you?"

"I'm just on my way to Bittman's Grocery where I have a part-time job delivering groceries." Again I notice the limp as we stroll along. It's his left leg, I realize, and he may wear a brace.

"Have you given any thought to helping us out at the camp? Dr. Crane from Camp Laurel only comes twice a week. You could come another two days. Then we'd have coverage more often than not." We pause on the sidewalk outside the grocery and my thoughts are interrupted when a family comes out with a basket of groceries and I have to move.

These are folks I don't know, a short man who, by the look of the blue scar on his forehead and the black grime under his fingernails, is probably a miner; his rail-thin wife, who wears a plaid dress that's seen better days; and two little boys in droopy striped overalls.

"Howdy," the man says, but the woman says nothing and looks away.

"I've heard the boys in the camps are pretty rough. People say some are ex-cons. Does that sound like a safe environment for a lady?" I ask.

"That's not true. Some are rough around the edges but no one is mean and no one who has a criminal record is allowed in the CCC. You'd be safe; I'd guarantee it. Besides, we could fill up your gas tank each time you came. We keep a big tank for the trucks and graders. You have a good vehicle? It would be a great service to the boys"—here he pauses for effect— "and the country."

I can't help it; I laugh and shock myself with the sound, realizing how little I laugh lately.

"The country?" I look up into his eyes, which are green with tiny flecks of gold around the pupils.

"Yes, you know: *My country 'tis of thee, sweet land of liberty.*" We are definitely flirting now.

"Sweet liberty!" I spread my arms out and realize that, despite my age and the wrinkles around my eyes, to this man from the camp, with my new finger wave and my yellow dress, I must be a sight for sore eyes, a stage star from Broadway right here in Liberty.

"Seriously, Miss Myers, we really need someone. The young men get injuries and sores that don't heal. I've driven to Torrington twice with kids who didn't really need to go to the hospital, but had to be seen by someone. If I can set up a meeting with the director on Thursday, will you come and interview? It might become a part-time job."

"Okay," I tell Captain Wolfe. "I promise I'll visit, maybe even Thursday, but I have other responsibilities—my grocery deliveries and a disabled man I care for. I would have to figure out what to do with him."

"I understand. All I ask is that you come for an interview." He salutes me smartly and limps away. I watch as he goes, wondering how he was injured, and if he, like my late husband, David, has nightmares of war.

Writing on the Wall

As I push through the glass door of the grocery store, I'm surprised to find pregnant Lilly downstairs sorting apples. Her quick, small, sensitive fingers feel for the bad spots and on each side of her she has a box, one for the perfect apples, another for the bruised.

"Lilly Bittman! What are you doing out of bed?"

"Oh, Becky Myers! I can't just lie around all the time. I haven't had any pain for a week and I *have* to do something. Anyway, who would tend the store while my husband is out making deliveries—"

Here, she pulls herself up, leans on the counter, and takes a deep breath. The light brown grocer's apron she wears almost drags on the floor and her sightless eyes roam the air in front of her. "I'm sorry. B.K. was going to tell you. He has to do the deliveries himself now. Money's that tight. The family that just left the store . . . They were here for thirty minutes, looking at the price of everything and finally left with two pounds of red beans and a sack of half-rotten apples that I threw in to be kind.

"We can still use you every now and then on Tuesdays when the shipments from Torrington come in and B.K. can't leave the store. I'm real sorry," she says again. "I know you need the money too."

I let out a sigh. "It's okay."

The truth is, I'm devastated. Without the delivery job, the doc and I can't make it. Sometimes there's money in helping at births, but it makes me so tense, I'd rather starve. Captain Wolfe's offer suddenly sounds very interesting, especially if there's money in it.

To change the subject, I go on the offensive. "You really should be upstairs, Lilly. It's okay to get up to use the commode or make yourself a sandwich, but I worry about you moving around too much. You aren't lifting those heavy boxes, are you?"

"Oh, no. B.K. fixed me up before he left. Your hair looks nice, Miss Becky. Been to Ida May's?"

I touch my head, remembering the luxury of the trim and perm at the salon, a luxury I now wish that I'd gone without, but how does the blind woman know where I've been?

"You're wondering how I can tell you've been to Ida May's? It's easy. By the smell of the perm! Who were you talking to outside? I heard laughter. That's rare nowadays."

Here my smile is genuine. "That's right. The man was Captain Wolfe from the Civilian Conservation Corps. Did you hear us?"

"Just a little. Not what you said, just your voices. Are you sure you should be consorting with him? The CCC men don't have a good reputation."

"Why is that?"

"I don't know, exactly. Mother Wade just says they're trouble-makers and riffraff."

"Well, I might as well tell you. They need a nurse at Camp White Rock. It would only be a few days a week, but it might help with money, especially if you don't need me for deliveries anymore. The problem is, I don't know what I'd do with the doctor."

There's a long pause as Lilly contemplates my situation. "If there's a job there, you should take it," she finally says. "You know yourself that jobs are few and far between. If you don't like the men or if the camp is too rough, you can always quit." A hopeful smile crosses her pretty face. "Maybe *I* could take care of Dr. Blum and you could pay *me* a little. Say, fifteen cents a day."

"But what if you start contracting again, or what if he tries to wander off?"

"I might have to tie a bell to his shoes so I could tell where he is, but B.K. is here most of the time. We might even find little chores for him."

"He can cut wood and carry things. Not much else. Children seem to enjoy him, though I don't understand why. I'll think about your proposition. The first thing is to see how the camp feels and if there's an actual offer from the director or it's just Captain Wolfe's grand idea. Maybe if B.K. thinks it's okay, I'll let Dr. Blum stay with you while I visit White Rock the first time. See how it goes. . . ." I move toward the door, anxious now to leave and get back to the farm.

"Wait," exclaims Lilly. "You forgot apples for applesauce." She pours half a bucket of the bad ones in a clean white sac that she finds under the counter, this without sight, and she doesn't drop one! I'm surprised when she moves toward me and takes me in her arms. "It will be okay, Miss Becky. We will all be okay. Even this one." Here she rubs her swollen belly. "We will get through this together."

17

Camp White Rock

"Isaac, today will be different." I use a soft schoolteacher voice as if I'm talking to a six-year-old and that's about how old Blum seems. He's gone from being a baby when we first returned to Liberty to being a first grader, but still that's progress. "After we make our last delivery, you'll stay with the Bittmans while I go to the CCC camp."

"You're to do as they tell you. They may have some chores. If there's nothing to do, just sit down on a box. This interview is important. They need a nurse at the camp and I need a job."

Who knows if Blum's even listening. He has the same blank stare as he always does.

The trip to the CCC camp takes longer than expected. Following Crocker Creek, which roars around boulders the size of an auto, I climb higher and higher with the mountainside falling away on the right. *Am I really going to drive this road in the winter?* Twenty minutes after passing Mrs. Stone's place, I see the first signs of my destination, a dark green arrow that reads CCC CAMP.

Here, I turn into a narrow forest drive and am surprised when it ends in a pine-ringed clearing holding multiple log structures and a row of what I think may be dorms, five in all. Young men are coming and going between the buildings. It's a whole little village of men, and I head for a group of fellows crowded around a tractor in a garage.

The corpsmen look over when I get out of the car, and though I don't think of myself as a femme fatale, I'm very aware of my femaleness.

"Excuse me," I say to the group. "Can you tell me where I might find the camp director?"

"Headquarters is two buildings down," an older man answers. It's Loonie Tinkshell from the Texaco station! "Howdy, Miss Myers. What are you doing way up this way?"

I really don't want to share that I'm interviewing for a job, but there's no way around it without seeming rude. "I'm going to talk to the director about employment as the clinic nurse, just a part-time position."

"Well, holy cow! I'm working here now too."

"I don't have the job *yet*!" I can't help but laugh.

"You'll get it!" "Yeah, you'll get it." "Good luck, lady!" a few of the young men chime in, and I smile. *The kindness of strangers*, my mother used to say, and it's true, especially in hard times.

Following Loonie's directions, I turn the Pontiac around and pull up next to a smaller log building across from the dorms. *Here goes nothing,* I say to myself, crossing my fingers behind my back. The many-paned windows reflect my tense face, and I practice a smile and smooth down my hair.

Mrs. Ross

"May I help you?" a big-bosomed woman asks as I enter the building. Her voice is higher than you'd expect from her size and her blue-gray hair is crimped and stiff.

"I'm Nurse Becky Myers. Captain Wolfe asked me to come meet the director today and talk with him about nursing services. I'm sorry I don't have his name . . . the director."

"The supervisor is out. You can wait if you want to." She looks at her watch, indicating it may be hours.

"Is the captain here? I've come a long way."

"No. They've both gone over to Camp Laurel." She gives me no further explanation and offers no tea or coffee, though I notice she's sipping something from a white mug with a green CCC insignia on it.

"I've come a long way," I repeat firmly, sitting down and making it clear that I'm not going home. That's all there is, no small talk or questions, and the woman goes back to her typing.

So, here I am and I hope this is not a half a tank of gas and a day wasted. I'm disappointed the men aren't here. I was pretty sure I told Wolfe that I'd come on Thursday, although now that I think of it, there wasn't an exact time.

While I wait, I take in the overly warm room. Directly across from me is a door labeled INFIRMARY and next to it a red-and-black poster with a photo of a strapping young fellow in a CCC uniform holding an ax. "A young man's opportunity to work, to learn, and to conserve our national resources," it reads, probably a poster designed by someone at the FAP, the Federal Art Project, a government program that hires unemployed artists.

From the handmade pine table next to me, I pick up the camp newsletter, *The White Rock News*, and open it to the humor page, but there's no time to read. The door bursts open.

To the Bone

"The doctor? Is the doctor here?" a fellow of about twenty shouts as four young men in bloodstained uniforms stagger in carrying an injured boy. From the looks of him, it's serious. His leg is covered in a crude bandage of white rags drenched in red and his face is alabaster.

The secretary rises so fast she knocks her chair over. "Oh, Lord . . . not another one!" She flings the infirmary door open to reveal four white metal beds with a scale in the corner and a blood pressure cuff mounted on a stand. I jump up, throw my pocketbook on the chair, and, without even thinking, begin to shout orders.

"Here, lay him down. Someone get my medical bag in the Pontiac. What happened?" The young men, by this time, are running out the door, either to get my bag, or more likely, to escape the scene of carnage, but I grab one by the shirtsleeve. "You! Explain!"

"It happened at the sawmill, ma'am. Awful bad. Halfway cut off. Where's the doc? Is the doc here today? Can he save his leg?"

"I don't know. I'll try." My informant is about to be sick so I let him slink away. "My bag!" I yell after him.

"Mrs. Ross, a pan of hot water. I'll need to wash the wound to assess the damage. Does anyone in the camp know first aid? Is there a medic?"

The round woman is now cowering against the wall. "Come on now, Mrs. Ross! Pull yourself together."

"No medic," she whispers.

"Call the physician at the other camp. Tell him registered nurse Becky Myers needs him here as soon as possible."

"There's no phone. It's a shortwave radio. I can try." Mrs. Ross starts for the kitchen to get water and then spins around like a top and points to the wooden CB set on a table in the corner. "Which first?"

"Water and clean rags first. Hold on the radio. This may not be as bad as it looks." Just then the young man who'd given me the report returns with my bag.

"This it, ma'am?" He's no longer so white and a cigarette dangles from the corner of his mouth.

"Yes, thank you, but you can't smoke in here. There's a pair of scissors and a packet of gauze in the satchel, get them out, please. Don't look at the wound if you can't take the sight of blood. I'm going to unwrap his leg." The young man runs to the door and flips his cigarette out into the yard.

Removing the crude bandage, I finally get a look at the injury. The cut is below the knee and down to the bone, but it's straight, not jagged, and there's no dirt or sawdust in it. Most important, the bleeding seems to have slowed.

The boy rummages around in my bag, pulls out what I need, and places it on the small pine table that Mrs. Ross brings in.

"What's your name, son? And what's the patient's name?"

"I'm Boodean Sypolt. His name is Jed Troutman. I didn't know there were lady doctors."

"Mmmmm." The injured man is coming to. He groans and then groans again.

"Boodean, hand me the blue bottle of merthiolate, the one with the cork. Also, I'll need the tin box of suture needles. I'm a nurse, not a doctor. A registered nurse."

"Fuck!" The victim shakes his head and there are tears in his golden-brown eyes. "What happened? Oh, fuck. What have I done?"

"It's okay, Jed. It's okay. I'm Nurse Becky and I'm going to give you a teaspoon of laudanum before I sew you up." This I do sparingly, since the liquid in the blue bottle is the last of Dr. Blum's supply. Within moments Jed falls back into a stupor, and I can get on with my work.

Boodean

For the next half hour, by the big wooden cuckoo clock on the wall, I cleanse the wound, carefully stitch the layers of muscle and skin back together, and anoint the deep cut with merthiolate. Boodean serves as my surgical assistant, cutting my suture when I need it and handing me the instruments, but otherwise concentrating on a poster above the bed, this one in green and yellow, exhorting the virtues of the Forest Army with an image of a tall evergreen and the Civilian Conservation Corps logo below it.

By the end of the procedure, I notice the young man is looking down at the surgical field and actually anticipating my next move. Finally, I'm finished. Boodean stretches his back.

"Nice job," I tell him, and when he smiles I notice one of his teeth is missing, the eyetooth, the one with the point. Otherwise he's a good-looking lad, with clear skin, kind eyes, and curly brown hair. His nose, which appears to have been broken at some time in the past, is the only other feature that mars his handsome face.

"Thanks," he says shyly. "I never did nothin' like that before. Will he still be able to work? His mother is counting on the twenty-five a month that Jed sends from his CCC pay. She's a widow with five other children."

"I'm sorry to hear that. He should heal okay, if he keeps his wound clean. Do you know each other from home?"

"Both our dads went down to Hawk's Nest to work on the tunnel they put under the mountain. Out of the four men from home who traveled together, my dad is the only one that made it back alive."

I'm familiar with the situation at Hawk's Nest. If you read the news, you couldn't miss it. In 1930, Union Carbide decided to improve their power plant by diverting the New River under Gauley

Mountain. To do this they hired unemployed Appalachians and blacks from the South.

It was a big scandal, even got hearings in Congress and in the federal courts. Four hundred men died, both white and colored, the largest industrial accident in the United States. Some, who had no family living close by, weren't even buried, they were just dumped over a cliff.

Dr. Blum had been livid. "The workers died of acute silicosis," he told me after attending a medical meeting in Torrington, where the tragedy was discussed. "The silica in the rocks coated their lungs and no one gave them masks or breathing equipment, although management knew enough to wear them. Those workers died within a year. . . . A waste of good lives. A crime."

Things like that used to really upset him, back when he had his mind.

The Major

I'm just washing up when Mrs. Ross cracks open the infirmary door. "They're coming!" she whispers. "Outside . . . the truck just pulled up . . . the captain and the superintendent."

After getting over her case of nerves when she first saw the victim covered in blood, the camp secretary has become my ally. I stand and straighten my hair. There's a spot of blood on my nylons but hopefully it's not too obvious.

The door bangs open. "Where is he? Is he okay? Why didn't you call me at Camp Laurel?" a loud nasal voice demands.

Mrs. Ross answers so quietly I can't hear her response.

Then the inner door swings back, and two men in uniform enter the infirmary. Captain Wolfe steps forward and shakes my hand. "Miss Myers. Thank God you were here. How's Jed? The boys outside said his leg was half cut off."

The man beside him is short and plump, balding on top, with his yellow hair combed over his freckled scalp. Both are dressed in army uniforms and they begin to perspire in the warm room.

"I'm Major Milliken," the superintendent introduces himself. Since I grew up in New England, I recognize his Boston accent at once. "I'm deeply grateful for your services, Nurse. Is the young man's leg okay? Do we need to transport him to the hospital? There will have to be a report filed. This is awkward, a civilian doing the surgery. . . ."

He paces the floor, mulling things over. "I wonder if we could submit the Pay Inquiry Form 2142 for the registered nurse before we submit the DA285," he says to himself and then turns toward his secretary. "Could we do that, Mrs. Ross?"

"Certainly, Major. Whatever you say. I'll do it right away. Post the employment 2142 this afternoon and the DA285 tomorrow."

"Hold on a moment." I'm not usually so forceful but things seem to be moving too fast. "Are you saying you're hiring me? We haven't discussed the pay for a registered nurse, the hours of employment, or what my responsibilities would be."

Captain Wolfe kneels at the side of the patient's cot, inspecting his dressing. He puts the back of his hand on Jed's forehead as a parent would, feeling for fever. "You okay, lad?"

"I gave him some laudanum," I explain. "The laceration was deep, but there will be no lasting deformity, except the scar of course."

"Young men don't mind scars." Captain Wolfe laughs, touching his own face. "It's their mothers and wives who mind. . . . Before we go too far, Milliken, don't you think you should interview Miss Myers and be sure she wants the job?"

"Oh, very well. Yes. Will you come into my office, miss?"

There's something about the *miss* that irritates me, but I let it go.

"I believe the current pay for registered nurses is thirty-five to forty cents an hour," the camp supervisor begins—no "How do you do?" or "Thanks for being here at just the right moment." "I can give you thirty cents an hour."

My inner eyes go wide at the insult, but I keep my face still. "Major, I just saved your enlisted man's life. If I hadn't been here, he might have bled to death. I can work for thirty-five cents an hour and no less.

"I'd also like dinner on the days I'm here, and Captain Wolfe told me the camp would fill up my gas tank and make minor repairs on my automobile if needed." This part about the repairs is a fabrication, but I don't care. The officious man annoys me.

"Agreed . . . Mrs. Ross," he calls, "Can you type up the offer and bring in the forms. This meeting is over. You'll need to make a list of supplies. There's already an account at the pharmacy in Liberty and anything they don't have we can order through the army quartermaster in Pittsburgh. I'll also assign one of the young men as your first aid officer. Can you come on Tuesday and Friday?" He doesn't wait for my response.

"The physician at Camp Laurel, Dr. Crane, will come Mondays and Wednesdays. Then we'll go uncovered on weekends and hope the medic can handle it. I'm going to add you to the payroll as an LEM. . . . That's the best I can do . . . Mrs. Ross!" He shouts these last words.

"An LEM?"

"LEM, locally employed man. We hire fellows to teach specialized skills—forestry, mechanics, driving heavy equipment. Most of the CCC boys are from cities and know nothing about working in the woods.

"We also hire cooks, carpenters, and unemployed teachers from the surrounding area. Headquarters in Washington has decided it will help the economy and keep down locals' resentment about the camps.

"Mrs. Ross!" he shouts again, though by this time she's standing right at his elbow. "Get Mrs. Myers's dress size and order her a surplus army nurse uniform. Make it two."

"I'd like Boodean for my assistant, if he's willing."

"Who?"

"Boodean, the young man who was here when you came in. I'd like him for my medic. He was very helpful with the wound repair and may have an aptitude for this kind of work."

"Agreed." The little man looks at his watch. "Can you stay and fill out the employment forms and the medical report? I have to go. It's three forty-five, and I'm teaching the class in business math at four."

Holy moly! I have to be in Liberty to pick Dr. Blum up by four thirty! Hastily, I make my report about the accident and my medical care and then turn to the employment form. Twenty minutes later, the secretary gives me a nod as I check on the patient in the miniature infirmary one more time. He still sleeps and Boodean sits at his side, but when I look around for Captain Wolfe he's nowhere in sight.

"Well, I guess I'm done, Mrs. Ross. Is there anything else?"

"No, honey. Thank the lord you were here. We'll see you next Tuesday."

As I hurry out the door, a chorus of deep voices startles me. "Hip, hip, hooray! Hip, hip, hooray!" Eight or nine young men rise from the steps where they've been keeping a vigil for their friend Jed Troutman. "Nice work, Nursie!" a short, bright-eyed fellow calls out.

"It's *Nurse Myers*," I correct, my face turning red.

"That's what I meant," the smart aleck answers.

Fall

18

Big Blow

It's Indian summer and each day is hotter and dryer than the last. Nights are in the fifties, days in the eighties. It's so hot even the goldenrod is drooping.

Lately, I've been reading the newspapers that Daniel brings over aloud in an attempt to stimulate Dr. Blum's mind. We sit at the table after our midday meal while I peruse the headlines.

"Listen," I say to him. "'RECORD HEAT. SEVEN DAYS IN A ROW. OVER NINETY IN IOWA AND A DROUGHT HAS SPREAD ACROSS EIGHTY PERCENT OF THE USA. IT'S RUINING THE RANCHERS AND FARMERS.'"

I turn to the comics and check out the latest *Li'l Abner* cartoon, then notice the caption on the next page under the photo of a short man in uniform who looks a lot like Charlie Chaplin.

"ADOLF HITLER, LEADER OF THE NATIONAL SOCIALIST WORKERS' PARTY, TAKES OVER GERMANY." I read the headline, but skip the article. "I don't know why we should care. Germany's so far away."

Outside the window it's another cloudless, sunny day. "Looks like a good afternoon to pick the last of the beans," I tell my silent partner. "We better get back to work." I find our straw hats and buckets and lead him out to the garden.

An hour later, a breeze ruffles my hair and within minutes I'm holding on to Dr. Blum's arm. The sky has turned dark and the wind is almost ripping my clothes off.

"Come on! We better get inside." I pick up our buckets, pull on Dr. Blum's arm, and head for the house. Small branches, torn from the trees, are flying everywhere, and then the rain comes, hard, cold pellets that sting.

"Is this a tornado?" I say out loud as we pull the blue door closed behind us. We have no telephone to call for help, not that anyone would come. No radio to listen to a weather report. No shutters to cover the windows. No basement to hide in. Then I remember the underground springhouse out by the barn.

"Blum! Come on!" He is sitting on the sofa staring into space, as if he doesn't hear the roar or feel the house shake. "We need to get to the springhouse," I shout into his face, shaking his shoulders.

"Blum, help me. Please! I can't do this alone." The doctor rises slowly like a man in a dream, and I lead him to the back door, where we stop under the porch eaves. Water streams down the hillside, already four inches deep in the low places. Then the thunder comes and the lightning.

CRACK! A tree somewhere close is struck and comes down. "We'd better go!" I shout. "I'll hold on to you." I push Blum down the three wooden steps but he stops again. I push him once more and that's when he does something wholly unexpected. He throws me over his shoulder and, like a fireman, heads for the only safe shelter we have.

We're halfway to the springhouse built into the side of the hill when the hail starts, chunks of ice the size of marbles. Even in Vermont, I'd never seen anything like this. Blum is slipping and sliding over the ice-covered ground. I'm still slung over his shoulder and I try to cover our heads.

At the entrance to the underground shelter, the doctor deposits me in the mud and I look up, expecting, perhaps, a smile saying "Surprised you, didn't I?" But there's just the same blank stare, as if his picking me up was a reflex that didn't involve his mind.

Thunder rumbles ever closer, with lightning right after it; we are in a war zone of light and sound and when I pull open the door, it blows off its hinges and sails away. Panting, we both fall inside, safe for the moment, watching nature go crazy in front of us.

Spared

Within an hour, the tempest is over, but it isn't until the sun comes out that I get up my nerve to look outside to see if our barn and house are still standing. They are, but pellets of ice still litter the ground.

The garden is a mess. It's good we picked most of the beans and tomatoes before the storm, because only one in three plants is left standing. The root vegetables, like carrots and beets, are okay.

When we crunch across the ice toward the house, I find that we do have a broken window where a branch from the old oak in front flew right through the glass. A row of shingles has also blown off, but these things are small. Already, Mr. Maddock and his tractor are coming up the road.

He pulls up near the house. "You folks okay?"

"Yes, thank you. And you?"

"Had to carry the missus down the cellar steps. Nearly fell. Lost a few chickens. They were outside and there was no way I could get to them. The cattle hid in the gulley down by the creek and the horses were locked up in their stalls."

"I didn't even think of *our* chickens. Good thing they were in the barn. I'll have to fix my roof, though. Water got in. And there's the one window."

"Mrs. Maddock says she's cooking up baked beans for your supper. You aren't to trouble about it." He looks at Blum, who is sitting on the porch staring into space again. You can tell it riles him. "Can't that man do anything to help you? Can't he get up and do something?"

"Not much. He can't do very much. He doesn't know how to help me."

Except once, I think, *one time today . . . when I really needed him.*

Rescue Party

By evening, Patience and Daniel also come up Wild Rose Road to check on us.

"Hello!" Patience yells, jumping out of the Ford. She's invented some kind of carrier for her little boy, a sling made out of bright cloth that she wears around her hip. It makes her look like a native from Borneo, but I doubt she cares. "Are you okay? Did you get much damage?"

From her cheerful expression you'd think she was talking about something dangerous but fun, a trip through the haunted house at the county fair or a roller coaster ride. I'm already up on the roof trying to tack down some wooden shingles over the hole while Blum sits on the porch bench.

"How you doing, old buddy?" Daniel says to him. "Hold on, Becky, I'll give you a hand." He crawls up the ladder. "Looks like you'll need a new window too. I might have an old one out in my barn."

When the work is done, Patience brings a basket of sandwiches out of their auto and I bring out Sarah Maddock's baked beans.

We sit on the porch eating companionably as the sun drops behind the green leaves and a V of geese overhead honks as they fly southward. Daniel offers the doctor a sip from his hip flask, but I put out my hand to stop him.

"You don't give a mentally handicapped person alcohol," I inform him, as if I'm the matron at a Rehabilitation Hospital for Disabled Soldiers. The vet looks puzzled and a little hurt, because he's been doing it all along, but Patience breaks the awkward silence.

"So it must have been scary. The worst storms always come from the west. Being on the east side of Spruce Mountain, we were spared. The hail was rough though. A stone the size of a baseball cracked Daniel's back windshield."

"It's okay." Daniel laughs, regaining his footing. "That rattletrap has seen better days and it didn't break all the way through. I just need the glass to stay together until the economy turns around."

"The hail was bad here too. Stones not so big, just the size of marbles, but they covered the ground like snow and the temperature must have dropped forty degrees in fifteen minutes. I was afraid the house might blow down. Was it a hurricane or a tornado?"

"Radio out of Wheeling says it was a freak tornado, only touched down in a few counties, but it did some damage."

Daniel stands. "Come on, old man," he says to Blum. "Let's drag those fallen branches under the porch. We may as well store the wood where it can get dry." He takes Blum's arm and guides him away.

I don't tell Patience about Isaac's heroic action when he carried me through the tornado to the shelter. It seems too unreal, as if I imagined it. I don't tell her that he actually seemed to understand that we were in danger. I don't her tell her that for a moment Dr. Blum seemed to be present, to be with me, to be back.

First Day

It's Tuesday, my first day to work in the infirmary at Camp White Rock, a blazing-hot morning, and as usual I'm in a rush. I assist Dr. Blum with his grooming. Shave him, brush his teeth, clean his fingernails, and check to be sure his trousers are buttoned. I want him to look nice because Lilly is watching him.

"You're going to stay at the store again this afternoon. Do you understand? The camp is the only opportunity I have to earn cash money. Please don't mess this up. Just sit where they tell you and try to be sociable."

I say this last part with a small grin, knowing *sociable* was not one of Blum's character traits, even when he was in his right mind. That's probably why his wife ran around on him. She was fun-loving in the extreme. Opposites attract, they say, and in this case it seems true.

I remember seeing her with a man at a restaurant in Charlottesville once, a handsome fellow with a new short haircut and sporting a seersucker blazer and white pants. It was summer and Priscilla wore a low-cut rose-colored dress, and he was touching her hand. I never told the doc about it.

When I get to Liberty, I drop Blum off at the grocery, and then stop at the pharmacy to pick up the supplies. When I hand Mr. Stenger the list, he reads it out loud.

> "1 combination hot water bag and enema syringe
> 1 male urinal
> 1 pair adjustable crutches
> 2 pair rubber gloves that can be sterilized
> 3 boxes adhesive plaster for making casts
> 4 rolls gauze bandage

1 glass thermometer
6 packs of Lifebuoy soap
1 box of lice powder
4 bottles of mercurochrome
1 jar Blue Itch Cream
1 large tube of Ben-Gay liniment
1 tin of milk of magnesia tablets
1 large bottle of Bayer aspirin
2 bottles of hydrogen peroxide
2 bottles of isopropyl alcohol
1 50cc bottle of morphine"

He stops and raises his eyebrows
"You preparing for the Battle of Gallipoli, Miss Becky?"
"You mean the narcotic? I may need it if there's a dislocated shoulder or a broken limb. When I was at the camp interviewing for the job, a boy came in with a deep laceration that had to be stitched, an accident at the sawmill."

"No, I didn't mean the morphine. I'm not questioning your credentials to give it, but all this is going to be expensive. . . ."

"That's fine. Colonel Milliken said to put it on the camp's account."

Stenger shrugs, rubbing his one lazy eye. "I guess the government's good for it, but the way the White House is spending, I wonder for how long." He moves into the back room to get some of the items off the shelf, but keeps up a running patter as I pet the orange cat on the counter.

"You know, some of the folks around are pretty riled up about the CCC camp. Say the men will bring trouble into Union County, but I think the Conservation Corps is all that's keeping this town alive. You know . . . Bittman's Grocery, not to mention Gooski's Tavern. Marion Archer got on as a reading teacher out at the camp, and I hear Reverend Goody is teaching elocution. Half the lads, they say, have never been to school, or at least not for long."

"Loonie Tinkshell works out there too."

"Real glad you found a position, Miss Becky, and I'm very happy to have your business." He wraps my supplies in brown paper as his lazy eye wanders toward the door, hoping, I imagine, to see another customer coming in. "Anything else?"

"This will do for a while."

"See the headlines?" Stenger offers just to keep me in the store.

I glance at the newspapers in the rack next to the counter. WAR CLOUDS DARKEN EUROPE and underneath, TESLA DISCOVERS NEW DEATH BEAM.

"What do you think of that?" Stenger questions.

"I don't know. It sounds dangerous." I glance at my watch.

"What if it got in the wrong hands?"

"Well, you know, Europe's a mess again. That Adolf Hitler's in power and it doesn't look good for the Jews. I guess Tesla is just thinking he could save a lot of lives, not have another Great War. One way or another the U.S. is going to get involved, mark my words."

"Oh, I don't think so. We Americans have enough trouble of our own. . . . I have to go," I say, excusing myself. "Don't want to be late for my new job." I throw him a smile and back out the door.

I wasn't honest with Mr. Stenger, didn't say what I really feel. I *hate war.* Like a dust cloud rolling across Oklahoma, it has taken almost everything I loved: my brothers and my shell-shocked husband, even my father, who died of a broken heart after his soldier sons died, one by a bomb, one by the Spanish flu that ran through the barracks like a mad fox in a henhouse.

It's no wonder I'm always waiting for the next calamity. Patience once called me Henny Penny, the chicken who runs around yelling, "The sky is falling! The sky is falling!"

If it didn't take so much courage to be a pacifist, I'd wear the white feather. I'd wear it proudly in my best hat or on my lapel, but in the last Great War, to be a pacifist was to be a traitor, and I couldn't have taken the ostracism.

Blum probably *could* take it. He didn't really care what people thought of him, but he was a physician at Walter Reed during the war, and even though he never saw combat, he saw the results . . . broken men whom he had to patch up and send back to their shattered lives.

It's funny, now that I think of it, how all the males I've cared about have been broken men, broken healers; my father who was addicted to booze, David who returned from the war but never left the horror behind him, and now Dr. Blum.

Linus

"Sorry, I'm late." I rush into the infirmary with the box of supplies, close the door, and pull on the white nurse uniform lying over the chair. I've brought my own starched nurse hat that I wore at Dr. Blum's office, but decide it looks silly and toss it in my bag. This is my first day in the clinic and together, Boodean and I (he's also dressed in white) look quite official when I come out into the waiting room and he leads the first patient in.

"Private Linus Boggs," he introduces the man. I sit down at a small desk in the corner.

"Welcome, Linus. I'm Nurse Rebecca Myers. What seems to be the problem?" The pale, blond twenty-year-old hides under his bushy white eyebrows, his oversized jaw clenched tight.

"It's his pecker, miss." Boodean doesn't have to consult his clipboard.

I nod toward the door to indicate that I need some privacy with the patient and he should leave, but my new medic doesn't get it. "It's crotch rot, is what he tells me. Needs some salve or something."

I take a big breath. "Ordinarily, Boodean, I'd like a private moment with the patients so they can explain their problem to me, then you can come in when I do the exam, but now that you've already offered your diagnosis . . ."

"It's not my diagnosis, ma'am. It's just what he told me. Right, Linus?"

The patient's face is by this time mottled red and I see tears in his eyes. "Mr. Boggs? Can you describe your symptoms to me? When did you first notice the problem?"

Linus turns to Boodean as if to say, "Is this horrible woman really going to make me explain all this?" My assistant looks at the ceiling.

The private clears his throat. "The problem came on last week, ma'am, but it's getting worse."

"Itching? Burning when you void?" I realize by his blank expression he doesn't understand the word *void*. "Does it burn when you pee . . . piss?"

"Nah, miss. Nothing like that! That's the clap, VD. This is more like an itch. I thought maybe it was crotch rot or crotch critters." (Lordy, I was expecting health problems like chicken pox, earaches, and infected wounds, not venereal disease and crotch critters. Maybe people in town were right and this isn't the place for me!)

"Well, Private, I'll need to examine you, either way. Can you lie down on the cot and unbutton your work pants. This won't take a minute."

I turn and begin to scrutinize the old blue, brown, and clear bottles of liquids in the cupboard behind me while the young man gets undressed. There's Cocaine Tooth Ache Drops, Hamlin's Wizard

Oil Liniment, and Estonia Seed Oil. *Estonia Seed Oil? Now what could that be for?*

"Ready." That's Boodean. When I turn around, I find Linus lying on his back, pants pulled down, face turned to the wall . . . and the biggest penis I have ever seen pointing right up at the ceiling. Boodean takes a chair in the corner and looks down at the floor.

It's not that I've never seen an erection. I've been married, had a few lovers while at school, and I worked at Walter Reed, but this is enormous!

I take a deep breath, pull on my red rubber gloves, and approach my patient, looking first at his protuberance and then at his testicles and groin with my magnifying glass, the Sherlock Holmes of penises. It doesn't take long to figure it out. There are no creepy crawlies, just a bright red irritated rash on his testicles and inner thighs, so bad he looks like he's been scalded and I'm actually happy, because now I know what's wrong.

"It's nothing bad, Linus, just a simple skin fungus. Luckily, I bought a jar of Blue Itch Cream at the pharmacy and there's a can of Gold Bond Medicated powder in the closet.

"You'll need to keep the area clean and dry and I'm going to give you some of the powder. Use it two times a day, sparingly. I have a jar of the salve too, but it's all I have for the whole camp, so we have to keep it in the clinic."

"Thank you, ma'am," Linus mutters, buttoning his work uniform khakis. "I'm greatly relieved."

"I apologize for having to examine you. I know it was embarrassing."

"Truly sorry you had to."

I laugh. "As a CCC camp nurse with all male patients, I imagine I'll have to do things like that from time to time. It's just part of the job." For the first time the patient actually looks at me and I see that he has a full set of teeth and a nice smile.

"Come to the clinic next Friday so I can see how you're doing. If you're not better, come sooner. The physician from Camp Laurel will be here on Thursday, if you'd rather see him."

"No, that's fine, ma'am. The worst is over. No woman's ever stared at my pecker except my mom and that was ten years ago."

The rest of the morning is less eventful. Boodean and I see cuts and burns, coughs and bellyaches, but nothing serious and no malingerers, as far as I can tell.

Finally the dinner bell rings. There's the smell of homemade bread drifting across the compound and just as Boodean and I are getting ready to go to the cookhouse there's a knock at the infirmary door.

A young man in a CCC uniform, with the motor pool insignia on the arm, walks in.

"Ma'am?" he says, standing at attention. "I'm Drake Trustler from the motor pool."

I recognize the low voice immediately. *Gravel in a stream bed.* Who does he think he's kidding?

Drake

"Nurse, I'm Drake Trustler from the motor pool and I've hurt my shoulder. Wanted to see about getting some Bayers."

Drake Trustler, my eye! It's Nick Rioli, Mrs. Bonazzo's driver. Baby-faced Nick with the kind eyes, the wide chest, and the gravelly voice. How dumb does he think I am? It's been months since I've seen him, but I don't forget.

"Boodean, you want to go on to the mess hall and get us some food? Get me some of everything, even dessert."

"You sure, Nurse Myers? I don't mind missing a meal now and then."

"You don't understand, *I* mind missing a meal! Now shoo." The medic backs out the door. "Get lots of everything!" I yell after him.

"So what's the scoop?" I challenge my patient. "You call yourself Drake Trustler now? Don't try any funny business with me, Nick. Here sit on this stool. Did you really hurt your arm?"

"Sort of. I wanted to talk to you before you saw me somewhere in the camp and called me Nick. I'm not Nick anymore. I broke with the Bazzano bunch. It was never for me. The only way I could ditch them was to disappear."

"So you just walked away?"

"Exactly. Once I got the missus and the children to White Sulfur Springs, I started planning my escape. You can't just quit the mob like it's a regular job; the mob is everywhere. We spent a few weeks at the Greenbrier and then went on to Roanoke, where she has family. The first night we were there, I left the keys in the Packard, loaded up a rucksack, and hit the road. It broke me to leave Joey, but I couldn't take him with me. Mrs. Bozzano would have hunted me down and had me killed like a dog.

"I didn't know where to go, but I caught the first ride that came along. Thought I might head to California, but everyone and his brother is trying to get there.

"I couldn't go north or south. There are mobsters all along the East Coast, and in the Midwest the thugs have taken over Pittsburgh, Cleveland, Detroit, St. Louis, and Chicago. I decided the mountains of West Virginia would be a good place to hide and started hitching this way." He paces the floor while I open my package from Stenger's and look for the Bayer.

"The third night out, I was camped behind a billboard outside of Hagerstown and I heard singing. It was coming from a truck full of CCC recruits broken down in the ditch.

"Fan belt was snapped. They'd fixed it, but the dummy that was driving had flooded the engine. Most of the fellows, a couple dozen, were pretty well liquored up, including the driver, so I got in and took over. Before he passed out, he told me they were headed for Union County. . . .

"Next morning, at dawn, when they all woke, cold and sick, the sergeant saw me behind the wheel and concluded I was one of the boys and a teetotaler. I introduced myself as Drake Trustler from Ohio. He was a kid I once knew in Meigs County who drowned when he was ten.

"Everything went fine until we got to the camp and they couldn't find Drake Trustler's paperwork. Mrs. Ross gave the driver hell for losing it and fixed me up somehow. I used my grandma's address in Ohio as my home. You have to have some sort of residence and kin to send your twenty-five dollars to or you can't be part of the CCC. Too bad for the fellows without family. This is a good place, plenty to eat, and work to do that matters. I've been here for three months now and I'm second in command of the motor pool."

He tells me his story while I make him a sling, get out two aspirin, and pour some Sloan's Liniment into a small vial.

"I'm sorry about Joey," I say when I'm done. "But I'm glad you got free of them. My friends told me later who the Bazzanos were. The mother didn't seem so bad."

"She's not ruthless like the rest of them, but she thinks she's entitled to whatever she wants. Johnny Bazzano spoiled her."

"Will Anthony and Frankie still try to find you?"

There are footsteps on the porch and I can smell the food before the door opens.

"You won't tell, will you?" Drake Trustler whispers.

19

Distraught

As I'm bumping home along Salt Lick, after my fourth day at White Rock, I see a strange sight and pull over on the edge of the road.

"Wait here," I tell Blum. "It's Daniel Hester. He looks upset. I'll see if I can help him." Blum stares ahead, as if he's not heard me, stares at the squished katydid on the windshield. "Sit. Stay," I command just because he irritates me.

"Daniel! What's wrong? Have you lost something?" The man is stalking back and forth along the road, staring down at the dirt and pulling his hair. Can I help?" I yell from the back of the auto. "Daniel?" When he finally looks over, I can see he's been crying. *What the hell?*

"Daniel!"

"I've killed her." He stops for a moment and then starts pacing again, up and down the shallow, dry ditch.

"Who? What? A cow? A horse?"

I know bad things happen in medicine. Dr. Blum has lost patients, and veterinarians must lose patients too, but what terrible mishap could have brought the man to this state?

"Daniel, I insist you sit down. You're upset, but whatever has happened cannot be that bad." I use my nurse voice, the voice I

would use if I were still on the wards and had to deal with a soldier
having a breakdown, but he doesn't respond, and when I reach out
to touch him, he pulls away. "Daniel? Daniel, what's wrong? Is it
someone's dog?"

"It's Patience. She's pregnant."

"I didn't know. She didn't tell me, but surely this is not all that
bad." The vet's hysteria surprises me. I thought he was a level-
headed man.

"She doesn't like to tell anyone because she's lost babies before,
but now she's bleeding. This is the way it always happens to her . . .
except for little Danny.

"I took her into Torrington this morning and Dr. Seymour, the
specialist, said she's going to lose the baby. He told us it's inevitable
and recommends an abortion before she hemorrhages, but Patience
refuses. She's lost two babies like this before, one when she was
sixteen, then another, our first together, the year you left Union
County. Little Danny is the only one who's survived.

"The placenta is separating, that's what Seymour says, but Patience won't give up. She had all but stopped bleeding a few days
ago, but now it's started again."

"How far along is she?"

"The physician thinks twenty weeks, but her cycle's irregular.
He's just going by her uterine size. That means four long months
in bed. That's *if* the bleeding slows down. As strong as Patience is,
she's not immortal. I should never have gotten her pregnant, and
I should never have . . ." Here he starts the pacing back and forth
again, as if he were chased by demons.

I am so shocked that I don't even notice Dr. Blum get out of the
car. He doesn't rush over, just moves in his slow, measured pace
as if sleepwalking, then sits on the ground. When Daniel marches
past him Blum sticks out his foot.

"What the hell!" The vet falls in the doctor's arms and sits up
again, but at least he's stopped the interminable tromping.

"Oh, God. Oh, God," Daniel moans, shaking his head.

My stomach goes cold. To lose Patience, to lose the Midwife of Hope River! It's unthinkable. I sit down in the grass with the two men and try to imagine what Dr. Blum would advise.

Bed rest, of course. If the placenta is only separating along the edge and Patience doesn't move around for the next fourteen to sixteen weeks, the baby and mother might survive, but if it breaks loose completely both mother and baby will die.

Daniel now rocks back and forth, his arms around his legs. The doc sits next to him like a tree stump. In the tall reeds, a small brown bird with an orange beak and very wise black eyes watches us.

"Where's Patience now?" I ask.

"At home in bed. Little Danny was napping."

I pull myself together. "Let's go to your house. Let's go see Patience. You can't stay with her every minute, but we have to work out a plan. For all we know she could be hemorrhaging . . . or out splitting wood, either one." Hester looks at me wildly and I bite my tongue.

Feel of the Earth

A few minutes later, we bump across the wooden bridge that spans the creek and into the drive. At the open door to the kitchen, Daniel raises his hand. "I'll go up first. Maybe she's sleeping."

"Honey? Patience?" he calls softly.

There's no answer.

"Patience?" he calls again louder and I hear his footsteps upstairs, clunking around, moving from room to room, opening and closing doors, getting more frantic. Then he stops.

"Daniel!" I rush up, imagining he's discovered the worst, his pregnant wife in a pool of blood, her drained body with the dead baby still in her, but when I get to their bedroom there's no blood on the sheets and no Patience either.

"Well, where the hell is she?" Daniel growls. "While, I'm mourning her possible demise and the devastating loss of another baby, she's outside picking posies?"

"Calm down, Daniel. You're distraught. Maybe she just went to the outhouse."

"No, look, the potty is right there. I brought it up before I left." A blue-and-white chamber pot, with a white lid, sits in the corner.

Dr. Blum now stands with us, looking out the window. I push in front of him to see what he's staring at and discover Patience Murphy lying on the green lawn below, her arms outstretched like a cross. Little Danny sits at her side playing with his red metal tractor.

"Oh my God!" Daniel rushes down the stairs.

"Slow down, Daniel. Get yourself under control," I yell, running after him. "She's alive and moving. I just saw her roll over. There's no blood on her dress."

I grab his shirt as he bolts toward the door and pull him back. "Take a few deep breaths. Don't make Patience more upset. Just go out there and sit at her side. We're going to talk. It may not be hopeless."

The man wipes his eyes and runs his hands through his ragged hair. He returns to the kitchen, pumps water in a tin pan, washes his face, and then steps out in the sun.

"Patience, honey. I've been looking for you. Whatcha doing out here?"

"Lying down like you told me." The midwife's shoulder-length brown hair is fanned out in the grass and she adjusts her wire-rimmed glasses.

I follow with Blum and we sit in a circle in the grass around her. "I meant lying down in bed. I thought you would lie down *in bed*." "It feels better out here," Patience says in a quiet voice. "I like to be in the sun and the wind, with the smell of growing things and the feel of the earth under my body. I think it might heal me."

Here I raise my eyebrows. Patience seems an intelligent woman, but she's so naïve. Surely, she doesn't imagine a placenta that's separating can knit back together just from sunshine and the touch of the sweet earth, yet I see peace in her face.

I decide to head things off, before Daniel starts to get hysterical again. Moving in close, I check Patience's pulse. It's rapid but not thready, indicating she's holding her own. Her skin is warm and dry. Respirations twenty-four. No acute distress.

"How much blood is there?" I ask. She pulls a blue cloth from under her skirt without embarrassment, and though it's covered with blood, I know, from my days as Dr. Blum's surgical assistant, it's only about a quarter cup.

"How are you feeling? Any pain? Any contractions? Are you light-headed when you stand?

"No pain yet. No contractions. Just the bleeding." She sounds so matter-of-fact, but looking into her eyes, I see the fear. If you've already lost two babies, you know the pain, the everlasting pain.

Commune

"Is there any hope, Becky?" Daniel asks, his eyes wide and sad.

"There's always hope," I answer, sounding more positive than I am. I look at Patience and continue. "This bleeding and your previous OB history make the prognosis for the pregnancy poor, but we should try to save it. It will be hard and you'll need to stay in bed for as long as it takes."

"It's probably due in March, the month of heavy, wet snow, one of the worst times for getting over the mountains and into Torrington," Daniel observes.

"But there's no way I can stay in bed that long!" Patience moans. "Who will deliver the babies? I have five women due in the next four months, and how can I take care of Danny? You have to work, Daniel. We live from hand to mouth just like everyone else. If you don't go on house calls, we can't eat . . . and then there are the payments for electricity, the telephone and the mortgage. . . ." She raises both hands, signaling her despair.

"We can't eat?" asks little Danny, looking over at us. The child didn't appear to be listening, just playing with his little red tractor, but he got *that* part.

"No, honey," Daniel reassures him. "We will always eat. We have food in the root cellar. Don't worry. Mommy and I will take care of you."

"Is there a woman you could get to move in with you?" I ask.

Patience frowns. "I can't imagine who. . . . We can't afford help."

"How about a girl from Hazel Patch or Liberty? You could provide room and board."

Out of the blue, Dr. Blum breaks his silence. "Isaac and Becky." We all turn with mouths open, shocked at the sound of his voice, as if a rock spoke or a tree.

"Us?"

"Oh, would you?" Patience pleads. "Could you come stay here? Just help us get through the fall and winter?"

Patience goes on as if "Isaac and Becky" were a normal suggestion from a normal individual. "We have the extra room downstairs and we have Moonlight, our cow, and a few chickens, plenty of milk and eggs and vegetables. We could all live together."

It sounds like it's almost decided, but I inwardly cringe. *There's no way I am going to share a room with Dr. Blum!*

"Please . . ." Patience pleads.

"It could work out well." That's Daniel, more muted.

"A commune, like Peter Kropotkin, the anarchist who advocated intentional communities in the twenties!" the midwife exclaims. She has told me a little about her radical days but I don't even know who Peter Kropotkin is.

Daniel rolls his eyes. "Don't get carried away, hon," he cautions, knowing his wife's idealistic tendencies.

I finally come out with my strongest objection. "I'm sorry. It isn't possible. Dr. Blum and I . . . We can't share a room."

There's dead silence and I notice that Isaac has wandered away past the outhouse, where he has stopped at the rail fence.

"Well then, he could bunk with Danny," decides Daniel. "We could bring one of the iron beds over from the house on Wild Rose. It's a big room at the top of the stairs."

Patience is looking at Hester. Hester is looking at me. I am looking at Danny. Better Dr. Blum with the little boy than Nurse Becky, I think. It's bad enough that I'm with Isaac almost every day, all day. I have to have some privacy, at least at night.

Across the yard the doctor leans his forearms on the cedar rail and stares out across the fields toward Spruce Mountain, where a few yellowing oak stand out against the green spruce.

"Please . . ." Patience asks again.

How can I say no? There's a life at stake. Maybe two.

Sleepwalker

It's a hot night and tomorrow we move from the house with the blue door that I've come to love to the Hesters' farm. I toss and turn, thinking about Blum and how he has been uttering a word or phrase now and then, wondering if eventually he will talk, but fearing he will never be normal. Finally, I tiptoe downstairs in my nightdress to get some air.

No moon yet. There's the Big Dipper, Orion's Belt, and the Seven Sisters. Those are the only constellations I know in an infinite universe with stars that go on forever. The wind in the big oak rattles dry leaves, and I forget about the chiggers and lie down in the grass.

I have always been humbled when I look up at the heavens. We think our problems are so big, but the universe is so much bigger and everyone on this planet has problems; it's part of being alive.

A few minutes later, I hear the creak of the screen door and watch as Dr. Blum, wearing only his long johns, steps out of the house. Maybe he's come out to pee . . . but no, he's sleepwalking and I'm only thirty feet away.

They tell you in nursing school, never wake a sleepwalker. The patient can get violent if disturbed. (David Myers, my late husband, would be a case in point. When I woke him, he nearly killed me.)

Like a ghost, the doctor shuffles right toward me, his head tilted back, looking up at the sky. Is he conscious enough to wonder about the stars, like I do? When he's only a few feet away, I shrink into the ground, pretending to be a log, afraid he will step on me, but somehow he senses my presence. The ghost plunks down next to me, but if Dr. Blum knows I am here he shows no sign.

I'm wondering what I should do, lie still or try to creep away, when he reaches both arms straight up toward the sky and opens his hands, like he's harvesting stars, plucking them from the black night. Stranger yet, he cups the stars and washes his face with them. Three times he splashes the starlight on his face and runs his hands through his hair. Then he takes a deep breath and, still in his sleep, holds the stars out to me. "Yours," he says.

We lie in the dark for a long time, maybe hours, until a sliver of moon rises over the mountains. Finally, Isaac begins to snore and I make my move. I tiptoe inside, retrieve the green quilt and come back to sit on the steps in the dark, a sentry guarding a man, who seems dead . . . but may only be hiding.

20

The Midwife's Instructions

"Just tell me," I insist, sounding braver than I really feel, "what I'm supposed to do when I go to a birth. I'll write it all down and memorize each step."

We've been installed in the Hesters' house for more than a week and Patience is staying in bed, as she should. Dr. Blum is downstairs at the kitchen table silently drawing pictures for Danny in a sketchbook that Daniel gave him.

"Okay, let's get to it," Patience says, becoming serious. "Mrs. Kelly always told me that most mothers could deliver their own babies if they had to, so try not to worry so much. The midwife is there for the two out of ten that might have trouble."

"*Two out of ten!*"

"Well, roughly. So, here's what you do. First thing, check the baby's heartbeat. After that, make sure of the baby's position. I always keep the woman up as long as she can stand it. The pain will be less and the contractions stronger. Do vaginal exams only if you have to. Maybe one at the beginning if you aren't sure about the presenting part and maybe another if the labor seems stalled. Of course, all your supplies and gloves should be sterile, but you know that."

"Okay, okay," I interject. "Let me catch up. I'm writing as fast as I can. . . . So after I assess that everything is normal, what happens next? Do I just sit in the corner and wait? Do I boil water? Do I go to sleep?" I say this as a joke, knowing Patience would never go to sleep.

"No. You give her support. Walk with her, be sure she is well hydrated and has nourishment to keep up her strength, nothing heavy like bread or pork and beans, but fruit, broth, tea with honey, things like that. And get your instruments laid out well in advance. Sometimes women will surprise you."

"I learned that with Dahlila."

"And while you're waiting, be calm, tell her she's doing great and try to get her to laugh."

"Make her laugh?"

"Yeah. Laughter is good for everyone. I didn't used to know that. . . . Oh, yeah, every hour or so check the baby's heartbeat again."

"Yes. Yes. Dr. Blum insisted on that." I am scribbling fast. I'll make an outline later.

Patience goes on to tell me how to support the perineum, how to check for a cord around the neck, how to deliver the shoulders without a tear, and how to get the baby to breathe if it has trouble. Then she describes what I do in the third stage of labor, the most dangerous time for the mother. She instructs me to be vigilant, watch for a show of blood, never pull on the cord, and so on.

"And I have a suction bulb in my birth kit." She tilts her head. "Which will be your birth kit for a while, Becky . . . if you are willing. . . . I know you're reluctant, but that's what makes you brave. Even when you are scared you do what needs to be done. . . . These are the women who are due in the next six months." She hands me a short list.

Brave! I think as I stare at the names and break out in a sweat. *Am I really going to be able to do this?* The first name on the list is Lilly Bittman.

"Childbirth is such an intense experience," the midwife acknowledges, putting a hand on my arm and looking into my eyes to encourage me. "Think of it. The moment a new person enters the world, everything changes. Everyone must move over to make room, every person, every rock, every tree, every star, and the midwife is privileged to witness the miracle."

Lilly

I'm driving too fast, I know I am, but if I don't speed up, Lilly is going to deliver without me. I run the one stop sign in Liberty, make a U-turn in the middle of Main, and pull up in front of Bittman's Grocery, trying to remember all the instructions I wrote down.

It's three A.M., and no one's around, so the U-turn doesn't matter, but I had forgotten that the grocery store would be closed at night and the way into the young couple's apartment is up the back stairs.

I make another U and cut down the alley, where I have to decide which stairs are the Bittmans'. I hadn't realized that all of the storefronts on Main have stairs in the back, but I finally decide the one with the lights on must be it and, grabbing Patience's birth satchel, I take the steps two at a time.

At the landing, I stop for a few moments to compose myself, pull back my hair, and straighten my top. If I had time to take my own pulse, I'm sure it would be one hundred and twenty! *Breathe,* I tell myself, like *I* was the one in labor. *Breathe.*

Then I knock twice on the back door. "'Bout time you got here!" B.K. laughs. (He sure is calm!) Maybe Lilly's not in hard labor after all, though on the telephone he certainly sounded like he thought she was.

"I came as soon as I could. You only called me forty minutes ago. How's Lilly?"

"Come in. You'll see." He leads me back to their small bedroom where I find the mother holding her newborn infant with her little boy in his pajamas sitting next to her on the bed.

"See how soft he is," the sightless woman says, showing her five-year-old, her face calm and radiant. "Oh, Miss Becky! I'm sorry I couldn't wait. The baby was coming about the same time you did that U-turn on Main, not more than five minutes ago. How does he look? I can tell he's healthy because he cried right away. Does he have all his parts? I mean, I know he has his boy parts, but everything else. . . ."

The young blind woman amazes me. "Did B.K. see me out the window, skidding around?"

"No, I heard you."

"You heard me while you were pushing the baby out? Weren't you screaming?" Here she laughs.

"No, I was singing right up until the end and then I gave a grunt and B.K. caught the baby . . . Well, not exactly caught, but supported it as it slid out on the bed."

"I helped too," announces Little B.K.

"What did you do?" I ask, just to be polite. Really, I'm horrified. The end result is apparently fine, but anything could have happened.

"I got the blanket and helped Pa wrap him up. There's still a cord on him, though. Ma said we couldn't take it off 'til you came." Here he turns to his mother. "What we gonna call him, Ma? He has red hair, but it can't be B.K.! *Not B.K.* That's already taken."

"Well, at least there's *something* for me to do. I can trim the cord," I tell them.

"Can I help?" asks Little B.K.

"I guess . . ." This is a request I've never confronted before.

I gently take the newborn out of Lilly's arms, but not before the mother kisses him three times, then I weigh him with Patience's hanging scale, assist Little B.K. to cut the rubbery blue cord with sterile scissors, and do my newborn exam.

The baby is perfect in every way, but one. He has webbed toes. I don't know how to tell the parents. They will surely be upset, so I put it off until later.

"You are to do nothing to the cord," I tell them, "except to change the dressing. It will fall off on its own in about two weeks."

"What about the afterbirth?" B.K. asks. "Shouldn't it be coming?"

"Yes, anytime now, yes." I shiver inside. The fact is, I was so concerned about missing the birth, I'd forgotten the placenta and thought my job was done. Patience told me the third stage of labor is dangerous for the mother, and here I am gabbing away.

"Are you feeling any afterbirth pains yet, Lilly?"

The blind woman pulls down the sheet, pulls up her nightgown and rubs her lower abdomen. There's very little blood on the bed, so I don't think the placenta has separated.

"Can't you pull it out? I feel so sweaty, I'd like to get up and wash." She pulls her damp curls away from her face.

Lordy! Fifteen minutes after giving birth and she wants to bathe? "No, we should wait. It won't be long." B.K. sits in the rocker singing to his older son, his long, thin legs up on the bed frame: *"Sleep my child and peace attend thee. All through the night. Guardian angels God will send thee. All through the night."* The boy is almost asleep so it's as good a time as any to give them the news about the baby's birth defect.

"Well, you were lucky," I tell the couple moving over to a stool next to Lilly, in case she gets upset. "The birth went fine. Sometimes there can be a cord around the neck and that can be danger-ous but all's well that ends well. . . . There is one thing about the baby I need to tell you though." Here B.K. stops singing and Lilly's sightless eyes get big.

"You probably didn't notice but your new son has webbed toes." I pause for their reaction and am surprised when they laugh.

"Oh, we looked for that right away," Lilly tells me. "All the Bittman men do! B.K. and Little B.K. and Grandpa. We just say it makes them good swimmers."

Retained

How is it that you always notice the tick of a clock when you are wait-ing? *Tick. Tock. Tick. Tock.* Lilly puts the newborn on the breast as easily as a sighted person. B.K. settles his five-year-old in his bed in the next room, then comes back with his guitar and strums a few tunes. He yawns. It's catching, and Lilly and I yawn too.

Tick. Tock. Tick. Tock. It's been forty minutes since the birth of their second son.

"Mmmmmm," Lilly moans, and I look between her legs expect-ing to see a gush of blood but there's nothing. "Mmmmmm," she moans again and I palpate her uterus. It's rock hard and at the level of her umbilicus.

"I think the afterbirth must be separating. Do you feel an urge to push?"

"No," Lilly says. "But it actually hurts more than my labor pains. It hurts quite a bit." I look between her legs again. Still no blood and the cord hasn't lengthened. B.K. yawns again. It's almost four A.M.

At four fifteen Lilly sits up on one elbow. "Miss Becky, I have to pee. Could I get up and use the bathroom? These pains are getting worse. I really have to do something!" Beads of sweat are on the mother's upper lip and her normally pale pink skin is chalky. She pulls her red hair away from her face and it looks like a skull.

I really have to do something, so I check the uterus one more time. It's now three centimeters *above* the umbilicus. Not a good sign. There must be blood building up inside.

"B.K., I think we should let Lilly pee. Maybe that's part of her discomfort, but I don't really want her to go down the hall. She might faint or something. Do you have an old-fashioned potty, you know, the kind that people use when they don't have an indoor bathroom?"

"Sure, right here. She used it when she was on bed rest." He pulls a white enamel receptacle out from behind the door.

I check again for any signs that the placenta is coming. Still no blood between the mother's legs. "Okay, Lilly, just take it slow and I will be right here if you feel woozy."

"I am a little dizzy, but just a little."

Oh, damn. I'm making such a mess of this. I should have gotten her vital signs before she got up. How is it that I know just what to do for a victim of trauma, a sick child, or a surgical patient, but I'm lost at a simple, uncomplicated home delivery?

I think I know the answer. Birth is a potentially dangerous situation, but in this relaxed environment, I lose my way. All this guitar playing and kissing and kids sitting on the bed gets me off track!

Slowly, we sit Lilly up. Slowly, we lower her legs off the side of the bed. Slowly, we help her squat over the commode. B.K. and I turn away so she can tinkle. But it's not a tinkle. It's a flood! Lilly pees and pees and pees.

"Mmmmmmm! Miss Becky, I really have to get this damn thing out of me! If you won't pull it out, I will. Where's the cord?" Lilly gropes around between her legs.

"No, Lilly!"

She finds what she's feeling for. "Uggghhh." *Plop.* The after-birth drops into the commode and blood and pee splash over everything. "Oh, thank goodness! But I think I made an awful mess." Lilly stands up without assistance and sits on a wooden bedside chair. Her uterus is now back to normal, firm, and three centimeters below the belly button.

I stare at the potty, nearly full of red. Would Lilly be upset if she could see this? It's impossible to estimate the blood loss since the blood is mixed with urine. Maybe two cups of blood, maybe four? I decide to go with three.

"Whew! I feel a lot better! Can I wash up and go to sleep now, Miss Becky? At least I didn't mess the bed."

"Sure," I say as if the whole prolonged third stage of labor was no big deal.

"I can't wait to tell Mama in the morning. She will be so flabbergasted!" Lilly says, grinning.

When I let myself out the back door, both mother and father are climbing into bed with their newborn between them. On the landing of their back stairs I stand for a minute looking down the alley at the halo of light around the gas streetlamps. Inside I can hear singing, a man and a woman. "*Hush-a-bye, don't you cry. Go to sleep, little baby.*"

Lilly's dark world is not dark at all.

October 10, 1934

Birth of Lilly and B.K. Bittman's second son, 6 pounds, 6 ounces. (I missed the actual delivery; it went so fast and the baby hadn't been named by the time I left.)

Lilly, blind since birth or early infancy, said she was singing as she pushed the baby out and that the birth wasn't painful at all. Hard to believe, but who am I to doubt her? This is the second time a patient has sung during labor and it should be written up in a medical book!

Little B.K. saw the whole thing and wasn't even disturbed. He asked to help cut the cord and I let him, a radical act for me, but he was so involved and curious, I couldn't see the harm.

The problem was the placenta. I was so intent on caring for Lilly and the baby, I neglected to get it out in a timely manner, almost causing the mother harm. I am sure that it was balled up in her vagina the whole time and she was building up blood behind it, but I waited more than fifty minutes before letting her get up to go to the potty and then it came out quite easily.

Baby was perfect in every way except the webbed toes, and I was afraid they would be upset when I told them, but they only laughed. Webbed toes are apparently a trait in the Bittman males. They are good swimmers.

October 10, 1934

Syndactyly! The word erupts, unbidden, from my mouth like hot lava out of a volcano!

Syndactyly is the medical term for webbed toes. I would tell Becky that little-known medical fact, but then she would realize I've been reading her journal. A sin, I know, but I can't help myself.

I'll explain how it happened.

The second week after we moved to the Hesters', while Becky was off at the CCC camp, Daniel and I got back early from the fields. As usual, he went up to see Patience and, having nothing else to do, I went into Becky's room. I found comfort there, the smell of her lilac lotion, a soft female presence.

Lying on my stomach on her green-and-blue patchwork quilt, the edge of something hard under the mattress rubbed on my arm and when I investigated, a flat book dropped out on the floor. I knew at once what it was and, opening the pages, saw Becky's neat script. I couldn't help it. Who could? I started to read.

I'll say it right out, I know it was wrong, but I have no intention of stopping. It's like looking through a window at another person's soul, a delicate person, someone you could learn to love, if you were not a monster like myself.

Now, in the back of Danny's sketchbook, I have started my own recordings. Words come to me, I find, in an easy way, as if all this time I've been thinking deep thoughts. It's like awakening after a deep sleep. You slide into consciousness wondering where you are, who you are, and what day it is.

21

The Sergeant

I've been going to White Rock Camp five weeks now and have found the job pleasant and mostly routine, nothing rough or threatening, as people in Liberty had implied. My cases, for the most part, are scrapes and bruises, headaches and sprains, a bad burn from the kitchen and frequent cases of bronchitis.

At noon today a sharp-looking fellow of about thirty-five walked into the clinic, leaned on the doorframe, and took in the infirmary. It's funny to say "sharp-looking" when all the men wear the same khaki uniform, but it's *the way* he wears it, his shirt tucked in and his pants low on his slim hips, his army hat cocked to one side.

Boodean clicks his heels, salutes, and backs up against the wall to give the older man space.

"I'm sorry," I announce. "We're just breaking for dinner. Can you come back at one thirty?" The man has the large soulful eyes and wide grin of Fred Astaire, and I half expect him to do a slow slide across the wooden floor with his hands out and then twirl at the end, but he takes a seat in Boodean's chair and stretches out his long legs.

"Afraid I can't wait, miss. I'm an L-E-M." He spells it out, as if it's a word he doesn't want to say in front of Boodean. "I'm in charge of the workhorses and this afternoon I have to teach the boys how to pull the fallen timber out of the ravine. It's a real fire hazard and we're just getting started."

"Lem? That's your first name?"

"No, Miss Myers. This is Sergeant Cross. He's an L . . . E . . . M like you, locally employed man," Boodean explains. "Lou is a foreman." He salutes a second time.

I take a long breath, inhaling the sweet smell of freshly baked cookies across the compound. "Well, I guess I can see you now, but we really need to hurry. I don't want to miss our meal."

"Thank you kindly, Miss Becky. Been hearing nice things about you from the boys." He looks me up and down.

"Sit down, Mr. Cross. Or should I say Sergeant Cross?"

"You can call me Lou."

"Please sit down, Sergeant Cross." (There's no way I'm going to call this fellow "Lou." He acts like he owns the place.) "So, what can *we* do for you today?" I say it like that, making it clear that the medic and I are a team and this is not a social call. Boodean pulls another chair in from the waiting room. "What's the problem?"

"Can I talk to you alone?"

"No, I'm sorry you can't. Private Boodean is my assistant. He records all my clinical notes and he understands that anything he hears here is strictly confidential." The medic immediately starts scribbling something on his clipboard.

"Well, I'm worried about a wart. It sounds silly and, Boodean, if you say anything to the fellows, I'll beat you bloody, but it's a big wart and it's causing me pain."

Right here I get nervous, hoping it's not another penile problem, some kind of venereal disease, but the sergeant goes on.

"I make a point not to limp, but sometimes at the end of the day, I can't help it. . . . I even tried stealing an onion from the cook and rubbing it on the thing and then throwing it over my shoulder, but it's been two weeks and nothing's happened. I'd like you to give me some medicine. I don't care how bad it tastes."

"Where is the wart, Mr. Cross?"

"On my damn foot! Pardon my strong language, Miss Becky. But it hurts so bad I can hardly walk. I'm not usually a bellyacher."

"Did you try going out in the garden at night, picking a bean leaf and rubbing it on the wart?" Boodean chimes in. "Then dig a hole with a silver spoon and bury it under a rock? My granny says that works every time." I look at my watch. The dinner bell rang half an hour ago and I'm afraid I'll miss my midday meal. In the mountains these old wives' tales are as common as dandelions.

"Well, let's have a look. Can you lie on the bed and take off your shoe and sock?" The man is wearing high regulation army work boots and it takes him a minute to untie his laces.

He lays his left foot up on the cot and I see what he's talking about, a black, crusty lesion the size of a half dollar on the ball of his left foot. It's a wart, I can tell, by the bumpy surface, and it looks like he's been picking at it, because there's blood on his sock.

"I see what you mean." The truth is, I'm shocked, and I immediately start wondering how to treat the eruption. Debridement comes to mind, but it will be painful; still, it's somewhere to start.

"Boodean, you go across the compound and have your dinner. You can get some for me, just whatever the cook will give you. Have you eaten, Sergeant?"

"Yes, miss. I ate before I came." He eyes me warily as I get out a scalpel, iodine, gauze, and a small basin. I pour a little water in the bowl and have the man soak his foot.

"Just rest your foot, sir. I want to soften the wart before I operate."

"Operate! Don't leave me, Boodean!" But the medic is already out the door.

"Can't you use some salve or something, Nurse? You're scaring me now."

"No, these warts are very stubborn, and onions, green beans, and salve are not going to do it. Here, take two Bayer while we wait. I want you to soak for ten minutes." I nod toward the cuckoo clock. So far, it seems to run on time, but I've never seen the cuckoo pop out.

I turn my back, step into the closet, and tear open one of the books I brought from Dr. Blum's box, *Diagnosis and Treatment of Skin Diseases*. Plantar warts. Plantar warts . . . I really don't have time for this. . . .

Invitation

Twenty minutes later, Sergeant Cross's foot has been scraped and is covered with gauze and Betadine.

"Tomorrow soak your foot again for ten minutes. Boodean can give you some Epson salts to take back to your cabin or you can come here. Do you have a cabin or do you bunk with the enlisted men?"

"We LEMs have our own quarters. I share a place with the head carpenter, the first log cabin up the creek. Come over anytime, or maybe you could do my treatments there? You know, make a house call?" He says this last part with a wink and a leer that curls up one side of his handsome face. I'm shocked by the proposal and truly can't tell if he's flirting or serious. Knowing his type, I decide he probably treats all women this way, but this is the kind of thing people in town warned me about.

"That would hardly be appropriate, Mr. Cross."

"Sergeant . . ." he says again, tying his boots.

Just then someone bangs on the infirmary door. "Can I come in?" It's the medic.

"Yes, of course. We're finished." Boodean enters with a basket of food from the cook, followed by Captain Wolfe.

"Hello," Wolfe says, removing his hat. "I hate to interrupt, but I need to know if Sergeant Cross is free to work. The men are waiting at the stables, the horses all rigged and ready." He consults his wristwatch, which I note is a gold Elgin, just like my father's.

"Keep your shirt on, Wolfe. I'll be right there. They can't start without me," my patient growls. "It's too dangerous. I told you before, I'll get there when I damn well can. . . . Pardon my language, ma'am."

"I'm not inviting you, Sergeant, I'm ordering you." It's obvious there's tension between the two. Sergeant Cross lurches up, steps into his boot, almost kicking the washbowl over, limps across the room, and slams out the door without another word.

"Sorry, Nurse," Captain Wolfe says, looking directly at me with his green eyes.

The rest of the afternoon is slow and I have a chance to read about plantar warts. The illustrations are appalling, but none so bad as the wart I just saw. Debridement is the treatment of choice, but toward the end, salicylic acid is cited as an experimental cure.

"Salicylic acid," I say out loud to the four walls. Boodean has gone out to the waiting room to beg Mrs. Ross for two cups of coffee. *Salicylic acid.* Maybe Stenger could make me some in a Vaseline base at the pharmacy.

As I leave, the sun is just setting and the camp is now full of overgrown boys, playing basketball, throwing horseshoes, smoking cigarettes, and shooting the bull. Even though there's a chill in the air and they have to wear jackets, when the work is over, the fun begins.

"Miss Myers?" Captain Wolfe approaches from the side as I'm putting my nurse's bag in the backseat, and he salutes me as if I'm in the service. "I want to apologize about the conflict in the infirmary earlier. It shouldn't have happened. Cross is a good worker, but a bit of a hothead."

"I figured that out," I say pleasantly, eager to get back to the farm to make sure Patience is okay.

"I have a favor to ask. I know I just met you, but I've been ordered to represent the White Rock Camp at a fundraiser for Eleanor Roosevelt's community experiment, Arthurdale. It won't happen for a few months and it's at the Hotel Torrington, but I'm supposed to bring a wife or lady friend, and I don't have one. Mrs. Roosevelt will actually be there. I wonder if you'd be my guest." He flushes in embarrassment.

"Arthurdale is the rural village that Mrs. Roosevelt is building in Preston County for the unemployed miners from Scotts Run, isn't it? I worked at Scotts Run as a public health nurse when I first came to West Virginia. What's the date again?" I ask this as if my social calendar is so full, I might be overbooked.

"New Year's Eve. It's a banquet and a dance. All the other CCC senior officers, Dr. Crane from Laurel Camp, and Major Milliken have wives."

I don't know what I'm doing. I have no dancing clothes, haven't danced since I was at Walter Reed and one of the doctors took me out. It's probably Wolfe's shyness that makes me say yes . . . that and the fact that Eleanor Roosevelt, the First Lady and tireless social reformer, might be there.

"Well, I guess I could. I don't usually go out with colleagues." (I don't usually go out at all.) "But under the circumstances, I could make an exception."

"Thank you so much, Nurse Myers! I haven't asked a woman out since my wife died four years ago." He straightens and salutes as I get in the Pontiac. When I look back he is grinning from ear to ear.

October 10, 1934

Salicylic acid is made from willow bark and is the main ingredient in aspirin. Hippocrates, a physician in 5 BC used it as a treatment for fever and pain. Funny how such thoughts come to me. . . . Just because I'm mute, doesn't mean my brain isn't working. On the other hand, I'm not sure I like it, this new affinity with words.

For so long there was comfort in silence.

22

Domestic Life

Though I'm not really good at it, or particularly enjoy it like some women do, since we've moved to the Hesters', I've put on an apron and become the chief cook. Patience gives me instructions and sometimes writes down recipes, which I keep on stiff cards in a little green box.

In the morning after the men water the stock and milk the cows, the Hesters eat upstairs in their bedroom and Blum and I in the kitchen. I am amazed at the progress the doc's made since we moved here. Except for his silence, he could be Daniel's hired hand.

All day, Daniel and Isaac are silently digging up the carrots and beets and storing them in the root cellar out back, or getting in hay, or insulating the barn for winter. Most of the time, they take Danny with them and let him play in the dirt, but sometimes he stays with Patience and plays on her bed. I know she feels isolated, so I try to visit often and bring her little jobs to do, like slicing apples or peeling potatoes.

In the evening, around eight, we gather in the Hesters' bedroom to eat popcorn made in a wire basket on the wood cookstove and listen to Patience read to us from her big book of Hans Christian Andersen fairy tales.

The family sprawls on the bed, Danny between his father and mother. I sit on the hard-backed chair and Blum stands next to the closet. When Danny begins to fade, Hester carries him to his room and I lead Dr. Blum to bed.

"Fly's in the buttermilk. Shoo, fly, shoo. Fly's in the buttermilk. Shoo, fly, shoo," Daniel sings to Danny as if it's a lullaby. *"Fly's in the buttermilk. Shoo, fly, shoo . . ."*

Afterward, I retire downstairs to my room to read a novel or sometimes the verses of Edna St. Vincent Millay.

As I turn off the light and snuggle under the quilts, I can hear Daniel and Patience in their room above me talking softly, sometimes laughing. And then silence.

Skip to my Lou, my darlin'.

October 17, 1934

Life has settled down at the Hesters' now that we have a routine. At 7 A.M. the vet gets up and lights the fire. It's the sound of the iron poker that wakes me. We rise about 7:30. I can dress myself fine, but I let Becky check my buttons and brush my teeth because I like her to touch me.

After the vet and I tend the animals and while he's busy straining the milk and Becky is making breakfast, I care for little Danny. He's an easy child to entertain, a bright little boy, who asks me to draw pictures for him in this sketchbook (my journal).

"Draw a cat," he orders. "Draw a dog. Draw a house. Draw a tractor." Simple enough. I would like to teach him his letters but that would require language, and though I have words in my head, I'm missing the connection to my tongue. Only rarely do I utter a sound. Dead men don't talk and I died the day my wife drove into the river.

Test

"Goddam!" The vet slams the telephone receiver down in its holder and Blum and I look up from the kitchen table where we've been finishing our coffee. (The doctor is able to eat on his own now, though sometimes I have to wipe his chin.)

"It's the Bishop brothers. They have a herd of cattle that needs to be tuberculin tested and want me out there this week."

"Who're the Bishop brothers?" I ask.

"You remember them. They're part of that crowd that jumped Blum and me at the Fourth of July picnic. A hard bunch, stingy with their animals, sour and unfriendly. They used to be in the moonshine business, until the G-men from D.C. shut them down. Five years ago or so, I had a run-in with them when their stallion, Devil, died." He pulls out a wooden chair and sits back down with us.

"The Bishops waited too long to call about a case of severe colic, and when the beautiful black Arabian died, they blamed his death on me and things got ugly. The three brothers were half drunk and it ended in a knock-down fistfight. I barely got out of there alive. They also dressed up like Klansmen and gave Patience and Bitsy a scare. A rotten crew if there ever was one."

"Can't you say no?"

"Nah, I'm the only vet around, and everyone is required by the state of West Virginia to get their herd tested. It's important. Fifteen years ago, one in twenty cattle had bovine tuberculosis. It was a big economic loss to the farmers, not to mention a threat to human health."

He reaches for his cup of coffee. "I was wondering when the Bishops would get around to calling me. Dreaded it! On the other hand, they don't really have a choice and neither do I. I took on the state contract. It's good cash money."

"Hey, Isaac, want to come with me?" he says, grinning. "Be my backup in case things get ugly?"

"I could come, too."

"You?"

"I mean, if a woman was there, they wouldn't get rough, would they?"

"Probably not. They aren't *that* crude. One of them, the oldest, Aran, has a common-law wife. The one I hate is Beef, a violent bastard. . . . I suppose you could help by writing down the test numbers in my ledger. If a cow tests positive, it's the end of it. It has to be killed right away and then the carcass burned."

I look at Dr. Blum sitting there in the wooden kitchen chair, staring into space, and imagine he and Daniel getting into another fistfight. "I'd better come."

The Bishops

Two days later, just as the sun is peeking over the mountains, Daniel, Blum, and I leave Patience with her breakfast on a tray and a pile of toys on her bed for Danny and head in the Model T toward Burnt Town. Hester explains that the little village was built along Crockers Creek a century ago and was completely destroyed by a forest fire, thus the name, Burnt Town.

"No one wanted to build there again. Superstitious, I guess. Too many people died. They say in these hollows, when a fire gets started, it roars up the mountains. The narrow valleys work like chimneys, just suck up the flames."

I look over the fields as we bump along in the Model T. The countryside is white with frost, our first really hard one, and everything is covered with little ice crystals. In the ditches the goldenrod stalks droop with their white fur, and red maple leaves are rimmed with white. Even the spider webs are covered with miniature beads of ice and shine in the morning light.

Finally, we turn off the main gravel road and bump down a rocky grade, across a branch of Crockers Creek and into a spacious farmyard.

There's a white farmhouse with a long front porch, a neat fenced-in vegetable garden, and something that looks like a chicken coop to the side. From Daniel's description of the Bishop brothers, I'd expected something more roughshod.

A dark-haired woman wearing a flour-sack print dress and a heavy green sweater is carrying a basket of potatoes across the yard. She stops to stare, and three hounds, chained to their dog-houses, bark viciously.

" 'Bout time you showed up, you old son of a gun," a stocky farmer on the porch calls out, then grins, saunters over, and reaches out his hand. "How you doin'? Ain't seen you much lately." I have a hard time reconciling Hester's story of the knockdown, drag-out physical fight after the Arabian stallion died with this sociable gent.

"Aran," Daniel responds with reserve. "I brought Nurse Myers to help with the record keeping, and Dr. Blum, you remember him? He can hold the steers while I do the testing. Are your brothers available to round up the cattle?" He scans the yard and I remember that it's the one called Beef he most dislikes.

"Yeah." Aran Bishop motions to our left where a short, thick man wearing hitched-up trousers and a red plaid flannel shirt moves slowly across the plowed field. A green John Deere sits in the distance. "Here comes Beef now."

The man called Beef strides up to Daniel and, bold as anything, shakes his hand, acting as if nothing has ever happened between them.

"Doc," he addresses him in a nasal voice. "Thought you were coming yesterday! Had them cows all penned up and you never showed. Let them loose for the night. They're all up at the back forty now."

"I told your brother, *today, November 17.* I was clear on that."

"Well, no matter." The older brother tries to smooth things out. "You're here now. Let's round them back up and get to work."

"Who's the skirt?" Beef jerks his head my way.

Daniel tightens his jaw. "Miss Myers. Nurse Becky Myers. She's going to write down the numbers while I do the testing. Dr. Blum can hold the cattles' heads."

"Yeah, and I get the butt-end where I can get kicked. Sounds fair."

Isaac steps forward and folds his arms across his chest. I almost laugh, wondering if he makes the tough pose on purpose or if it's just by accident.

Thirty minutes of drinking coffee in silence on the porch with Aran's common-law wife and I spy the men and dogs across the field driving a stream of cattle toward the barn. Dr. Blum is walking along with them, waving his arms back and forth like a windmill.

"Thanks," I say to my quiet companion. "It was very neighborly of you to keep me company." She must be in late thirties, a tough-looking lady with a lined face and dishwater hair that she keeps twisting in ropes. She responds with a stiff smile, but still doesn't speak.

It's quite an operation going on down at the barnyard. The men are driving the livestock into a pen. There's shouting and swearing as the big animals occasionally step on someone's foot. Once, a cow forces Daniel up against the fence, almost crushing him, but Aran pulls it away.

"Cocksucker!" says the vet, shocking the pants off me. My

woman companion laughs. The man called Beef herds the cows into a long chute, three at a time, using a whip, and he smiles when the leather hits the animals' backs.

"Must be time for me to get to work." I set my heavy blue-and-white mug on the porch. "Thanks again. . . . I'm sorry, I didn't get your name."

"Cora."

"Thanks again, Cora."

One by one, Daniel injects each animal with a small amount of purified tuberculin antigen just under the skin. He reads the cow's number from a clip behind its ear and I write it down. In three days we will return. If the animal has TB, a welt will appear where the needle went in, and the cow will have to be slaughtered.

We work together, becoming more efficient as time goes on, and finally the yard clears and the animals run off. The whole thing takes about two hours, and by the time we're done, the men are exhausted so I offer to drive home.

"So we'll see you in three days? What time? We'll try to have the animals rounded up," Aran offers.

"About nine," the vet answers.

"Better be here when you say you will," threatens Beef.

Or what? *You'll beat us all up?*

23

Visitor

I take another sip of spearmint tea, made from Patience's dried herbs, and stare out the kitchen window. There's a wind coming in from the north and it's cold. The sky is pale blue and the trees are all bare, all except the spruce on the mountain.

The experience at the Bishop brothers' farm yesterday intrigues me, and I can't help thinking about how functional Dr. Blum seemed, almost like one of the guys. I must remember to keep on challenging him, to not let him get away with being an invalid. Like a child, he needs new activities to build up his skills. That's why I asked Daniel for a pocketknife.

Now, Dr. Blum sits in the rocker near the Hesters' wood heater stove, whittling a stick. There's a pile of shavings in a basket at his feet that I plan to keep for starting fires. At Walter Reed they called it "occupational therapy," and it seemed to do the disabled vets good.

The sound of a motor whining down Salt Lick Road pulls me out of my reverie and a truck bumps across the bridge. It's Mr. Maddock, and all I can think is it must be some emergency. He starts out the minute I open the door. "Ma'am," he blurts out. "Ma'am, I wonder if I could trouble you . . ."

"Come in. Come in. Please." The frigid air explodes through the doorway and I watch as he pulls off his black hat, then steps out of his work boots. I have never seen him without his hat before, and his hair is thick and peppered gray. "Can I offer you some tea?"

The farmer stares at Blum. "No. No, thanks. Is he okay with that knife?"

I smile. "Yes. He's not cut himself once or done anything inappropriate. Dr. Blum used to be a surgeon, you know, and was handy with scalpels." I say this last part with a smile, but Maddock doesn't get the humor. "How can I help you?"

"It's Mrs. Maddock. She's in the family way . . . and I'm worried." Here he looks down at his wool socks, green with brown toes, probably knitted by his disabled wife. Patience knits too, but I've never learned.

I picture his wife, a polio victim of about fifty, who's been paralyzed from the waist down since she was in her early thirties. "Are you sure? Some women miss their monthlies when they're close to the change." I can see he's embarrassed.

"Yes, Sarah thought the same thing, but yesterday we both felt it move. I wonder if you could make a home visit. Mr. Stenger at the pharmacy said you'd be the one, since the midwife had to take to bed."

"How old is your wife?"

"Just forty-seven."

"Certainly, I'll come. Do you want me right now?"

"If you're not too busy . . . I could drive you and bring you back."

"I need to get a coat and hat, and I guess I have to bring Dr. Blum. Dr. Hester is away."

"You have to bring the doctor?"

"Yes, I can't leave him here alone," I explain. "There's no one to watch him. Mrs. Hester must stay upstairs resting."

"Well, I guess . . ." Maddock hedges and I remember how

protective he is of his wife. He steps back in his boots, but he stops and turns before he goes outside.

"I know you aren't a fortune-teller, Miss Myers. You can't predict the future, but I can't lose Sarah. Childbirth can be hard on an older woman, and we both know there can be trouble with the baby. Just tell us what you think. That's all we want."

The man looks at me for a long time, and I can't be sure, but I think there are tears in his watery blue eyes.

Sarah

"Sarah," Maddock yells at the door of the two-story white clapboard farmhouse on Wild Rose Road. "Are you in the bedroom? I'm bringing Miss Myers in to see you. Dr. Blum is here too." He stands blocking Isaac, as if the sight of him would cause his wife to faint.

In truth my charge has become quite handsome. He stands tall and straight, has good teeth, and though his hair is receding, it's dark and curly. He has a strong jaw and beautiful eyes, or they used to be, before the light went out in them.

"Yes, I'm in here, honey, lying down."

We enter a cool, dark interior, furnished with a leather settee and matching chairs, a fringed blue lamp, the kind David and I had in our little house in Brattleboro, and a flowered blue carpet.

Mr. Maddock indicates the closed door of a downstairs bedroom. "That way," he instructs me. "Can the doctor drink sarsaparilla? I have some in the fridge."

"Sure, just set the bottle in front of him to give him the idea. And can you take off his boots?" I lay my hat and wool coat on the sofa and tap on the door. "Sarah? It's Nurse Becky. How are you doing?"

"Oh, come on in. I'm fine. Just a little tired. Tired of doing nothing. You know how Mr. Maddock is! He'd have me confined for the whole pregnancy, if he could." Sarah laughs and I can't help myself, I laugh too. She's a pale, soft, thin woman with gold and silver hair pinned back on the sides, and she wears a hand-knit blue cardigan with darker blue flowers embroidered on the front.

"So, are you okay? Your husband seems awfully worried."

"Kiddo, I'm ecstatic. When I became paralyzed and lost my first baby, we never tried to have another one, but we weren't trying not too, either. I assumed the high fevers during my illness had just made me sterile."

"Another baby? You've given birth before?"

"Yes, years ago. We don't talk about it."

"Was it stillborn or a miscarriage?"

"No, the baby was fine, but I was terribly ill. I had polio and the paralysis was moving up toward my chest. If it got to my diaphragm I would stop breathing. The doctors thought I was certain to die, so they talked Mr. Maddock into letting them do an emergency cesarean section and he gave our little girl to my cousin who'd never been able to get pregnant."

She recites all this without emotion, but when she ends I see the side of her mouth twitch one time, an expression that tells me she still feels the pain.

"No one thought I would live, and then when I slowly recovered over the next twelve months, I couldn't ask for the baby back, could I? What's even sadder is that both my cousin and the little girl passed a few years later during the Spanish flu epidemic."

I lay my medical bag on the carpeted floor. "May I?" I say, indicating the bed.

"Sure." Mrs. Maddock smoothes the covers so I can sit down

next to her. "So here we are with another chance," she goes on. "My husband's terrified, won't let me lift a finger, but I think it's good for women to be active during their pregnancies, don't you?" We both look down at her skinny withered legs, white against the white coverlet. She shrugs and covers them with a lap robe.

"Well, as active as I can be anyway. It's not like I can go out and throw hay to the cows." Here she gives me a pleasant smile, showing that she has a sly sense of humor. She is a sensitive, intelligent woman, someone I would like for a friend, if I had time for friendship.

"No, I agree. Unless you're bleeding or having pain, you should be up moving about, doing your normal activities. How far along are you?"

"I don't know. I haven't had a monthly since July. I was always regular before and I thought I was having hot flashes, though, looking back, it was a horrible summer, maybe I was just hot."

"Let me examine you. If you really are four or five months' pregnant you should be showing by now. You think you felt the baby move yesterday?"

The pale woman smiles. "Yes. Yes. We both felt it." She pulls up her housedress and shows me her belly, which is rounded, but not the way it should be. I press down gently around her belly button. No hard, round ball of uterine muscle. I palpate lower. *Still no firm ball.*

"What are you feeling for?"

"It's called the fundus, the top of the uterus. Where did you feel the baby move?"

She points to an area just above the umbilicus and to the left. *Too high.*

"Sarah, I don't think you conceived this summer. I don't know how to say this but Mr. Maddock wanted my honest opinion. I don't think you felt movement way up there. Your uterus is still very small. You're either not pregnant or you're very early." I stop to let my words sink in and am surprised to see tears well up in the woman's green eyes. The room darkens, though there's no change in the light, and the smile that had illuminated Sarah's face fades. "So I'm not with child?" She says it like this, in the old-fashioned way.

"Well, I'm not positive, but I'd say no, unless you just very recently conceived. Any morning sickness or breast tenderness?"

Mrs. Maddock shakes her head no.

"You can go to Torrington and get the A-to-Z test where they inject a baby mouse with your urine if you really want to be sure."

"I don't think so. . . . Will you tell Mr. Maddock? He will be relieved. He was so worried that having a baby would hurt me."

I stare at the woman, who wipes her moist eyes and turns toward the window.

"I'm sorry," I murmur and then leave the room.

At the kitchen table I find the two men silently drinking sarsaparilla. "Mr. Maddock," I begin abruptly, wanting to get it over with. "I can't be sure, but I don't think your wife is pregnant. At least, if she is, she's not far along. She hasn't been sick or had any breast soreness, and her womb is still small." The men look up, Blum paying special attention and Mr. Maddock looking confused.

"But we both felt it move!"

"I know. I know. You felt something, maybe a gas bubble, but the baby couldn't have been as high as where Sarah showed me."

The man twists his lips, trying to keep from crying, then clears his throat. "Is Sarah okay? She would be a good mother. I was just so worried about the pregnancy being dangerous for her."

"She's disappointed. You'd better go to her. We'll find our way home. It's only a mile."

It's a silent walk down Wild Rose Road and around Salt Lick, but then with Blum it always is. Tiny hard raindrops pelt our faces, and at the Hope River the smoke of three campfires rises in the mist. I blow on my hands because I forgot my mittens and Dr. Blum gallantly gives me his.

Dancing Dress

This morning when I take Patience her breakfast she looks rather blue. I'm sure it must be torture for an energetic person like her to lie in bed all day, but sometimes she gets under my skin. At nine A.M. she's still wearing her flannel nightgown and her hair is a mess.

"About time to get dressed, isn't it?"

"What's the point, Becky? I won't be going anywhere. Why bother? I'll just stay in my nightclothes."

"You think that will make you feel better?"

She has copies of the *Socialist Worker* all over the bed. It's become her main interest, cutting out the reports about the labor unrest, stikes here, battles there. Recently she told me about a textile workers' strike in Rhode Island, the largest one ever. There were 420,000 men and women on the streets.

"No, it won't make me feel better."

"So what will it be, then, the red frock or blue?" I indicate two housedresses hanging on pegs next to the window.

"Red, the blood won't show," she answers bitterly.

"Speaking of dresses, I have to find one. I've been invited to a dance." My news has the desired effect.

"A date?" Patience pushes up in bed so suddenly, I worry she'll start bleeding again. "Why didn't you tell me? With who?"

"Calm yourself. It isn't *a real date*. Captain Wolfe at the CCC camp asked me to go with him to a benefit for Arthurdale Community. You know, Eleanor Roosevelt's pet project, the one that was in the newspaper. All the other men have wives, and when he said the First Lady would be there, I couldn't say no. It's New Year's Eve, a long time from now. Do you have anything I could wear? Maybe I should have refused."

"Are you kidding? You *have* to go. Think of it, the *president's wife* right here in West Virginia! And she's a real liberal crusader too! Leave it to me. I'll come up with something."

Later in the afternoon, I take a bucket of warm water upstairs and wash my friend's hair, which cheers her considerably. "Any bleeding?"

"Not today."

"Is the baby still moving?" Here she smiles, a burst of sunlight.

"Of course. As old Mrs. Potts would say, 'The infant is right lively.' I miss Mrs. Potts. Are you going to be my midwife, Becky? I know you love childbirth!"

Now it's my turn to smile. "I guess . . . I visited Sarah Maddock yesterday. She thought she was pregnant. Hadn't had a menstrual period for five months, but I don't think she is."

"Was she sad?"

"Yes, I think she was. Mr. Maddock seemed sad too, though he might have been relieved. He was so worried about his wife's health. They both knew at forty-seven she had a chance of having a baby with problems. I told them they could go to the hospital in Torrington and have a test to be sure, but I doubt they will. The sad thing is, they thought they'd already felt movement, and I really think Sarah would like to be a mother. She'd had a baby before, did you know?"

"I did. She told me one day when we were having tea, but I've seen that before, women thinking they felt the baby when there was no baby. Probably a gas bubble."

"That's what I said. Is there something I should have done differently? I hated to disappointment them. What if I'm wrong?"

There's a pause, long enough to hear a red-tailed hawk in the distance, and Patience pushes out a sigh. "I don't think there was anything else you could do. She's pregnant or she's not, and either way, I think she'll be okay. We are all stronger than we think."

October 21, 1934

"We are all stronger than we think." That's what Patience said, but are we? Faced with grief and guilt, even the toughest person can crumble. I cite myself as an example.

I was never a sensitive soul. Thick-skinned, you might say. I took care of people, but didn't particularly care about them, even Pris, my wife. She was a beautiful woman, and her beauty fascinated me, like a crystal ornament twirling in the sunlight, but I wouldn't call it love. It's only now that I can admit that.

24

Results

"I just hope none of the Bishops' cattle have a positive test," the vet worries as we bump down the rutted road onto the the Bishop farm. There's a wet wind, but we've dressed for the weather, with knit caps, winter jackets, and long flannel underwear.

As they promised, the men have the animals ready in the barn, and all four of the Bishop brothers are present so there's no job for me except to circumvent a fight.

"Cigarette?" Cora asks, holding out a pack of Pall Malls. Her light brown hair is long and lank with bangs down to her eyebrows, and her voice is low for a woman. Probably the cigarettes.

"No, thanks. I don't smoke." We're sitting on a bale of hay watching the men work, and she puts the cigarettes away as if she's made a social blunder.

"I've always been afraid to smoke," I admit.

"My gran says it's good for you, that the smoke clears your lungs."

"Lots of people say that."

"Hey, watch it, George!" Beef yells at a man who seems to be his younger brother. "You stomped on my foot."

"Well, sorrrrrry!" George mocks him. It's cold in the barn and steam comes out of his large red mouth.

"They say you're a nurse." That's Cora.

"Yes, I work part-time at White Rock CCC Camp."

"The Bishop men hate the CCC camp. Hate the boys there too. Say they're a bunch of pansies, parading around in uniform as if they were some kind of heroes."

"They're just regular fellows, earning money for their families and staying off the streets. Young men get into mischief if they don't have work to do."

"The Bishops hate them because the camps are run by the government. They hate anything to do with the government, hate Roosevelt, hate Herman Kump, the governor. I hate them too. The feds killed my pa. He was a moonshiner, until they gunned him down. This was back during Prohibition." The girl rattles on as if she's had no one to talk to for months. "That's how I came to live here. The Bishop brothers were moonshiners like Pappy and took me in when he died. Now I'm Aran's woman. Do you think we could still have a baby? Him being older like?"

My attention is on the men.

"Number twenty-three?" Beef snarls, looking up from his notebook. "Speak up, George. You got rocks in your mouth?"

"I said twenty-five!"

"Well, shout it out."

"Fuck you! It ain't easy pulling on a cow's ear while reading a metal clip."

"Do they always go on like this? The brothers?"

"Yeah. They're a quarrelsome bunch. You get used to it." Cora pulls the pack of Pall Malls out again and lights one, then pinches the wooden match head to be sure it's not hot before flipping it across the barn floor.

"So, you think I could still have a baby even if Aran's an old man?"

"How old is he? He looks fit."

"Forty-five."

"I would say yes. Does he want to be a father?"

The woman smiles shyly and blows smoke over her head so it won't get in my eyes. "Yes, he does. Is there anything special I should do?"

"Goddammit!" It's Earl, the bald one this time, the one who looks like Beef without hair. Things are getting tense, and there are still eight more cows to go. So far all the injection sites are negative.

I turn back to Cora. "Well, you want to eat a lot of healthy food, milk, meat, vegetables, corn bread, and beans. Then you want to have relations often." I don't know why I don't say *intercourse*. It's not like Cora is a church lady or something.

"Like every day?"

"No, three times a week would be fine. Also, don't drink moonshine."

"Not at all?" Cora asks.

"Women who drink too much alcohol have funny-looking offspring and they're not too smart."

"What *should* I drink?"

"Milk. It's good for your baby's bones and, also, the midwife says, raspberry tea. You can pick the leaves now if you can find a stand of berries, then put them in a tea ball or a little bag of gauze to steep in boiled water. Do you have a tea ball, one of those little metal things on a chain that you dip in your cup?"

"Aran will get me one." The woman's pale face lights up. "He loves me that much!"

"Last cow," yells Hester. He leans over her flank, studying the area that he'd shaved three days ago. "Blum," he calls. "What do you think?"

"Why the fuck are you asking him?" Beef complains. "You're the vet. He's just a walking vegetable." The whole group is tense because they know if there's one positive result the cow will be sent to the slaughterhouse and the rest of the herd quarantined for a month.

"The doc doesn't speak but that doesn't mean he's dumb." Daniel defends his friend with a jaw as tight as a steel bear trap. "He's given the Mantoux test to hundreds of soldiers at Walter Reed. This animal has a red spot that's almost five millimeters."

The barn is silent. Even the cattle have stopped mooing. Blum leans over and stares at the mark while we all hold our breath, and then shakes his head no, meaning it's not reactive.

"Woo-hoo!" the brothers crow, and throw their hats in the air.

"I'm getting cold. Are we almost done?" I stand and do a fake shiver, ready to get us out of the Bishops' barn before a real quarrel starts.

Daniel takes the hint. "I'll send the forms into the West Virginia Department of Agriculture. Clean bill of health for your herd, Aran. Congratulations, everyone! They look good."

"Thanks," says Earl.

"Sorry we gave you a hard time," offers Walter.

Beef just turns around and plods away. There's something familiar about that walk, a discouraged look, and I wonder if Beef is troubled by nightmares of explosions in trenches, men crying, and blood.

November 9, 1934

Working with Daniel is a comfort to me, and I wonder at the ease between us, an ease I haven't felt for a long time. We work for the most part in silence and that's part of it. I've been mute so long, my tongue is frozen in place, and words only come out when there is some kind of pressure.

At times, it seems to me, the loss of Priscilla and the death of the drug detail man on the same day were my undoing; one I thought I loved and one I knew I hated. The confluence of those feelings propelled me into such horror that I just shut the doors on life and went away. It's easy enough to do. Easier than suicide.

Tax Sale

It's a raw day as I head for the camp and I'm surprised as I pass Mrs. Stone's place to see a line of trucks and horse-drawn vehicles heading into her drive. Curious, I decide to follow them. At the gate there's a sign: FARM AUCTION. MOUNTAIN FEDERAL BANK.

Since my grocery deliveries have dried up, I haven't visited the old lady once in more than a month and now my heart freezes. How could I have let this happen? If I had been Patience, I would have raised holy hell about the gas company's harassment. I would have driven to Charleston and picketed on the steps of the State Capitol until I got justice, but now it's too late.

I park behind a cart with two mules and wander over to the barn where a crowd of fifty men has churned the grass into black mud. These neighbors, I think, are like vultures, here to take advantage of Mrs. Stone's weakness. I don't exactly know how these sales work, but I figure someone's about to get Mrs. Stone's property for a song, and it probably involves the gas company.

Near the barn door, the old lady stands next to the auctioneer, a stout fellow with a wide face, wearing glasses and a bow tie. She's dressed smartly in a gray coat with a gray lambswool collar. They consult a document laid out on an old wooden table. Standing over on the porch of the house is Sheriff Hardman and two suits from the bank. The sale begins when a man in a denim jacket brings out a nanny goat and two frolicking kids with droopy ears.

The auctioneer steps up on a podium. "We'll start this tax sale with the stock, then the machinery, then the land, and lastly the contents of the house. What am I offered for this good milker, a purebred Nubian that gives a gallon of milk a day and her two offspring, all in excellent health?

"Do I hear three dollars? Three dollars, now three, now three, will ya' give me three?" I'm surprised when the crowd stands silent and no one raises their hands. The auctioneer is confused and the bankers seem concerned.

"Okay now, gents. Loosen up. Let's try two. Two-dollar bid, now two, now two, will ya' give me two? Will you give me two, just two greenback bills?"

"Two bits," says Mrs. Stone in a little-girl voice.

"That's unheard of! Do I hear a dollar? One greenback dollar! Now one, now one. Will you give me one?" He goes on like this for five more minutes, but the wide gray sky just muffles his singsong. Finally . . .

"Call the sale!" someone yells, and the auctioneer, having no other bids, has to close.

"Sold for one quarter," he yells with disgust and knocks his gavel on the table. "Unbelievable! Why she's worth twenty times that much!"

Mrs. Stone hands the quarter to one of the suits, takes her animals back in the barn, and the sale goes on. Twenty goats all sold to Mrs. Stone for ten cents, or two bits, and each time her voice gets stronger.

I begin to understand that this auction is rigged. Not one of these neighbors plan to buy the old lady's farm; they're here to make sure no one else does.

The auctioneer leads the crowd to the farm machinery. "What

am I bid for this 1920 John Deere? It's a beauty. Not a speck of rust on her," he begins without spirit. "Do I hear twenty? Twenty greenback dollars. Now twenty. Now twenty. Who will give me twenty?" Again no one bids. "Do I hear ten?" The bankers rub their clean-shaven chins and wipe their spectacles. This sale isn't going as planned, and there's no way anyone is going to get the two hundred dollars in back taxes that someone has decided Mrs. Stone owes.

I look around the crowd, wondering who the oil and gas man might be and see One-Arm Wetsel, Mr. Hummingbird, and Charley Roote, the old veteran who was one of my grocery delivery customers, along with a dozen other familiar faces.

"Do I hear ten, ten, ten?" Dead silence. The auctioneer shakes his head and looks at the bankers. One of them shrugs. The John Deere goes to Mrs. Stone for three dollars.

I stay until the actual land comes up for sale, and for a minute I think the farm is lost. The auctioneer starts the bidding at two hundred dollars and is down to one hundred dollars when a man with slicked-back hair wearing a pin-striped suit exits a late-model Graham and walks toward the front. This is it, I think, the company making its move.

The oily-haired weasel starts to raise his hand to bid, but is immediately surrounded by farmers who, without even touching him, make their point clear. Mr. Hummingbird towers over him at almost seven feet tall, and Charley Roote strolls over and opens his jacket to display a pistol tucked into his belt.

"We don't think you really want to buy this farm, mister," Charley growls, boring into the fellow's eyes. "It wouldn't be healthy. We think you want to get right in that shiny auto and go back where you came from. Understand?"

The farm goes for five dollars, sold once again to Mrs. Stone. Thinking it over, I realize she's spent about twenty dollars in all, and now she's clear and free of the bankers, tax men, and the oil and gas company . . . at least for a while.

Penny Auction

By the time I get to White Rock I'm two hours late.

"About time you got here," Boodean chides me. "Lucky the brass had to go to Camp Laurel for a meeting. What happened, car trouble?"

"I'm sorry. Did I miss anything?"

"Nah. Just a bellyache and a boil. Then Lou Cross came in for some more of that salve you had made for his wart at the pharmacy. He says it's really working." Mrs. Ross holds out a cup of fresh coffee and I tell them about the farm auction, but no one is as excited about it as I am.

When I get home, I get a better reaction. Eager to narrate the story, I run up the stairs to tell Patience and she gets so worked up, Daniel has to tell her to calm down.

"This is great. This is great," she keeps saying. "The people are taking control! They're fighting back."

"I've never seen anything like it," I continue, enjoying her enthusiasm. "The farmers stood up to the bank, and Mrs. Stone got her land back. Then they chased the oil and gas man off the property. The auctioneer didn't even bother to sell the household contents, because by then he knew they were beaten. The whole thing must have been fixed by someone. . . ."

Daniel, who reads the paper religiously, enlightens us. "I've heard about these sales in the *Times*. They're called penny auctions and started in the Midwest. Nationwide, they estimate, a quarter million farms have been foreclosed on, so the farmers are getting organized."

"But they don't have a union, do they?" That's Patience, always a union supporter.

"County agriculture societies seem to be the instigators," Daniel goes on. "Or sometimes they're spontaneous. However they happen, the locals bid ridiculously low and some won't bid at all. If an outsider or a land speculator shows up, things can get rough. There have even been a few deaths, though no one was charged. The banks walk away with a fraction of what's owed and the farmer gets his land back. This may be the first penny auction in Union County, but it won't be the last."

"After it was all over," I share with a smile, "I saw the old lady wave at Mr. Roote, so I think maybe he was the one who got the other farmers to show up. She was almost gay, and he was standing very tall."

25

November 25, 1934

Today I have been thinking about my life as a physician, and I'm not proud. I could enumerate my wrongdoings, each omission or co-mission seared on some twisted lobe of my brain, but the list is too long. I'll just tell you one event that sticks with me. There were so many. . .

Mary Proudfoot comes first to mind, the MacIntoshes' cook, an African queen. Back in 1930, when we still lived in Liberty, she was carried to my small clinic after her fall down the MacIntoshes' back stairs. I knew something was fishy, but chose to ignore it.

Mrs. Proudfoot, a highly respected colored woman, was as strong as an ox. At six foot tall she was my equal. How does a woman like that just fall down the stairs at one in the morning? And why was she fully dressed at that time of the night?

William MacIntosh, the coal baron, had brought her to me in his Oldsmobile. The man was upset, almost crying, and smelled strongly of booze. This was no surprise. Though it was still Prohibition, anyone could get liquor when he wanted.

The cook was unconscious, her pupils dilated and unequal, and she had bloody spinal fluid coming out of her nose, a sure sign of an intracranial bleed. I should have done *an immediate craniotomy, but I called the funeral wagon and sent her to Robinson, the Negro physician across town.*

Robinson was a good doctor, don't get me wrong, that wasn't the problem. He'd trained at Meharry, and we'd had many discussions sitting in the dark on his back porch, sipping his homemade apple wine and talking about new medications and different approaches to surgery, but Mary Proudfoot died on his operating table before he could perform the surgery. The delay in transfer cost the woman her life.

What kind of physician does that? And why? Was it laziness? Was it because of her color? Was it because everyone in town knew MacIntosh had lost his fortune and didn't have a red cent to pay me? Whatever the reason, I beg Mary's forgiveness and Robinson's too.

First Snow

Snow, like feathers, falling softly, down and down and down. "I hope the installers from the Mountain Farmers Telephone Co-op come today, although with this snow they might not," I worry out loud.

"I lived for a long time without a phone before I moved here." That's Patience, resting back on her pillows. She has good days and bad days and I never know what each will be. Lately she's taken to knitting little things for the new baby, tiny booties, a sweater, and this seems to cheer her, give her hope.

"But it would be so nice to know that you had a pedestal phone like Lilly's on the bedside table." I hold out a blue-and-white-flowered chipped teapot filled with hot water. "Raspberry tea?" She nods her head yes. We're eating breakfast up in her room off a wooden tray that I constructed myself and then painted with flowers.

"I hate leaving you alone today. Daniel and Blum are out on a call. We don't even know when they'll be back. What if you need something? Maybe I should quit my job."

"No, Becky. You can't quit. You've done a lot for us, just moving in. I'll be okay." Patience turns, smiling. "I love the snow."

"So do I. I grew up in the north country, Brattleboro, Vermont."

"I was raised in Deerfield, Illinois, near Chicago," Patience offers, and I realize how little we know about each other.

Then there's silence as we both stare out the window.

The roof of the barn is covered, the lawn, the meadows, the branches of every tree and shrub. And the snow is still coming. Up on the mountain, the fir and spruce are dark against the white. Here and there a golden oak that hasn't lost its leaves brightens the scene.

"So beautiful," Patience whispers. "You asked me about my previous births the other day. . . ."

"Don't talk about it if it makes you sad."

"It's okay. I think it's important that you know. You *are* my midwife." Here she gives me a sly smile, teasing, because she knows, unlike her, I'm a reluctant midwife.

"I've been pregnant four times. I abrupted my first when I was sixteen. I was an orphan and conceived unexpectedly with my love, Lawrence, an art student in Chicago.

"He was killed in a train wreck on his way to tell his parents that we wanted to marry. I read about it in the paper and lost the pregnancy a few days later. The baby was stillborn and, having plenty of breast milk and no other employment, I became a wet nurse."

I listen without comment, but my eyes widen thinking of so much sadness. *To lose your lover and your child in one week! How could she endure?*

"What happened to your parents? Couldn't you turn to someone in the family?"

"My only grandma died of consumption, a slow, lingering death, then my father, a first mate on a freighter, died in a storm on Lake Michigan, leaving my mother and me deep in debt. A few years later, when I was twelve, Mama died of TB. She hemorrhaged in her sleep and I found her in her bloody bed in the morning. That left me alone and that's how I got sent to an orphans' asylum in Chicago." She recounts all this as if describing the weather, a drought, a blizzard, a flood.

"Is this too much for you?" she asks, squeezing my hand. The midwife has noticed tears in my eyes.

"No, I'm just amazed. I had no idea you've had such a hard life."

Patience laughs. "We all have hard lives, Becky. Don't you know that? Sometimes you just have to take your wounded heart out, stitch it up, stuff it back in your chest, and go on. . . ." Here she pauses and I picture myself doing that. Stuffing my wounded heart back in my chest.

"Anyway," Patience continues after smoothing her hair. "I mourned deeply, but I was young and eventually fell in love again. This time, the man was a union organizer for the United Mine Workers in Pittsburgh, Ruben Gordesky. We married and were together seven wonderful years until he died in the Battle of Blair Mountain when he was only thirty-five, along with a couple of hundred other union men. I thought I'd never love again, then Daniel came along and we conceived our first time."

Here she gets a faraway look in her eyes. "We weren't married or even engaged and since I'd never had a baby with Ruben, I assumed I was barren. . . . It was just something that happened in the middle of a thunderstorm. Oh, that sounds so bad!" She smiles and raises her eyebrows.

"Here I was, trying to establish myself as a reputable professional and then I get pregnant and I'm not even married. I was distraught. The community would never accept me as a midwife.

I even thought of taking some herbs that would make the baby go away, but I decided I deserved to be happy. If I wanted a baby, I would have one, to hell with what people would think.

"Daniel found out I was expecting and we decided to marry. We had a date for the wedding and everything, invited the Maddocks and the Dreshers, one of Daniel's big clients. Well, the wedding came off, a quiet one in town with Judge Wade, on a snowy day like this, but I abrupted a second time months later, went into painful contractions out in the fields bringing in the hay. I should have known better. By the time I got to the house, the baby came out on the kitchen floor in a pool of blood. I named her Rosie, because she was so red, and I buried her behind the barn on Wild Rose Road with that other baby. You remember, the dead premature baby someone left in a carton at your clinic?"

I let my breath out and consider coming up with an excuse to get out of the room, but Patience needs to talk, so I hold my seat. When something traumatic happens to you, whether it's the loss of a limb, the loss of a lover, or the loss of a child, talking it through is part of healing.

"After that," she continues, "I thought for sure that I couldn't have children, but within six months I was pregnant again. This time, Daniel and I went to Torrington to the specialist and were told that I must have a blood disorder. He was pretty sure I would just keep losing babies and wanted me to have a termination and get sterilized.

"He told us it would be too hard on me emotionally and physically to keep losing a baby every year. In a way, I think he was right, but Danny Boy stuck and he was worth everything. So despite the bleeding with this pregnancy, I don't give up hope." She rolls over and puts her head in my lap and I stroke her hair. Outside the window, the snow falls and falls.

November 26, 1934

Reading about Patience's life in Becky's journal, I am stunned. Who could have known the difficulties she's lived through? I'm stunned and ashamed.

How is it that Patience could lead a life of so much pain and still be a beacon of hope, while the loss of my wife destroyed me? Am I really that weak?

The thing is, it wasn't just grief. There was the guilt, the overwhelming guilt. And it wasn't just her death. There was Teeleman, the drug rep. A double murder.

Thanksgiving

"I'll say the blessing," Daniel announces when our Thanksgiving feast is placed on a table next to Patience's bed. "Lord, we thank you for this bounty and for these friends. . . . Amen." It's a short prayer and we have a white tablecloth and candles that Patience insisted on. We have all dressed up; the men, even Danny, in long-sleeved shirts and ties and Patience and I in our second-best dresses.

Ordinarily, we begin our meal without preamble, and I'd thought Daniel was more like Blum, a skeptic when it came to God, but I guess I was wrong. Little Danny folds his hands, making a church and then a steeple, and there are tears in Patience's eyes as she looks at her rounding belly. Maybe she's saying a prayer for her unborn child. The fetus is now around twenty-eight weeks, too early yet, much too early.

Outside, the snow falls again, tiny white flakes and there are three inches on the ground, but it won't amount to much, which is good, because I have to go to work on Friday.

"Do you want to carve the ham?" Hester asks Blum. I'm always surprised when he treats the doctor as if he's normal, an intelligent companion who's just lost his voice, rather than a handicapped patient who has lost his mind.

Isaac takes the carving knife and slices the ham neatly with his nimble surgeon's hands. We also have fried trout from the river, home-canned green beans, mashed potatoes, and a pumpkin pie with whipped cream that I made myself with a recipe Patience gave me. All of the food is from our garden or the farm animals, except for the flour, sugar, and lard, and this pleases me, because, for the first time, I had a hand in growing it.

"Milk?" Patience asks pouring for everyone. I hold out my cup and am happy that I don't have to go to work at the CCC camp today. I worry about the boys when I'm away too long, but they have the day off too, so unless they get into some kind of shenanigans, at least there won't be any serious accidents.

I take in the room, the flickering candlelight on the faces of my friends. We don't have much, but for this day, this week, we have enough and we are safe in each other's care.

Winter

26

December 15, 1934

The day of Priscilla's accident did not start out well. When I kissed her at breakfast she turned away. It was just a husbandly kiss on the cheek, but it offended her somehow and she brushed me aside with a sour expression.

"What's wrong?"

"You smell bad," she said, and it hurt me. "And I'm sick of you, Isaac."

Priscilla was a very dramatic woman and said such things regularly.

"Sick to death of me?" I tried to jolly her out of her bad mood, but this time it didn't work.

"Sick enough to file for divorce," she announced.

I turned slowly to assess her expression. Though we'd had a few hard times in the past, divorce or separation had never come up before.

There was no twinkle in her eye, no smile. She stared at me with disgust, as if I were a fly in the honey. Then she leaned over and pulled a sheaf of papers out of the kitchen drawer. "Divorce Decree" it said on the top in fancy calligraphy and under that "Petition for Dissolution of a Marriage."

At first I just blinked, then I sat down and reached for her hand. "Darling, you can't mean this. I know our marriage *hasn't always been easy, but it's nothing you can throw away without talking."*

"Watch me!" she slashed back.

Christmas Past

Christmas approaches and I find myself sad. It's not that I'm more lonely than usual; in fact, quite the opposite. There's the Christmas party at the camp where Starvation MacFarland cooks up a big feed, and the men put on a skit of Charles Dickens's *A Christmas Carol*, with Loonie Tinkshell as Scrooge, and Boodean as the Ghost of Christmas Future, and upstairs, Patience and Danny are already making paper chains for the tree; it's just that I keep thinking of Christmas in Vermont.

When I was a child and my mother was alive, the holiday season was quite a to-do. Starting in mid-December, she and the cook, Ingrid, would begin baking cookies, some for us, but mostly for the church bazaar and various less advantaged families that mother had taken under her wing.

We decorated the doorway and the banister up the curved oak stairs with boughs of cedar and holly, then covered the ten-foot fir in the living room with colored glass bulbs, delicate carved ornaments from Russia, and the hand-blown icicles from England. Then there were the parties and finally the year-end Christmas service at the church. I miss singing the old carols.

Not since David died have I felt the same way. It's as if the little candles on the Christmas tree in the white Victorian on Elliot Street were blow out, but the flames still flicker behind my closed eyes, flicker yellow and white.

December 19, 1934

Today I cried, not a lot, and not loudly, just the kind of tears that spring to your eyes so suddenly, you don't have time to hold them back.

I'm addicted to reading Becky's journal, all her secrets, her self-doubts, her dread of childbirth, her work at the CCC camp, stories about Patience . . . and I feel guilty, of course, but not guilty enough to stop.

Lately, it's gotten so bad that I actually wait for Becky to leave and for Hester to go out to the barn or up to his wife, and then I step silently into her private space, pull her journal from beneath the mattress, and read what she's written the previous day.

It was when she talked about Christmas that tears came to my eyes. Becky has such a tender heart and I could picture her, a shy girl at Christmas, pale and backward. She's not so backward now, the nurse of a barrack full of young men at the CCC camp.

And another thing—I didn't know Becky could sing. I like to sing too, but no one has ever heard me, no one alive now anyway, not since the day Priscilla went into the river. Priscilla, the star at the top of my Christmas tree . . .

Christmas Eve

"Watch it, Blum." That's Daniel.

"Don't drop me," Patience squeals.

What in tarnation?

I fling open my bedroom door to find a strange procession. Daniel backs down the steps, gripping the legs of a wooden chair, which is tilted at a forty-five-degree angle. Patience sits on the chair like the Queen of Sheba, and Dr. Blum supports the back, followed by Danny who scoots down on his bottom.

"Be careful!" Patience laughs again, as if it's a big joke. She's dressed, bare-legged in a red silk kimono with dangling red cut-glass earrings that catch the light.

"What do you think you're doing?" I inquire.

"Patience wanted to come down to sing Christmas carols around the piano," Hester explains.

"I'll recline on the sofa. What's the difference, lying down here or lying up there? It's Christmas Eve."

"What if they drop you?" I roll my eyes.

The men groan, their faces red from the exertion, and when they reach the davenport, Patience, giggling like a schoolgirl, quickly slides over onto it.

If I didn't know better, I'd say the woman has had something to drink and I don't mean lemonade. Hester carries around that little flask. . . .

"There! Isn't this nice?" Daniel proclaims. "Blum, bring the cookies."

In the corner in a bucket is a six-foot newly cut spruce that the men brought in earlier this afternoon, and the room is filled with its fragrance. "Let's put the decorations on. Did you bring down the paper chains Danny and I made and the lights and the box of glass balls?" Patience asks.

I leave the room while they begin the process of putting on the ornaments and lights and return, after a major search, with the one decoration I've had with me all these years: a glass nutcracker on a golden string, made in Holland and brought to me by my soldier husband when he returned from the Great War. Isaac wires it near the top, next to a wooden angel that Patience says belonged to her old midwife teacher, Mrs. Kelly.

"Shall I dim the lights and plug in the tree? Everyone ready?" Daniel asks. Patience makes the sound of a drum roll while he reaches for the prong, and instantly the room is illuminated by the large red, blue, gold, and green bulbs. The midwife claps her hands like a little girl and hugs Danny, whose eyes are round with surprise. When I look over at Blum, he is looking at me, this time as if he actually sees me.

27

Caroling

"*O Christmas tree. O Christmas tree!*" Patience begins, and Daniel slides onto the piano bench to bang out the tune. I have never heard him play before and assumed that only Patience knew how. "*Your branches green delight us!*" We wing through the English version, then Daniel sings the German.

"*O Tannenbaum, O Tannenbaum, Wie true sind deine Blätter!*" My grandmother who came from the old country taught me," he explains, then reaches for an old hymnal and hands it to me. I draw a kitchen chair next to the sofa so that Patience and I can share. We all know the first verse and sometimes the second, but without the words in front of us we can't remember the rest.

Blum still stands next to the kitchen door and I squeeze past him to bring in another chair, and then lead him over so that if he wanted to, and I'm not saying he would, he could share the hymnal with us.

"How about 'Silent Night,'" Patience suggests. "*Silent night. Holy night. All is calm. All is bright*," we sing the old words. Patience looks up at me. "Thinking of the Virgin Mary, having a baby alone in the stable?"

I shrug and smile. Actually, I was thinking of my husband, David Myers, remembering our last Christmas together. I tried so hard to make it nice for him. . . .

"How about number 214?" Daniel asks. " 'Hark! The Herald Angels Sing.' . . . No, wait a minute. I've got something special on the stove." He returns with a tray of four mugs and a glass of sweet warm milk for Danny. "Rum toddies!" He passes them all around and this time I don't say a word about Dr. Blum not drinking alcohol.

"Daniel first seduced me with rum toddies. They're dangerous drinks. This was back when we first met. He came to my house on Wild Rose Road and brought cream and liquor. It was still during Prohibition and it was Christmas Eve." He grins his lopsided grin, she smiles, and I raise my eyebrows.

"*Nothing happened*. See you've shocked Becky," the vet jokes.

The music starts up again. "Hark! The Herald Angels Sing"; "The First Noel"; and then one I don't know, "I Heard the Bells on Christmas Day." For a minute there's silence, then finally I rise to give Patience a good night hug. My embrace is stiff, for I'm not much of a hugger. "Merry Christmas."

"Come here, you two." Daniel jumps off the piano bench and enfolds both Dr. Blum and me into his arms, squeezes so hard I hear the bells ringing.

"Me too. Me too!" Danny hollers until we open the three-person circle and let him in. Patience yawns and rubs her growing belly. "It's Christmas Eve, Danny. Come hang up your stocking and see if Saint Nick will bring you a present. I'll sleep down here and keep an eye out. Did we save old Mr. Claus a few cookies?" Danny runs upstairs to find a sock and, returning, hangs it over the back of a chair. Isaac brings in gingersnaps for Santa on a plate.

"Good night, all," I say again. "And off to bed, Dr. Blum! I'll brush your teeth in the kitchen. Thank you for a lovely evening, both of you." I stand and take the doctor's arm, then turn to look at the tree one more time. In its simplicity it's as beautiful as any we had in Vermont.

"You'll turn off the Christmas lights won't you?"

"Yes, *worrywart*." Patience smiles and I can't help but smile back.

She's probably right. I worry too much.

Silent Night

After I get Blum settled, I perform my ritual lock check. This is something the Hesters don't do, and since I sleep downstairs it seems only prudent. Before I latch the kitchen door, I open it and look out. The flurries have stopped and new snow covers every rock and stump, the fence rails, and branches. An almost full moon shines through the ragged clouds and I suck in air so cold it makes my lungs hurt.

Inside, I hear singing. Daniel has come back down to sit next to Patience, with only the Christmas lights on. The closeness between them makes me feel lonely. Will my life always be this way? I didn't used to mind and actually thought it was easier to be single, and maybe it is, but seeing them together makes me wonder.

When I'm fifty will I be alone on Christmas? I picture myself in an apartment in the city somewhere, maybe back in Washington D.C. or maybe Boston. . . . I attend a Christmas Eve service at the National Cathedral, then come back to my rooms, have a cup of tea, and go to bed. . . . No rum toddies, no caroling, no tree. Why would I bother? The bleakness makes me shiver.

Back in my room, I take off my clothes, fold them over the back of the rocker, and pull on my long flannel gown. "*Silent night. Holy night,*" Patience and Daniel sing. "*All is calm. All is bright.*" Upstairs I think I hear another voice. Could that be Dr. Blum? Such beauty. Such sadness. Such longing.

December 24, 1934

Tonight I sang to myself in bed. "Silent night. Holy night. All is calm. All is bright." Danny was asleep in his crib. Becky was downstairs in her bedroom and the Hesters were sitting in the dark parlor next to the lighted Christmas tree, crooning carol after carol in their sweet alto and baritone. I added my contribution in my rusty, unused voice, not that anyone heard me.

I was thinking about Becky and feeling just a little bit happy. I like it when she brushes my teeth. I could do it myself, but she doesn't know that. What a sensual thing. She holds my head under my chin and orders me in that brisk nurse voice to open my mouth, but her hands are gentle. Sometimes I close my eyes. Despite my wanting to lock myself in a cell of silence, the human touch seduces me.

Christmas Morning

"*O come all ye faithful,*" Daniel bellows at the top of his lungs as he bangs around in the kitchen. I lie in bed, waiting for the house to warm up, listening to him putter, first getting the fire going, and then putting the dogs out. Beyond my window, the snow is falling again, this time in hard little pellets. It's the first really big storm we've had and the Hesters say the lack of snow is bad for the soil. We need more moisture.

Oh, well, I'm awake anyway.

As I come out of my room dressed in gray slacks and a red cardigan sweater, little Danny bounces down the wooden stairs in his footie pajamas. "Did Santa come? Did he?"

"In here, honey." That's Patience. She still reclines on the sofa, where she spent the night. Behind Danny comes Dr. Blum, clunking along in his sock feet.

"Did Santa come?" Danny asks again.

"Looks like it." Hester laughs, pointing to the child's stocking with something bulging in the toe. Danny pulls out an orange that I got at the Bittmans' store on discount and a little bag of marbles.

Then he discovers a red metal wagon under the tree. In the wagon is a delightfully carved rabbit with wooden wheels and a pull string. There are also a couple of other wrapped presents, and I put my small offerings under the spruce branches along with the rest. Daniel reaches around behind the sofa and plugs in the lights again.

"Danny Boy, slow down," he hollers as the child runs through the kitchen pulling his new toy. "Bring the rabbit to your aunt Becky and show her what Uncle Isaac made for you."

"The doctor *made that*?" I knew he'd been carving little animals, but nothing so large or so fine.

"Great, isn't it? He's been working on it for a couple of weeks," Daniel praises his friend's work.

I stare at the toy and run my hands over the carving. The bunny even has whiskers made with small wires. His eyes are carved in detail with black buttons for pupils. I turn to Blum to see if he is watching, but he only stares at his hands.

It takes us an hour to open our presents and we pass them around and remark on each one. I remember the Christmas scramble at my parents' home in Brattleboro when I was a girl and my brothers were teenagers. We had a *mound* of packages under the big tree, but none were more appreciated than our few this morning.

Blum has even carved something for me, a small angel, each feather on her wings detailed with his knife blade. She's holding an infant in her arms.

"It's beautiful, Isaac. Thank you." He smiles and the room lights up. It's been so long since I've seen that wide grin. "I mean it. You're very talented. Thank you."

My gifts to the others are mostly hand-me-downs, a rose silk bed jacket I've had for ten years, but rarely used, for Patience. (She loves it.) A gray wool scarf for Dr. Blum that I bought at a church flea market in Liberty. I drape it around his neck and he surprises me when he reaches up and touches my hand. A bottle of ether for Daniel that I thought he could use for his animal surgery. This has been boxed in the back of the Pontiac since we left Virginia.

He grins and holds it up. "This stuff costs a fortune."

"It's from Dr. Blum and me together," I explain. "We don't have any use for it."

Finally, for Danny, a picture book that I illustrated myself, the story of the Tin Soldier. It's the first time I've used my watercolors since Dr. Blum got sick, and I sewed the pages together with twine.

Daniel and Patience must have exchanged gifts on Christmas Eve for she still has on the red crystal earrings and also under the tree are a stack of handmade white handkerchiefs, with Daniel's initials on them. Patience has also knitted socks for everyone, with yarn from old sweaters that she took apart.

The last gift is a parcel wrapped in brown paper and tied with a red ribbon for me. I open it, wondering what it could be, and am astounded to discover a soft, red velvet floor-length dress with a low, beaded neckline. My mouth falls open and a little noise comes out.

"Do you like it?" Patience asks. "If it doesn't fit, I still have time to make changes."

"Oh, where did you find it?" I rise and hold the dress up to my chest, letting the fabric flow. As it falls, I see that the red velvet is really two colors in panels, one a little darker than the other, but sewn together so they harmonize.

"I made it."

"You made it? How could you?"

"With a needle and thread and a pair of scissors," she says, laughing. "Out of two other flapper dresses my friend Nora left me. Her men friends often bought her clothes."

I've heard about this Nora, the protégée of Mrs. Kelly, the midwife and teacher from Pittsburgh. I say "protégée," but what I mean is lover.

There are more women like that than one would think. At Walter Reed I knew several nurses . . . and then at Vassar, a professor or two. Even in Brattleboro, the widows Mrs. Case and Mrs. Honeycutt were a known couple for twenty years, but no one ever talked about it.

"I can't wait to try it on. Now I will have to go to the ball for sure."

"You weren't thinking of getting out of it?" That's Daniel. "And breaking the poor captain's heart?"

I shrug sheepishly. (It *had* crossed my mind.)

"Come on," Daniel says, changing the subject. "One more gift. Out in the kitchen." We all rise, except Patience. Danny is hopping around and leads Isaac into the pantry where two rough white feed sacks cover something bulky on the floor.

"Go on, Blum," Daniel commands. "Unwrap it."

The doctor leans down and pulls off the cloth. Underneath is a strange metal contraption, a tool of some sort about three feet long with an electric cord.

"It's a lathe for woodworking," Daniel announces, all smiles. "You can make bowls and plates and spindles and canisters with it, and these are the chisels." He holds up a flat box of six sharp-looking instruments.

"We might even be able to sell some in Torrington where people have more money or we could swap for goods around here. I got the lathe for setting a broken leg on a Morgan filly."

"Do you really think he can handle such machinery?" I ask, nodding at the doctor. "It looks dangerous. A pocketknife is one thing, but this is massive."

"Weighs seventy pounds," says Daniels. "Had a hell of a time getting it in the house last night. Anyway, if he can drive, I think he can manage this."

"But he can't drive. Not since. . . ."

Daniel clears his throat.

"He can't drive, *can he?*"

"Just the tractor so far . . . I didn't mention it?"

December 26, 1934

Daniel spilled the beans and now Becky knows I can drive. What else does she know? Does she know about my fight with Priscilla the day she died?

It was at breakfast when Pris handed me the Petition for Dissolution of a Marriage.

"Just sign it," she said. "I want nothing else."

"Priscilla, can't we talk? What is it? Another lover?" I asked this only because I'd heard men say such words on stage, not because I had any real suspicion. Her silence gave me the answer.

"*You mean it? There's someone else. Sit. Please!*" I heaved myself onto the sofa and pulled her down with me. She turned away, stared out the window.

"*I met him in Charlottesville at the inn,*" she says in a monotone, not looking at me. "*You know I go to lunch there sometimes. He's everything you aren't—open, friendly, fun . . . and good in bed. You don't have a sensual bone in your body.*" (She stuck the knife in there.)

"*We started having lunch once a week; just friends at first, then we went to the movies . . .*" Here she trails off, letting me imagine the rest, the flirtation, the trysts in a hotel room. "*He's a traveling detailer for Eli Lilly. John Teeleman. You've met him. He's been to your office.*"

"*The hell he has! Why did he come there? To mock me while he screwed my wife?*"

"*Just sign the papers. We don't need a lawyer. I'm leaving with John for Baltimore tomorrow.*"

"*Priscilla. Pris. Listen to me. This isn't right. I have to be in the operating room at Martha Jefferson in an hour. I can't sign like this. We have to talk some more.*"

"*The papers will be here when you get home, but I won't.*" That's all she said, then she locked herself in the bathroom.

Three Legs just came over to me and leaned his head against my knee. Pris said I wasn't sensual, but it's not true. I ruffle the dog's yellow fur and put my face against his big lump of a head.

I touch all three dogs, and I often hold Danny on my lap at the table. I breathe in his little-boy smell, feel his blond hair under my chin.

28

December 29, 1934

This morning, early, I was called to the home of Zachary and Petunia Cole on Aurora Ridge. Since the weather had been bad, Daniel offered to drive me. I was much relieved by his presence, and thinking the birth might be fast, he took a nap on the sofa.

Two hours later a 7-pound, 10 ounce baby girl was born in a posterior presentation. Sunny side up, Patience calls it. Present were the father, the patient's mother, Olivia, and her sister Daisy.

On inspection, I was distressed to find a deep vaginal laceration, and in the kitchen discussed with the father the possibility of transporting his wife to the hospital in Torrington. (Just thinking of taking Petunia out in the weather, of separating her from her baby, made me cringe.)

In the end, the vet offered to do the sewing, and though I thought it might be embarrassing for Petunia, she was actually grateful not to have to make the hard trip through the snow. Hester showed me some things about approximating the layers of the tissue and muscles, and I think maybe I could do it myself if I ever have such a tear again, which, of course, I hope I won't.

Cinderella

"Can you tuck your hair behind your ear on one side?" Patience asks me. Danny is sitting on the bed leaning against his mother, enjoying the fashion show. He's wearing a navy blue sailor hat with a daisy on top. It's quite an outfit and I don't know what Daniel would think, but Patience loves it.

I stare at the midwife in the mirror. "What's wrong with my hair the way it is? Ida May did it just yesterday and said it was swell."

"It's fine. I just thought it might look more appealing."

"Patience! I don't want to look appealing. I'm a nurse and a representative of the White Rock CCC camp." For some reason this makes us both giggle. I laugh so hard I'm afraid I might pee. It must be my nerves.

"Pretty!" Danny says, getting off the bed and stroking the long velvet skirt.

It's a cold, windy evening, not quite dark yet, with just a sliver of sunset over the mountains. Daniel and Dr. Blum have gone out on call. Sheriff Hardman's favorite dog is whelping, and I'm upstairs in the Hesters' bedroom preparing for the winter ball. My heart does a flutter when I hear the sound of an auto coming up the drive.

"Oh, Patience. I don't want to go! I haven't been out on a date with a man for years."

"Stop it, Becky. You said yourself it's not a date, but a chance to see Mrs. Roosevelt."

I take a deep breath. She's right. I'm getting carried away. I grab my long burgundy wool coat and a crocheted peach scarf that Patience lent me and go downstairs to open the door before the man even knocks.

"Well, don't you look nice!" The captain stands on the porch in a black tuxedo with a silk collar and a black tie. I had been worried

I might be overdressed and am relieved to see that the form-fitting red velvet gown is just right. Without knowing why, I tuck a lock of my hair behind my right ear.

"Patience, my friend, made the dress for me. I'd introduce you, but she's in the family way and confined to bed for the rest of her term. Her husband, Dr. Hester, is a vet and is out on a call. . . . Have you been to the Hotel Torrington? I hear it's lovely."

I'm nervously prattling on as he takes my arm and leads me to a spotless older model dark blue Ford. He must never use it or he's spent most of the day polishing the chrome. "Nice auto, Captain."

"Please call me Norm." He starts the engine. "Had her a few years, but I keep her in the garage at the camp. Mostly I use one of the CCC trucks if I have to go somewhere. The boys at the motor pool washed and shined her for our outing."

It takes us almost three hours to get to Torrington. The roads aren't too bad, but there's a snowdrift on Hog Back Mountain and for a few minutes, as we slip and slide, I fear we're going to have to get out in our fancy clothes and shovel, but we make it through.

The captain tells me he grew up in Ohio, and for most of the way our conversation is entirely about the camp and the local area. I'm pleased that I can give him a little synopsis of the mining wars in West Virginia since it may help him understand some of the tension among the CCC boys. It still matters whose pappy stood with the UMWA and who fought the unions, tooth and nail.

He also was unaware that the state was split in its loyalties during the Civil War. More than sixty-five years later, half the citizens still think of themselves as Confederate and half are loyal to the Union.

At last we cross the iron bridge over the distant end of the Hope River and enter the small city, or what is called a city around here. The Torrington Hotel, the tallest building on River Street, is lighted up like a fairy castle, and when we pull under the canopy, the bellhop runs over, assists me getting out, and takes the car around back.

I slip my arm through the captain's, partly because he holds it out for me and partly because I'm shaking inside so much, I need someone to lean on. How did I get myself into this? I only accepted the invitation because I didn't want to hurt the poor man's feelings, and now I would give anything to be home reading Edna St. Vincent Millay.

The Ball

We enter a lobby carpeted in red and paneled from floor to ceiling in gleaming oak. A coat girl beckons us over and takes our wraps. To the right, a curved marble stairway leads to the next floor, and through glass doors at the end of the room we can hear an orchestra and a male vocalist doing a rendition of a Richard Rodgers tune, "Isn't It Romantic?"

At the open double doors we pause to get our bearings. Golden chandeliers hang from the ceiling and the area is ringed by small round tables covered with white tablecloths, each with a candle and floral arrangement.

A maître d' takes the invitation that the captain removes from his breast pocket and seats us at a small table near the front. Ten feet away is a raised platform with a long table and an American flag. I see now that the band is playing from the balcony and already some people are dancing.

"It's been a while since I've been to a larger town," the captain remarks, as he runs his hand over the scar on his right cheek. I resist an urge to ask how he was wounded.

"Me too. I feel a little awkward."

"You don't look it. You look beautiful."

I swallow hard. No one has called me beautiful in a very long time. "Thank you," is all I can think to say. "I wonder who will be sitting up front. At least we have good seats."

"Oh, I imagine someone like the mayor, the regional head of the Conservation Corps, maybe some other Washington politicians, and Mrs. Roosevelt."

"Do you really think she'll come? I mean she's so important."

A colored waiter pours water into our crystal water glasses and explains that dinner will be served a bit later, buffet style at the rear of the room, because they're still waiting for the guest of honor. "And yes, ma'am, Mrs. Roosevelt will be here! You can count on it. She loves this place, stays here all the time when she's doing her work for the miners. Knows us all by name."

"Thank you," Captain Wolfe murmurs as the maître d' stiffly beckons the chatty waiter away with a white-gloved hand.

"I thought the superintendent was going to be here with his wife?" I comment, looking around.

"He was supposed to be, but his wife wanted him to come home for the holidays. Between you and me, I don't think she likes this mountain life very much. Want to dance?"

The band begins "Stardust." "*And now the purple dusk of twilight time— Steals across the meadows of my heart . . .*" Already five couples have entered the floor. I let out a long sigh. I got myself into this, and you can't come to a ball without dancing.

The Queen

Captain Wolfe leads me onto the oak parquet floor with his hand on my back and accidentally touches my bare skin, but moves down to the velvet respectfully. For a man with a limp he's not a bad dancer; in fact he's quite graceful. Just as we're returning to our table, there's a rustle near the double doors in the rear and a parade of dignitaries marches in, led by an imposing gray-haired gentleman. The band switches to a rousing version of "The Stars and Stripes Forever" and everyone stands.

"Governor Kump," Captain Wolfe whispers. Behind him, arm and arm with another woman is none other than Eleanor Roosevelt! Almost six feet tall and looking like a queen, she passes our table wearing a long flowered dress with a three-foot string of pearls around her neck, probably real. Her hair is held back in an old-fashioned style and she has a little overbite, and from the light in her eyes she strikes me as an intelligent woman, full of curiosity.

Her companion is tall too with short dark hair and an aquiline nose. She's wearing a plain black dress with no ornament except a golden brooch, and her movements are fluid and athletic. This must be Lorena Hickok, Mrs. Roosevelt's special friend, the one people whisper about.

Following the First Lady and Lorena is a bald man in a white jacket with a red cummerbund escorting a platinum blonde wearing a sleeveless silver gown and silver high heels. The blonde illuminates the room like the sun splitting through clouds, and from a distance she's a ringer for Mrs. Priscilla Blum, the doc's wife.

The patriotic tune stops, the band switches to a quiet waltz, and everyone sits down except the people at the back tables, who are now escorted to the buffet. Waiters serve the guests of honor and I study them as they eat.

Mrs. Roosevelt interests me the most and I can't keep my eyes off her as she focuses her attention on each individual at her table, as if he or she were the only person present in the huge hall. Lorena stares at the crowd. No shyness there. She looks right at us and catches my eye.

What is she thinking? Does she mock us, we small-town folk?

But then I remember, she's the journalist and social worker from Wisconsin who encouraged Mrs. Roosevelt to champion the cause of the impoverished coal miners of Scotts Run. She's the driving force for the completion of Arthurdale, a woman of commitment and compassion.

"Can I get you a glass of champagne while we wait for our food?" Captain Wolfe interrupts my thoughts. "There's a bar in the back."

"Oh, yes, thank you," I murmur, turning from the celebrities.

"How's the dinner line look?"

"About like the line at the chow house at White Rock." He heads for the bar and I again make note of his rugged handsomeness. You hardly notice the limp, and even in his tux you can tell by his tanned skin that he's an outdoorsman.

Twenty minutes later, when our turn to visit the buffet finally comes, I'm feeling just a little bit tipsy. Even before Prohibition I didn't drink much. Maybe a glass of wine before dinner on special occasions, but since David died there haven't been many occasions.

By the time we get back to our places, the governor is ringing a little bell, the chattering stops, and he introduces the First Lady. Mrs. Roosevelt puts her napkin on her chair and steps to the podium. Her voice is surprisingly high for a big woman, and she starts without preamble.

"We have come here tonight to celebrate the work of the Civilian Conservation Corps in the Mountain State and the beginning of Arthurdale, our miners' community. Could everyone involved in the state CCC camps please rise?" About a third of the audience stands, and my face turns scarlet as we receive applause.

"I imagine a great many of you could give this talk far better than I, because you have firsthand knowledge of the things you've had to do to get these programs running, but I, perhaps, am more conscious of the importance of the Civilian Conservation Corps in the history of our country. . . ."

She goes on to talk about Arthurdale and her mission of providing alternative employment for the out-of-work miners, but it's not the words I'm listening to. You cannot help but be inspired when the wife of the president of the United States says you are doing something important.

Mrs. Roosevelt ends her short talk with a bang: "President Roosevelt's Tree Army is marching from Oregon to Maine, from California to Florida, from West Virginia to Wisconsin to save our country from despair and you are part of it! We are all marching together from sea to shining sea!"

Here the band comes in with "America the Beautiful," as if it was planned, and we all stand up again. "*America! America!*" we sing. "*God shed His grace on thee. And crown thy good with brotherhood. From sea to shining sea.*"

Oh, how Patience would love this!

29

Drop into Darkness

Outside the glittering fairy castle, fog has turned to snow, big, wet flakes that drive down the brick streets and bore into our coats as we wait for the bellhop to bring around our car. The red canvas awning over the double oak doors rattles and Wolfe almost loses his hat.

Not six feet away from the canopy, a trio of bedraggled men in worn and patched clothes stands in the sleet wearing cardboard placards. Their thin faces are red from the cold and one man can't stop coughing. The signs around their necks tell their stories and, trying not to make eye contact, I read them while we wait.

FAMILY MAN, AGE 44, 5 CHILDREN. NEEDS A DECENT JOB, NOT HANDOUTS. EMPLOYED IN WHEELING AT THE IRONWORKS 14 YEARS.

VETERAN, 47, ACCOUNTANT AND SHIPPING MANAGER. MUST FIND WORK.

SKILLED CARPENTER. AGE 50. WILL WORK ANYWHERE. HAVE TOOLS. SICK WIFE AT HOME."

How humiliating for these proud men to stand here. How desperate they must be to do this in front of those they see as rich and advantaged.

Across the street I notice a canteen with a hand-painted sign over the window: FREE SOUP, COFFEE, AND DONUTS FOR THE UN-EMPLOYED. OPEN 24 HOURS.

A line of about twenty stands outside in the snow. These three must have come from that food line when they heard of the fancy ball going on inside the hotel. Whether it's a demonstration or a sincere effort to catch the eye of someone who can actually help, it's hard to tell.

I steel my jaw and let out a breath. In a way I am angry. How dare they ruin our sparkling evening! On the other hand, I feel like crying. What terrible times we live in. . . . The newspapers tell us the economy is getting better, but these men show us it's not improving nearly fast enough.

I only hope Mrs. Roosevelt doesn't have to walk by the trio. She is so idealistic, with her "sea to shining sea" speech. The sight of the men would bruise her.

The bellhop appears with Captain Wolfe's Ford. He gets out of the auto, bows low, and opens the door for me, but I have to brush by the unemployed men to get in. They smell of cigarettes and bodies that need washing.

"Sorry about that, Becky." Norman breaks the long silence as we cross the iron bridge and head back toward Liberty. (We are on a first-name basis now.) "I hated for you to see that, a bad ending to a lovely evening."

Yes, we are all sorry—the bellhop, Captain Wolfe, and I—but what can we do? It's the failure of runaway capitalism.

My own thoughts shock me. I sound like Patience Murphy and I remember back in '28, even before the Crash, how Dr. Blum carried on about what he called *too easy credit*. It's ironic that the only thing he didn't pay cash for was his house and we saw what happened there—he lost it.

The snow is heavier as we head up the mountains, and the dark closes around us. No other vehicles are on the road, but I'm strangely unworried. There's something about Captain Wolfe that inspires confidence, as if his hands on the steering wheel translate to safety.

"I was thinking about the men and their signs," I say, breaking the silence. "Do you think they were really looking for work or just wanted to make a point?"

"They could find work if they wanted to."

"Do you think so? It shocked me, really. In Union County we see the traveling families with all their possessions strapped to their trucks, the hoboes camping down by the Hope River, and the men waiting for work in front of the courthouse, but they don't seem truly hungry. Those men did.

"At least out in the country there's a way to get food," I continue. "There's trout in the river, berries to pick, wild greens in the fields, deer in the woods, and the opportunity to plant a garden if you have a little plot of land."

"Survival of the fittest," Captain Wolfe says. "It's each man for himself and his family. That's why I like the CCC camps. Those boys want to work and they are willing to work hard, but the bums outside the hotel are just looking for handouts."

"But they're too old for the camps, in their forties and fifties. What do fellows like that do?"

"There's the Public Works Administration. They're building a new highway in Pennsylvania."

"But everyone can't get work with the relief programs. I've heard unemployment in West Virginia is over fifty percent . . . in a few counties, eighty."

"Survival of the fittest," Captain Wolfe says again, and then we are silent until we pass through Liberty and cross back over the Hope, where we can see the tents that are pitched in the shelter of the stone bridge. Men are huddled around campfires in the snow and mud. . . .

"The roads are bad. Do you think you should stay the night at the Hesters' house and go home in the morning? You'd be welcome, I'm sure, but all we have is a sofa."

"No, I'll be fine. It's clearing up."

We slip sideways on Salt Lick as we plow through a drift, but finally make it home. As he walks me to the door an awkwardness closes around us.

"Well, I had a lovely time." I thank my escort as I stand shivering on the walk and I'm surprised when he takes my hand.

"You're a beautiful woman," Captain Wolfe says. "Perhaps just a little too soft-hearted. . . ." When he smiles, his white teeth gleam in the porch light.

Norman pulls me to him, holds me against his chest, and I think I could rest there forever. Comfort. Safety. "You are a beautiful woman," he says again.

When the low clouds open, the half-moon breaks out and illuminates the white world, a world of light and promise.

January 1, 1935

There's something I don't like about this man, Wolfe. "Captain Wolfe" Becky calls him. I watch the two of them from my dark bedroom upstairs, watch them stand in the snow after their return from the ball. She's shivering in her thin wool coat and he takes her in his arms, holds her in the moonlight for a full two minutes.

Becky is too innocent. And I fear he will hurt her. Cut her tender heart open like an apple, and take a bite with his sharp teeth. When the captain walks away, I can hear his saber rattle against his injured knee.

Prison

It's New Year's Day and I think we all have the post-holiday slump. The house is quiet and there's a center of gloom around Patience's room. Each day I take her vital signs, listen to the baby's heartbeat, and measure with my fingers how much the fetus has grown. I record the amount of fetal movement, the amount of bleeding, and whether there are any contractions.

The baby is strong, but Patience is not. When I really look at her, I notice that her face is drawn. Her skin is too pale. Her arms are too thin.

"So? What did you do then?" Patience questions me. I have just told her about the unemployed men picketing outside the Hotel Torrington.

"What *could* I do? There was a line of vehicles waiting and more people coming out of the hotel. We had to get in the auto and leave."

"Well, you should have done *something*, at least given them a few coins?"

"Their signs said they didn't want handouts. They wanted *work*, decent jobs."

Patience let's out a sigh and rubs her face. "It's been so long since I've been anywhere but this bed, I forget how hard it is out there. So long as we have food and warmth, I think everyone else does."

"Where do you want me to put this?" I'm holding up the beautiful gown.

The midwife shrugs. "It's yours. Put it in your room." I can't tell if she's mad at me for not doing something to help the jobless men or just upset because *she* can't do anything.

"I'm sorry," she explains. "I've just got the blues again and I'm envious of you, going out to help people, going to births, going to dances, meeting Mrs. Roosevelt. I feel like the Count of Monte Cristo, locked away in a dungeon."

"I didn't exactly *meet* Mrs. Roosevelt. She just stopped at our table and thanked us for representing Camp White Rock. She shook our hands and moved on. She shook everyone's hand."

"I know. You told me."

Patience is lonely, discouraged, and bleeding again. Not a lot, just a little red on her pad. I look over at the calendar hanging on the wall next to her bed. On each numbered square, Patience has made an X, marking off the days like a prisoner. Now we face January—dark, cold, and lasting forever.

Sheriff Hardman

Captain Wolfe puts his dishes and silverware in the bin by the mess hall sink, then stops to chat with the cook, Starvation MacFarland. (I don't know how the man got his name; no one is starving here!) The captain laughs at something Starvation says, then turns to look out across the mess hall.

We haven't spent much time together or gone on another "date," but every few days he comes by the infirmary to ask me if everything is going okay or if I need any more supplies, and once on a dry, sunny day when the temperature rose above fifty and we weren't busy, he drove me up the back trail in a CCC truck to show me the wooden fire tower the men are building on top of White Rock Mountain.

I had never been up there before and the view of the mist and the mountains rolling on, ridge after ridge, took my breath away. Below us, the granite cliffs dropped two hundred feet, and in the distance steam rose from the ice-covered river.

Working on the tower above were eight young men, carrying timbers, balancing on scaffolding, hammering, sawing, bolting the wooden structure together. The fellows looked so small at the top, like little plastic soldiers.

"How high is it?" I asked.

"One hundred and fifty feet. It will be nearly one seventy when they finish the lookout cabin at the top. I'll take you up there someday when it's safe."

I wrinkle my nose. "Maybe not."

"Afraid of heights?" The captain laughs.

"Just a little."

"Miss Becky!" A voice breaks me out of my memoires. It's Mrs. Ross calling me in her high voice, as she stands just inside the mess hall door. She's wearing her winter coat and hat and I realize I've never seen her in the cafeteria before. She prefers to bring her own lunch and eat at her desk while listening to supervisor Milliken's big band records on his Victrola. The minute we return, she turns off the machine, as if it's her guilty secret. "Miss Becky!" she calls again looking around the mess hall.

"Over here!" Boodean yells and the short round woman rushes across the crowded room. By the look on her white face, I have no doubt something's wrong. Perhaps one of the boys has been injured.

"Oh, Nurse Myers! I hate to interrupt your meal, but Sheriff Hardman from Liberty is in the main office and needs to speak to you." All heads turn and the hall gets very quiet. Most of these young men have had hard lives and know that a summons from the sheriff is never a good thing.

Captain Wolfe strides over. "Is there a problem, Mrs. Ross?"

The poor lady is so upset she's shaking all over. "The sherriff wants Miss Becky, *now*. Says he tried to reach us on the two-way radio, but couldn't get through."

"I'm sure it's nothing," I reassure. "I'll be right over, Mrs. Ross."

"I'll come with you." That's Wolfe, the protector.

Outside, rain comes in from an angle and I pull my burgundy wool coat closer. The sheriff paces on the clinic porch. He takes a drag from his cigarette, blows out steam with the smoke, and tosses it into the snowbank.

"What's this about, Bill?" Wolfe starts out, and I'm surprised that the captain knows the lawman by name.

"There's a woman in labor and Daniel Hester, the vet, called and asked me to get Miss Myers," Hardman explains. "Can you come, Nurse? It's way out in Hazel Patch."

"A birth? A delivery?" Even in the chill, I begin to perspire.

"Yes." The sheriff looks at me funny, wondering what else it could be. "One of the colored ladies. The midwife told the vet that it's her second child and she expects a quick delivery."

"Go," says the captain. "Don't worry about your automobile. One of the boys from the motor pool and I will drive it out later."

"Let's hit it," says Hardman, opening the door of his squad car. I grab my nurse's bag out of the Pontiac and climb in with him.

"Oh, dear!" says Mrs. Ross, fanning away a hot flash.

30

Livia

"So, do you know what's going on?" I ask Sheriff Hardman as we skid out the CCC gate.

"Sorry, didn't get the details." He activates the flashing red lights on either side of the front doors, and then takes off on a small dirt road, a shortcut to Liberty. It isn't until we're within a mile of town that he turns on the siren and I feel like I'm a G-man on a Prohibition raid. In another half hour, we're following a rail fence into Hazel Patch.

This is the first time I've been to the Negro community, and as we wheel through the neighborhood, the siren blaring, small, tidy farmsteads fly by. Most have a barn and farm animals and enough oak and maple trees for a woodlot out back. There are goats and sheep, a few cows and even some horses, and it strikes me that this is what Mrs. Roosevelt is trying to create at Arthurdale, only the people have done it without government help.

At last we pull into a short drive and stop in front of a weathered clapboard house where a small dark man stands on the front porch waving. Apparently, he's expecting us, because he shows no surprise as a police car with red lights pulls into his yard.

"It's coming!" he shouts. "The baby's coming!"

With no time to thank the lawman, I grab my nurse's bag and run into the house where three colored women push me into the bedroom.

"The midwife's here. She's here!" they tell the very lean mother who half sits in bed, rhythmically swinging her head back and forth. She's gripping the white sheets, making a low noise in her throat, and an infant's head, with dark curly hair, shows at the opening of her vagina.

I take a deep breath. "Hello . . . I'm Nurse Myers the home health nurse. I'm sorry . . . the sheriff didn't give me your name."

"Mmmmmmm," the mother groans. The short man who was waiting on the porch and who I assume is the father makes a brief introduction.

"Sorry, I'm Homer Lewis and this is my wife, Livia. Now that you're here, I'm going to escape down to the Reverend's house. This is women's business." He kisses his wife and steps out in a hurry.

"Okay, Livia, one or two more pushes and the baby will be out. If you can blow through the next few pains, I'll have everything ready." What I'm thinking is, *this looks easy.* I don't even need to get vital signs or a fetal heartbeat. It will all be over in minutes.

"Ladies." I turn to the three birth attendants, a light brown wisp dressed in a yellow shift; a graying, almost black grandmotherly type; and the third, a coffee-colored girl who could be the laboring woman's sister. She has the same narrow face, high cheekbones, and almond eyes, and it suddenly strikes me that even though they are all called Negro, they're as different as a pale Norwegian, a swarthy Italian, and a red-faced Irishman.

"Ladies, this is what I want you to do. . . ." I give orders like the boss on a PWA road crew and within minutes we're set up and ready for the birth.

"Okay, Livia, time to push."

The laboring woman doesn't answer but growls with the next pain, the sound of a mother elephant calling her young.

There's timelessness when watching a labor and we slip into the stream. I check vital signs. I check the fetal heartbeat and all is well, but after another ten contractions I look at my watch. This isn't right. The head hasn't moved and it's been forty minutes. I need to take action, but what should I do?

"Livia, I want you to stop pushing for a few minutes." I turn toward the others. "A phone? Is there a telephone?"

"The closest one is at the Reverend's house. Reverend Miller," offers the gray-haired lady, her eyes big and round.

Damn! (A silent curse.)

"Okay, then, I need someone to run to the Millers' home and call Patience Hester, the midwife. Who can that be? Who will go?" The young woman in yellow raises her hand.

"Okay, what's your name?"

"Daisy."

"So, Daisy, here's what I want you to say. . . ."

She bundles up and takes off, a deer chased by a pack of hounds, slipping and sliding in the gray slush. Once she falls, but she looks back, grins, and keeps going. "Tell the Reverend a few prayers couldn't hurt," I call after her, but I don't think she hears.

It's only then that I notice the weather, low clouds boiling over the mountains and into the valley. Daisy runs into the wind.

The Midwife's Advice

Patience told me when you don't know what to do, wipe the mother's face, so I return to the bedside with a cup of sweet, hot tea, reach for a cool rag, and follow my friend's advice. Livia's eyes flutter open and with my little finger I moisten her chapped lips.

"How much longer, midwife?" she asks me. (*Midwife!* I feel like an imposter.)

"I want you to rest another twenty minutes, then we'll start pushing again."

"Is my baby too big?"

I lean across the bed to palpate the uterus. "I don't think so. About six pounds."

"My other one was seven." We look at each other.

Only a few weeks ago, Patience talked to me about obstructed labor. "While you sit on your hands," she advised, "try to think what could be wrong. Are the contractions too weak? Then strengthen them. Is the mother too tired? Try to get her to rest. Is the baby in a bad position? Correct it."

I run over these options while I check the fetal heart rate, then look at my watch again. *Where is Daisy? I hope she understands the importance of bringing the midwife's message back as fast as she can.*

To fill the time, I do something I've never done before. I brush Livia's dark hair between contractions. She lets out her breath and sinks back on the pillows.

"Thank you, Miss Becky. Why is it you have to go through labor to be treated like a queen?"

"You *are* a queen. I've never met a woman who was so brave."

"I'm scared. All I can do is pray. My body is one solid prayer for my baby." She starts to contract again just as a horse with two riders gallops up to the house.

"Did you get her on the phone?" I meet Daisy on the porch, impatient to hear.

"I talked to the vet, who ran upstairs and talked to his wife, then came back with her message. The midwife says, '*If you can't shift the baby, shift the woman.*'"

"What?"

"If you can't shift the baby, shift the woman." The girl takes a few more deep breaths and looks right at me. "That's what her husband reported. He said those are her exact words, *'If you can't shift the baby, shift the woman.'* "

"That's all? That's all she said?" I reenter the house, shaking my head. Outside the window, a few snowflakes drift down.

"Shift the woman!" Grandma repeats with a toothy grin. "You know. Shake her up. Get her moving."

The Power of Snowflakes

I decide to trust Patience.

"Livia." I kneel down by the bed. "How are you holding up?"

"I can't do this much longer."

"Well, you aren't going to have to. The midwife sent word that we must get you moving. We'll try different positions, and if that doesn't bring the baby, we'll head to the hospital in Torrington." There's a hush in the room.

"Oh, no! We can't go there." Livia begins to cry. "You don't know what it's like. The colored hospital is down in the basement. Old people go there to die, but only if they have no kin. I can't go there! *I won't.* I'd rather die here, where people care about me."

I am struck dumb by Livia's words. No one is going to *die*! Not if I have anything to say about it.

The first thing we try is walking. I thought this might be too un-comfortable, with the top of the baby's head sticking out, but strangely it's not. When Livia gets up, she actually feels better and she tells us her back pain is gone. I have her push standing, with my hands positioned under the baby's head. We try squatting. We try hands and knees. Still no change.

Outside it's getting dark and has begun to snow hard, big wet flakes that slash against the house and cover the west side of the trees. From far away there's the sound of a vehicle gunning through the thick white.

Daisy lights a kerosene lantern, sticks her head out the bedroom door, and says something to the people who've just arrived, but I pick up only a few sentences. "She wants to take her to the colored ward in Torrington. You have to make her understand, that just isn't going to happen."

I shake my head, let out a long sigh, and keep going. A few minutes later the familiar words of the Lord's Prayer come through the wall. (I'd told Daisy to tell the preacher that a few prayers couldn't hurt. They must have formed a vigil.) Then both male and female voices break out with, "Onward Christian Soldiers," a strange choice I think to serenade a woman in labor, but it actually gives us strength.

> *"Onward Christian soldiers, marching as to war,*
> *With the cross of Jesus, going on before."*

Livia's face and whole beautiful brown pregnant body are now slick with sweat as she pushes and pushes with no results. The rest of the women are working hard too, so I open the bedroom window a few inches to cool us.

"Oh, can you smell it? Can you smell the snow?" Livia exclaims turning her head toward the fresh air. "I want to go outside!" She looks around for her slippers and Daisy finds them for her as if this was the most natural thing in the world, but I'm horrified.

"Oh, I don't think so! The snow is really coming down."

"I know. That's why I want to go out there. I need to feel it on my skin, on my arms and face. I need to feel something different than the pain between my legs."

I stand in front of her to block the way. "It really can't be recommended. Women in labor never go outside, certainly not in the snow. You might catch pneumonia. Now how would that be when you have a new baby?"

Livia isn't listening. She's moving toward the door with determination, and if I don't move, she may plow me over.

"Can't you stop her?" I plead with the others. Daisy shrugs and throws a man's plaid bathrobe over Livia's shoulders. As I follow the little band through the parlor, I see who's been singing.

It's the Reverend and Mildred Miller; Homer, the father; the horseman; and three other ladies kneeling in front of the sofa. Cypress, the grandma, breaks from the birthing team to join the prayer group, but I grab my worn wool coat and the rest of us press onward.

Outside, the temperature is not as cold as I'd thought, but the snow swirls around us like feathers. Then it occurs to me: what if by some miracle, the baby starts to come? I run back inside for a blanket, not that it's likely to happen, but I'd rather be prepared.

Livia heads toward the split cedar fence with Daisy and Georgia, the three looking up as if they've never seen snowflakes before. The mother-to-be stops, reaches out to touch the inch of white on the rail, takes some and washes her face. She bends her head down and licks it with her tongue. The others, laughing, follow her example. It looks so fun, I'd like to do it myself, but someone has to be sensible.

Livia takes off her robe and steam rises up as the snowflakes fall on her hot body. She puts one foot up on the lower fence rail and leans back to catch the feathers in her mouth and that's when it happens.

"Ugggggh," she groans, as if she were the earth pushing a whole tree out of the ground. "Uggggggg!"

Both young women turn toward me, mouths open. "Get her back in. Get her in!"

We make it as far as the living room. Here, Cypress throws a quilt on the floor. Mrs. Miller puts a pillow under Livia's head and I catch a healthy male child, already crying.

The preacher, Homer, and the horseman, who I later realize is Nate Bowlin, the guy who helped the preacher bring us some wood, stand in the corner, faces turned away, murmuring a prayer.

"Thank you, Lord Jesus!" says Cypress, taking the infant and wrapping it in a kitchen towel. "If you can't shift the baby, shift the mother!"

The third stage of labor is a blur. I deliver the afterbirth, cut the cord, get Livia back in bed, and examine both the mother and baby. Then, while everyone celebrates with apple cider and sandwiches that Mildred has brought from her house, I slip out into the dark yard and walk toward the fence. Tiny flakes tickle my face as I look into the gray sky and let the tears come.

I have lived under the presumption that there is great pain in this life and you must move carefully or you will get hurt, but I see today that sometimes pain brings great joy, like labor contractions bring us the baby.

I walk over to the fence, lean forward, and lick snow off the cedar rail. And the joy makes up for it all.

January 8, 1935

Male infant, 6 pounds, 9 ounces, born to Livia and Homer Lewis of Hazel Patch. The labor was a hard one. I arrived and it seemed as if the birth would happen any minute—a crown of dark hair was already showing—but the mother pushed for two hours and still had no baby.

Embarrassed to have to do it, I asked one of the support ladies to run through the snow to call Patience for advice and she brought back the strangest suggestion. "If you can't shift the baby, shift the mother." It was Livia's grandmother who interpreted the message. The midwife meant we had to try all kinds of positions until something changed.

I see now the wisdom in that. If I were with Dr. Blum and we had an obstructed labor he could just do a cesarean section and pull the baby out, but without a surgical option you have to be creative. The whole thing made me wonder how many of the cesareans we did were truly necessary if we had just let the woman out of bed and helped her to move and try different things.

In the end it was Livia who led the way. She insisted, despite my objection, on going out in the snow, and when she propped one foot up on the fence rail, something happened and the baby shot out.

There were a couple of minor tears near the top of the introitus, but they were superficial and didn't need stitching. Blood loss was heavy, 400 cc, but I didn't have to use Mrs. Potts's hemorrhage medicine. Present, besides Livia and her husband, were her support team, Grandma Cypress and women friends Daisy and Georgia. (The Reverend, Mrs. Miller, and several other church members prayed for us in the living room.)

We were promised another load of wood as payment and Cypress presented me with a handwoven sweet grass basket, half as big as a washtub, something she had learned to make from her aunties when she lived in Charleston, South Carolina. I left feeling exhausted but elated, as if I were carried on the wings of great love.

31

January 19, 1935

"Scalpel," Daniel orders, after shaving and then cleansing the bovine's side with betadine. He holds his right hand out and I, like a good surgical nurse, hand him the knife. We are standing in a dim barn just off Salt Lick a few miles past Horseshoe Run. Walter Pettigrew, the farmer, holds a kerosene lantern over his head. His neighbor, a bull of a man named Mr. Simple, holds the rope around the Jersey's neck.

The vet talks as he works. "If you have to do a cesarean section on a cow, try to do it with the animal standing. If they go down on you, it's a lot more work and more dangerous too. For cattle, local anesthesia is sufficient."

"I would have called you sooner, Doc," Pettigrew interrupts, "but we ain't got much money and what I have I need to feed the kids. I thought maybe if I left her alone she could do it."

"I understand, Walt. Things are tough all over."

"Now watch this," Hester goes on. "I've cut through two layers of muscle with the scissors. . . . This is the hard part. . . ."

With his bare hand he reaches into the animal's body clear up to his armpit and struggles around. All I can say is, delivering a 90-pound calf is much harder than a human infant.

Thirty minutes later, our gear already stored in the trunk of the Ford, we're leaning against the back stall *as the cow and her baby get acquainted. The calf butts her mother's udders and latches on. Daniel laughs and nudges me with his elbow. "I love that. Never get tired of it."*

"So," asks Walter, clearing his throat. "What do I owe you?"

"Twenty dollars for the surgery."

"Whew! I ain't got that kind of cash, Dr. Hester. Things are pretty tight." The farmer rubs his face.

"I know," Daniel responds. "I figure this time, we did the surgery for the fun of it. What do you say, Blum?"

Daniel's kindness shames me. Why wasn't I like that when I used to practice medicine? It's not like I worshipped the Almighty Dollar; I just didn't want to be taken advantage of . . . that's how I was raised.

Now I see the other side of things. Being poor makes you more sympathetic to the poor.

Fall from Grace

The weather has cleared and it's unseasonably warm for February, almost balmy, so I'm in a good mood until, on the way into camp, I'm almost run over by a covered CCC truck speeding out the gate. Somebody ought to be reported for reckless driving, I think, but when I recognize Captain Wolfe at the wheel with Boodean at his side, I know there must be trouble.

Mrs. Ross stands on the porch of headquarters with her hand over her mouth staring up toward White Rock Ridge.

Normally when I arrive in the morning, the men have already been at work for several hours in the garage, the carpentry shop, the kitchen, the sawmill, the forge, the stables, or out in the woods. Today, clusters of corpsman stand in groups smoking, all looking toward the mountain.

"What is it?" I ask Mrs. Ross, hurrying up the porch steps.

"An accident."

"What sort of accident? I saw Captain Wolfe and Private Boodean speeding out of camp. They almost ran me off the road. Are they taking someone to the hospital? What happened?"

"We don't know yet. That fellow over there . . ." She points across the compound. "The one with red hair sitting on the bench with the superintendent came down with the report that someone fell from the tower. Someone fell."

Oh shit! I almost say, but I bite off my words before they jump from my tongue. "Did they take the stretcher? Should I try to go up there? I could get Private Trustler or someone from the motor pool to drive me."

"No. The captain said for you to stay here. They did take the stretcher, and he wants you to be ready."

Be ready. Be ready, I say to myself, but ready for what? I decide to pull out gauze and bandages in case there's a wound. I also lay out casting material to prepare for broken bones, and a bottle of laudanum, which I most likely will need, in either case. Then I go back out on the porch and pace.

Major Milliken comes over and salutes me. "Nurse Becky. I'm glad you're here."

"Who is it? What happened?"

"Don't know him. The kid who came down the mountain with the message is so upset, all I could get out of him was 'A fall! A terrible fall!' He gave me a name, though: Linus Boggs. Mean anything to you?"

"He's been a patient here." *The white-haired guy with the giant pecker!*

Five minutes later the sound of a vehicle speeding toward camp and honking its horn alerts us that the men are back. They screech to a stop in front of the infirmary.

Broken

"Nurse Becky," Boodean yells. "Probable fracture of the left arm, head injury, and contusion to the torso. Pupils equal and reactive. Patient semiconscious but in pain." His report is so organized and lucid he could be a physician in the emergency room of Massachusetts General.

"Bring him in. Boodean. Be gentle, there may be more injuries than are obvious."

Captain Wolfe, Boodean, and a few of the others slide the stretcher out of the truck.

"You'll have to fill out an injury form," the supervisor calls. "This won't look good. There's been too many damn injuries in the CCC camps lately. You'll have to fill out the DA128."

"I'll take care of it." That's my medic. Wolfe and Milliken stand back by the door.

"You know, gentlemen, I think Boodean and I will be fine now. As soon as I've made a full assessment I'll come out and let you know the extent of his injuries so we can decide whether to get the physician at Camp Laurel or head for the hospital in Torrington."

The two leave without comment and the room feels bigger.

"Mmmmmmm," moans the patient, his straight pale hair matted with blood. "What happened?" He's coming around and that's good. He can help me figure out the extent of his injuries.

"You're here in the infirmary at the CCC camp. Do you know your name, sir?"

"Sure, Linus Boggs from New Martinsburg, West Virginia. How'd I get here, what happened? I feel awful banged up . . . My arm! God, is it broke? And the back of my head? Hey, why'd you cut my shirt and trousers off, Boodean? Are you playing a joke on me?" He tries to sit up. "Oh, shit, that hurts."

"Lie back down, Private. I need to do a full examination. Just lie there and be quiet. Do you need some pain medication?"

"Couple of Bayer wouldn't hurt." The medic gets up and gets the man two aspirin and with shaking hands gives him a sip of water. Boodean seems strong, but he's just twenty years old, a kid, facing disaster and doing a great job.

"Okay, Boodean. I'm going to start my examination at the top and work toward the bottom. You make notes. First the head." I pull up Linus's eyelid and look at his very pale gray-blue iris, the color of the sky at dawn. "Pupils equal and reactive to light . . ." I feel his skull through the thick blond hair.

I move on down, checking both arms. I think I feel crepitus in his right forearm so I will probably set it. He can move both his legs and his reflexes are fine. I palpate his liver and kidneys and then his pelvis. That's all I know to do, and while Boodean cleans the blood off him and attends to the young man's scraped torso, I check his exam notes, add a few of my own, and then go out to Milliken's office.

"Is he okay?" Mrs. Ross asks.

"I think so."

Milliken and Captain Wolfe are sitting in the major's office smoking their pipes. "He has a broken arm but it's a closed fracture and not displaced, so a simple plaster cast should do it. Bruises will show by tomorrow.

"He needs to be observed, because he hit his head and we want to be sure there's no concussion. Right now he's lying in there talking to Boodean. He must have asked five times, 'What happened?' Short-term memory loss is common after trauma, but it's Dr. Crane's decision if he should be transferred. I guess we're ready to call him. Can you get him on the shortwave radio, Mrs. Ross?"

The physician from Camp Laurel asks the appropriate questions. "Is he stable?" "Is he conscious?" "Are there any signs of internal bleeding?" "What are his vital signs?" His voice is low and clipped, a Midwestern man.

"Well, if there's no change for the worse, I'll come over tomorrow and see the young man," he decides. "It's my regular day. Sounds like he's one lucky bastard and you are too, Major! No death report to fill out!" He chuckles like this is funny. "We had one here the other day. Hell of a thing, one of the lumber crew fell into the saw. Someone said he was drinking. He was dead before he got to the clinic."

Captain Wolfe catches my eye and lets out a long sigh. It's clear he thinks the physician is a jerk. I give him a small smile. After the adrenaline surge I'm exhausted, but I still have four hours of my shift to go and there are other sick men who need tending.

"Let me know if anything changes for the worse, Nurse Myers," Dr. Crane orders. "The medic should stay with him tonight. I wouldn't give him any laudanum. If the pain gets worse, I want to know at once." The physician signs off, "Over and out."

Starvation's bell rings at the mess hall. "Dinnertime," says Milliken as he pushes himself up with his pudgy hands. "Thank you, Miss Myers. Ready for some grub, Earl?"

"Would you like to join us, Becky?" the captain asks, using my first name. "You did a heck of a job in there."

"Thank you. I'll eat later. I still have to cast his arm. I'm just glad he's okay. The boy must have crashed into a pine tree or something that broke his fall; otherwise I don't know what would have happened." (Actually I *do* know what would have happened: he would have broken his neck and died.)

I slip back into the infirmary, tell Boodean what Dr. Crane said, and send him off to the mess hall. Since it's a clean break and the bones don't need to be repositioned, setting the limb isn't difficult.

I get out my plaster bandages, soak them in water in a white enamel bowl, and wrap the forearm from elbow to wrist until the limb is encased in a hard white sheath. Linus Boggs is almost asleep by the time I finish.

"How does that feel?" I ask him.

"Fine. Just fine." The young man yawns.

"Any dizziness? How's your headache?"

"Not too bad, Nursie. I just want to rest."

"Okay then, Linus." I let the *Nursie* pass. "I'll be right here."

The corpsman's respirations are deep and regular and his color is good. Once or twice he snores. When he tries to turn his head he moans in pain. That is one lucky fellow.

32

Hero of the Day

An hour later, Boodean returns. "I'm sorry it took me so long," he says. "The boys had a lot of questions. . . . Everything okay?"

"Fine. Did Starvation save me anything?"

"Of course! You're the hero of the day!"

Crossing the muddy yard, I notice the balmy air has turned chilly but it doesn't dampen my spirits. My training stood me well, and once I started the head-to-toe assessment, I knew just what to do.

As I enter the huge room, all the men stand and cheer, and I think about the warnings I got before I came to White Rock. There is nothing shady or rough about these fellows and I realize how fond of them I've become.

Wolfe is still sitting with Milliken at the officers' table and he beckons me over. In front of me is a plate of baked beans, white bread with butter, and collard greens.

"How's he doing?" Milliken asks.

"Fine. Sleeping now. Did you hear any more about the accident?"

Captain Wolfe shakes his head. "There were four men on the

tower, four on the ground. Nobody saw how it happened. Boggs was almost at the top, where they were constructing the cabin, and he must have slipped, maybe the wood was wet. He crashed down the ladder and through the scaffolding and then hit the ground. It's amazing he lived. The cook left some apple pie in the kitchen. Want some?"

"Sure," I say with my mouth full.

"*Nurse Becky!*" A carrot-headed corpsman waves frantically from the main double doors. I look up, trying to decide whether to swallow my pie or spit it out. "Come quick! Boodean says you have to come quick!"

Captain Wolfe and Major Milliken follow as I run across the compound, but I slam the infirmary door in their faces. Whatever's happened, a crowd of observers isn't going to help.

"What!" I ask, but I shouldn't have bothered. *Linus is seizing.* Mouth stretched wide, he looks like he's screaming but no sound comes out. His eyes are rolled back, showing the whites. His knees are drawn up and he keeps rubbing the left side of his head with his cast as if he's trying to pull off a vise.

There's no way I can get vital signs, nothing I can do but protect him from falling out of bed and hurting himself worse. Boodean is already trying to thrust a tongue blade, wrapped in gauze, crossways in his mouth, something he must have learned in his first-aid class.

"I didn't do anything, ma'am. I swear I didn't," he defends himself, his eyes wide with fear. "I took his vital signs like you said and wrote them on the clipboard. I was just settling down to read the camp newspaper, when Linus made an awful noise. He was holding his head like it was going to explode and then he fell back and started shaking all over."

The seizure lasts ten minutes and then Linus Boggs from New Martinsburg is dead.

Washing Death Off

It's dark by the time I cross the Hope River, and the campfires of the homeless under the bridge throw flickering light on the stonework. I'd stayed two hours after the boy expired, cleaned up his soiled underclothes, washed his body, and with Boodean's help wrapped him in a clean sheet for the undertaker. Then I finished my nurse's notes, filled out the death report, and called Dr. Crane on the shortwave radio.

"You did what you could," the physician said, trying to comfort me. "It wouldn't have mattered if I'd been there. Without a neurosurgeon and an operating room, he couldn't have been saved. Even if you had tried to get him to Torrington, that's a three-hour drive and he would have seized and expired in the truck. You did what you could," he said again. "I'll contact the next of kin." And that was the end of it.

Now I walk through the Hesters' side yard toward the house, carrying my little black medical bag. Daniel and Dr. Blum are waiting on the porch and don't say a word, not that the doctor ever says much.

"Do you want to talk about it?" Daniel asks, gently leading me inside. I shake my head no. "Mrs. Stenger called," he goes on. "She heard about the boy's death from Sheriff Hardman, who got the shortwave radio call and had to notify the mortuary. . . . Patience wants you upstairs. Can you take her some tea?"

This seems like an odd request, but ever the nurse, I carry the tray up to her room. The midwife is waiting for me.

"Sit here," she commands, patting the side of the bed. I haven't the strength to argue. "Did you eat?"

"I'm not hungry. . . . Oh, Patience. He shouldn't have died," I let loose the tears. "I went to lunch, so sure I'd done a good job and that he was going to be okay. I set his arm in a cast and everything. The physician at the other camp said his death was inevitable, that I wasn't to blame, but it shouldn't have happened. He was just a kid, really."

Patience pours hot water in a cup, but forgets the tea ball, and instead takes a cloth, dips it in the warm water, and wipes my face. Tenderly, she wipes my hands and neck. She pulls up my sweater and undoes my bra. She drops a long white flannel nightgown over my head, like I'm a child, and pulls me down on her bed.

"You can sleep here."

"I'll be better downstairs."

"No, you won't. You'll sleep with me. It's healing to lie next to someone after a great loss. Once I had a woman die in labor; she seized too. Eclampsia. I slept with Daniel that night. He washed the death off me."

There's no arguing with the midwife. We sleep together in her bed, both in our flannel gowns, Daniel politely taking the sofa.

In the night I dream of falling. Linus and I are falling from the tower. The earth is rushing toward my face, but Patience catches us.

February 27, 1935

I am worried about Becky. The death of the young man, Linus, has hit her hard and she's withdrawn and not herself. If a pan drops or little Danny makes a loud noise, her head jerks up as if expecting disaster. At meals her hands shake.

I have lost patients; every physician has. If you work in the medical field long enough, you will lose a patient whether you are a physician, nurse, midwife, or vet, but you can't blame yourself.

Easy to say and I say this now, but I blamed myself plenty after the pharmaceutical man expired. The thing is, I never should have operated on him. As soon as I heard his name, I should have thrown down my scalpel and insisted the nurse find another surgeon. The trouble was, he was in shock, and if I hadn't tried, he would have died anyway. That's what I tell myself now, but I doubted it then.

I watch Becky closely, worried the death of the corpsman will be too much for her and she will slip into the same black hole that I did after Priscilla and John Teeleman died. The sky is gray. The woods are gray. The snow is melting and dirty and gray.

Leicester Longwool

"I'm so glad you don't have to go to the CCC camp for a few days, Becky. It was nice of them to give you the time off. You need to rest," Patience says. We are all up in the Hesters' bedroom listening to her read a bedtime story from her Hans Christian Andersen book, and Danny, in his blue footie pajamas, is snuggled between his mother and father where he can see the pictures. Blum and I sit in the extra chairs.

Patience is right. I need the rest, but not just sleep. Since Linus's death, my confidence has gone and I find myself expecting disaster wherever I turn.

"Once upon a time, an old poet, a really nice and kind old poet, was sitting cozily by his potbellied stove eating apples . . ." The phone downstairs rings shrilly two times and a cold dread runs through me. *Not a birth. Not a birth.* After Linus's death, I feel so weak, as if all the courage has drained out of me. There's no way I could go out in the cold and face another mother alone.

Daniel groans, jumps off the bed, and stomps down the stairs to the telephone. "Hester here. . . . How long? . . . Okay. . . ." I can't hear what's said on the other end, but he clumps back upstairs. "Well, Blum . . . looks like we're needed."

"Oh, hon, do you have to go out?" Patience asks.

The vet shrugs. "It's one of Walter Schmidt's sheep, his prize ewe. You know him, hon. His wife died of pneumonia a couple of years ago and he's raising his boy and taking care of the farm alone. The ewe is carrying triplets. Huge. Why don't you come, Becky? It will be fun and it won't take long. Patience will be okay for a little while, won't you, babe?"

"That's okay. I'll stay and put Danny to bed," I offer.

"No, go," insists Patience. "It will do you good, after witnessing death, to witness new life. It will be healing. Danny's almost asleep already. Just take him to his crib, Daniel."

I've had an afternoon nap and everyone has been so kind to me, I have no good excuse to stay home, so thirty minutes later, Daniel, Dr. Blum, and I pull into a small farmyard on Elk Run. In the clearing, the lights of the Ford illuminate a henhouse, a barn, and a two-story log dwelling, and I'm surprised at the humble setting. When Hester mentioned the *prize ewe*, I'd assumed we'd be going to one of the bigger spreads.

The vet gets out his doctor's bag and hands it to Blum, then the two men head for the barn. I follow, unsure what my role will be.

"Hello!" Hester booms out. "Hello!"

A child wearing a woolen knit cap and a plaid wool jacket peeks out the double barn doors. Inside, there's a kerosene lantern hanging from a beam and in the center of the circle of yellow light a farmer kneels next to the biggest sheep I've ever seen, a strange creature with strings of long, curly wool hanging all over it.

"Is the lamb dead, Pa?" the little boy asks.

"No, watch. It's still wiggling." He turns toward the door.

"Hester, thank God you're here. Hated to call you at night, but this ewe is really suffering. She's the one I got at the auction last year, a Leicester Longwool. Can't afford to lose her. Been laboring now for five hours. I can't get her to stand on her feet and she's stopped straining, a bad sign."

"Have you been inside to feel around?"

"Yes, but only once. I remember what you told me when you came out to help with the foal last spring. A farmer should go in once and if he can't figure out what to do, *right then*, he should call the vet." He sits back on his haunches and smiles, and I notice one of his front teeth is missing. Except for that, he's a handsome man with a brown mustache who reminds me a little of Hemingway. "I know it will cost me an arm and a leg, but I can't find the head and there's three legs presenting."

Daniel throws his coat to me and hangs his hat on a post, then walks over and squats next to a bucket of steaming hot water and begins to scrub his hands and arms with a bar of lye soap. "These are my assistants, Dr. Blum and Nurse Myers. You know them?"

The farmer looks over, but the sheep is so exhausted she doesn't even lift her head. "Nice to meet you. I've heard you were back," he says this to Blum and then tips his hat to me. "Nurse Myers . . . This is Martha." He stokes his ewe's head and puts his forehead to hers.

Gopher

"I'll need the rope in the trunk, Becky. Can you get it, please?" Blum is now taking his turn soaping up. "Oh, and bring the old blanket."

Now I see what my role is. Gopher! *Go for this. Go for that.*

I push open the big doors and the little boy follows. "Can I help you?" He's a pleasant little fellow of about seven, who wears tiny spectacles and his voice is deeper than what you'd expect.

"What's your name?"

"Petey. Peter Schmidt, I mean."

I open the trunk of the Ford and feel around in the dark for the blanket. The ropes are harder to find. They turn out to be a bundle of cord and I hand this to Petey. As we reenter the barn, the doctors are waiting. The little boy hands the cord to Dr. Hester, who hands it to Blum. I shake out the old wool coverlet. "Here?"

"Little more toward her back side." The vet points with his boot as he rubs some lubricant on his right hand, all the way to his elbow, then lies down on his side on the old lap robe. With the three-foot-long cord, a slipknot at the end, he works his way into the ewe's vagina.

"Well, this is a *challenge!*" He smiles his crooked smile. "Good thing you called me. It's going to be tricky. The first thing I have to figure out is which lamb the legs belong to." I'm surprised when Petey comes over and leans up against me. Maybe he misses his ma, I think, imagining what it would be like to be the mother of such a child.

"Baaaaaa!" Martha cries. "Baaaaaaaaaaa!" She struggles to get up, but Blum and Mr. Schmidt hold her in place. The farmer whispers something into her ear to keep her calm. Other than her cries there's only the hiss of the Coleman and the snorting and footfalls of other larger animals in the dark recesses of the barn.

"Mmmmmmm," the vet moans. "She's straining against me. Trying to push my arm out. This is a real puzzle. Another rope please."

Blum fixes a loop at the end of another cord and hands it over. If I ever had any doubt that Isaac can understand, it's obvious that he does. He even anticipates what the vet will need next. Daniel screws his face up as the ewe tries to expel him. "Baaaaa!" She shakes her head and almost gets up.

"Let her," Daniel orders. "Let's see what happens." Blum and Schmidt back off as the sheep springs to her feet. Hester still holds the ends of the cords. "I've got them attached to two fetlocks that I *think* are from the same lamb, so let's hope I'm right. We'll let her strain again and see if we can help her."

I look at my watch. It's now ten P.M. Petey yawns, but Daniel's guess is right: the first lamb comes out with traction from the cords and the next two lambs follow without a problem. In a little more than thirty minutes, three miniature sheep are wobbling around in the straw, trying to get to their mother.

"By God, that was slick! Thanks for coming out, Hester!" the farmer expresses his appreciation. Then in a much quieter tone, "I can't pay you anything now, but you know I'm good for it." The vet doesn't show his disappointment, but hearing Patience talk, I know they have bills to pay too, the mortgage on the Hesters' large farm, for one.

"That's okay, I know how tight cash money is. You'll get it to me when you can, or we'll work out a trade."

Back in the Ford, we all sit up front, me sandwiched between the two men. I smile in the dark. Patience was right. I'm glad I came. Seeing a birth when I have no responsibility is uplifting. Linus is dead. He has left this earthly home for a new one, but three fuzzy new lambs are born. Life is a circle, renewing itself, one way or another.

It's almost midnight as we drive home and there's a light snow, big white flakes coming down from the west. Hypnotized, I watch them dance in the headlights. It's so peaceful; twice I fall asleep and when I wake I find my head on Blum's shoulder. The second time, his arm is around me.

Finally, we bump across the wooden bridge and into the yard.

"Better check the stock before bed," the vet says as he turns off the engine.

The minute Blum opens the passenger-side door I know something is wrong.

33

Red

What alarms me as I stand outside the Hesters' stone house is the sound of Danny crying from his dark bedroom upstairs while the light is still on in Patience's room. "I'll see what's going on." I enter the kitchen and take the stairs two at a time while the men head for the barn.

"Patience?"

"I'm sorry. I'm so sorry."

I push open the door. *What in heaven's name?* My first thought is that someone has spilled paint on the bed, but that's absurd. Patience is lying in a pool of her own blood, and the red spreads down the sheets to the floor.

Tears run down the midwife's white face and she speaks slowly as if drugged.

"I shouldn't have done it. . . . I was having bad stomach pains and thought it was because I was constipated so I convinced myself maybe I could have a bowel movement in the commode if I squatted and strained. When I got up, the blood came and I realized the pains weren't from being blocked up. Oh, Becky, I'm so scared!" She lets out a sob, just as Daniel enters.

"God in heaven!" His face turns gray. "Fucking hell. Fucking hell," he curses, looking around at all the red, as upset as the time we found him in the ditch saying he'd killed his wife. "Oh, Patience, honey." He collapses next to the bed, kneeling in the blood and taking his wife's face in his hands.

Blum now stands in the doorway wiping Danny's tears, but when he takes in the scene, he whips around so the child can't see. It's not easy to estimate the amount of blood when it's spread all over the place, but from all the surgeries I've assisted with, it looks like a couple of pints. The human body I remember contains eight to ten. If she loses much more, she'll go into shock.

I put my hand on her uterus. It's rock hard but there's a baby inside, so old Mrs. Potts's hemorrhage tincture can't help us. "Daniel, quit blubbering and let's find out what's going on. Can you take her blood pressure?" I fly downstairs, grab my medical kit, and return, flinging the cuff and stethoscope across the bed.

"Patience, listen to me. Take slow, deep breaths. I'll do a vaginal exam and see if we have time to get to Torrington." I'm surprised to hear myself speak with such authority. I almost sound like a midwife.

"Oh, Becky. The pain. It's here all the time and it just gets worse with contractions. I feel like I'm going to rip apart."

"I know, Patience." I suck in a big breath and blow out through my lips. "I know. But breathe. Breathe like this. In . . . Out . . . In . . . Out." I demonstrate and she copies while I sit down on a corner of the wet bed, warm with Patience's life fluid, and pull my red rubber gloves over my shaking hands.

Abruption

"Blood pressure, seventy-six over fifty. Pulse one twenty," Daniel spits out. He's quit crying and wipes his face and nose with a clean corner of the sheet.

I slide my fingers into Patience's vagina and another blossom of blood spurts out. Blum now stands at the door again, but without Danny. Somehow, he's gotten the child quieted and back in bed, probably gave him a cookie.

"I'm abrupting. I know I am. The placenta is shearing off," Patience whispers. "I've already lost two babies this way." Another twisting pain comes and she stops to get through it, sweat beading on her brow. The contractions are two minutes apart.

"Only four centimeters dilated," I report to the group.

"Shit," says Daniel. "I was hoping for eight or ten."

"Check our baby. Check the heartbeat." That's Patience. She's weak but still with us, the infant her chief concern.

"Do you think we can make it to Torrington?" Daniel turns to me. "The snow's really coming down now, but I could put chains on."

I take Dr. Blum's stethoscope, place the silver headpiece over my brow, and lean down to listen to the fetal heart rate. At first I hear nothing and hold up my hand to quiet the room. Then from underneath Patience's rapid pulse, I catch a slower *tick tick* and tap the air with my finger to show them the rate. Daniel looks at his watch.

"Eighty," he announces. "Too slow?" Patience starts crying again.

"Oh, save my baby, Becky. I'll push now! I can push! I don't care if my cervix rips." She sits up in bed and another half cup of blood spurts out of her.

"What's it supposed to be!" Daniel yells at me.

"One hundred and twenty to one hundred and sixty."

Patience begins to breathe as if she's been running, gulping for air. "Daniel, turn up the light. It's getting dark," she cries and then collapses back on the bed. He reaches over, his face almost as white as hers, and takes her pulse again.

"One eighty, maybe. I can barely feel it."

Shock

"Time to go," Hester says, pulling himself together. "We have to cut. We have to do a cesarean section. Here, Blum, give me a hand. We'll move Patience down to the kitchen. The bottle of ether is in the hall closet. Becky get the table ready and pull it away from the stove. Ether is flammable. Then build up the fire and put on a pot of water."

"Daddy?" It's little Danny calling from his room.

"Not now, honey. Go to sleep. Mommy's sick and we have to take care of her. Be a good little boy."

"Daniel, can you do this? Patience is your wife," I question. "Maybe I should do the surgery. I don't want to, but I think I could. I've seen the operation so many times. *She's your wife, Daniel.*"

"We don't have time to argue, Becky. She's going into shock. Just do as I say. How different can a woman be from a horse or a cow? I'm a veterinarian surgeon. *A surgeon.* The question is, can *you* do the anesthesia? That will be critical. Can you do the ether?"

"I have an anesthesia certificate from Walter Reed and I've done anesthesia for Dr. Blum." I whip around and fly down the stairs. (He's right! We don't have time to discuss things.)

Within minutes, I've laid out Blum's old surgical instruments, which fortunately were still wrapped in sterile cloth from a year ago. Patience is stretched out flat on the kitchen table and tied down with whatever we can find, apron strings, Daniel's and Blum's belts, and the long peach scarf that I wore to the ball.

It's important that Patience not be able to move when she enters the excitable phase of the ether administration. I take a paper cone and sprinkle the anesthetic on it, not too much and not too little. This is familiar territory to me and I know how many drops from experience. Patience is still unconscious and still losing blood, not cupfuls, but in a slow trickle. There's a trail of it down the stairs and across the oak floorboards.

Hester has scrubbed with soap and warm water from the reservoir on the side of the cookstove, and so has Dr. Blum, though god only knows what good he will be. Maybe Daniel plans to have him hold a retractor.

As soon as Patience is under, I nod to the doctors. Daniel stands with his scalpel above his wife's belly and I can see that he really has no idea where to cut, side to side or up and down.

"On a woman you start midline about three inches above the umbilicus and go straight through for another three toward the pubis," Blum shocks us with his unused voice, a rusty pulley in a well.

Daniel holds the scalpel out to him. "Please, man, I'm begging you. You do it. I know you can! Save my wife. Save our baby if it's not too late."

Patience moans and I give her a little more ether. "Daniel, cut! Or Blum! Someone cut now!" I command. "This baby can be out in five minutes." It's then that I see something I could never have imagined. Blum steps up and takes over. With one swift movement he slices through Patience's pale skin.

"Scissors," he commands, but I'm already holding them out. He snips through the abdominal muscles, then opens the tough peritoneum with his hands and the shiny pink womb lays exposed like a giant egg.

"Scalpel." Delicately, he makes a hole in the uterus. More blood clots and fluid spurt out, spilling over the sheet and onto the floor. Blum enlarges the hole, then dips his right hand deep into the Patience's body, feeling for the fetal head. He grapples this way and that, like a man digging for gold, but then changes course.

Daniel just stands there, but I'm already holding out a warmed baby blanket, waiting for an infant that I'm sure will be floppy, but pray will still be alive. Finally, Isaac gets ahold of the feet, delivers the infant as a breech, and plops the limp, bloody baby into my hands. It's over in only four minutes.

34

Raggedy Ann

It's funny how fast you can move if you have to. I hold the tiny infant against my chest and run for the parlor, where before we started the surgery I had built up the fire in the heater stove and laid a blanket and some supplies on the sofa. "Breathe, baby. Breathe." I talk to the tiny girl as I scoot across the slippery kitchen floor. Not only is she depressed from the anesthetic, but also weak and pale from blood loss, like a balloon that's lost air.

The first thing I do is place her on the flannel blanket, then I go to work. In the other room, I can hear Blum saying something to Daniel as he delivers the placenta and begins to quickly suture the uterus back together again.

I dry the infant and rub it all over. There's a pulse, but no reaction to stimulation, no startle, no cry. She just lays there, floppy as a Raggedy Ann doll. "Come on, baby. You are *not* going to die. I've had enough death for one week!" I try Patience's trick, the Breath of Life, and blow on the infant's umbilicus. Still nothing!

Finally, I take the Asepto, suction her airway, and place my mouth over hers. Three quick, light puffs as Patience once showed me. Not too hard—you can damage the delicate lungs. Three puffs and then wait five seconds and then try again. Finally, the baby lets out a cry. I am so grateful I cry with her.

"Okay, little one! Okay, baby. Keep breathing." I rub her thin skin all over with a dry towel as she turns from blue to pink, but her troubles aren't over. When I stop stimulating her, she stops breathing.

Now I know what we have to do. Keep touching her. Keep talking to her. I don't care how long it takes. I'll sit up all night if I have to.

"Becky? The baby?" That's Daniel calling from the kitchen, and I step back through the door.

"A little girl." I move closer to watch the end of the surgery. "She had trouble getting started and looks about three pounds, but has good muscle tone, good reflexes, and good color. Now we just have to keep her warm and keep stimulating her so she won't forget to breathe. How's Patience?" As I talk I keep patting the bottom of the little bundle in my arms.

"Weak, but she'll make it. Infection is what we'll have to worry about." The two doctors close Patience's skin, their four hands working together like dancers who've danced this dance before, the curved needles swooping back and forth across the midwife's alabaster body.

Dr. Hester clips the suture and holds the skin closed, Blum does the stitching, as slick and competent as I remember. Finally, they're done. They cleanse the skin one more time, then lay on two layers of cotton wool.

"Here, Daniel. Why don't you sit down by the stove and hold your baby? The anesthesia will be wearing off soon and we'll have to control Patience's pain with laudanum. Dr. Blum and I can finish the dressing."

I look at Patience so still and white, but I'm already thinking about her recovery. We must get fluids into her as soon as possible and then good food, chicken broth, and liver. What she needs is blood, but blood transfusions are still experimental, and even if they were available there's no hospital nearby that could give them.

Patience moans and flips her head back and forth. She twists her mouth around like she tastes something bad, but these are all good signs that she's coming around.

"Patience, it's Becky." I place my hands on each side of her face. "You're okay. You're okay, my friend. You're okay and so is the baby."

Daniel comes over with the newborn in his arms and pushes a wooden chair in close so he can sit down. There are tears streaming down his face and I'll admit, my face is wet too. He holds the baby a little higher, as the mother's eyes flutter open. "Look, my love. We did it. It's a miracle. She lives. Thank god! She lives."

Circle of Prayer

The crisis is over, but now the hard work begins. The first night, the three of us, Daniel, Blum, and I, sit up together as if prayer could keep the baby and mother alive. First, we transfer Patience to the sofa while she's still under the influence of the opium, and then we take turns rubbing cooking oil on the infant's skin and keeping her warm. If ever she turns blue or stops breathing we double our efforts. Only once do I have to breathe for her as I did right after her birth.

As we hold our vigil, I watch Dr. Blum, still shocked at how he returned to himself when we needed him. He doesn't say anything, just sits there, silent as usual, but he's present, and when I hand him the baby so that I can catch a few winks he takes her gently and begins the massage.

A quarter of the midwife's life fluid is on the bed upstairs and another quarter on the kitchen floor, so I'm determined not to let Patience lose any more and now I can be liberal with Mrs. Potts's hemorrhage tincture. I thought maybe Dr. Blum would ask me what's in it, but once the emergency was over he went back to his old silent self.

The main thing with Patience is to keep the uterus firm and to hydrate her. We start with the herbal mixture, blended with honey and warm water. Water. Water. Water. Tea and water. By morning she's still weak but alive and we begin with warm milk. Daniel goes out in the hall and telephones the Reverend in Hazel Patch.

Right after breakfast, the troops arrive, first Preacher Miller, quiet and serious, and his wife, Mildred, a bundle of energy. She throws off her long coat and rolls up the sleeves of her white blouse. She's even brought her own flowered apron.

"Oh, my. Oh, my," Mrs. Miller sighs. "You should have called us last night. We would have circled you with love the minute we heard. And Dr. Blum did the surgery? That's what you said? Praise Jesus, our prayers are working. You know we hold him in the light every Sunday. Just think, not even a year ago he was like a child." She's all smiles and gives the doctor a hug. He smiles too, but just barely and doesn't hug back.

"Now, honey, tell us what you want us to do. I can stay all day and all night, and there will be several others here as well. I suppose half of Liberty knows by now if the telephone operator is her usual self."

I give her the worst job. "We are all so tired, can you clean up the blood?" Mrs. Miller doesn't hesitate. While the preacher tends the stock and splits more firewood, she takes my red rubber gloves and a bucket of water and goes right to work, starting in the kitchen and then the stairs and then the Hesters' bedroom. By evening you wouldn't know that the tidy home had been the scene of a near tragedy.

"The baby?" Patience asks, and I know that she's back. Then she notices Danny standing next to her, patting her hand. "Oh, Danny. Mama's so glad to see you. I missed you."

"Uncle Isaac gives me cookies."

Dr. Blum rises from the rocker where he has been tenderly massaging the baby and holds her out to her mother, but when Patience reaches out, she drops back in pain.

"Don't sit up yet," I admonish. "Do you want to try to breast-feed? I can help you get started."

"For sure!" Patience smiles, and it's as if the sun has come out at the end of a long, rainy day.

February 28, 1935

When Patience abrupted, I was surprised I could still operate, but there wasn't much choice. "Please!" Hester begged. "Save my wife. Save our baby!" What else could I do? There's no way Daniel was able to do it. He was trembling all over and he didn't even know where to cut. I'm an asshole, but not a total asshole.

Surgeons have an unspoken rule that we do not operate on our loved ones . . . or our enemies. Emotions run too strong, cloud our judgment, and make our hands unsteady.

On the morning Priscilla told me she wanted a divorce I had thirty minutes to cool down before I got to Martha Jefferson, but I used it, instead, to fuel the fire.

Who was this John Teeleman from Eli Lilly? Even his name enraged me.

Drug detail men came and went in the office, and my brother and I gave strict orders to the staff to let them stay only ten minutes. I imagined Teeleman as affable, always ready with a laugh or a funny story, calling me by my first name as if we were pals. "So what do you think of our new elixir, Isaac, have you had a chance to prescribe it?"

Okay, I'll admit I was shaken to the core. My home and marriage had just exploded and lay in rubble at my feet. Was I really that bad of a husband?

Maybe I wasn't much fun. She had me there. When I wasn't practicing medicine, I was reading medical journals, playing solitaire, or sleeping, but a physician who works ten hours a day needs a little mindless relaxation, doesn't he? He needs his sleep too. . . . Okay, I was a selfish jerk.

Priscilla used to beg me to go into Charlottesville, to eat at a nice restaurant or see a picture show, but I was too tired, too edgy. I craved peace and quiet. Maybe I deserved to be dumped, but still she couldn't really mean it.

In the parking lot of the hospital, I pulled my collar up against the sleet, took a few deep breaths, and cut through the emergency room. A few minutes later, I walked into the OR as if all was routine.

Surgeons are trained to do this. Nothing must interfere with our concentration. Lives depend on it. If you can't pull the curtain down on your personal feelings you don't belong at the operating table.

35

Healing

Recovery has been slow, but this is not unexpected. Each person heals in his own way and in his own time. You can be supportive, but you can't make it happen.

It's more than one week since Patience delivered, and day by day she's getting stronger. We don't have to beg her to eat anymore; she knows what to do, and unlike before in the late months of her pregnancy, when she seemed to be fading away, she now has something to live for.

Patience is not allowed to do any work, not even to take care of Danny, only herself and the baby. Danny has had a few temper tantrums, but Blum handles them well, silently swooping the little boy over his shoulder and taking him out in yard.

The doctor has pretty much returned to his old silent self. He's fixed up a swing in one of the willow trees, and I realize, by looking at the new leaves on the willow, that we have been in West Virginia for almost a year. The long weeping willow branches are budding with yellow and the trees are bright balls of sunlight.

Most days, Patience just lies on the sofa listening to the radio, though the news isn't good. It's mainly about the nationwide drought, the devastation of the Midwest by wind and dirt, and the rising unemployment rate, now 25 percent nationwide, much worse in West Virginia, though in rural areas we can at least live off the land.

Patience likes Will Rogers's show out of Pittsburgh best. Will rambles on about politics and the common man, not quite a Red, but not a capitalist either. "The short memories of the American voters is what keeps our politicians in office," he said, and it made Patience laugh so hard I thought she might bust her stitches. Even Dr. Blum smiled.

After our midday meal, Patience sometimes gives the baby to Daniel and sits at the piano playing old show tunes. (She once was a chorus girl on the stage in Chicago, though it's hard to picture that now.) Then she goes upstairs, taking each step slowly, to nap with Danny and breastfeed the baby. No cooking. No cleaning. No gardening. No attending deliveries.

At first, because of the dehydration and blood loss, she had almost no milk, but she's determined to nurse and always feeds first from her breasts to build up her supply. Afterward we give the baby a bottle of Borden's canned formula mixed with Moonlight's milk.

Hester is concerned about the dangers of the tuberculosis bacterium, even though our cows have been tested, and he insists that his baby will have only top milk, heated to one hundred forty-five degrees for thirty minutes and later stored in the Frigidaire as the USDA recommends.

I, on the other hand, am concerned about the dangers of postpartum infection and check Patience's incision each day. She's a setup for septicemia, but so far, so good. Some angel must be watching over her.

At first I was worried that Patience might slip into mother depression. I've seen this before after a difficult delivery or sometimes for no reason at all. It happened to the Hamlin girl in town, five years ago. She tried to slit her wrists in the bathtub. Fortunately, Dr. Blum was able to save her, but she had to be taken to the State Lunatic Asylum in Weston and may still be there.

On warm days, I assist Patience in going out and sitting in the sun on the porch. Despite all science has to offer, fresh air and sunshine are still the best medicine.

They named the baby Mira because she was a miracle.

Return to Work

Today I returned to my job at the CCC camp. I'd called Sheriff Hardman and asked him to leave word with Supervisor Milliken, via shortwave radio, that I wouldn't be able to come in for two weeks because of a family emergency, but when I showed up, there was hell to pay.

"So *nice* of you to join us, Miss Myers," Captain Wolfe greets me, standing with his hands on his hips on the porch of the administration building. "What was the big emergency? Your *doctor* have a serious relapse of muteness?" Boodean and Mrs. Ross pretend not to listen.

"Can we speak in private?" I head for the infirmary and close the door behind him.

"What is your *problem*?"

"What is yours? I stood up for you, helped you get this job, and then you leave for two weeks!"

"I sent a message through the sheriff that we had a medical emergency. What did you expect me to do? Leave a critically ill mother and premature baby? I figured Boodean could cope with minor problems and the doctor from Laurel would cover both camps the same way he did before I was hired."

"Well, it wasn't that easy. Dr. Crane quit ten days ago and went back to Ohio. It's been a zoo around here. Four kids were almost killed in a truck accident and I've been going back and forth to the hospital in Torrington. I've been trying to help Private Boodean in the infirmary, doing my job and yours too. One night we had four men sleeping here. I had half a mind to come out and get you or just fire you right out, and I would have if I'd been in charge, but Milliken said to wait. There aren't many other nurses in Union County."

The captain can't stop himself. He goes on and on. "You signed on for this job. You have responsibilities. In the middle of everything, we've had an outbreak of mumps in the camp. This place is a mess. Look around. Do you think Boodean and I were coping?"

He's right. *The place is a mess.* Two extra cots crowd the small room, there's a pile of clean linen on a chair, and a pile of dirty linen on the floor in the corner. Bottles of medication and gauze cover the desk.

We glare at each other, neither wanting to be the first to look away, and silence thickens the air. I'm eager to get to work and clean the place up, but not while Wolfe is still standing here. His face is red and I imagine mine is too, a far cry from the night he told me after the ball in Torrington that I looked so beautiful.

Finally, there's a timid knock at the door.

It's Boodean. "We have our first patient, Nurse Myers." The captain spins on his heel and leaves without another word.

Within ten minutes after Wolfe's departure, Boodean and I have the extra cots collapsed and stored against the wall, the medications back on the shelves, and the dirty and clean linen put away, but I am still steamed.

What makes me feel so bad is that maybe Wolfe is right. Maybe I should have driven out here and told him personally what was going on. Maybe I *could* have come back to work sooner.

Fever and Chills

There isn't much time for further self-recriminations. Within five minutes Boodean escorts our first patient through the door.

It's Drake Trustler, aka Nick Rioli, the mobster's driver, and he looks terrible. His face is pale with dark circles under his eyes and he's lost so much weight his CCC uniform droops from his shoulders. I try to remember when I last saw him. It must have been before the camp Christmas party.

"Miss Myers." He gives a little military salute. "Glad to have you back. I haven't been feeling so well."

I take a seat behind the desk and my assistant picks up his clipboard.

"Do you think you're getting the mumps? I heard several of the men had it." (Mumps are quite serious for adult males and can make them go sterile.)

"Not likely. Me and my brothers had the mumps in 1919. We were awful sick. I remember because my pop had just gotten back from the war."

"Well, tell me what's wrong then. What are your symptoms? Does it involve your bowels? Are you able to eat?"

"Oh, nothing like that. I eat all I want and I keep it down. Don't *feel* much like eating though." He starts to cough and puts a blue kerchief to his mouth. "It's more like my chest hurts and I'm not sleeping well. I wake hot and then chill. I'm worried I've got pneumo."

Without even asking, Boodean gets out my thermometer and stethoscope. He shakes the glass rod vigorously and pops it in the patient's mouth before I have a chance to ask any more questions.

Two minutes later, as Boodean holds the glass tube up at eye level, his eyebrows go up. "One hundred and one degrees," he reads out loud.

"Is that high? What's it supposed to be, ninety or something?" Drake questions.

"Yes, it's a little high." I run my fingers down his neck looking for swollen glands and then lay the back of my hand on his forehead, feeling the heat. "You didn't have a cigarette on the way over, did you?"

"Nah, I never smoke. My father died of consumption, so none of us kids did."

"Can you take off your shirt?" The medic steps over to the wood stove, opens the damper, and throws in two logs to warm the room up.

The patient coughs again. When he stops, I place the bell of my stethoscope over his left upper chest and am startled to hear a familiar rattle. I listen again. Yes, it's still there, a rattle on the in breath and not only that, there's a high-pitched wheeze on the out breath too. "Can you cough harder? Clear your airway?"

"Yeah, I feel it, a squeaky door, every time I breathe." The man leans over, his elbows on his knees with the kerchief over his face and hacks a few times, but when I listen, the rattle's still there and so is the wheeze.

"You know, Drake. I think it's a good idea to keep you in the clinic overnight. It's probably warmer here than in the bunkhouse, and tomorrow I'm going to get Captain Wolfe or someone to take you down to the hospital in Torrington for a chest X-ray." Boodean gives me a strange look.

"Oh, no, Miss Myers! My mother told me never to get an X-ray!" Drake argues. "She knew a lady who got brain cancer that way. I'm sure I'll be better tomorrow. Just sleeping here will help. It *is* cold in the bunkhouse and in the garage I'm on the concrete floor under the trucks all the time."

"Drake, that's a common misconception about X-rays, but I'll consult with the captain and the supervisor to see what they think. . . . If you don't mind, why don't you sit in the reception area while we fix up your bed." I open the door to tell Mrs. Ross, but find the room empty.

The mechanic slowly pulls his uniform shirt on and then slowly buttons it.

"What was that roll of the eyes you gave me when I told Trustler he might need an X-ray? Do you disagree?" (The medic and I are readying the room for Drake's overnight stay.)

"You're the doc."

"Come clean, Boodean." My little rhyme makes us both laugh.

"Okay, the truth is, it cost White Rock Camp plenty when they had to send those four boys down to the hospital, the ones that were in the truck accident. If you'd been in the camp, it might have been avoided. The supervisor and captain won't take kindly to another medical expense, especially if it's really not necessary. Trustler looks like shit, pardon my language, but it's probably just the croup."

"You didn't listen to his lungs. I've heard sounds like that before."

"Like what?"

"Like pleural effusion."

He stares at me blankly.

"Fluid *outside* the lungs."

I step to the door of the waiting room. "Hey, Drake, do you want to go back to the bunkhouse to get your pajamas and whatever else you need?"

"Drake?"

The man has fainted and is slumped over in his chair.

"Drake!"

Blessing

"I may have to make a trip to Torrington on Monday," I tell Patience as I set the table for our noon meal. "I had a corpsman faint in the clinic yesterday." She sits nursing the baby on one of the wooden kitchen chairs. "It's Drake Trustler . . . Nick Rioli, the driver for the mob crew from Pittsburgh. . . . Remember, I told you about him, how he's turned his life around and is now one of the lead mechanics in the camp motor pool." Patience shifts the baby to the other breast and touches her little girl's cheek.

"She's really growing isn't she?" I observe.

"Four pounds now. Pretty good, huh? And I'm not giving her the Borden's anymore."

"You look like you're feeling stronger too."

She gives me a little smile. "Did I ever thank you for saving my life . . . and Mira's? You're such a blessing to us."

"Me? It was Daniel and Isaac who did the c-section."

"Daniel told me it was you who said, 'Let's go. We have to go *now!*' It was you who resuscitated the baby."

"You do what you have to do when someone you love is in danger." This surprises me and I blush. I had never said that before, not even to myself, that I love Patience Hester. She doesn't blush. She just looks at me steady and then changes the subject.

"So you might go to Torrington?"

"I might have to, but it won't be easy. Drake is convinced X-rays cause cancer."

"I've heard that too."

"Heard what?" Hester kicks his rubber boots off, returning from the barn, along with Blum and little Danny.

"X-rays causing cancer . . ."

"Where do people come up with this stuff? That was twenty years ago," Daniel scoffs.

"Mrs. Kelly thought they were dangerous too," Patience puts in. "She told me that Thomas Edison wouldn't have an X-ray machine in his lab after one of his scientists got radiation burns and had to have both arms amputated."

"Well, that's a true story, but they're safer now. Why are we talking about X-rays, anyhow?" He runs his hand along the back of Patience's neck and leans in to kiss his baby. Blum plunks Danny in his wooden high chair and sits down beside him.

"What ray?" the little boy asks, but no one answers him.

I put the corn bread and beans on the table and bring fresh milk and butter from the Frigidaire. "I was explaining, I have a sick man at the camp and we may have to take him to Torrington for a chest X-ray."

Here Blum looks as if he's interested, and a familiar light flickers in his blue eyes, but he doesn't ask questions or offer an opinion. It's as if the night of the surgery, when he returned for a few hours to his old self, never really happened, or it was a dream.

"So what's the big deal? They do X-rays all the time." That's the vet.

"The young man doesn't want one. Thinks they cause cancer. It's going to be a fight."

"Well, good luck with that one. The captain's a military man. I'm sure he can issue an order."

The Hesters bow their heads and close their eyes preparing to say the blessing and Blum and I do too. Since Mira's birth it's become a familiar ritual for us.

Daniel starts out and Patience and I join in, but Blum is mum. *God, we thank you for this food. For rest and home and all things good*. . . . I open my eyes to see what Blum's doing and find him looking at me. It's a curious moment, unsettling, and then it is over.

36

Hannah

For two days a spring storm, rain and then ice, breaks the limbs off the trees in the yard and higher up in the mountains. I try to call Sheriff Hardman to have him radio Camp White Rock that I can't get in, but the phone lines are down and the thought of meeting Captain Wolfe's ire if I don't show up for clinic tomorrow makes my stomach hollow.

Outside, nothing moves but the tinkling branches. It's late afternoon and we're cut off from the world, and I'm just thinking of doing a watercolor of the crystalline trees when the distant sound of a vehicle alerts me. *Who would be out on an evening like this?*

Running to the window, I look down the road and see a tractor with two people on it, both bundled in rubber coats, knit caps, and scarves around their faces. Looking closer it appears there's also a child. The tractor stops at the Hesters' drive and bumps over the wooden bridge.

"What in heaven's name?" That's Patience, who was awakened by the motor's sound and has come down the stairs to stand next to me.

"Come in! Come in!" she calls from the porch. "Watch the ice.

It's a bad day to be out on the road. Is there some way we can help you?"

"Well, I hope so!" a young woman answers. "It's us! Hannah and John Dyer." She whips down her scarf and pulls off her cap to reveal two long black braids and a cheerful pink face.

Her husband, a Scandinavian-looking fellow, removes his hat too and, grinning, unwraps the youngster, a girl of about five, a small female replica of her mother, the same black braids and everything. "This is Mary. I thought she could play with Danny."

I'm still wondering why this young couple would travel over the dangerous roads to make an apparent social call when Hannah brings out a flowered tin box. "Oh, and we brought refreshments. Couldn't have a baby without cookies! I hope you don't mind. I figured it would be better to come to you than to make you come out in the storm."

(Now I know who the young people are. This is the couple Patience told me about that delivered so beautifully in their farmhouse down by the Hope River five years ago.)

"Well, isn't this nice! How're you doing, Hannah? Are the pains very bad?" Patience gives the mother a hug, looking right in her eyes.

"I'm fine, but the contractions are getting harder. Can we get some music going? I brought a recording of Cab Calloway with 'Minnie the Moocher' and another of 'The Saint James Infirmary Blues.'" She whips off her Mackinaw to reveal a very pregnant abdomen. "Where's your gramophone?"

"I'm sorry, we don't have one. We have a radio though. Becky, can you find something out of Pittsburgh or Wheeling? Try WWVA." I sit down next to the wooden console and fool with the dial but all I can get is the news, then it fades into static. "Sorry," I say. "The ice storm must be interfering."

"Oh, no! We *have* to have music. Maybe we should go home again. Sing, John! I was counting on music!" There's urgency in her voice and she begins to whirl around like a top. The husband throws his coat on the floor and takes her in his arms.

"One, two, three," he chants as he leads her in a waltz. "One, two, three." Then he begins to hum "The Blue Danube."

Whirling Dervish

As soon as the contraction is over, Patience leads the mother to my bedroom.

"Hannah likes to dance through her pains," she enlightens me when I return with a pot of hot water and the sterilized rubber gloves.

The young woman is lying on her back, half naked, while Patience listens to the baby's heartbeat. Her five-year-old, Mary, leans on the edge of the bed all eyes. *No modesty in this family!* Then without warning the woman gets frantic again. . . . "Hurry. Hurry. Hurry! I can't stand to lie down when the pains come."

"One more minute. I just want to verify the baby's position," Patience responds, pulling on the exam gloves, but Hannah won't wait. She holds out her hands to John, who pulls a long white ruffled skirt over her head and they are off, swooping in graceful arcs.

"*Oh, John, go faster!* We have to outdance the pain! Can't we jitterbug or polka?"

Just then the kitchen door opens and Blum and the vet blow in from the barn. "What's going on? I saw the tractor." That's Daniel.

"Hannah and John Dyer. Hannah's in labor but we need music. Can you give us a polka?" asks Patience.

Things are moving too fast for me. The mother is a whirling tornado, taking over the whole house, and without Patience's calm I'd be blown away in the storm. I lay out the birth supplies in my bedroom, which I assume will be the birth room, and then, grateful not to be in charge, crawl up on the parlor davenport to be out of the way.

Singing along in German, Daniel sits down in his work clothes and begins to bang out a lively tune. *"So ei-ne Liech-ten-stei-ner Pol-ka die hats. Die macht Rabatz, mein Schatz! Ja ja ja! Ja ja ja! Ja ja ja! Ja ja ja!"* I have no idea what the lyrics mean but it's a rousing tune and soon John and Hannah are doing the polka, joining in with the "Ja ja ja!" They swoop and turn, occasionally bumping into a chair.

Suddenly, Hannah stops and looks down between her bare feet at a pool of clear fluid on the floor. "Whoops!"

Quick as anything, Patience runs to the kitchen for a dishtowel and wipes the mess up. "Better work your way back to the bedroom," she instructs, but nobody's listening. The piano music goes on, punctuated by another rousing "Ja ja ja!" Even little Mary gets into the song, jumping up and down, and I can't help myself, I'm singing too. "Ja, ja, ja!" Blum stands in the kitchen doorway eating a cookie.

Suddenly Hannah's eyes pop open and she digs her fingernails into John's shoulder.

"Oh, my God. Something's coming!"

Surely not!

Patience runs to the bedroom for her gloves and kneels down. "It's the head, Hannah. Don't push. Can you walk to the bedroom?" Hannah can't walk, but she can waddle, so she waddles down the short hall into my room, lies on her side, and in three pushes delivers a very pink baby boy. His eyes, like his mother's, are wide with surprise.

That's all there is to it. The mother delivers the placenta, the midwife drops it in the chamber pot, and I put a pad between the patient's legs, though there's very little bleeding.

"Do you want to nurse?" Patience asks.

"You betcha! Come up here, Mary," Hannah calls to her daughter. "You have a little brother." John is sitting there too, and the sunset, shining orange, comes through the window, where the storm clouds have cleared.

Meanwhile, Danny and Mira sleep upstairs through it all, and Daniel keeps playing, but he's opened a hymnal and changed the song.

"Joyful, joyful . . . We adore thee, God of glory, Lord of Love. Hearts unfold like flowers before thee . . . opening to the sun above."

March 5, 1935

Precipitous birth of 8-pound John Lincoln Dyer Jr. to Hannah and John Dyer of Hope River . . . born at the Hesters' house after an ice storm. It was like nothing I had ever seen before. No crying, no screaming, just dancing and music. Not long after her water broke, Hannah just pulled up her long skirt and squirted her baby out.

Hester played the piano, first a German polka he learned from his grandmother and later the "Ode to Joy" by Beethoven. Except for the mother's frantic insistence that we keep the music going, there was no way to know that Hannah was in hard labor, and I see now that the urgency in the mother's voice, no matter what she asks for, comes with the urgency of the baby to be born.

Present were John and the little girl Mary, Patience and me, Dr. Blum, who stayed in the kitchen, and Daniel Hester, who played the piano. We were rewarded ten dollars, for which we were grateful, especially since we didn't have to go out in the cold.

37

Sing a Little. Dance a Little.

I awake to the sound of water dripping and, when I look out the window, find it's raining. The water coming down the drainpipe is like flute music. Maybe spring really is here!

By midmorning the storm clouds pass and I'm able to drive into Liberty.

"How are the roads?" I ask Boodean when Sheriff Hardman finally gets a connection to the camp on the shortwave.

"Bad," Boodean answers. "One of the trucks slid into the creek."

"I guess I better not try to get there then."

"Don't even think of it. Nuthin' but mud and slick as . . . well you know. You'd be foolish to try."

"How's everything else? How's Drake?"

"Still the low-grade fever, chills, and the cough. I've been bringing him four meals a day, but he just picks at his food. Captain Wolfe agrees we need to get him to the hospital in Torrington, but he says we should wait until tomorrow. Can you meet us at Stenger's Pharmacy at nine fifteen? Can you do that?"

I agree to the plan. We talk a little about a patient with a spider bite who came into the clinic yesterday and then, "Is the captain still mad at me?"

I hear a long indrawn breath. "Yes, ma'am."

"Oh, Boodean! What do I have to do to get back in his good graces?"

"Sing a little. Dance a little."

"Boodean, I'm serious!"

"Me too. Sing a little. Dance a little. Over and out."

Then just static.

Namesake

I arrive, as instructed, by nine fifteen and stand in the window of Stenger's Pharmacy watching for Captain Wolfe and Boodean. Snow is already flying again, but not so it would stick, just big, lazy flakes coming down like confetti.

"How's Patience?" Mr. Stenger asks, staring across the counter, one eye on me, one eye wandering toward the window. "I haven't seen her for a long time."

"She's getting better."

"Dr. Blum was there and did the surgery, that's what I heard. A hemorrhage, was it?"

"Yes." It doesn't surprise me that the pharmacist knows some of the details of the birth. I expected it. In a small town word gets around.

"Got something that might perk her up." Stenger holds out a small brown bottle, labeled Dr. Blaud's Iron Pills. "This is the real McCoy! It would do Patience a lot of good."

"I usually don't hold with patent medicines," I hedge. "Dr. Blum used to say that most of them are a bunch of hooey." I don't know why I invoke Dr. Blum's words. He's no longer an authority on anything.

Stenger continues like a pitchman. "Usually I agree, but I can vouch for this. It actually has iron in it. Does wonders for women with heavy monthlies too."

I take the bottle and give it a shake. "How much?"

"It's a gift. The midwife took care of my mother one summer when she had ulcers on her feet, the best nursing she ever had."

"Well, thank you. We'll give it a try. Patience is still rather weak and pale, though she's gaining ground. . . ."

Just then the little bell on the pharmacy door rings and Willa Hucknell and her flock of little blond wrens flutter through the door. For a minute I think of hiding. I've been such a bad friend. I just stopped seeing her when the deliveries dried up, completely forgot she was pregnant, and almost forgot about the bruises.

On the other hand, she never contacted me either, so maybe she feels awkward too. Knowing everyone in town saw Alfred hit her at the Fourth of July picnic probably still hurts, and I have to admit that with Patience's birth and Linus's death, Willa never once crossed my mind.

"Miss Becky. Miss Becky!" the girls cry, coming up to me. "Where's Dr. Blum?"

"He's home," I reply. "How are you, Willa?" I can tell she's a lot stronger. Her face is pink and her yellow hair, which is now cut short in a bob, is shiny and clean.

"Never been better. Want to see something?" Apparently, she holds me no ill will because she opens the bundle that is pressed close to her chest and shows me a beautiful baby. "It's a boy, *finally!* Alfred Junior." The white-haired infant looks at me with round gray eyes.

"Do you like him?" the oldest girl, Sally, asks.

"I do. He's beautiful, but why didn't you call me when you went into labor, Willa? I would have come. Who delivered him, anyway? Did you go to the hospital in Torrington?"

"Oh, we didn't go nowhere, did we, Sally? He's three months yesterday."

"You had the baby at home, with no help? Was Alfred there?"

"No, he was off working."

"I helped her!" Sally Hucknell crows. "I helped her. Ma calls me her little midwife."

"You?"

"Yeah. Ma said it was the easiest birth yet. She just lay down, told me what to do, how to check for a cord, and ease the baby out and get it to breathe. I was the first one to know he was a boy, and when Papa got back from his coal mine, he was so happy to have finally got his namesake."

"His coal mine?"

Sally starts to tell me something, but Willa shakes her head no. Outside there's the blare of a horn.

"That's my ride, Willa. I'm so happy for you. I'll come by and see you when I have time." I look at Alfred Jr. and all the happy, loving little girls. Have I so misjudged this family; let the bruises on the mother's face stain the whole picture?

"Can you bring Dr. Blum too?" Sally asks and is echoed by her sisters.

Willa reaches out and touches my hand, and the little boy baby gives me a smile.

The X-ray Machine

"Good morning, everyone," I greet the men as I climb in the front seat of the captain's personal auto.

Wolfe doesn't even say hello. He glances at his watch and pulls away from the curb. "The roads are bad. We've got to move or we're going to be late for the appointment." Drake, looking like death warmed over, is lying on his side in the back with Boodean. He wears his khaki CCC uniform, which is now two sizes too big.

"How's he doing?"

"Maybe a little better." That's my medic trying to sound optimistic, but I can tell by his eyes that he doesn't really think so.

The rest of the trip is about what you'd expect. Snow in the higher elevations and fog as we come over Hog Back Mountain. Captain Wolfe doesn't say a word except to swear under his breath when we slide in the mud.

"How long has this man been ill?" Dr. Fisher asks me as the hospital nurse and Boodean assist Drake Trustler to back up against the cold glass plate mounted on the X-ray machine. It's a shock to see how weak Drake is. His once muscular body is skin and bones and his forehead is beaded with sweat.

The doctor's assistant is dressed in a white surgical gown with a white puffy hat, and I'm glad I wore my army nurse's dress and white shoes so I look somewhat professional. Boodean is also dressed for the part in his crisp CCC uniform with the medic patch on the shoulder. The captain stays in the waiting room reading the Torrington paper.

"He's been sick about a month, maybe longer." I hand my report to Dr. Fisher, a tall man, about six-foot-three, with coal-black hair that is greased down and combed straight back. He tosses the file on a desk without looking at it and stuffs the earpieces of his stethoscope into his ears.

"Lungs sound like shit!" he announces in a voice too loud.

My face turns red, but I remind myself that I've heard much worse language at Walter Reed. I wouldn't be surprised if Dr. Fisher is an ex-military man. He has that way about him.

"Yes, rales and rhonchi when he inspires and exhales," I respond, but the man cuts me short and motions his nurse to position the patient.

The intimidating X-ray machine is about six feet high, a steel frame with black metal in back and black glass in front. The nurse positions Drake behind the glass, and I must admit, the fearsome medical equipment looks like a medieval torture device.

Dr. Fisher, wearing elbow-length black leather gloves, turns a knob next to a red blinking light and sits down. With a whir, a motor moves the sheet of dark glass against Drake's chest, pinning him in, and all I can see are his eyes, boring straight into mine.

I know what he's thinking. *My mother said never, EVER, get an X-ray!*

Spring Again

38

Break in the Weather

"There's a nakedness to the land when the snow melts off," Patience muses. "Have you ever noticed? The yard is littered and muddy, a tin can here, a pile of tomato stakes there, chips of firewood and blown-down branches, but already the grass is greening; the green of Ireland, Mrs. Kelly would say."

We sit with Danny on the front porch, drinking cold milk and eating gingersnaps. It's only fifty-six degrees by the thermometer but feels like summer, and the men are in their shirtsleeves out in the garden clearing tall weeds.

"I always listen for the bird sounds. To me, that's the first sign of spring," I answer.

A few minutes later, Patience starts up again. "So, how was your trip to Torrington with Captain Wolfe? Did you talk to him about the way he's been treating you?"

"Tense. The road was bad on the way there, so we didn't talk at all. Even Boodean, my medic, was silent."

"So? Is it TB?"

"I don't know. The physician wasn't sure. There's some scarring of the lungs, he said, and some pleural effusion, so he's sending the plates to a specialist in Pittsburgh and wanted to keep Drake at the hospital until he gets the results.

"I felt so bad. Drake *really* didn't want to be admitted, but the report should be back in another three days and we'll go get him. It's going to cost the camp an arm and a leg."

"What will you do if the report says tuberculosis? Weren't all the boys tested before they enrolled?"

"They *were* all tested . . . *all but Drake!* Remember, I told you he just climbed in the CCC truck around Hagerstown and no one even noticed he hadn't joined up at the processing center? I'm worried about him, but not just him—I also feel responsible for the rest of the corpsmen. When I hid his secret, it never occurred to me that he hadn't gone through the usual health screenings. Now, if TB spreads through the camp, there will be hell to pay, and think of the reaction in Union County. The locals don't like the CCC boys much anyway."

"Try not to worry so much, Becky. Even if he has TB, it doesn't always spread. Most of the things we worry about never happen."

I take a deep breath and let out my air. She's probably right. Most of the things we worry about never happen.

"Look, Danny," Patience says. "There's a robin sitting on the fence post, his red chest shining, his yellow beak open. . . ."

The Runaround

I am furious! I'm so mad I could spit. Today, after leaving three messages I finally spoke to Dr. H. A. Raymond, radiologist at West Penn Hospital in Pittsburgh.

"So sorry," he said, "for not getting back to you sooner. I was in Boston speaking at the New England Roentgen Ray Society's yearly meeting." (He waited to be sure I was properly impressed.) "Can I give my report to the camp physician?"

For god's sake! We have no physician! I wanted to shout, but I kept my temper. "This is Becky Myers, RN. I'm the nurse for the camp infirmary."

There was a long pause with only static on the line, and for a minute I thought we had lost the connection.

"You don't have a supervising physician? Well then, who's in charge? There must be someone."

"*I'm* in charge. We had a part-time doctor, but he went back to Ohio. Meanwhile I deal with all the medical emergencies and illnesses, nothing my medic and I can't handle."

"Well, I can only give the report to a physician . . ." he says, as if it's a federal law.

"All I need to know is, does Mr. Trustler have TB?"

"Trustler, you say? I thought you were calling about William Taylor at Camp Wolf Rock, in Pennsylvania."

"This is *Camp White Rock in West Virginia*," I explain. "I've been calling every day. We have reason to believe *Drake Trustler* has tuberculosis. He's hospitalized at Boone Memorial in Torrington, West Virginia, until we have a definite diagnosis, and it's costing the CCC camp a bundle."

"Did you do a sputum culture?"

"Of course, but the lab at Johns Hopkins said it would be two to four weeks until we have the results."

"Well, I haven't seen Drake Trustler's images yet and, regardless, you will have to find a supervising physician willing to talk to me."

At this point I hung up. I did! I know it was unprofessional, but I just couldn't stand it! What will I do now?

March 14, 1935

I have been thinking about this compulsion to share Becky's thoughts. Why do I do it? Why can't I stop?

The thing is, I'm not sharing her thoughts. It's more like stealing and I don't understand it; I never had a need for intimacy before.

I had a wife and I have had lovers, but not many friends and even those I had, like Dr. Robinson, the colored physician, have never shared their inner life with me. Not that Becky shares willingly. As I said, I am a thief.

Daniel Hester is my friend, I must not forget, but ours is a bond based on work. We work in silence and enjoy each other's company. I know his next move and am ready to assist him. We laugh together and I've patted his back a few times when an animal he was trying valiantly to save didn't make it, but we never communicate about anything personal.

And another thing, this Dr. Raymond, what an asshole, refusing to give the results of the X-ray to Becky, saying he can only give them to a physician. I have half a mind to go up there and knock his block off.

Missing

"So where could he be? You think he just got in your Olds and drove away?" I ask.

Hester, Patience, Danny, and I are sitting down to supper and have said our brief grace.

"How long has he been gone?"

"All day, I guess." That's Patience.

Daniel interrupts. "I was tuberculin-testing two herds in Grant County. Patience thought Blum was with me."

"Yes, I just assumed he was with Daniel, until Daniel got home and asked where my Oldsmobile was. All day I'd been puttering around the house and hadn't been out to the driveway to notice."

I'm worried about Isaac, of course, but also angry. I've been at work and assumed all was well. He's never wandered off before, not since that time when he joined the soup line in Liberty. Certainly he's never taken a vehicle, although at Christmas the vet divulged that Blum could drive a tractor. I let out a heavy breath. If a man previously thought to be catatonic can do a cesarean section, who knows what else he is capable of.

"Honey, drink your milk." That's Patience speaking to Danny, who grins, takes up his tin cup, and dribbles white down his chin.

"He'll come back," Daniel reassures. "Can you pass me the butter?"

It's the stillest part of the night and I am still awake, thinking about what could have happened to Isaac. Did he run off the road? He might be injured and trapped behind the wheel, though Daniel and I drove to Liberty and back looking in all the ditches. We even drove up Wild Rose Road to check the house with the blue door. No Oldsmobile. No Dr. Blum.

The irony is that, even though I've felt burdened by having to care for him for so long, now it seems I've grown to care *about* *him*. I think of his kindly ways with children, of his beautiful woodworking, of his companionship with Daniel, of his surgical skill when Patience was hemorrhaging. He is Isaac Blum, but a new Isaac Blum. Even his body is different; muscular and brown, a farmer. But where is he now?

Unexpected

At dawn, I wake to the sound of Danny laughing up in his bedroom. "Uncle Isaac. Uncle Isaac is home!"

Then Hester, "Dammit, man! You gave us a scare! Where the hell did you go? Becky and I drove around half the night looking for you." (This is an exaggeration. We only drove into Liberty and back, then up Wild Rose Road.)

There's no answer, of course, but what is Blum playing at? Stealing a car, leaving us for twenty-four hours, and then sneaking home like a teenager and crawling in bed! I throw on my bathrobe, ready to stomp upstairs and confront him, give him a piece of my mind for making me worry all night, but as I rush through the kitchen a file folder on the table catches my eye.

WEST PENNSYLVANIA HOSPITAL is stamped on the front. It takes me a moment to realize what I'm looking at. It's Drake Trustler's X-ray report.

Did Dr. Blum drive to Pittsburgh? No, it's not possible! How could he find the way? How did he communicate with the hospital personnel? He can barely talk, unless he's been faking the whole time. I pace the cold kitchen floor. Did he pretend to be a physician from the Civilian Conservation Corps? I'm still riding the wave of my anger and am unsure how to react, but before I can go off the deep end, I take a big breath and I flip open the folder.

Dear Doctor *(The name of the unknown camp physician is left blank.)*

Thank you for sending me the roentgen images of Drake Trustler's lungs. The chest X-ray confirms the presence of multiple small (<10 mm) nodules in the upper lobes. Using the ILO classification system, these are of profusion 1/0 or greater. . . ."

I skip to the bottom of the report with a sinking heart, looking for the summary.

. . . producing so-called classic "eggshell" calcifications. I believe this is a clear case of silicosis and not the tuberculin bacillus.

Thanks again for this consultation,

Respectfully yours,
H. A. Raymond, MD

Silicosis. I whip through the report a second time and am stunned. Not TB? Silicosis! But how could Drake have contracted silicosis? He's only twenty-four. Usually, it's a chronic disease of old men or miners like those at the Hawk's Nest disaster. Then I remember that Drake once told me he worked alongside his father and grandfather at a brick factory in Ohio before he ran away. Could the lungs of a young boy be more susceptible to the disease than a man's? Is this good news for Drake or another death sentence? I really don't know.

"Becky! Isaac's back," Daniel calls down to me. "He just went up to Pittsburgh to West Penn Hospital and had a hard time getting back."

I tighten my jaw and don't answer. What can I say? I am shocked and I'm furious. I am also happy. Drake doesn't have TB and Isaac is safe. The S.O.B.!

March 19, 1935

Becky was mad as hell when I returned from Pittsburgh, though the Hesters took it in stride. What did I imagine? That she would be grateful? But no . . . (and I guess I can't blame her) she was steamed. For nearly 24 hours she had no idea what had happened to me.

The thing is, when I read in Becky's journal about the radiologist's ridiculous refusal to give her a diagnosis for the boy Drake Trustler just because she was a nurse and not a physician, I was ready to punch his lights out. If a patient is ill you need to take care of him, and this bit about having to give the report to an MD is pure bullshit.

All day, I thought about Becky's problem. I had a little money saved from the wooden bowls I crafted on the lathe that Hester sold for me at the flea market in Delmont. There were three cars in the drive . . . Becky needed the Pontiac to get to work. Hester needed his Model T to make his rounds, but I figured Patience wasn't going anywhere, so that left the Olds for me.

I let Becky put me to bed just as usual. I could do it myself, of course, but I like her to touch me. So gently she holds my chin and opens my mouth to brush my teeth, then pushes my hair from my eyes. I lie on my back and she straightens my pillow and pulls up the covers. For just a split second, her breast brushes my chest as she bends over me, but she doesn't notice. She's a nurse and I'm just a patient to her.

Before sunrise, I made my move and tiptoed downstairs with my good clothes on. Not wanting to alert the household, I pushed the Oldsmobile out into the road before I turned on the ignition.

Getting Trustler's X-ray result was easy. I'd driven to Pittsburgh plenty of times when I used to take Priscilla shopping. Funny how things come back to you, just like when I did Patience's surgery. The body remembers. The hands remember.

At West Penn Hospital, when I introduced myself as Dr. Blum and said I was from White Rock CCC Camp, the report was handed over without question. It took all of three sentences to get what I came for. Coming home was more difficult.

I ran out of gas at the West Virginia border and had to walk ten miles back to Uniontown, Pennsylvania, but the Texaco station was closed. Then it took me three hours to find a farmer willing to sell me five gallons of gas and I had to walk the ten miles back.

I arrived home to a dark house about two A.M., took off my shoes, dropped the folder on the kitchen table, and cat-walked up the stairs to bed. I was never in the military, but I now know how soldiers must feel when they make it back to camp. As I fell asleep I smiled to myself. Mission accomplished.

39

Asylum

"I'm sorry I've been so withdrawn. The thought of Drake having tuberculosis was really upsetting me," Captain Wolfe opens up. "My wife died of TB, but silicosis, that's different. There's hope."

We are in his sedan, driving to Torrington to pick up Drake Trustler and I am elated. Silicosis, I've read, is serious, but at least it's not communicable, and Drake can come back to the camp.

"I didn't want to do it," he goes on, stroking his scarred cheek, and for the first time telling me about his dead wife. "I didn't want to put her in the tuberculin asylum, but the doctors said it was her only chance. The cool mountain air would soothe her lungs and isolating her would keep me from getting it.

"I drove her up to Cresson near Johnstown, Pennsylvania, in the middle of winter. It was the nicest sanatorium I could find. She had her own room and everything. Caroline was a teacher, an elementary school teacher, and she loved children, though we never had any ourselves, a beautiful, delicate woman. They say that happens. The good die young. . . ."

He looks over with tears in his eyes and it strikes me that the man is still in love with his wife. I think about my husband, David. Do I still love him?

The captain goes on. "I went up to see her every other week and the last day is like a hand-tinted photograph imprinted in my mind. It was a beautiful spring day, but something was off, the yellow of the forsythia was too yellow, the grass was too green, the red on her handkerchief too goddamn red.

"I left with a bad feeling and the next day she died, *died alone.*" The captain wipes his eyes. "If Drake had had TB, I couldn't have stood it." After that there's silence.

"Drake can't stop talking since he's been back at the camp. It's like he's been given a new life," Boodean confides later that afternoon when we'd sent Drake over to the cookhouse for supper.

"Well, I'm sure he was worried about TB. Everyone knows tuberculosis is incurable. The thing is, Boodean . . . " Here I lower my voice. "Silicosis isn't much better. It's not contagious, which is a plus, and the deterioration is slower, but in the end . . ." I stop, hoping my meaning is clear enough.

A few minutes later, Drake comes back into the infirmary whistling. His color is better, he gained five pounds while in the hospital, and we intend to keep the weight on. Mrs. Ross even got him some smaller uniforms so he doesn't look like a scarecrow, and she plans to bring him pound cake that's full of eggs and cream from her farm every week.

"From now on, until it gets warmer, Drake, I want you to sleep in the clinic, and the major says you can be Mrs. Ross's assistant, sending out the twenty-five-dollar checks to the boys' families and doing other little jobs for her."

Drake just chews his gum and smiles.

"Then in a couple of weeks, the captain plans to station you in the new fire tower during the day, a nice easy job, so you can get your strength back and continue to heal. A corpsman from the motor pool will drive you up with your lunch, and you'll sit in the lookout station with a shortwave radio and binoculars, looking for signs of smoke and calling in anything suspicious.

"That's swell, Nurse Becky. I know I'm blessed that I don't have TB. I was pretty sure you'd have to send me to one of those sanatoriums, like where my grandpap went to die."

"March through May is fire season," Boodean interjects, "and the fire index is higher this year because we didn't get the heavy snows, so it's not like this job is a piece of cake.

"Before the oak and maple leaves pop out and provide shade, the forest floor is as dry as a tinderbox. One spark from a steam engine or an untended fire and it's all over. Thousands of acres can burn in a day."

"That's why us boys are ready and trained," Drake adds with pride. "It's part of the CCC mission . . . to stamp out forest fires. Yee-ha!" He laughs, proud, but still making fun of himself.

April Fool

Today is April Fools' Day and the doctor and I have been home in the little house at the end of Wild Rose Road for three days. It was hard coming back. I miss the Hesters, but Patience is well and doing fine; in fact she attended a birth on her own the day I went into Torrington. An easy one, she told me, right on the outskirts of Liberty, so she didn't have to drive too far. It was Ida May's cousin Betty Lou Cross, having her third, and now all the women on Patience's list are delivered. In a way this gives me peace, but also a feeling of emptiness, like something important has gone out of my life.

So now here we are, back where we started, but it's not a happy landing. I watch Blum out in the garden turning over the soil with a garden fork, and I'm still pissed as hell. All this time, he could drive, find his way to Pittsburgh, go to a hospital, and pick up a report, while I have been taking care of him as if he were a prince! What a fool I've been! And how did I not realize that the man was so functional? It can only be that I was still treating him like an invalid while clearly he was recovering.

And another thing: how did he know where to go? Patience didn't seem as surprised as I was. She knew he'd been driving the tractor and even the Model T when he went out on calls with Daniel, but neither of us can remember talking about *which hospital* or *which radiologist* was causing me grief. For the first time, it occurs to me, with a turn of the stomach, that he has been reading my journal.

The son of a bitch!

April 3, 1935

Becky is on to me. She's moved her journal and she's acting strange, so she must have realized I've been reading it. The problem is, reading her thoughts has become a compulsion, and even though I know I should stop, I find myself drawn to her room, like an opium addict to laudanum.

I peek under the mattress and find the journal gone. I search her drawers and the top of her closet. I can't stop. There are footsteps on the back porch and quickly I dart across the hall to my own room and lie down on the bed. If she peeks in, will she think I'm sleep? Will she see my heart pounding?

Upright

"Hip, hip, hooray!" we all cry. Today Mrs. Maddock walked!

Mr. Maddock, who was once an engineer, invited us all over, even Dr. Blum, whom he apparently no longer fears, to witness the demonstration of a pair of leg braces, much like President Roosevelt's, that he's made for Sarah. She was able, using the wheelchair for support, to walk down the garden path to the driveway and back again. Maddock hovered behind her in case she fell.

"I have been practicing standing for weeks," she tells us, straightening the collar on her pretty flowered dress. "Holding myself up with the help of the braces, on the backs of chairs and the back of the sofa. I figure if FDR can do it, so can I, but I still get very tired. I don't know how the president does it!"

"He has a handsome young man who pretends to be his body guard stand next to him to give him support," Daniel explains. "Look at the photos of him in the newspapers giving a speech or waving to the crowd, there's always someone at his side."

"Well, I have my guardian angel, Milton." She plunks back down in her wheelchair and Mr. Maddock pushes the conveyance up the side ramp to the porch, where we find celebration refreshments on a white wicker table—lemonade and sugar cookies that Mrs. Maddock has made herself.

Whenever I have been in Sarah Maddock's home, I've appreciated all the adaptations Mr. Maddock has made to accommodate his wheelchair-bound wife and wonder if he will have to remake all the shelves and cupboards now that she can walk. In the kitchen, pantry, and water closet everything has been built low, so that Sarah can reach from her wheelchair. It's amazing what disabled people can do if given the appropriate tools.

"Saw fire warning signs on Salt Lick today as I came into Liberty," Daniel mentions, munching a cookie. "I guess the CCC boys put them up. Surprised we haven't had more trouble with the corpsmen. In some towns they raise holy hell."

"Couple of boys got drunk at the bar a few nights ago," I add, "and Sheriff Hardman put them in the drunk tank overnight, but that's the only trouble I've heard of. Captain Wolfe and the superintendent run a tight ship."

"That's good," Daniel agrees. "Got to make those boys tow the line." Here he looks at Blum as if this were an inside joke and I swear Blum actually smiles, the bastard!

April 14, 1935

For months we've been listening, as Daniel reads aloud from the Torrington Times, about the conditions in the Great Plains, how it's estimated that 100 million acres of farmland has been lost to the winds, and I'll admit I thought it an exaggeration, but there's something to be said for hearing about it firsthand.

Mrs. Rumer, who went out by train to Arkansas for her older brother's funeral, told Daniel what she'd seen, as we sat drinking lemonade on her porch after testing her cattle for TB.

"When the dust cloud came over the horizon, it felt like a shovelful of sand was flung in my face," she began. "We were out in the yard and could hardly make it back to the house. Cars along the road came to a standstill. I saw it with my own eyes. . . . My sister-in-law and the children live with the red dust, day in and day out.

"They can't escape it, and my brother George had to live with it too, until it killed him. 'Dust pneumonia' the doctors

call it. The red grit gets deep in the lungs and then you fever
and die, especially old people and children.

"They eat dust, sleep with dust. Watch dust strip their
hope away."

And then yesterday there was no doubting the stories.
Hester and I were working out in his garden (we've been
trading days back and forth from my garden to his) when a
wind came up and strange orange clouds began to boil over
the mountains.

We'd heard on the radio out of Wheeling that it was
storming in Ohio, so we weren't surprised about the clouds,
but the color, that was another thing! On our way across
the barnyard, heading for the house, the sand hit us full
force.

Next thing, lightning, and then the sky turned copper
red. The air became heavy with grit. I couldn't believe it.
We were getting some of Mrs. Rumer's dead brother's
farm.

Then on the news today everyone's talking about the
"Dust Bowl" and "Black Sunday," the biggest dust storm yet
and the only one that made it all the way to the East Coast.

Apparently, an Associated Press newsman and his
photographer were caught just north of Boise City and
got pictures of the black clouds as they blotted out the sun
and rolled across the prairie. The reporter's the one who
coined the name "Black Sunday," dirt in the air so thick, you
couldn't see through it, and some of it made it all the way to
our mountains! Damnedest thing.

Scoundrel

A few years ago, I'd have been glad not to hear doors banging, children crying, voices in another room, but now that we've returned to the house with the blue door it's the silence that gets me. With only the doctor for company, it's quiet as a mausoleum. Even our three-legged dog doesn't bark unless a deer walks right past him.

The worst part is my relationship with Blum. Since I realized he'd been reading my journal, I don't brush his teeth anymore or lay out his clothes. I cook for him, so he won't starve, but that's all.

What bothers me most is the suspicion that it wasn't just once that he read my journal but many times. Thusly, I have doubled my effort to locate a good hiding spot. So far, the loose floorboard under my dresser seems the best place. I don't think he can possibly find it, but still I keep picturing him with the little leather-bound book open over his knees.

Yesterday at breakfast, I finally came out with it.

"Blum, you are a bastard and a dickhead!" (Those were the only words I could find.) "After all I've done for you, you creep into my room and look in my journal. What kind of man are you?" That's what I said. He just hung his head, didn't answer. Not that I really expected him to.

The idea of leaving him has come to me lately. If he can drive to Pittsburgh, he's much more functional than I imagined. But if I left, *where would I go?* I still have my job at Camp White Rock and I could move into town, but I don't make enough money to afford it.

On the other hand, I have become fond of the farm at the end of Wild Rose Road, the daffodils, the brook, the oak in front just budding out. This is our second spring here and the early crops have already been sowed. And then there's the chickens, only six of them, but they all have names, Mary, Martha, Madeline, Molly, Maria, and Minny. Minny's the littlest, a red Bantam that lays brown eggs. What would I do with them if I left?

I suppose I could tell Blum to leave. Tell him to wrap his few clothes in a bundle, tie them to a stick, and hit the road like a hobo, but then I'd be here alone. That would *not* be a good idea, not with the homeless men drifting over the land.

Just yesterday two rough-looking fellows came to the door and the hair on my neck rose up like a cat's. Bums, I thought, looking for handouts, but it turns out I was wrong.

"Would you like to buy some nice hard coal, ma'am?" the bearded one asks, taking off his dirty cap. His hands are almost black and there's soot on his nose. They lead a jackass loaded with burlap bags of the black gold. "Two bits a bag; burns nice and hot."

"Where'd you get it?"

"We dug it ourselves. We're no thieves if that's what you're thinking."

"You dug it? I thought all the mines had closed in Union County."

"They did. MacIntosh Consolidated went bust five years ago. Horse Shoe barred the gates and evicted us from our mining shacks this December, but the coal is still down there. It belongs to the people, same as air or water." (This must be what Sally was talking about when she told me her pa was working his coal mine!)

"Listen, lady," the thin dark man holding the jackass growls. "It will be cold again this winter, and you'll be sorry if you pass this up. If you don't want it, someone else will. Mrs. Hester, the midwife, sent us up here. She took four bags yesterday and Mr. Maddock took three today."

I'm suspicious . . . "Is this what they call 'bootleg coal,' from those diggers over in Pennsylvania? I read how out-of-work miners are digging pits on the hillsides and how the cops arrested some two hundred men, but the jury wouldn't convict them."

"Damn right! Pardon my French, ma'am. Some call it bootlegging, but Sheriff Hardman calls it sensible. We have wives and kids to feed. Do you want some or not?"

My mind spins like a top. The price is good, but technically the fuel *is* stolen. On the other hand, Mr. MacIntosh, the coal baron, died by his own hand at the beginning of the Depression and his widow, Katherine, and her little boy moved back to Baltimore, so they've given up on Appalachia. Now the coal is just sitting there and the miners are only scratching a living from the earth, same as Dr. Blum and I.

I make a snap decision. It's not cold now, but it will be this winter. "I'll take the rest of what you've got, all four bags and I'll take more if you're ever up this way."

"Well, thank you, ma'am. Where should we put it?"

I show the men where we keep the firewood under the porch and run upstairs for a dollar. Returning, I grab two biscuits from the kitchen and wrap them in a piece of newspaper.

"Here," I say, after turning over the money. "For your journey home, in case you get hungry." The men look surprised.

"God bless you, lady," the dark fellow says. "You and your man." He looks over at the garden where Isaac is hoeing potatoes.

Here I almost choke. *My man!* If they only knew how close I am to getting rid of him!

April 17, 1935

I miss Becky. She has cut me off, called me a dickhead and a bastard. Not that I didn't deserve it. The worst part is, I know reading her private journal was wrong, but I've never felt so close to anyone and now I'm alone again.

The problem is, I can't say I'm sorry. Reading her most private thoughts has changed me. Something deep inside has been touched.

What if she were reading my notebook?

I think I would be glad.

Drought

I wake just as the sun is peeking over the mountains, thinking about President Roosevelt's fireside chat last night. The Hesters had us over to dinner and just like old times we sat around the radio listening, along with all the other worried Americans. In his quiet, reassuring way, Roosevelt talked about the Public Works Project, about getting people off the dole, about a new program called Social Security. Most important, he gives us hope that these dark days will not last forever.

Outside my window, leaves in the old oak rattle so hard I get out of bed thinking it's rain, but it's just a strong, hot wind, coming up from the valley. Too bad; it's been two weeks without a drop.

Blum has already made breakfast, leaving a bowl of porridge on the table for me and is out in the garden wearing a pair of cut-off blue jeans, transporting water from the spring to our delicate seedlings. It's important because by seven A.M., it's already eighty and the ground is bone dry. Three-quarters of the states are now experiencing drought, and West Virginia is one of them. Not enough snow this winter, they say. Not enough rain this spring.

I watch from the kitchen as the doctor carries two buckets at a time, then bends with a tin can and carefully gives each plant a drink. He's working without a shirt and his body is lean and brown, but that only makes me hate him more.

An hour later, as I approach Camp White Rock, already twenty minutes late for work, I'm surprised to see more men without shirts, about a dozen of the CCC boys, just outside the gate, marching into the wind along Crockers Creek, armed with axes and folding shovels on their belts. The Forest Army, I think, like in the yellow-and-green CCC poster in the infirmary. "Hi, Nursie!" the young men shout.

I pull over and roll down my window. "What's going on?" I ask Lou Cross, my patient with the plantar wart, who is leading the troops.

"Working in the woods, miss." He tips a green cowboy hat that is definitely not part of the regulation CCC uniform. "Going to dig a trench up the ravine and cut brush for a firebreak. It's a big project. We have two natural barriers from a wildfire, the cliffs and the stream, but we're vulnerable as hell on either side, pardon my French."

"I don't think there's been a fire around here for ten years."

"Makes it worse, especially this year when there's not enough rain. Too much dead timber and dry brush."

"What's the gun for? In case you have a mutiny in this heat?" I ask with a smile. He has a pistol in a holster strapped to his hip.

"Copperheads or rattlers," he says, pulling down his hat to keep it from blowing off. "Keep up, Morris! Roland, quit looking at the birds, we have a lot of work to do. Watch the ax, Snake! That thing could hurt someone."

You can see why the fellows admire Lou; he's a natural leader, comfortable with himself and comfortable with the young men. It's apparently just Captain Wolfe who finds him irritating.

40

Desertion

When I finally get to headquarters, Mrs. Ross is all in a dither. "He's gone," she says. "He just packed up and left. No good-bye or anything, just a note with his forwarding address." She frantically paces back and forth.

"Who?"

"Milliken," Boodean answers. "His wife came all the way from New England yesterday. Drove by herself. We think she gave the major an ultimatum: 'Come home now or don't come home ever.' He took off with her in the night."

"Oh, what will we do now!" Mrs. Ross twists around, flapping her arms like a chicken in a burning henhouse.

"I'm sure Captain Wolfe will step forward until they send someone. Maybe they'll make him the superintendent." I try to comfort her. "That would be nice."

"Not likely." Wolfe steps out of Milliken's office. "I was trying to get someone in the main office at District Five to tell them Milliken is AWOL, but our antenna for the shortwave radio blew down this morning. Not the first time."

"Did Major Milliken say anything to you? Is this a desertion or can he just resign?" I ask.

"No, I didn't have a clue, except anyone could see he wasn't happy. They'll probably find him at home in Newton, Massachusetts."

"So who will be in charge?" That's Mrs. Ross again. She's the kind of woman who can't manage without a boss. "I could drive into town and telephone District Five. Kind of hate to in this wind."

"I guess I'm in charge for now. I think we can manage for a day or two," says the captain with a laugh. "Eventually we'll get someone on the shortwave and they can figure it out. Meanwhile, I'll have Mac in the welding shop come over to try to fix the antenna. Where's Drake?"

"The fellow from the motor pool already took him up to the fire tower and the cook sent his lunch," Boodean puts in. "This is his third day on White Rock Mountain and he doesn't mind it at all. He's almost his old self again."

"Good," I respond, wishing I knew more about silicosis and vowing to read up on it if I can find the topic in one of Blum's old books.

"Nurse!" I hear a man call out as he stomps up on the porch. "Need help here."

I can tell by the voice it's the cowboy, Lou Cross.

Snake

"Shit!" a corpsman swears, hobbling into the infirmary with Lou Cross supporting him. The young man has his CCC shirt wrapped around his left lower leg and there's blood leaking through and dripping onto the wooden floorboards. Boodean grabs the door as it crashes back in the wind.

"Watch your language, Snake! A lady is present. . . . Sorry, Miss

Myers. This is Snake Nelson," Lou Cross introduces him. " 'Fraid
he's had a little accident. Cut himself with his own damned ax.
Deep one too. Hope you can fix him. I'd hate to try to get to Boone
Memorial in Torrington today. That hot wind must be forty or
fifty miles an hour, could blow a truck right off the road. Can I
leave him with you? I need to get back to the unit. Our goal is to
get a trench up to the cliffs by dark."

Boodean already has Snake lying down and is gently unwrap-
ping the injured leg.

"Sure," I say, turning to wash my hands in a bowl. Through the
window, I watch as Lou mounts his horse and gallops back to the
road.

"Okay, Private Nelson." I pull a chair over to the bedside and
look at the wound, then turn to the medic. "It's bad, a deep cut
on the shin, right down to the bone, but at least there's not much
contamination. We'll need catgut suture, five percent carbolic acid,
and gauze dressing."

"Looks like you got yourself a week of enforced rest, Snake."
This time I call the man by his nickname, still having no idea what
it means.

"And, yes, bring out some laudanum too, Boodean. He'll need it."

Smoke

"You smell that, Boodean?" We've finished our morning clinic,
a short one with only Snake's deep cut, and are battling our way
against the wind to the mess hall.

"Yeah, corn bread."

"No." I tilt my head back and flare my nostrils. "Smoke."

"Hope the cook didn't *burn* the corn bread," Boodean worries. "I'm hungry as a *wolf*."

"You talking about me, Private Boodean?" The captain laughs, holding his hat down, catching up with us.

"No, sir," Boodean explains. "I was describing my appetite. *Hungry as a wolf!* Any word from District Five?"

"Not yet. I have two welders on the roof, but the wind is so strong, every time they think they've got the aerial fixed something else comes loose. Last I heard they made a brief connection with Camp Laurel, but reception was so poor they couldn't communicate. I guess we can get along without a superintendent for another twenty-four hours."

"Do you smell smoke?" I question the captain.

He takes a long sniff and looks around. "Not really. Must be something from the kitchen." I take another sniff to make sure, but the faint hint is gone.

Boodean is right, Starvation MacFarland did make corn bread for dinner, along with beef stew; plain fair, but tasty. Starvation has also made donuts dipped in sugar for dessert. I don't know if all the CCC camps feed their men so well, but the fellows at White Rock have nothing to complain about.

As we return to the clinic, I raise my head again. There it is, the smell of woodsmoke! "Come on, Boodean. Don't you smell it, the smoke?"

He looks around and takes a few breaths. "Could be the men are burning trash. . . . Probably shouldn't, not with this wind. And there's a patient on the porch, smoking a fag."

Frustrated, I ask the camp secretary to come out. Maybe women have better noses. "Do *you* smell smoke, Mrs. Ross? Like woodsmoke?"

She looks at me out of the corner of her eye, as if this is some kind of a test and she wants to give the right answer. "Maybe a little . . ."

"See," I tell Boodean as we enter the infirmary. "Mrs. Ross smells it too. Can you find the captain and ask him to have some of the boys investigate? After that, check with Drake at the tower, see if he's seen anything?"

"Not likely to reach him," the older lady reminds me. "The shortwave radio still isn't working. The two fellows trying to fix the antenna were going into Liberty for a part. If they don't find one there, they'll try Delmont."

I let out a sigh. So there's no way to communicate with the outside world and no way for Drake to communicate with us either, but that's really not my worry.

"Okay, Boodean, bring in the next patient."

Fire

By three o'clock, there's no doubt about it. There's a fire somewhere, and though the sky is still clear, even Boodean can now smell the smoke. The captain is tense and has called in the four camp officers. I stand listening at the open door as Wolfe takes a seat behind the superintendent's desk.

"Listen, guys. I know this isn't regulation, but without Milliken someone needs to take charge. Until we're able to contact District Five, I hope you won't mind if I step up."

Loonie Tinkshell makes a joke. "It's your funeral!"

"Right," says the captain. "So here's what I need you to do. People have smelled a whiff of smoke for a couple of hours. It's getting stronger and if I'm not mistaken, there's a haze coming over the mountain. We need to take about twenty boys off their usual assignments and get them out looking for the source. They need to go all the way up to the cliffs and maybe a little way over the mountain. The fire may be on the other side.

"The cook can keep his crew, we have to eat"—here there are a few chuckles—"and Lou Cross still has his guys out building a fire trench, but that's a big project and will take the whole day. Maybe some of the men from the sawmill could look for him. We need to be on the alert. Otherwise, it's business as usual. Surveying class tonight, Ed?"

"You betcha."

As the camp officers leave, the captain steps out on the porch, runs his hands through his hair, and stares at the sky. I go out and stand beside him, trying to keep my nurse's uniform from blowing up over my knees. "The smell's getting stronger and the wind too," I observe. "And look up by the cliffs, there's an orange haze."

The captain goes back into headquarters and returns with his binoculars. "Son of a bitch, Milliken! He would pick today to abandon ship," he grumbles, adjusting the focus of the lens. "There's smoke all right and it's thick at the base of the cliffs. Probably came from the west side of the ridge. The whole damn county might be burning, and with our shortwave radio out, we're the only ones that don't know it.

"Boodean!" he shouts. "Get on the bullhorn and alert the fire suppression teams. I want two trucks of men dressed in protective gear, with their tools in their hands, water packs full and on their backs in front of headquarters in twenty minutes. *This is not a drill.*

"After that, you better work on the radio. I don't care if you have to send a monkey up the pole, see if you can get Drake Trustler and the ranger station in Delmont."

He turns to go back to the superintendent's office but stops for a minute to squeeze my hand. That's all. One small squeeze but it means a lot. *I'm glad you are here,* the touch says. *I appreciate you. We are friends.*

Flames

Twenty minutes later, two trucks loaded with firefighters dressed in long-sleeved green shirts, heavy army pants, and gray metal helmets pull up in front of headquarters singing over the roar of the wind, a popular Cab Calloway song. *"Hi de hi de hi de* hi—*Ho de ho de ho de* ho.*"* They act like they're going to a Sunday school picnic instead of what will probably be a brush fire.

The drivers and foreman get out to consult with Captain Wolfe. My medic is still up on the roof fiddling with the antenna and Mrs. Ross is inside repeating in her high voice, over and over into the radio mouthpiece, "This is CCC Camp White Rock, does anyone hear me? Urgent message. We believe there may be a forest fire. This is CCC Camp White Rock, does anyone hear me?"

"Boodean, take these," the captain shouts over the roar of the trees bending back and forth in the hot wind like wild women dancing. Leaves and small branches fly through the air and it reminds me of the time last spring when we had the tornado, but there's not a cloud in the sky.

My medic leans over the roof as the captain stands on the porch rail and hands up the binoculars, a recipe for a fall, if you ask me, but I keep my worries to myself. "Can you see the fire from up there?"

We all wait while the medic crawls to the peak of the building, stands up, and scans the mountainside. "To the left," he says. "I can see flames in the ravine to the left. A ground fire . . . Holy shit!" We all turn where he points and watch as the top of a pine in the distance bursts into flames.

"Go. Go!" Wolfe shouts while the drivers and foreman run to their trucks and head out of camp. The corpsmen have seen the burst of flame too, but it only increases their enthusiasm.

"Hot potato! Let's hit it," one fellow yells. Another starts up an old army song. *"Over hill, over dale. We will hit the dusty trail! And those caissons go rolling along."*

Myself, I'm not thrilled or enthusiastic. I'm scared. Lou Cross said we were sitting ducks with all the dead timber around us and I'm afraid he's right. Unfortunately, he and his crew started up the ravine on the right side of camp and the fire is coming down the left.

"Mrs. Ross, keep trying to connect with the outside world," Captain Wolfe commands. He grabs a bullhorn and begins to walk around the compound. "All personnel to the flagpole, immediately!"

I follow after him, not sure if I'm *personnel*, but wanting to know what the next step will be.

"Men, we have a critical situation. There's a fire about three miles away in the ravine between White Rock and Medicine Ridge. We have to send everyone. We'll start digging trenches about a mile from the camp. The fire suppression teams are already out there. I'll pull Lou Cross and his crew over to the left, if he hasn't already gotten there.

"I need someone to go with me to get Drake Trustler down from the fire tower. It may be a lost ride. Who volunteers?"

Loonie Tinkshell raises his fist. "I'll go."

"Okay, then. Every man follow your team leader. Get shovels, axes, rakes, anything you can find, buckets of water and burlap sacks. We'll beat the flames back if we have to," he shouts against the wind. "And be careful as hell."

Waiting

Now, except for the roar of the wind and Mrs. Ross's calls for help on the shortwave radio, it is quiet. Boodean has been forced to come down from the roof or the wind was going to blow him down. Snake Nelson, the boy with the leg wound, still sleeps on a cot, under the influence of the laudanum.

I lay out gauze to cover wounds or burns, and Boodean runs

to the laundry for clean towels and washcloths and then to the
kitchen for salt and ice to make saltwater packs to cool the men's
skin, but other than that we are as ready as we can be.

"What do we do now?" Boodean asks me. "Sit and wait?"

"No, we should set up an ambulance system, some way to transport corpsmen if they get injured."

"Really?"

"Yes. I want you to scour the camp for an available vehicle,
maybe a pickup truck with a metal hood. Metal, not canvas; it
could catch on fire. We'll make a couple of pallets in the back and
load the stretcher, then you take ambulance down the road, closer
to the flames where the men are working.

"If anyone gets hurt, do first aid at the site, bind wounds, put on
splints, whatever you can to stabilize the patient before you move
him, but stay away from the fire. Don't get hurt yourself."

The secretary stands up and starts yelling into the mouthpiece
again, "This is CCC Camp White Rock. Can you hear me? Can
anyone hear me?"

For a few seconds there's static on the line, but then it stops.
"Can anyone *hear* me? There's fire on the mountain. This is CCC
Camp White Rock calling. We may need help."

Outside on the porch I scan for a blaze as the day darkens. It's
only four o'clock but it could be nine, the smoke is that thick.

Heat

"Uhhhhhhaug." Snake wakes up crying. "Oh, Nursie. My leg
hurts so bad! Can I have another few drops of that medicine? It's
mighty good stuff." The man sounds half drunk.

"Look, Snake. I know you're in pain, but I can't give you any more laudanum. We have a disaster on our hands and I might need it for another patient."

"What disaster?"

"A fire, a real wildfire. Everyone is out fighting it. There's only you and me, Mrs. Ross, the cook, and few of the kitchen staff left in the camp. Anytime now, Boodean may return in our makeshift ambulance with an injured or burned corpsman. All I can give you are two Bayers."

"It's okay," Nelson answers pushing up and hopping over to the window to look. He uses a chair to support himself and stares out the glass, then he hops back to bed. "I guess I could use a Bayer. It would help some. Wake me if there's anything I can do, Nurse Becky."

There is nothing like waiting for imminent calamity. I run over all I have done and consider my skills. I really don't think I am qualified to run triage at a disaster site. Not only am I not a physician, I'm scared. My way of handling it would be for all of us to get in the trucks and get the hell out of here, but I'm sure Wolfe wouldn't think of it. The camp is his responsibility and he is a warrior, not Chicken Little like me.

While I kill time, I pace the clinic, investigate Colonel Milliken's office, and then return to the porch, where the setting sun has turned the billowing smoke clouds bloodred.

41

Burn

At first I don't hear the sound of the motor coming toward the clinic. The wind is that loud. It's the headlights piercing through smoke that alert me. Boodean and our ambulance! Quickly, I look over our meager supplies and rehearse what I know about burn injury.

If the burns are only red, like sunburn, cover them with cool cloths. They will heal in four days and leave no scars.

If the burns are partial thickness with blisters, we must protect them with cool cloths, being careful not to disturb the eruptions. Hydrating the patient is important, with a little salt water, but only in very small amounts because you don't want the patient to vomit.

If the burns are full thickness, going right through the skin, and covering much of the body, the patient is critical and may go into shock. Many won't make it.

The truck bumps to a stop.

"Becky!" a hoarse voice cries, as a man dressed in a filthy CCC uniform with a blue bandanna tied around his mouth and nose staggers into the waiting room. "It's me, Boodean." He carries the body of another man who also has a bandanna over his face. The patient's pants have been burned off and the skin on his legs is blistered and black. He wears a familiar Elgin watch.

"My God. It's the captain! What happened?" The victim groans as I try to absorb some of his weight and we half drag him into the infirmary.

"It was terrible." Boodean pulls off his mask. "I found Captain Wolfe staggering down the road with Drake's body over his shoulders. Before he passed out he told me he'd driven up to the fire tower to bring Trustler down, but found the corpsman collapsed on the trail, overcome by smoke and badly burned.

"It's hell out there, Miss Becky. The fire is spreading and trees are crashing over the road so that Captain Wolfe had to abandon the truck and come down by foot."

"Drake Trustler, where is he? Still in the ambulance?" I stand up and head for the door, but Boodean grabs my arm and won't let go.

"Becky, don't. Drake's gone. We have to concentrate on Captain Wolfe."

I can hear Mrs. Ross sobbing in the other room. "No!" she says over and over. "No!" She had become quite close to Drake when he was her assistant.

"Are you sure?" Tears come to my eyes and I don't try to hide them. "Drake was trying so hard to get well, to get over his lung problems."

Boodean looks straight at me. "*He was trying to get down the mountain to alert us about the fire. He died a hero. That's what's important.*"

"What happened to Loonie? I thought he was with Captain Wolfe."

"He was planning to go up with him, but the captain ordered him to stay behind and fight the blaze. The trench is halfway down to the creek, but the fire is moving fast. Can you take care of Wolfe alone? I have to get the men from the kitchen to go back and help. We need everyone!" He stops to get a drink of water from the bucket.

"Do you think we should send a couple of the corpsmen out in a truck to try to get to a telephone? Mrs. Stone's farm is only twenty minutes away."

"The flames are fifty-feet high, Becky. They're fanned by the wind so they flatten out, then swoop to the earth and catch on the dry underbrush. The boys would never make it. They'd be blown off the road or the gasoline in the truck would explode. If I ever wondered what hell would be like, I know now!"

Terror

"Mrs. Ross, can you help me?" I call. "The first thing we must do is get the rest of the captain's burned clothing off."

"Oh, honey, I don't think I can." The poor lady wipes her eyes with her wet hanky, and peeks through her fingers as if trying to make the vision of the scorched captain go away. "He was such a nice man. They both were."

"Don't say *was*, Mrs. Ross. Drake is gone, but the captain's still alive. Just get over here and help me! This probably won't be the only burn victim we'll get tonight."

"I can help." It's Snake sitting up on his cot.

I give up on Mrs. Ross for a minute. "Here, Snake, I'll get you a chair and you cut the rest of his trousers off. Be very gentle. I'll take off his boots. Look at the leather soles! They're almost burned through!"

When I first see the brave captain's legs, I let out a long sigh.

From the top of his boots to the top of his knees his skin is black and peeling. His upper thighs have a mass of blisters and his hands too. His face isn't so bad and neither is the back of his legs or his trunk.

I share what I know with Snake. "The first rule of thumb, when assessing burn injury is . . . if more than thirty percent of the body is covered in burns, the patient will lose too much fluid and go into shock, so our task is to try to keep that from happening." Wolfe moans and I give him a few drops of laudanum. "If he makes it though the night, we must worry about infection. This will be a close one."

"Hello! Hello!" Mrs. Ross is on the shortwave radio again, cranking away. If only the wind would calm down, she might be able to make a connection. "Can anyone hear me?! This is CCC Camp White Rock. Dammit! Pick up! We have a wildfire here and we need help!"

Snake and I look at each other, and though our situation is dire, we can't help but smile. To my knowledge, no one has ever heard Mrs. Ross swear before.

I call the panicked woman over. "Mrs. Ross, I want you to run to the kitchen for sugar." She looks at me as if I've lost my mind. "When you come back I'll show you how to feed the captain saline-sugar water with a dropper. We want to get a cup in the captain every hour," I explain. "With so much of his skin gone, he's losing his life fluids." The secretary bustles off, happy to have a job that doesn't involve looking at a scorched body.

Outside, the sky is crimson, a towering inferno. Sparks whirl up as another pine explodes and the blaze takes flight like a flock of red birds. I notice my breathing is way too fast.

Terror, the word comes to me. We are afraid, but the fire is afraid too and is fleeing the men across the mountain.

Devil and the Deep Blue Sea

When we hear the horn blast the second time, we are ready. Snake can't do much lifting, but I've found him a crutch and he's fixed another cot with clean sheets and a pillow. Mrs. Ross is still feeding the captain fluids drop by drop.

This time, Boodean brings back three patients, but thankfully they are all ambulatory, another burn victim, a second fellow with a dangling arm, and a third, Loonie Tinkshell, who just needs to lie down because he can't catch his breath.

"It's terrible out there, Miss Becky," Loonie pants. "Hotter than Hades. . . . Fire jumped the creek . . . burning across the fields. . . ." He gulps air two or three times, just to get through one sentence. "You're going to need more cots. I'll go to the dorms. Get you some more blankets and pillows."

"Loonie, just rest. Just stop talking and rest. Someone else can get the pillows. Here, take a drink of water and lie down."

"He's right, though," Boodean tells us as he stays to get the three men situated. "It's hell out there and the fire is spreading. If the boys can just get the trench finished in time, we can save the camp. Then we'll just keep beating the flames with wet burlap sacks if they try to skip over." He talks about the fire as if it had an evil mind of its own and he doesn't say what will happen if they *can't* get the trench finished.

"Unfortunately, we've lost contact with Lou Cross and his crew. It's too dark and too crazy to do a roll call, and no one has seen them since morning. On the other hand, we got a couple of people coming in from Liberty the back way. Had to go all the way to Delmont to get in here. Apparently, one of your emergency calls got through to Sheriff Hardman, Mrs. Ross. . . . Gotta keep moving." Before I can say good-bye, the medic rushes out the door.

"We need music," Mrs. Ross says, and at first I think she's lost her marbles. "Something to soothe us. The one thing the superintendent didn't take with him was his Victrola. How about Count Basie, 'Between the Devil and the Deep Blue Sea'?"

The melody is a nice touch and between feeding the captain the sugar-water and restarting the recording, Mrs. Ross now has a full-time job. She even manages to make us some coffee.

I give the man with the dislocated arm a sling, some Bayers, and a pallet on the floor. Then I turn to the burn victim. Phil Otter is his name, though I have no time to write any nurse notes.

"A burning branch was about to crash right down on the three of us and I reached up my hands to toss it aside," he recounts. You can tell he is proud of his action. Snake, my new assistant, gently cleans and dresses his blistered hands. Then we wait, wondering who the reinforcements could be.

An hour passes on the cuckoo clock and it's now ten P.M. Captain Wolfe moans in his opiate-induced sleep, and I sit down next to him to take the saline-sugar dropper from Mrs. Ross. The water is all we have to keep him alive.

I have always wanted to touch the scars on the captain's handsome face and I do now, touching them with one finger. "If you make it until morning and we can get you to the hospital there's hope," I whisper as my tears fall on his pillow. "As bad as it is, there's hope. I know you're a fighter. Hold on."

Reinforcements

"Incoming!" Snake announces, sounding like a soldier in a war movie. He's referring to the sound of a horn blaring over the music.

"Ready." I stand up and shake myself to get the blood stirring. "Mrs. Ross, take over Captain Wolfe's drops."

This time an extra man is with Boodean, the Reverend Miller, and the two of them assist a young carrottop over to a chair and give him a wooden box to support his foot. "It's his leg, maybe a break," Boodean tells me. "How's the captain?"

"Still with us. Mrs. Ross is trying to keep him hydrated. . . . Hello, Reverend. I'm amazed anyone could get in here."

"Nice to see you again, Miss Becky," the preacher says, tipping his hat. "Brought Daniel Hester and some of our faithful from Hazel Patch in the hack, even a couple of the homeless fellows I found under the bridge over the Hope, anyone I could round up in a hurry. Had to come clear around through Delmont. Left the recruits with the CCC men, but I'd be no good fighting fire. I've had lung problems since I was a boy." He rolls up his sleeves and looks around for something to do. "Figured if nothing else, I could help around here or ride with the ambulance man."

"We got to get back," Boodean says, looking out the window and pulling on the pastor's arm. "I think we've almost got the fire licked but no one can find Lou Cross and his men. I'm getting worried." Here Loonie Tinkshell sits up from his place on the floor.

"I'll go look for him," Loonie says. "I'm fine now, right, Nurse?" Stepping forward, I listen to the mechanic's heart and lungs. "You're fine. Just be careful!"

"Need some joe, Boodean?" Mrs. Ross holds a mug of steaming coffee.

"Thanks." The medic paces back and forth, his hands around the cup to keep them from trembling.

"Are you okay?" I whisper.

"Just tired."

"I mean it. *Are you okay?*" He shakes his head no. "Then stay here. Loonie and the Reverend can make a few runs."

Boodean looks at me hard and shakes his head no again. Then goes out the door.

Tourniquet

With Mrs. Ross's help, I have five more pallets set up in the waiting area and I stand on the porch, nervously looking up at the cliffs that glow white against the scarlet sky. It's then I remember that I forgot to ask Boodean where Drake Trustler's body is. It shouldn't be alone. *I don't want it to be alone*, but there's no time to think about that now.

The ambulance arrives with horn blaring again, followed in the distance by the wail of a siren. Boodean and Reverend Miller jump out of the cab and run around back. "We got a leg wound here! Awful mess. Hemorrhaging!" Boodean shouts as they carry in one of the cook's crew, a copper-haired fellow I've seen in the kitchen.

"Hang in there, Rusty!" the Reverend pleads. "The Lord is with you." Then turning to me he whispers, "He was run over by one of the CCC trucks. Driver backed right over him, felt the crunch, then pulled forward and drug him for thirty feet. Couldn't see a damn thing in the smoke and confusion."

Boodean's face is white and the Reverend's ash gray, and I instantly see why when I get a look at the injury. The foot at the end of Rusty's leg is turned inward at a ninety-degree angle. Bones protrude through the torn flesh, the toes are mangled, and blood is spurting from a major artery in the ankle.

"Tourniquet," I command, and when no one responds I pull on Snake's pants. "Your belt! Your belt! We'll use it for a tourniquet." I'm sure my eyes are wild. I haven't seen this much blood since Patience abrupted, and if we don't stop it soon the man will expire. Mrs. Ross covers her face and runs from the room.

"Get vitals, Boodean." Outside, the sound of the siren gets louder, and I realize where I've heard it before. It's Sheriff Hardman from Liberty.

Doors to the squad car slam and several people enter the infirmary, but I don't look up. I'm too busy tightening the belt, trying to put pressure on the boy's leg just above where the torn flesh begins. As hard as I pull the belt, the bleeding doesn't slow.

"Prepare for surgery," a familiar voice says. It's Dr. Blum.

Gates of Hell

In our little clinic, the night from hell is just beginning. Around nine P.M., a violent rainstorm moves in, which dampens the flames, but the thunder is so loud and close to the camp that it rattles the window glass. Lightning jabs the still-smoldering mountainside and then in the middle of everything the camp's generator goes out.

"Shit!" curses Blum, a needle and needle holder in one hand. He waits, thinking the power will come back on, looking at me over his cloth surgical mask across the superintendent's desk, our makeshift operating table. The power doesn't come back on.

Snake has to hobble out into the storm on his crutch to look for a kerosene lantern, but it takes at least five minutes before he gets back, looking like a drowned rat. Meanwhile, I have both gloved hands deep in Rusty's torn flesh, trying to reduce the open fracture and Sheriff Hardman is mopping up blood. "Good thing I got you here when I did, Doc."

"Praise the Lord!" That's the pastor, who helps Snake through the door, grabs the Coleman, and lights it.

"Had to threaten him with bodily harm," the lawman chuckles.
"That's not quite the whole story," mumbles Blum.

"Had to pull my gun and order him to gather up his doctor stuff
and get in the squad car."

"That's not quite it," Blum says again. "I told you I would come,
didn't I?" He silently holds out his gloved hand as if I will know
what he wants. I take a guess and hand over the scalpel. "The part
about the gun is true, though, and you enjoyed it, Hardman."

This is more than Blum has said in the last year, and he sounds
almost like a regular Joe, but the banter doesn't last. Two trucks
pull up, horns blaring, and Daniel Hester slams through the door.

"Head trauma and burns," he announces. "One of the CCC
fellows found a colored boy under a fallen pine. It was so dark, he
almost stepped on him. I don't think he's going to make it."

"Boodean!" I look away from the surgical field. "Where's Boodean?" The medic pokes his head through the door, tears in his
eyes and I fear he is about to unravel. "Boodean, help the vet. Get
the patient's vitals. Try some smelling salts on yourself."

"I'll be with you in a minute, Daniel," Blum says over his shoulder. "I've stopped the bleeding here. . . . Suture and needle holder,
Nurse . . ."

When I look down, Rusty's foot is not part of his body.

42

Afterburn

"In the end we saved many, most of them really." I'm standing with Patience, the day after the fire, in the camp laundry room, our makeshift morgue, looking down at the dead. "We've already transferred ten men to the hospital in Torrington," I tell her. "One of the first was Captain Wolfe; but he died in transport."

"Oh, Becky. I'm so sorry!" Patience reaches for me, expecting me to cry, but I am done with tears and am only numb. When I touch my own skin I am numb. Even my bones are numb.

"Thirty-five were treated in the camp's infirmary for everything from heat exhaustion to burns to broken bones. Three of those required surgery. It was amazing to watch Dr. Blum. The whole time the electricity was out, he moved among the wounded and the burned in the kerosene light like a Civil War surgeon. You heard one of the boys, Rusty, lost his foot? It was too mangled and Blum had to amputate. I've never seen so much death and horror."

I am staring at the row of corpses lined up on the concrete floor wrapped in white sheets like babies. Patience has cared for them all. I offered to help, but she told me to go back to the clinic and take care of the living.

Gently she washed each body, changing the water in her white basin over and over, leaving the gauze over the burns or wounds. She closed the dead men's eyes, put a rolled-up washcloth under their chin to keep their mouth shut, and then bundled them tight in a white sheet with only their feet sticking out; four bodies with white feet and two with brown. Little paper tags are tied on the toes and labeled with their names in Patience's neat writing.

"Where's Daniel?" she asks me.

"He went into Liberty for medication and supplies, Bayers, gauze, more laudanum, and some Silvardene, a new drug that's supposed to prevent infection. Dr. Blum had used it at the hospital in Charlottesville."

I lean over and read aloud the names of the six men, starting with one of the coloreds.

"*John Doe.* Who's this?"

"No one knows. Head trauma. A tree fell on him and someone found him after the storm. We think he's one of the homeless men who joined the firefighters. Probably has a family somewhere who'll never know he died a hero."

I continue reading. "*Drake Trustler . . . Captain Norman Wolfe . . . Nate Bowlin . . .* I met Nate Bowlin at Livia's delivery in Hazel Patch," I observe. . . . "And another time when he and Reverend Miller brought us some wood."

"The boy was like kin to me," Patience says. "Bitsy married his brother, Byrd. Nate was a real sweet kid, planned to go to college at Howard University next fall." She takes off her wire-rimmed glasses and wipes her eyes with the back of her hand. "The first of his family to go on to college."

The death count goes on as we stare at the row of bodies. *Percy Bishop . . . Clarence Mitchell.* This last name is familiar. . . .

"Lucy's husband. Lucy with the twins! Clarence Mitchell."

The sadness almost brings me to the floor. "Poor Lucy," I whisper. "Poor Lucy and those three little kids."

"You know this one too. Percy Bishop." She points to a short, thick body wrapped in her neat white shroud.

"I don't think so."

"The Bishop brothers? Beef?"

"Beef, the son of a bitch? What was *he* doing here?"

The midwife looks at me as though I've lost my mind. "*Fighting the fire.* Don't speak ill of the dead, Becky. Men came from all around. Daniel told me that Beef died trying to save Clarence Mitchell. Smoke inhalation." She puts her arm around me. "Death is the great leveler, and in the end, death takes us all, the weak . . . the strong . . . the angry and loving. Mrs. Potts, used to say that some of us get nine days on this earth, some get ninety years, there's no telling. . . . People like us should know that."

"People like us?"

"Midwives," says Patience. "Healers."

Feeding the Army

Twenty-four hours after the first men left to fight the wildfire, Starvation has the wood cookstove going and is prepared to feed the Forest Army, but when we enter the mess hall, it's as quiet as a church at midnight.

The corpsmen eat their eggs and pancakes, but have no appetite. Years later, they'll tell stories about the Wildfire of '35, but today they have lost good friends, have lived through a nightmare, have battled an inferno, and a motion picture of it still rolls behind their dark eyes.

CCC officers, corpsmen, and volunteers from the surrounding farms, both black and white, sit together, and I recognize a few faces. The Indian man, Mr. Hummingbird, looks up and waves a tired hand. One-Arm Wetsel is sitting with Reverend Miller, and John Dyer, the young polka-dancing father. Even the bearded, bootlegging coal miner who came to the house and his short, dark companion are here. As we walk past the tables I catch a few muted snatches of conversation.

" . . . They estimate five thousasnd acres burned, maybe more."

" . . . The only green left, between here and the Hope, is the hundred acres around the camp."

" . . . It was the rain that saved us."

" . . . Did Lou Cross and his crew ever report?"

Patience and I had planned to just get coffee, but it smells so good we end up eating a whole breakfast.

"Excuse me," Patience says when we're almost finished. She stands and walks toward the kitchen to talk to the bald-headed cook. I can't imagine what she's saying. "More pancakes, please"? "Thank you for the nice meal"? She comes back with a clean, empty mason jar.

"What's that for?" I ask, thinking it may have something to do with the burial preparations.

"My breasts," she whispers, smiling, as if I would enjoy the joke. "They're so full, I need to go somewhere private and get the milk out before I get a breast infection. I left the baby and Danny with Mrs. Maddock."

"What are you going to do with the milk?"

"I don't know. Put it in a pitcher next to Mrs. Ross's coffee?" Here we both start laughing so hard I almost choke.

Rescue

Back at headquarters, the big news is that Lou Cross and his crew have at last been rescued. Loonie Tinkshell sits on one of the wooden chairs in the waiting area projecting his voice so the men can hear through the open infirmary door.

"I went out to look for them and in a little gully about a quarter mile west of the trench, I heard a sound. Standing in a rocky area at the side of the ravine, I could hear water dripping somewhere, so I began to explore. That's when I slid down the mining shaft. It must have been one the bootleggers' coal mines. Their holes are all over these hills."

Here the porch door swings open and, who should limp in, carrying a mug of steaming coffee but Lou Cross himself, still wearing his cowboy hat. He has on a clean uniform and, of course, looks quite dapper.

"There you are, you son of a bitch." He slaps the mechanic on his back, pulls up a chair, and straddles it backward. "Pardon my French, ma'am, but he's my friggin' hero. We were more dead than alive when he slid into that hole.

"Here's how it happened . . ." he begins, like a storyteller. "My boys and I found the bootleggers' mining shaft about the same way Loonie did and it saved our lives," Lou continues. "We were headed across the west slope, trying to meet up with the rest of the camp when the fire pounced on us like a cougar." He smacks his hand hard on the back of his chair to make his point. "Smoke so thick and air so hot, we dropped our tools and ran, but there was no way we could outrun the flames.

"Arthur, hunched over and coughing, was in the lead one minute and the next he was gone. Fell right into the hole. Lucky for all of us, the slope was only a forty-five-degree angle, not straight down, but there were boulders at the bottom. That's how Arthur broke his ankle." I look across the waiting room and see a small, pale young man with his lower leg in a cast, Dr. Blum's handiwork. Arthur grins and raises his hand, in case some of the group don't know him.

"The rest of us were able to slow our descent by digging in

our hands and heels. If it hadn't been for that mineshaft, we'd be goners. The fire was right on our tails, drawn up the ravine like creosote in a tin stovepipe . . . Whoosh!"

"When I dropped down into the pit, I was kind of scared." This is Loonie Tinkshell, continuing the narrative. "I wasn't sure what I had found. 'Hello!' I called into the black. 'Anyone down here?'

"'Hell yes!' Lou answered me. I couldn't stop laughing."

"The worst part was the heat," Arthur, the kid with the cast, observes. "It was like we were trapped in a cooking pot. The twelve of us crowded away from the opening, got as far back as we could, but the shaft ended right there.

"Lou ordered us to take off our shirts, wet them with what we had in our canteens, cover our heads, and get down on the floor. The sergeant lay nearest the opening to keep any of the fellows from bolting out of there. Threatened to shoot us if we tried."

"Well, I know how men are," Lou gets back in the narrative. "We'd rather take our chances out in the open than be cornered. On the other hand, I was certain anyone who tried to break for it would be burned to a crisp. Turns out I made the right decision, boys! *We are all still alive* . . . Praise the Lord!"

"Praise the Lord!" the men echo.

43

Red Sails at Sunset

The days after the fire are only a blur. I walked and worked through a daze of acrid smoke, Boodean, hollow-eyed, at my side. In a lull between vital signs and dressing changes, I found my medic sitting in the corner of the superintendent's closet listening to Count Basie, tears streaming down his face.

"You okay?" I could see that he wasn't so I sat down on the floor beside him. "Is there something I can do to help?"

"Nah. Thanks, Nurse . . . I'm just tired. Don't tell the fellows I was crying, okay?"

"I'm tired too. It will take us some time to get over this. You were a hero out there, Boodean. You know that? You saved a lot of men's lives."

"I didn't save Drake Trustler or the captain or that colored kid Bowlin. He died in my arms."

"No, we didn't save everyone."

"I don't think I can do this anymore, Miss Becky, be a medic. I'm not cut out for it." Boodean Sypolt breaks down then, crumbles like a little boy, all the pain and death and suffering pouring out of him in great gulping sobs. I turn up Count Basie so that no one can hear.

Dr. Blum stayed with me for three days. There were the wounded and burned to care for, and he slept in the dorms and ate in the mess hall, while I slept in the infirmary to be close to the men.

Side by side we worked as he talked, gave instructions. It was almost like old times. He even comforted the corpsmen in a kind but stiff way. Then one morning he insisted I get out of the clinic.

"Go up to the captain's bungalow and get some rest," he encouraged. "If you don't take a few hours, you're going to get sick, and the patients still need you."

He knew from experience that such an approach always works on me. *Get rest, not for yourself, but so you can better take care of others!*

Nearly ten hours later, I woke to a hazy orange light pouring through the four-pane windows in the captain's log cabin. The sun was fading to the west, and one thing I've learned is, you get spectacular sunsets after a big fire.

On the homemade oak table beside the captain's bed, rests a book of poetry and a framed photo of a beautiful woman. I reach for the book, where a ribbon marks what he must have last read, a poem by Elizabeth Barrett Browning: *"How do I love thee? Let me count the ways. . . ."*

Then I pick up the photograph and stare into the woman's eyes. What was her name? Caroline . . . I remember now. His wife was a blond schoolteacher with a heart of gold. The captain wasn't thinking of me when he read that poem, but his wife.

"And if God choose," the sonnet ends, *"I shall but love thee better after death."*

I roll on my side, kiss the captain's wife on her forehead, and put her photo back on the table. Then I kiss the captain's pillow and smell his scent, now gone forever, a man who could have been my lover.

Wherever they are, they are together, Captain Wolfe and his

wife, Caroline, flying hand in hand, sailing over the tops of the White Rock Cliffs through the red-golden light.

Torched

Before Blum and I leave the camp, the new major, sent over from District Five, calls both of us into his office. "You need to rest. You're exhausted," he tell us, sitting behind the desk we'd done an amputation on a week earlier. "I'm going to ask for a nurse from Camp Roosevelt in Virginia to come over for a few weeks, so you can take some time to recover."

"That's very gracious." The doctor clears his throat. "But speaking for Nurse Myers, will her leave be paid?" My mouth falls open and my cheeks redden. I wouldn't have had the nerve to ask.

"Gadzooks, yes! And I'm going to put in for a position for you as an L.E.M. too."

Dr. Blum looks puzzled.

"Locally employed nan. I understand the camp hasn't had their own physician for a couple of months. Maybe we can work out a schedule, if you're willing to alternate with Nurse Myers."

The doctor doesn't respond, and for a moment I think he's gone mute again, but finally he speaks. "Yes. Certainly. But I'll need to discuss it with my other employer." *Who the hell is that? I think. Hester?*

Patience had gone home with Daniel in the Ford and left the Pontiac for us, and I'm so tired I don't even notice when Blum slides into the driver's seat. We leave the green forest of the camp and enter the nightmare remains of hell. All along the road are the blackened monuments to the wildfire, black spikes without branches reaching into the sky.

Crockers Creek is almost overflowing with rushing brown water. "The ground can't hold the rain after a burn like this. The rain put out the fire, but it doesn't heal the earth. Not yet," Dr. Blum says, taking the tone I've heard before: learned professor. "The soil will be fertile, full of minerals and nitrogen, but the ashes coat the ground, so the water can't penetrate."

I'm just going to ask how he knows these things when something catches my eye, a stone chimney, standing alone where there should be a house.

"Stop!"

Blum puts on the brake and pulls up next to the metal skeleton of a swinging bridge. Across the roaring creek there's no house or barn where there should be. No family with little girls.

"Fuck!" exclaims Blum. "Where are the Hucknells? Their place has been torched. The fire must have swept over on the swinging bridge and burned across their land. You can see it didn't go much farther."

I don't respond. My breath is knocked out of me. What happened to the family? The whole place is gone. Blum shifts the Pontiac into gear and speeds on to Liberty. Near the bridge that crosses the Hope, the scene changes again.

On one side of the river are charred forest and fields, a black-and-white world; on the other, a town with green lawns and flowers. It's the same all the way home, green on one side of the river, black on the other.

The Hucknells

We stop at the Hesters' before going home, and as I enter the kitchen I smell something good. Patience is baking bread. Danny

plays with his tin truck on the floor and the baby sleeps in the
sweet grass basket that Cypress, the grandmother from Hazel
Patch, gave me.

"Oh, Becky!" Patience greets me. "How *are* you? Where's
Isaac?"

"Out at the barn, searching for Daniel."

"You look so tired. Coffee?" I know what she means. No makeup, stringy hair, droopy army nurse's uniform. I've not changed
for days.

"I'm okay . . ." I trail off and then start up again. "We went past
the Hucknells'."

"Yes, the Hucknells . . ."

"Their house is gone. That was one of my old delivery stops.
What happened?"

"I thought you knew."

"No, nothing. What happened?" I ask again.

Patience looks puzzled and moves toward me. "You didn't hear?
Alfred and Willa and their baby boy died in the fire."

"No!" Patience catches me as I drop, and helps me into a kitchen
chair.

"Oh, Becky, I'm so sorry. It's been almost a week and I thought
everyone knew."

"What happened? How could that happen? And what about the
girls?"

"Alfred carried the girls out of the house, one by one, when he
saw the fire had jumped Crockers Creek. It was in the paper and
everything, an interview with the oldest child, Sally.

"He carried them through the burning fields down to the creek.
Remember how the wind roared that night? The wooden boards
on the swinging bridge were already in flames. He made each girl
lie in the water with a wet blanket over her head.

"It was good thinking. The water saved their lives. Then he
went back for Willa and the baby. When he got them as far as the

creek bank, he ran back to the barn to free the frightened horses and cows."

"But you said the parents and the infant died."

"Willa slipped on the steep bank and lost hold of the baby. She couldn't swim. Couldn't reach the baby in the brown water. The oldest girl saw it happen, but it was dark and the current was strong. Within minutes, they were both swept away.

"The creek saved the girls but took the baby and their mother. Their bodies were found two days later in the rocks down by the gravel pit . . . I'm sorry. Am I telling too much? Should I stop?"

"No . . . finish."

"Alfred was apparently caught by a burning beam in the barn. . . . The girls found him when they thought it was safe to come out of the water. Can you imagine, finding your father, burned and dead? Twenty-four hours later, Reverend Miller picked them up on his way back from the CCC camp, the four little orphans, walking along the road to town barefoot in their nightgowns."

The tears that come out of me for the next hour, my head bent down over the kitchen table, would flood the Hope River. Patience stays with me the whole time, patting my back. I'm not just crying for the little girls, but for everyone, and not just the victims of this fire, but all the victims of all the fires, all the victims of this hard, hard life.

When Blum comes in from the barn, his eyes are red too.

44

Graveyard

I've not been feeling well and I know Isaac notices. He has even begun cooking and cleaning the house. Sometimes I go out in the garden and weed, even if it isn't needed, just to sit with the plants. Sometimes I lie down in the meadow, down by the creek, looking up at the sky, just to feel the comfort of the earth. Secretly, I fear something has been burned out of me, something that will never grow back.

Despite all the many losses when I was young, I thought if people did what was right and played by the rules, all would be well, but life, I've learned, doesn't work that way, and death and pain come on relentlessly whether you are good or not.

It has been a week of funerals. On Saturday we went to Clarence Mitchell's service at the Saved by Faith Baptist Church. I couldn't stop crying. When I went up to Lucy Mitchell, instead of easing her grief, I bawled on her shoulder; it was that bad.

Willa's girls are staying with Mrs. Stenger, and she told me in private, "I'm too old for this. The littlest ones have nightmares and the older ones fight. I hate to think of them going to an orphanage, but they have no family and I have my own brood of five to care for."

I didn't go to the Bowlin boy's memorial service at Hazel Patch and neither did Dr. Blum, though Patience invited us to join them. I'd only run into the young man twice, when the pastor brought us wood and then again at Livia's birth, and Blum didn't know him at all.

While the Hesters are at the Hazel Patch chapel, I walk out behind the barn to look at the graveyard where Blum has been digging the graves. There will be eight in all, each seven feet deep. Next to the empty holes, there are three little graves with tiny wood crosses.

The first cross is for the premature baby that was left in a cardboard box at my Women and Infants' Clinic, another lifetime ago, when I didn't understand how such things could happen. Now I know. Life is cruel.

The second is for the baby Patience lost before she moved to West Virginia, the one she delivered prematurely in the back of the horse-drawn ambulance in Chicago, when she was sixteen. (There are no remains in this tiny grave, but the midwife needed a place to remember.)

The third cross is for the baby Patience made with Daniel during a thunderstorm and then birthed on the kitchen floor.

All the victims of the fire who have no family plots will be buried in this place tomorrow. Captain Wolfe, Drake Trustler, the colored homeless man John Doe, Willa Hucknell, Alfred Hucknell, and the baby, but Patience has also convinced the Hazel Patch folks and the Bishop brothers that Beef and Nate Bowlin belong here too, with the other heroes of the Hope River Wildfire. When the midwife makes up her mind about something, she's very convincing.

Blum has started carving a sign, to be mounted on two cedar posts, that will read, HOPE MEMORIAL CEMETERY.

May 9, 1935

I am out digging the last grave behind the barn in the spring sunshine and all the time I'm thinking about my own grave, the one I jumped into the day Priscilla died. What was it that propelled me into that black tomb? What happened that made me turn my back on life? I'll try to explain, though it may not make sense. The thing is, I was beyond sensibility.

Looking back, the words of the circulating nurse in the operating theater come back to me through a dark tunnel. "You won't be happy about this, Dr. Blum. They're sending a patient up from the ER, a hot abdomen."

I was just finishing my third surgery of the day, a hernia repair, and was anxious to get home. Whether Priscilla would be there was the question.

"Dr. Gross says the man is in critical condition," the RN goes on. "You're the only surgeon still in the hospital, so the case comes to you."

Pissed off, I changed, rescrubbed, and reentered the operating room, just as the anesthesiologist was putting the patient under. As the nurse gave report, I waited, scalpel in my gloved hands. I had done hundreds of appendectomies and a couple of dozen ruptures.

"This is a patient in his late thirties, found in front of a downtown hotel with fever and chills, acute abdominal pain. Temp 104, pulse thready at 120, blood pressure 100/40 and dropping. The ER suspects a ruptured appendix or a twisted bowel. There's no known next of kin, but the name on his business card in his wallet says John Teeleman, Eli Lilly."

I almost dropped my scalpel. John Teeleman, the man who had been screwing my wife?! Rage overcame me. My hands shook, sweat beaded out on my brow. Fortunately, everyone else in the operating theater was concentrating on getting the man's blood pressure up and no one noticed.

"Epinephrine," the anesthesiologist ordered, and a nurse inserted the drug into the IV. "You'd better cut now, Blum," he said to me.

The rest of the surgery was a blur. My first look at the patient's abdomen revealed a well-healed vertical scar from sternum to public bone, so he'd already had surgery sometime in the past.

I know I made a small incision over McCurry's Point and opened the fascia. I remember opening the peritoneum and being surprised when I encountered massive adhesions, probably the result of an old war wound. The appendix had already burst and purulent fluid was everywhere. It must have been as I was cutting through the scar tissue that I nicked the abdominal aorta. I couldn't be sure because the visual field was compromised with a waterfall of blood.

"Suction!" I ordered, though the scrub nurse was already sucking.

The anesthesiologist tried to start a second IV line.

I opened the abdominal incision wider, searching for the bleeder.

The nurses tilted the table to shunt what was left of the Eli Lilly rep's life fluid back into his heart.

I fought for John Teeleman's life, as his blood drained red on the operating room floor.

"Thanks, Dr. Adams," I shook hands with the anesthesiologist when it was all over.

"You tried, Isaac," the circulating nurse said, giving me a one-armed hug.

But did I? To this day, I don't know. Sworn to protect life.

Did I try hard enough or did I intentionally kill the patient with that slip of the knife, execute John Teeleman, the man who was fucking my wife?

Sunday Dinner

"These are *some* apple fritters, Isaac!" Daniel exclaims.

"More, please!" says Danny, agreeing with him. "More, with apple butter!"

There's a cool wind outside and we're sitting in the kitchen around the table in the little house with the blue door. Tomorrow is the burial in the new graveyard, and Dr. Blum cooked the meal.

"You're going to put me to shame, man," Daniel goes on. "All I can make is fried eggs and bacon."

"Isaac has been feeding me very well. Somehow I just don't feel like cooking."

The doctor doesn't say anything, but he smiles, and I realize how, despite the anger I had toward him about my journal, my feelings have softened. Maybe the fire melted my heart. With that thought, the tears come again and I have to leave the table.

Patience follows me out behind the barn where the graves are ready for the ceremony.

"Are you okay, Becky?" Patience asks when I wipe my eyes.

"I guess. I just can't stop crying. It wasn't like I was *in love* with Captain Wolfe, but we were close friends and maybe I *could* have loved him. And Drake Trustler, he was so brave and such a good spirit. I can't believe he's gone. The others I didn't know well, but still it's so sad.

"You should have seen the boys the day the of the blaze, Patience. The Forest Army went off in their trucks, singing as if the fire were a Sunday School picnic. I'm not kidding. They were singing *Hi-de-hi-ho*, never knowing the hell they would face. They were just kids really. I keep hearing their voices. *Hi-de-hi-ho. Hi-de-hi-he.*"

The midwife doesn't say anything, just puts her arm around me as we stare into the empty holes, seven feet deep and seven feet long.

"But you know what really gets me? *Willa.* I cry for her and I cry for the baby and I cry for Alfred, the wife beater, who loved his little children so much he would walk through fire to save them."

May 10, 1935

The day John Teeleman died, I left the operating suite like a man in a trance and was surprised when Priscilla ran up to me in the ER waiting room.

"How is he?" She grabbed at my coat sleeve.

"Who?"

"Don't play dumb! John Teeleman, my lover."

"How did you know?"

"When I went to the Inn to meet him, the bellman told me they brought him to Martha Washington Hospital. How is he?" she asks again and pulls at my lapels, her face so close I can smell the fear.

"He didn't make it." (I don't mean to sound cold, but I'm just so exhausted it comes out that way.) "Bled out during surgery."

"No!" Priscilla pounds on my chest, hits me over and over as she screams in front of everyone in the waiting room. "No! You killed him, you son of a bitch! You killed him on purpose!"

"It wasn't like that, Pris," I try to explain. "There were adhesions. Massive infection. He was already critical. We couldn't stop the bleeding...." But she rages on, not caring who hears.

"You killed him!" Every eye in the waiting room is on us, so I pull her roughly outside.

"You killed him. My only chance at happiness! You fucking waste of a man!" That's when I slap her. It's not like I meant to or even thought about it before my hand moved, but my palm makes a red mark on her cheek.

"Pris!" I yell, but it's too late, she's already running across the parking lot, careening carelessly, blinded by tears.

"Watch the ice, Doc," Jackson, the colored maintenance man cautions as he lights a cigarette on the hospital loading dock. I don't answer, but throw my black bag on the seat of my Pontiac and follow Pris's little roadster out to Locust. By the time I make the turn, she's a half mile ahead of me, disappearing fast.

Thirty minutes later, I cross the iron bridge over the James, pass through Perrysville, and pull into the drive of our brick home. I'm thinking I'll beg her forgiveness, but her car isn't there. It's already on the bottom of the James River.

An accident they called it, but I thought differently and have never doubted she drove over the bank on purpose.

How long does it take a person to forgive himself? Two lives lost because of my stupidity. Maybe you will say I'm too hard on myself, but I was a hard man in those days, and I set my own punishment: death for a double murder ... and for a coward who doesn't have the courage to kill himself, death while alive, madness.

45

Now I Lay Me Down to Sleep

The turnout for the burials is more than we expected and I'm glad
the four of us spent some time last evening constructing makeshift
benches to seat the next of kin and older folk. There were horse-
drawn carts and vehicles parked all over the yard.

The little Hucknell girls find Dr. Blum and cling to him, insist-
ing he sit up front on the benches. Only the eldest, Sally, cries, and
Isaac puts his arm around her and holds her close.

One by one, the coffins are lowered into the graves by the CCC
men. There are eight freshly dug holes and nine dead, because we
planned to bury the baby with his father, Alfred Hucknell.

Boodean is here and Starvation MarFarland, and Snake and
Loonie Tinkshell and a few of the others, even Rusty on his crutches
because, as he told me, even though he lost his foot, he wanted to
thank Dr. Blum for saving his life. The new superintendent seems a
little lost, but Lou Cross takes care of everything.

"Ashes to ashes. Dust to dust." Reverend Miller says a few
words about death and heroes and reads the Scripture. I picture
the ashes left from the wildfire sifting across the land, acres and
acres of drifting gray ashes. The service closes as Mrs. Miller,
wearing a long purple gown and a strand of pearls like Eleanor

Roosevelt, sings a hymn and we all join in on the chorus. "*Will the circle be unbroken? By and by, Lord, by and by? There's a better home awaiting. In the sky, Lord, in the sky.*"

Afterward, everyone gathers at the homemade tables for potato salad and baked beans, apple pie and cold milk and coffee. The Hazel Patch faithful are present and Mrs. Miller comes over and gives me a hug. The Bishop brothers and Cora are here. From across the crowd Cora winks at me and points to her belly. She's wearing a new blue dress and her hair is done up on her head, like a proper lady. The CCC guys sit by themselves, all in uniform, until the Reverend and Sheriff Hardman go over and join them.

As everyone gets in their auto or carts to leave, Blum, Hester, and Maddock walk out across the fields toward the creek and I think how good it is to see Isaac acting like a regular man, a man who has friends. Even before his collapse, when he was a functioning physician, I don't think he had friends. Come to think of it, neither did I, not many anyway, and not close.

From where I stand toward the back of the cemetery, I can look down Spruce Mountain toward the Hope River. We are on the green side, and I see, on the other, blackened forests and fields all the way to the west.

The golden forsythia bush next to the barn rings like a churchbell.

Flowers

"No one brought any flowers for the graves!" Patience says after everyone is gone and the four of us are taking down the homemade benches and tables. "Let's go get some. Come on!" She is pulling my hand. "Here," she says to Daniel taking her baby out of the sling and handing her over. "You take the kids. We have to find flowers!"

It's almost dusk. I'm dead tired and would just like to lie down, but I do what she says. In the field by the barn we find daisies and mustard and phlox. We pick and pick until we have enough for all the graves.

"Isaac is carving the sign for the cemetery. What do you want it to say?" I ask as we turn back.

Patience doesn't hesitate. She must have had it all planned.

HOPE MEMORIAL CEMETERY

DEDICATED TO THE HEROES OF
THE HOPE RIVER WILDFIRE OF 1935
"WE ARE ALL STRONGER THAN WE THINK."

Back at the gravesites, we kneel again and spread out our flowers, a blanket of color to cover the dead, white, yellow, and pink. Patience surprises me when she makes the sign of the cross. "Mrs. Kelly," she shrugs as if that explains it. "She was Catholic."

I think about that . . . how little parts of those we love are alive in us, even when the beloved is gone.

"What happens to them?" I ask. "Drake and Beef? The captain and Nate Bowlin? The Hucknells? Are they just flesh and bones to molder under the earth or is there something more?"

"More," the midwife says firmly.

"You sound so sure."

"Look around you," she says pointing down into the valley where the Hope reflects the sunset, a ribbon of red, and I'm crying again, but this time for the joy of it.

46

The Itch

Today was my first day back at work and though the sun was shining and I was happy to be returning, the drive there depressed me. On both sides of the road, as I approached White Rock, there was nothing but blackened forests and fields, and then around a bend there was the camp, an island of green that stood like a testimonial to the men who fought to save the trees.

"Boy, am I glad to see you!" Boodean exclaims as I walk into headquarters. Mrs. Ross greets me with a cup of coffee and two new starched nurse uniforms and that gift lifts my spirits some. "The nurse from Virginia treated the lads okay, but wouldn't let me do a damn thing. Said I wasn't a *real* medic." You can see her words hurt him.

I make a list of supplies we need from Stenger's Pharmacy and then we get busy with three patients one after another, a case of poison ivy, a boil the size of a half dollar that I let Boodean lance, and finally, just before lunch, a new man who worries me, Joe Morgan, who'd just transferred in from a CCC camp in Pennsylvania.

"I don't know what's wrong, ma'am," the very tall, thin corpsman tells me. "I'm thirsty all the time. I even have to get up at night to drink and I can feel my heart pounding. Not only that, I'm losing weight, no matter how much I put down my gullet."

I suspect he has diabetes, but when Dr. Blum comes he will decide.

Finally it's chow time. When Boodean and I enter the mess hall, tears spring to my eyes. These young men, the Forest Army, many from the poorest and most disadvantaged homes, are my knights in shining armor.

Snake, the boy who almost chopped off his own leg, strolls over to our table, with only a slight limp. "The trees finally came," he tells Boodean. "Morning, Miss Becky. We're going to start planting this afternoon."

"Trees?" I ask.

"Yeah, the new super ordered a boxcar of jack pine and some wild grass seed to prevent erosion on the hillsides. It's one of the missions of the CCC camps, reforestation, and boy do we have a lot of *reforestation* to do!" You can tell he likes the way the new word sounds.

"Do you want to go with them?" I ask Boodean. "Sounds like fun."

"I wouldn't mind."

In the afternoon clinic, I see some of the corpsmen injured in the fire, per the routine of the substitute nurse, and at the end of the day, Rusty hops in supported on his one foot and two crutches.

"Howdy, Miss Becky. Nice to see you back," he greets me cheerfully.

"My mother and father in Indiana sent you a note. He hands me an already opened envelope and I pull out a five-and-dime greeting card with a hummingbird on the front. Inside it says simply, *"Thank you. Our sun is our hope. You saved him."* Son is spelled wrong, but it doesn't matter, I know that Rusty is their shining sun and it brings tears to my eyes.

"Aren't you going home, Rusty? I'm sure you could. They would give you medical discharge. I can fill out the papers if you want."

"No, I'm happy here. I get three squares a day, medical care, and my ma gets her check. It means a lot to them back in Indianapolis.

"Major Langford, the new camp superintendent, gave me a sit-down job in the woodshop, learning to make furniture. I can do it all on a low bench so I don't have to stand, and he's looking for someone in Pittsburgh who can make me an artificial foot. My only problem is the itch."

Here I raise my eyebrows. Another case of the crotch itch?

"Where exactly does it itch?" I ask, thinking this will be awkward if I have to examine his privates with Boodean off planting trees.

The young man looks confused. "My foot, of course. My left foot. The one the doc took off!"

"Oh." I start to giggle and I can't stop. "It's called *phantom pain* when a limb is removed, but I guess you have phantom itch!" Now Rusty is laughing too.

"Go ask the cook for ice to put on your stump the next time you get the itch and dunk your stump in cold water to numb the nerves." With my home remedies I'm getting more like the midwife every day.

Offering

Home . . . I'm going home. My auto has been tuned up and filled with petrol by the motor pool guys. I have twenty-five dollars cash money in my pocket, my vacation pay, and two new army-issue nurse uniforms.

It isn't until I pass the Hucknell place that I roll down the window and slow the Pontiac. It's a sight from a CCC poster.

All across the scorched earth, CCC corpsmen march in a line, planting tiny jack pines. The boys have their shirts off, with burlap bags of seedlings tied to their belts. They take a few steps, slash a hole with their ax, kneel down, put the seedling in, stand and stomp the soil around it, then take a few more steps and do the same thing again. Someday, fifty-foot pine trees will grow here, reaching up to the sun, a memorial to the Forest Army.

Forty minutes later, I wind up Wild Rose Road, looking forward to taking a walk and lying on the grass down by the stream, but something looks different.

I can't make it out until I pass the Maddocks', but as I get closer I see that there's a new picket fence around our front yard. I love picket fences, but who put it up? Surely Patience and Hester don't have time for such fancies.

Jumping out to inspect, I find that each picket is handmade, painted white, and not only that, on the pointed end of each staff, someone has carved a delicate daisy. Our house is encircled with flowers!

There's only one person who could do this and I run inside, prepared to thank him, but the parlor is empty, the bedrooms are too. "Isaac!" I call. No answer. Just to be sure I poke my head in the kitchen and am shocked to find a mason jar filled with lilacs on the table. It just about floors me and I plunk down in one of the wooden chairs to take it all in.

What's gotten into the man? You'd swear we were courting. It's then I notice a child's sketchbook. *Confessions of a Silent Man* it says on the cover in Blum's neat print. Has the doctor been keeping a journal too? Did he leave it here for me? It seems obviously a gift, along with the flowers and the beautiful fence, but what if I'm wrong? What if he left it on the table by mistake? If it's not meant for me and I read it, I'd be as rotten as he was. . . . I lift up the cover and glance at the first lines.

"Syndactyly! The word erupts out of my mind like hot lava out of a volcano. Syndactyly is the medical term for webbed toes. I would tell Becky, but then she would realize I've been reading her journal."

Gratitude

All afternoon I hold back and then about four I open the doctor's journal and begin to read. By eight o'clock, it's too dark to see and I wonder vaguely what's happened to Isaac. Probably off with Daniel helping with lambing; it's a busy time of year. I get up to light the kerosene lamp and start a fire in the cookstove. I have no intention of cooking, but the house is getting a little cold. So far, I've read up to: *I miss Becky. She has cut me off, called me a dickhead and a bastard!*

I take a big breath and tighten my mouth, remembering when I said those words. I really should stop reading, not because I'm doing something wrong. I'm sure now that Isaac wanted me to read his journal, but I fear hearing his thoughts will have unintended consequences. The words are drawing me in, drawing me closer to a man I never really knew. Still I go on, wanting to hear what he will say next.

Outside the night grows dark and the spring frogs sing. Where could Isaac be? For so long I resented his presence, even tried to think how I could get rid of him. What if he just packed his stuff and hit the road, and the sketchbook is his parting gift?

I continue to read, but leave the last few pages because I don't want it to end. What will I do then? And how will I talk to this new Isaac when he comes back. (*If he comes back*, the old worried Becky thinks.)

I lay the sketchbook aside. Somehow, I now *want* Isaac to read my journal, read all I've written since I found a new hiding place, so before retiring, I hang a lantern on the porch and leave him a present, my journal, next to the flowers. . . .

Upstairs at my bedside, I stand for a moment in my nightdress and then do something I haven't done in a long time, kneel down on the floor.

The prayer is one word. "Thank you. Thank you for repairing what was broken, what was torn, what was bleeding.

Thank you.

47

May 16, 1935

Early this morning, as soon as Becky left for the CCC camp, I began installing the picket fence that I'd been working on in the loft of the barn for the last month. It only took a few hours because the staves were finished last week; all I had to do was put in the posts, screw on the crosspieces, and nail up the wood. While I was working, I tried to decide if I should leave my notebook for Becky. In a way, I felt she deserved to know who I am, a broken man, trying to knit the bones of my life back together.

Finally, I did it. I left my journal on the kitchen table, and to be sure she noticed, went out in the field and picked her some flowers. I had never picked flowers for a woman before.

Just as I finished, Daniel Hester sped up Wild Rose in his beat-up Ford. "Can you clean up, Blum? We got trouble. Judge Wade just called from Liberty. Social services out of Charleston are coming into town this afternoon to take the Hucknell girls away. They're going to split them up. Dump them into four foster homes in four separate counties."

"The hell they are."

"Well, we'd better get going if we want to stop them. I

already alerted Maddock and he's putting on his Sunday best. You talk with Becky about adopting Sally?"

Here there's a pause. "Not yet. I was mulling it over. You know me, I'm not much of a talker."

"Dammit, Blum. We discussed it with Maddock for a couple of hours after the burial. You said you'd talk. Can you call her? Adoption is a big commitment."

"There's no phone at the camp, remember..."

"Well, hell! We have to act fast. Patience thinks it's a great idea, and she said Becky would too. If we take the twins and Maddock takes Sonya, Sally could live with you."

I recall how Sally clung to me at the burial service, how I wiped her tears. "No, we have to do it. I'll just hope for the best. If Becky doesn't agree, I'll be a solo father like the widower, Walter Schmidt. He does okay with little Petey." Hester turns the Ford around and I run for the house for a clean shirt and tie.

"So, fellas, what can I do you for?" Linkous asks when we're seated around his desk. He's trying to talk like a good ol' boy, but everyone knows he went to law school at Yale.

Daniel cuts short the chitchat. "We want you to draw up adoption papers for four children and we need them today."

"You need them today? What's going on, boys? This is mighty short order. My secretary took the day off to see her sister in Torrington."

"I can type," I interject. (I might as well say something. The last time the lawyer saw me, Becky was wiping drool off my chin.)

"Well, well, Dr. Blum. I heard you were back with the living. You can type, huh? So what's the deal?"

"The Hucknell children? You heard about them?"

Linkous whistles. *"Everyone has. It was in the paper. A tragedy. Real shame. How're the kids holding up?"*

"They're doing as well as can be expected, but we just heard that the girls are due to be picked up by the Children's Home Society out of Charleston today and then placed in four different foster homes all over the state." That's Daniel making a long story short.

"At the funeral the other day, the three of us had discussed taking the sisters, but we didn't know things were moving so fast. We need to make our adoptions official before the social workers get here."

Linkous whistles again. *"Any next of kin? We'd have to get approval."*

"None," adds Maddock. *"Judge Wade investigated. He's the one that got in touch with the Children's Home Society a few weeks ago."*

"So do you know these children, any of you? Do your wives agree? Women do most of the raising."

"I've known them for a long time," I put in. *"Nurse Myers and I were friends with their mother and used to visit them regularly."* I don't mention that I haven't really talked about the adoption with Becky, and before Linkous can sense my discomfort, Daniel breaks in again.

"Patience and I will take the twins, Sunny and Sue. We have an extra bedroom. The Maddocks will take Sonya, and Blum will take Sally, the oldest. She has a bond with him. We all live within two miles of one another so the sisters will see each other every day."

"Have you talked to Judge Wade about this?"

"Yes," says Daniel. *"He called us this morning and that's our next stop."*

"It all sounds good to me, except Blum you haven't exactly

been a model citizen for the past year. Do you even have a job?"

"He works as my assistant," Daniel reveals.

"And I'm starting at the White Rock CCC camp as their part-time physician in a few days."

"I heard you were mighty helpful the night of the wildfire. That has to count for something. . . . Well, men, let's get to work. I'll look up the form for adoption and you start typing, Blum, but you'll have to type one copy for each of the girls with carbon paper behind it. This has to be perfect, so don't make any mistakes. If you erase on the carbon it looks like shit."

Maddock and Hester go on to Judge Wade's, and I sit down at the Remington. Three hours later, the other two are back and I'm on the last line of the third form. I said I could type, but I'm only using two fingers. Daniel looks at his watch.

"Judge Wade's fine with it, but we have to be in court in an hour. Mrs. Wade put in a good word for you, Blum."

"Shhhh. I have to concentrate. One more document to go."

"Did you stop by the Stengers'?" Linkous asks. "Tell the girls?"

"Shhhh!" I say again and the three go in an adjoining room and close the door.

It isn't until a quarter to four that we have the forms ready. West Virginia Petition to Adopt they read at the top. The three of us straighten each other's ties, and then, with Linkous in the lead, run across the street to the courthouse.

"Where's the fire?" the sheriff asks, poking his head out of his office. "You still talking, Blum, or do I have to come out and harass you?"

"Nice to see you, Hardman!" I respond, letting him know that I still have my tongue.

We skid into the courtroom just in front of the social workers, two gray-haired ladies in almost identical navy suits and black pumps. The Stengers sit in the front row of wood benches with Sally, Sonya, Sunny, and Sue, who are all dressed in starched print dresses that must be hand-me-downs from the Stengers' own girls. They even have shoes on.

Linkous presents the petitions to adopt even before the ladies get seated. Judge Wade looks the forms over and asks the Stengers if they think this is a good idea.

"We know all the parties involved and think they are fine people," Mr. Stenger offers.

"It would be a terrible crime to separate the sisters," Mrs. Stenger adds. "In my opinion it would cause lasting psychological damage." I always forget Mrs. Stenger has a college degree and can sound like a professor when she wants to. No one mentions that Becky and I aren't man and wife.

Things are going just as we hoped when Judge Wade decides that he ought to at least get the social workers' input and I inwardly cringe. Bad idea.

"So, Mrs. Jenkins and Mrs. Quinn. Do you have anything to present to the court?"

"I certainly do." The taller of the two comes forward with four manila files. "Considerable effort has been spent in finding these placements. It's not easy to locate foster homes for females. In hard economic times, everyone wants males to help with the farm work. Girls are seen as a liability."

"That's enough of that liability talk!" interjects Mrs. Stenger, reminding the woman with a fierce glance that the *four little sisters can hear what is said. "Just let the judge see what you've got."*

"Mmmmm," Judge Wade says, thumbing through the paperwork. "I see. A chicken farmer and his wife. A widowed dressmaker. The owners of a roadside café, and a couple that plays with a blues band out of Wheeling. This the best you could do?"

The tall lady lifts her chin defensively, but doesn't answer the question.

"Well, I'm sorry, ma'am, but the petitioners have you beat. We have a doctor, an engineer, and a veterinarian here. All have their own property and the little girls can stay right here in Union County. All four petitions to adopt approved!"

He pounds his gavel three times. Then with a grin, pounds it three more, and we all stand and cheer. I am so happy it's all worked out I forget, for the moment, that I still have to tell Becky.

After that, we go back to Stengers' for dinner, pack up the girls' things, and drive home. They don't have much. Everything they owned or loved burned up in the fire.

It's a long, dark ride back to Spruce Mountain and to keep the girls from being anxious we sing songs. As we get closer to Wild Rose Road I'm getting anxious myself, contemplating the enormity of what I have done.

I suppose the Hesters could have taken Sally, along with the twins, but it seemed too much to ask. Now here I am, a father, and if Becky agrees, she's a mother, but are we a couple? Can we be a family?

Hester stops at the Maddocks' first and Milt has to carry Sonya inside because she's asleep.

"Sally and I will walk from here, Dan. It's a nice night," I say, standing next to the Ford.

"Sunny and Sue, give your sister a hug. Sally's going home with Dr. Blum. We'll all see each other tomorrow," Daniel instructs, and when they reach over, the little girls have tears in their eyes.

"Good luck," Daniel whispers and I know he is thinking of Becky.

It's after ten as Sally and I amble the rest of the way up Wild Rose Road, and I'm glad that Becky will be asleep. Before I left, I hurriedly fixed up my bed for Sally and laid a little wooden doll I'd carved under her pillow.

"Does Miss Becky like me, Dr. Blum?" Sally asks in a soft voice, taking my hand. Above us the Milky Way trails like a scarf across the black sky and the spring frogs sing in the wetlands. "She loves you. She loves you like a mother and she doesn't even know it yet." I reach up and grab a handful of stars and give them to Sally. She takes them in her little hand and presses them to her heart.

Passing through the arched gate in the picket fence, I realize that with the hectic process of getting the adoption accomplished, I'd almost forgotten about putting it up. Becky has hung a lighted Coleman on the front porch, and I take it as a good sign that she's seen the flowers and accepted the gift of my journal.

"Here, Sally," I whisper. "Sit on the sofa while I take off our shoes." Through the kitchen door, I notice that my sketchbook is gone and in its place is Becky's leather-bound journal with the little red ribbon marking her place.

"Be quiet now. Miss Becky is asleep. I'll show you your room." We creep up the stairs, she changes into her nightdress, and I tuck her in, something I've never done before, tucked a child into bed.

"I like the doll," she tells me. "I'm going to name her Willa."

"Do you think you can sleep? I could sit here for a while."

"I'm okay. Thank you."

"I'll be downstairs on the sofa if you need anything." I give Sally a kiss and step out of the room.

"Isaac?" Becky calls in a soft voice from across the hall. "Isaac?"

Home

"Isaac? Who's with you?" Blum stands at my bedroom door in the shadows and I beckon him in. There's just enough starlight to see each other.

"Sally Hucknell," he whispers and closes the door.

"You brought her home?"

"I brought her to *our* home. I might as well get it over with. I've been scared to tell you. We officially adopted Sally today. Judge Wade signed the papers. The Maddocks and Hesters took the other girls. Your name's on the document. I can get it off later if you want. Did you read my journal?"

The man can see that I did. It's open on my bedside table and he has my journal under his arm.

"I'm sorry I didn't talk to you about the adoption." He sits on the edge of the mattress. "Hester, Maddock, and I discussed it after the burial, but I was still getting my nerve up to mention it to you. Then the vet found out this morning that the social workers were coming today and they were going to split the girls up. We had to move fast or it would be too late. If you don't want any part of it, I can do it alone."

I take his hand and have him lie down. Even fully clothed his body warms me. "I guess it's okay. We can try. She's a nice little girl and she needs a family. Are we a family?" There are tears in my eyes, but I don't think he sees.

What is a family? I ask myself. *They come in so many different forms and it's been so long since I had one.*

"Becky," Blum whispers again. "I'm sorry. Sorry for everything."

I answer by turning over and pulling him around me, his front to my back, spooning together.

We sleep all night like that, neither moving, the cells of our bodies weaving together.

48

Mother

"Miss Myers, would you braid my hair? Mama used to braid my hair, but Mrs. Stenger had so many children with us there, she didn't have time." It's Sally, standing barefoot at the bottom of the stairs, wearing a pink flour-sack dress, her long white-blond hair uncombed. She's holding a wooden hairbrush. Blum left the house before sunrise to assist Hester with a prolapsed uterus in one of Mr. Dresher's cows and I have been upstairs reading his journal again. What strikes me is all that silence. A year of silence.

"You can call me Becky." I take the brush and have her sit on the braided rug in front of me. "One pigtail or two?"

"Just one, straight down in back . . . I don't like to call grownups by their first names. It feels rude."

"Right. I had an Aunt Petunia once who wanted me to call her Pet. I couldn't do it. How about *Aunt Becky*." The girl thinks it over.

"Should I call Dr. Blum *Uncle Blum*?"

"No, his name is Isaac. I think you should call him Uncle Isaac." This girl needs some decent clothes. I pull Sally up in my lap. She's a big girl, not a baby, but I'm already thinking like a mother.

A mother . . . I say to myself . . . I never saw myself as a mother. Certainly, I never wanted to be pregnant or give birth. Sometimes I envied women with children, the physical closeness they had to their little ones, but here I am with Sally in my lap and the feelings of wanting to provide and protect her are undeniable.

Mother, I think. Mother is about love. It doesn't mean the one who gives birth. It is the one who braids your hair.

Communion

The Hope River runs clean and clear again, the ash and debris from the wildfire gone. For a few weeks even the homeless abandoned it. Now, as we wind ourselves through the willows, I notice a few of the traveling people are back, but in smaller numbers; only two camps, one white and one black, constructed away from each other in ramshackle wood shelters with hobo stoves made of tin and clotheslines tied to the trees.

The men nod as we pass but the women, wearing ragged, dirty housedresses, turn away, ashamed to be seen looking so destitute. These are not vacationers camping along the river for the fun of it; they have nowhere else to go.

It's been only a few weeks since we adopted the Hucknell children and we three families have gathered on the bank of the Hope for a Sunday picnic. Even Sarah Maddock has come, wearing her braces and leaning on a walker that her husband ordered from Sears. Reverend and Mrs. Miller are here too, with a boy and a girl from Hazel Patch, to talk about their school.

"It would actually help us to have you participate," Mrs. Miller says. "There are only twelve students, ages five through fourteen. It's a cooperative, certified by the Union County Board of Education. The closest other school for coloreds is on the far side of Delmont."

"And the Hazel Patch folks won't mind white children at their school?" I have to ask the question.

"Heavens no!"

"Then it's settled," Daniel comes in. "We'll all volunteer and you can expect four new pupils in the fall. . . ." He turns to the children. "Now, how about a game of Duck Duck Goose?"

While the kids and the men play the silly circle game, Patience and I wander downstream. She made a new sling, a smaller flowered one, so that she can carry Mira everywhere, and we find a flat rock where she can sit with her bare feet in the water and nurse the baby. I lie there looking up at the clouds and listening to the river as it sings below.

"How are you going to do it?"

"What?"

"Be a midwife with a baby, a toddler, and two school-aged children."

"I've thought about that. It will be harder, but maybe you'll help me." Here she grins. "I know how you love childbirth."

I can't help but smile back. "Helping women have babies when *you're* in charge isn't so bad."

"So you'll be my partner, like Bitsy?"

I don't answer at first, trying to pull all the pieces of my life together, mother, nurse, midwife. Then I shrug. "I guess I could."

Patience cheers and kicks water up like a little girl. "Yay!" And the drops come down like diamonds, sparkling in the sun.

"Dinner!" It's Mrs. Maddock calling from the riverbank.

Our picnic, on blankets, isn't exactly a feast, just whatever we could throw together; potato salad from Patience, deviled eggs from me, fresh home-baked bread and bean pickles from Mrs. Maddock, and cold milk from Moonlight, the Hesters' cow.

I'm waiting for someone to say grace and am surprised when Sally begins. "God is great. God is good." All the little girls chime in. "And so we thank Him for this food." I catch Isaac's eye and well up with tears.

Chain of Fools

"Who wants to wade to the other side of the river?" Daniel jumps up when we've eaten our fill. "Who's with me?" Most of the children raise their hands and start taking off their shoes.

This is an adventure. None of us has ever crossed the Hope before, except over the bridge into Liberty. Daniel and Blum are scouting for a shallow place and immediately I start thinking of danger. Someone might drown! But then I see Patience kicking off her boots and handing the baby to Sarah Maddock for safekeeping.

Fools come in all sizes, those who heed no caution and those who heed too much. I unlace my shoes.

"Are you going across, Sally?"

"I don't know. I'm afraid."

"I'm scared too, but there's a bunch of us. I think we'll be all right."

Even the Reverend and Mrs. Miller come in. We are all barefoot with our pants or skirts hitched up high, and then two more children from the homeless camps run over. They want to join the fun, and their parents, seeing the number of adults participating, wave them on.

Here we are. Can you see us? All holding hands, brown and white together, a chain spanning the river? Daniel leads the way, little Danny on his shoulders, with Mr. Maddock at the end, thirteen of us crossing the Hope, ice-cold water up to our knees and no one falls.

Baptism

The other side of the Hope River is not beautiful. The ground is bare and brown where the flames scorched the earth, but we can look back at the green where we came from. For a while we lounge on rocks or play in the sand, the boys and girls wading and splashing in the cool shallows.

Then as the kids become hungry or bored, the grownups begin to shepherd them back. Braver now, they cross in twos and threes. Sally returns hand-in-hand with Mrs. Miller, who has become her friend.

"When you come to our school, Sally," Mildred Miller confides, "I will be your teacher. Have you ever played with colored children before?"

"Not until today. I never touched a brown hand before today, but my daddy told me that there isn't no difference. He said we're all the same under the skin, same blood, same heart. He worked with plenty of coloreds in the PWA."

I think about that. Despite his violence, Alfred Hucknell gave a legacy of equality to his daughter.

"Dessert, everybody!" Sarah Maddock calls, getting her famous strawberry cake out and cutting pieces for the children, even the homeless kids.

Isaac and I are the last to leave.

"Come," he says, standing. He reaches for my hand and we wander down the bank away from our party, where the river runs fast and deep. There are rocks here as big as autos and I'm hoping he doesn't want to go for a swim. I'm not that big a fool.

"Look! The land is already healing." He bends down and pulls me to my knees next to the river. "Green plants growing up through the ashes . . . some of the seeds had probably sprouted before the fire, but some were dormant and released by the flames." He's talking like a professor again.

"Shhhh," I say, putting one finger to his lips. "Shhhh. Just worship. From devastation comes new life."

We look into each other's eyes, but it's too much for me and I shift my gaze.

This is a man I've lived with since his wife died and he fell apart, a man I worked with for seven years before that, but a different man now, rising from his own ashes. And I am a different woman.

"Lying with you that first night when I first brought Sally home," Blum says, "I felt I'd come home myself."

I wrap my arms around him. "You are home." We stay like that, kneeling on the ground for a long time.

Finally, Isaac breaks the silence, "Do you think a person can be born again?"

"You mean born into Christ, like religion?"

"No, not that way. Just you open your eyes and you see everything fresh and in a new way." We are still locked together and I stare out over his shoulder at the green trees and the sparkling grasses on the other side of the river, trying to understand what he means.

"I was in a dark cave of my own making," he goes on, "and you rolled away the stone. Not everyone gets a second chance."

"It was a very heavy stone," I joke, but he isn't joking.

"Come here." I gesture, as I let go of him and crawl across the sand to the edge of the water. "Lie down." He looks at me funny but does what I say. "On your back."

I cup both my hands and drip cold water over his head, run my fingers through his hair. He doesn't struggle. I don't have to hold him.

"What are you doing?"

"I'm baptizing you."

"Baptizing me?"

"In the name of the sun, and the trees, and the holy water."

Then Isaac Blum grabs me, pulls me right down on him so that our bodies are one, and in the shallows of the Hope, we baptize each other.

About the author

About the book

Read on

Insights,
Interviews
& More...

Meet Patricia Harman

PATRICIA HARMAN, CNM, got her start as a lay midwife on rural communes and went on to become a nurse-midwife on the faculty of Ohio State University, Case Western Reserve University, and West Virginia University. She lives near Morgantown, West Virginia; has three sons; and is the author of two acclaimed memoirs. Her first novel, *The Midwife of Hope River*, was successful around the world. ～

2

Interesting Facts about the CCC Camps

FORMED IN THE DEEPEST PART of the Great Depression, the Civilian Conservation Corp was one of President Roosevelt's first New Deal programs. He believed that this "tree army" would revive the rural economy and keep urban youth "off the city street corners."

By 1933, 40 percent of working-age U.S. citizens were unemployed. From 1933 to 1942, the CCC program, coordinated by the U.S. Army and the National Forest Service, employed three million of them to plant a billion trees, build fire towers and fire trails, construct dams and state parks, and correct soil erosion on forty million acres of land.

The Civilian Conservation Corp accepted only unmarried men between the ages of nineteen and twenty-five whose families were on relief. The men were paid thirty dollars a month, but twenty-five dollars of it was sent home to their mothers. In return, the government provided everything the participants needed, including clothing, tools, and training.

Over the course of the Great Depression, 500,000 young men were enrolled in the corps and 2,600 camps were built from Maine to Oregon. White Cliff Rock camp, featured in the book, is fictional but typical of many mountain camps.

Usually, the men lived in tents to ▶

Interesting Facts about the CCC Camps
(*continued*)

start with and then constructed cabins and dorms from local materials. Most of the boys had never been more than a hundred miles from home before. As can be imagined, there were sometimes conflicts that had to be dealt with in a military manner, and the camps weren't always popular with locals who viewed the outsiders with suspicion. Though planned to be multiracial, the country wasn't ready for that, and in the end separate camps were designed to house African-Americans as well as Native Americans.

It took a few years and a lot of

National Archives and Records Administration

national publicity to sway the public, but eventually with Eleanor Roosevelt's support, the young men of the tree army became the heroes of the New Deal. ᶜᵕ

National Archives and Records Administration

Reading Group Discussion Questions

1. When Becky returns to Liberty in 1934, she is broke and finds out that Dr. Blum's home has been sold for back taxes. Currently, many families have lost their homes to foreclosure. Have you ever been poor or nearly destitute? How do you think you would react?

2. Dr. Blum's disability is frustrating to Becky. Even though she's a nurse and a friend, she doesn't really have to take care of him. What would you do? (Keeping in mind that he has no family willing to take him and there were no adult social services available during the Great Depression.)

3. Becky came from an affluent family. She has never had to want for anything. It's hard for her to accept the charity of Mr. Bittman when he gives her the box of rotten apples. . . . How do you think you would feel?

4. Patience, the midwife of Hope River, is comfortable with the noises and smells and sights of childbirth, but Becky finds them unsettling and downright scary. How do you feel?

5. Facing the hard winter, Patience tells Becky that they will all have to pull together and somehow they will get through. In our mobile society, what place do family and community play in your life?

6. If you, like Patience, had to stay in bed for three months to keep from losing your baby, do you think you could do it?

7. What do you think about the friendship between Dr. Hester and Dr. Blum? How does the vet help Dr. Blum heal?

8. How does Blum's experience being helpless and poor change him?

9. How do we heal one another? Have you ever had an experience when a friend played a big role in helping you heal physically or emotionally?

10. Have you ever heard of the CCC camps? How do you think they would benefit society today?

11. What is it that the Hazel Patch folks have that many others in Union County do not?

12. The forest fire of 1935 left death and destruction in its wake. Have you ever faced a natural disaster? How did it change you? ∽

Have You Read?
More from
Patricia Harman

For more books by Patricia Harman
check out . . .

THE MIDWIFE OF HOPE RIVER

Midwife Patience Murphy has a gift:
a talent for escorting mothers through
the challenges of bringing children into
the world. Working in the hardscrabble
conditions of Appalachia during the
Depression, Patience takes the jobs that
no one else wants, helping those most in
need—and least likely to pay. She knows
a successful midwifery practice must be
built on a foundation of openness and
trust—but the secrets Patience is keeping
are far too intimate and fragile for her to
ever let anyone in.

Honest, moving, and beautifully
detailed, Patricia Harman's *The Midwife
of Hope River* rings with authenticity as
Patience faces nearly insurmountable
difficulties. From the dangerous mines
of West Virginia to the terrifying
attentions of the Ku Klux Klan, Patience
must strive to bring new light and life
into an otherwise hard world.